ROBOSOLDIERS
THANK YOU FOR YOUR SERVOS

◉◉◉

ROBOSOLDIERS

THANK YOU FOR YOUR SERVOS

an anthology edited by

STEPHEN LAWSON

with a foreword by
Major General (Retired)
STEPHEN R. HOGAN

ROBOSOLDIERS: THANK YOU FOR YOUR SERVOS

This is a work of fiction. All the characters and events portrayed
in this book are fictional, and any resemblance to real people or incidents is
purely coincidental. The views expressed in this publication are those of the
authors and do not necessarily reflect the official policy or position of the
Department of Defense or the U.S. government.

A Baen Books Original

Baen Publishing Enterprises
P.O. Box 1403
Riverdale, NY 10471
www.baen.com

ISBN: 978-1-9821-9190-0

Cover art by Kurt Miller

First printing, June 2022

Distributed by Simon & Schuster
1230 Avenue of the Americas
New York, NY 10020

Library of Congress Cataloging-in-Publication Data

Names: Lawson, Stephen, 1980- editor.
Title: Robosoldiers : thank you for your servos / edited by Stephen Lawson.
Description: Riverdale, NY : Baen Books, [2022]
Identifiers: LCCN 2022009785 | ISBN 9781982191900 (trade paperback) |
ISBN 9781625798664 (ebook)
Subjects: LCSH: Science fiction, American. | War stories, American. |
    Artificial intelligence--Fiction. | Robots--Fiction. | LCGFT: Science
    fiction. | War fiction. | Short stories.
Classification: LCC PS648.S3 R59 2022 | DDC 813/.0876208--
dc23/eng/20220304
LC record available at https://lccn.loc.gov/2022009785

Printed in the United States of America

10 9 8 7 6 5 4 3 2 1

DEDICATION

This volume is dedicated to two men, my two grandfathers.

If you read my bio at the end of the book, you'll understand that history rhymes even when it doesn't exactly repeat.

I never met my father's father. He was a Navy man. He'd been through some things, and he drank. And so I never met him.

My mother's father retired from the Air Force and went to fly for the airlines. He taught me to fly in his Cessna 170 when I was very young, and he pinned my wings on when I graduated from flight school at Fort Rucker. When I was in the Navy I showed him on a map where the carrier I was stationed on was moored, and he said he could probably land the Cessna on the flight deck.

"They'd shoot you down," I told him.

He just smiled and said, "Oh, I bet they wouldn't."

They were both a bit mad, perhaps. I'll leave it at that for anyone who knows me.

Understanding where we've come from helps us understand where we are, and where we might be going.

Thank you to both of you for your service and for the children you raised.

CONTENTS

Foreword by Major General (Retired) Stephen R. Hogan ix

Editor's Introduction by Stephen Lawson xiii

Higher Ground by M.T. Reiten 1

Today I Go Home by Martin L. Shoemaker 25

All Is One by Doug Beason 51

Edge Case by Richard Fox 77

Manchurian by Sean Patrick Hazlett 97

Resilience by Monalisa Foster 129

The Rules of the Game by Phillip E. Pournelle 153

My Dog Skipper 2.0 by Weston Ochse 183

Uncovered Data by David Drake 217

The Handyman by T.C. McCarthy 229

The Pinocchio Gambit by Brad R. Torgersen 247

Nightingale by Stephen Lawson 269

Operation Meltwater by Philip A. Kramer 297

About the Authors 327

FOREWORD

I find it fitting that I am writing this on the twentieth anniversary of the September 11 terror attacks against the United States. It's appropriate—in addition to the obvious—because September 11, 2001, has personal significance to me, as it was within a few days of the midpoint of my thirty-six-year service as an officer in the US Army.

During eighteen years of peace, followed by eighteen years of war, I have certainly witnessed major advances in the technology used by our nation's military. It is worth noting that the majority of this technological development and implementation came after 2001— the necessity of warfare bringing exponential growth in technical hardware, and at an unprecedented pace. Existential threats stimulate adaptation here, as they do in biology.

Technological advancement at the necessity of warfare is not a peculiar or unique notion, as military campaigns have advanced technology throughout the history of the world. Innovations in weapons, battlefield management, logistics, medicine, and even something as seemingly insignificant militarily as sanitation, have all come about because of the battlefield. Technology in the profession of arms is quite literally survival by supernatural selection.

These advancements survive and become mainstream—the majority adapted for civilian use—despite rigidity of senior soldiers, who have historically been resistant and slow to realize their benefit. I wonder sometimes how many American soldiers died during the US Civil War because the generals on either side refused to adapt to the increased accuracy of the rifled musket relative to its smoothbore predecessors; how easily Europe was conquered during the formative stages of World War II because those armies could not adapt to the technology of the armored combustion engine; how the parachute, and later the helicopter, provided commanders with a third method to envelop the enemy and gain surprise vertically; how predominant air power has become as the driver of operations, and the method by which the greatest lethality can be cast upon an opposition. Those pioneers that saw this wisdom—those soldiers like Emory Upton, Adna Chaffee, James Gavin, or Billy Mitchell—were regarded with suspicion or even as heretics by those who were stuck mentally in the rigidity of their own training and experience.

In 2005, on a semi-guided tour of the Tomahawk Building, which was located in the center of the International Zone, Baghdad, Iraq, I became enamored with the technological might of this nation. This building, pre–US invasion, served as the equivalent of the Pentagon for the Iraqi Armed Forces. It was nicknamed the "Tomahawk Building" because of the dozen or so Tomahawk missiles that were used to make useless this key facility minutes after the war had started.

What I found completely compelling is that this was executed by sailors of the US Navy, manning their stations hundreds of miles away, likely absent any personal gratification from the significance of the attack. Holes in the roof were precisely struck, a uniform distance from one another. With this technology, and the others that were once thought too radical, inertia followed that predicted the eventual result of this invasion.

This technology, while still compelling and awesome, has been eclipsed by new innovations that will continue to change the face of warfare. The 2005 capabilities that awed me are still available, and still awesome, but now fall into the category of "old school."

Forays into space; warfare against rival computer systems; drone technology; intelligence and targeting systems; advancements in medicine, logistics, management; "over the horizon" capabilities; and others turn yesterday's science fiction into today's science fact. The possibility of "smart" systems to be utilized by the individual soldier and which enable his tactical survival, to those that have theater, strategic, or global implications have advanced to the point that the future of warfare is literally in the hands of those with minds great enough to dream of them today. There are literally no limits to what can be accomplished, with the only commonality being the necessity to accommodate the hostile environment.

I began my military career in 1983. If I had been given insight then on the advances in battlefield technologies that we would see in 2021, I would find such notions literally unbelievable. Except for one machine gun—the M2 Browning .50—literally everything from the Army I joined has been replaced or improved by something with greater technological benefit. My challenge as a young soldier would reside totally in not being rigid in what is known, and what is, as yet, unknown.

The field of military robotics is rapidly advancing, and rightly so. Robots reduce risk to their human counterparts and can survive in conditions where human soldiers cannot. The fear of creating a weapon beyond our control, or the replacement of the human element in detaching oneself by distance with "over the horizon" capability, occupies the same space in our collective consciousness and moral anxiety that nuclear weapons did during the Cold War. That said, the necessity is very clear—US national interests demand that we must remain one step ahead technologically or find ourselves at the mercy of those who evolved more efficiently than we. We adopt rigidity at our peril.

Science fiction has certainly become science fact since 1983. The future of warfare belongs to those with imaginations large enough to see it.

—Stephen R. Hogan
Major General, USA (Retired)
September 11, 2021

Stephen Hogan has served our nation in numerous military capacities since 1983. Most recently, General Hogan served as Commanding General of both the Kentucky Army and Air National Guard and as the Cabinet Secretary/Executive Director of the Department of Military Affairs. After retiring from the military in December of 2019, General Hogan founded The Arlington Group to continue protecting our communities (tag-ky.com).

EDITOR'S INTRODUCTION

As with many things, I didn't intend to be the editor of this anthology. *Robosoldiers: Thank You for Your Servos* came to me as sort of a joke, and I thought about putting it at the top of the story of a washed-up combat veteran robot who gets adopted by a teenage girl and they save the world together. I still might write that story, but it's going to have a different title. I figured there were a few veterans in the science fiction community who could imagine great and terrible things for the future of military robotics, and that it'd be nice to have their ideas in one volume with a title like the one on the cover. So I pitched the idea to one of the editors at Baen and asked for a slot for one of my stories if he would edit it. The verdict came back that the title and concept were fine, but all the editors had a full load, and that I should edit it instead. So I did.

I have a few friends who are civilian scientists and programmers too, and I'm really pleased with the ideas they brought to this anthology. I loved his debut novel, so I wanted a story set in the world Martin Shoemaker created for *Today I Am Carey*. He delivered with "Today I Go Home," a story that reminds me so much of Isaac Asimov's best short fiction.

Monalisa Foster's "Resilience" is gritty and harsh, yet optimistic and genuine. Every time I read her work I'm left wondering which bits are partially autobiographical and which are purely fiction, though I'm always too afraid to ask. It's quite good, though.

The anchor story in this volume, "Operation Meltwater," is the sort of thing I've come to expect from Philip Kramer—hard science laced with his unique humor in an engrossing adventure tale.

What you're getting in this book is the best and most entertaining idea factory and military futurism we can offer you. You're getting all-domain warfare—land, sea, air, space, and cyber. You're getting hypersonic delivery vehicles, human-machine teaming, wetware, nanomachines, artificial intelligence, explosive ordnance disposal, nuclear weapons, and hunter-killer robots of all shapes and sizes. Best of all, you're getting them from experts in their various fields.

M.T. Reiten is a former Army Captain who works at Los Alamos National Laboratory, which was founded in 1943 to design and build the first atomic bomb.

Doug Beason is a retired Air Force Colonel who's also worked at LANL, and is a former White House staffer, among a ton of other roles which you can read about in his bio. I first met Doug at the Writers of the Future workshop in 2017, in which he was a contest judge and I was a neophyte writer who'd just made his first pro sale.

Richard Fox is a veteran Army officer who delivered some amazing technical detail and white-knuckle suspense with "Edge Case," a story of human-machine teaming in EOD. There's also a great subtle joke in his story that I didn't get until I was halfway through editing.

Sean Hazlett, who edited Baen's *Weird World War III* and the upcoming *Weird World War IV*, is a veteran Army officer and holds a master's in Public Policy from the Harvard Kennedy School of Government as well as an MBA from Harvard Business School. His fleshing out of some far-reaching problems in US-Chinese competition left me in deep contemplation for days.

Phillip Pournelle—son of science fiction legend Jerry Pournelle—is a retired Commander from the US Navy who now does strategic analysis and wargaming at the national level. His story, "The Rules of the Game," is everything you'd expect from someone with those credentials.

Weston Ochse is a Special Forces veteran, and to be honest, I think he redacted most of his bio before he sent it to me. You'll know an authentic jungle story with authentic carnage when you read it, though.

David Drake, the Baen legend, was an enlisted interrogator in Cambodia.

T.C. McCarthy is a former CIA weapons expert and is a regular speaker at USSOCOM (US Special Operations Command) and other commands on future warfare topics.

Brad Torgersen is our multiple-award-winning writer and the only warrant officer I could find to write in this. For anyone who's served with Army warrant officers, you'll know they're remarkably hard to find until absolutely needed, as stealth seems to be a part of the secret warrant officer creed. I needed Brad for this, though, and he delivered with "The Pinocchio Gambit."

And then there's me. I didn't set out to be a commissioned officer. After a five-year stint in the Navy and four years spent getting a B.A., I just wanted to fly helicopters for the National Guard. I wanted to be a warrant officer, like Brad. Unfortunately for me, the colonel in charge of deciding if I'd get to go to flight school at Fort Rucker needed RLOs (Real Live Officers, a snarky term in the aviation community for pilots with extra responsibilities). So I agreed to be an RLO, and in exchange I get to fly.

I know you'll like the others' stories, because I do. I've gotten immersed in twelve separate worlds while editing this thing—worlds that frightened me, made me think, and made me wonder at what might be possible. I just hope my story keeps pace with the rest in this group. The team you see in the table of contents wasn't selected by accident or with an open call. They're the best at what they do, and it shows.

HIGHER GROUND
M.T. Reiten

"Trust your NCOs."

That was the standard advice 2LT Nina Miller got before commissioning. Now she was climbing the nearly vertical rock of a peak in the Hindu Kush Mountains. At one point, she'd had orders to NATO HQ in Brussels before being diverted to this shithole. The 'Stan Part II. Most wars got a sequel—and just like movies, the sequels always sucked. Nina stumbled and slipped to a knee in the powdery, wind-whipped snow.

"I can carry you, ma'am." Uniform Four trudged behind her. A massive armored chest held up by sturdy legs. An impassive helmet with sensor strips like slits in a knight's visor and antennas like wolves' ears on the side. Long, gorilla-proportion arms held the large Pelican case outstretched, reverently, as if delivering a holy relic to an altar on top of the world. Uniform Four paused, perfectly gyro-stabilized among the rocks.

"Yeah, I got it." Nina struggled to regain her footing, shifting the M4 Bullpup slung against her chest. She was out of breath in the thin, clean air. She wished she had an NCO to lean on, but the OIC of Combat Outpost Murphy had instead sent the Guardian to accompany her to the commo site up the hill. Up the hill turned out to be up half a fucking mountain.

Down slope, COP Murphy stuck out like a busted wart. Crumbling Hescos in a vague perimeter among jagged mountain rock. Sandbagged huts of graying plywood and desert tan transportainers huddled inside. A slightly frayed American flag snapped from an antenna mast. And the captain huddled inside his listening post warm and safe, unwilling to roust any of his troops out of their racks to accompany her, a fresh lieutenant from joint HQ, on a one-hour mission. Two hours tops, she had promised him. The bastard had spent too much time among his enlisted soldiers.

She turned her attention back to Uniform Four. Before today, she'd only seen the human-shaped M-1 Guardian fighting machines in recruiting videos. Uniform Four was one component of the Autonomous Platoon Engagement System, basically a power armor suit inhabited by an AI. The latest, greatest evolved sentience, capable of rational inference and supposedly self-aware. ES 2.0, ubiquitous as all hell Stateside, was tricky when put into a weapons platform. AI-inhabited robots were prohibited on US soil per the so-called "Terminator Laws," but were allowed for overseas military operations. Four of them made up an APES and packed the same punch as a tank platoon back in the day. Uniform Four's intimidating first impression had given way under closer inspection. Its ceramic armor was gouged in spots. The stink of ozone wafted from fiber-strand musculature, hinting at compromised insulation. She was certain she detected Sharpie touch-up marks covering worn metal. But Uniform Four was respectful and knew the path to the top of the second-highest peak in the area. Not exactly an NCO, but it would have to count.

"Let's knock it out," Nina said.

"Yes, ma'am." His deep baritone clearly identified Uniform Four as male.

"So the AIs conduct the patrols here?" Nina checked with the Guardian unit. He trailed directly behind and didn't offer suggestions, so she assumed she was going the right way.

Uniform Four hesitated before answering, "Yes."

Nina turned into the grit-laden wind hissing against her goggles. Icy pellets of snow or bits of weather-blasted rock, she couldn't tell. She tucked her chin into her neck gaiter and shifted her daypack before continuing the zigzag climb. Two degrees per three hundred meters in altitude? She turned up her gloves and boots, but the thermal points barely registered. Even though she exerted herself, she felt the cold in her core the moment she stopped and sweat wicked away the little warmth she had generated.

Thankfully, Uniform Four carried the Spitfire intelligence boxes she had brought from Kabul. There was no way she could hump those over this terrain without help. The Guardian had an e-mag rifle—basically a portable rail gun that could shoot through buildings—clamped on his back and ran off a catalytic fusion unit, so he could operate for weeks before swapping in a new power supply. His onboard hyper-spectral imaging and battle awareness suite equaled any recon vehicle. The Guardian units cost more than she was worth a couple times over and were typically brigade assets. The one thing lacking was the officer to give the order to fire. She had been given command authorization. Although temporary, this was a unique experience for a signal officer. And the AI didn't give her the rash of shit a human NCO was obligated to dump on a fresh second lieutenant. Mostly. Except for freezing her ass off, this wasn't nearly as bad as it could have been, all things considered.

The wind died down as they approached the flat area near the crest. Uniform Four released a pair of micro-drones. They whirred away like lost hummingbirds. A minute later, he announced, "Area clear."

"Sons of Talib are active out here?" Nina mused as her breath coalesced around her face. "I thought we were out of fighting season."

"Standard procedure, ma'am," Uniform Four replied with a matter-of-fact intonation. She had no way to tell where the Guardian was looking. His helmet sensors gave no clues. His posture, despite the humanoid shape, was distinctly odd, as though he were moving from one video game action pose to the next.

Nina got to a level area near the twelve-digit grid coordinate she had been given and used the map on her issued phone to orient herself. She looked up from her forearm to gauge the horizon, which seemed to curve under the weight of the surrounding mountains. The gray curtain of a snowstorm was moving down from the north, but she expected to finish her task before it arrived. To the west over jagged peaks was the Salang Tunnel, the main north-south supply route for the newly minted Alliance of Afghan States. A little to the northeast was a cell tower on the highest point, a backup ground-based trunk. It had grown in strategic importance with the satellite situation going to hell up in orbit. Below her to the left was a deep bowl-shaped valley, walls pocked by abandoned mine shafts once run by Consolidated Rare Earths. A meandering path wound through snow-topped boulders down the hill toward tailing mounds and rusty rail tracks below. At her feet were the autonomous data-monitoring units she was sent to replace.

She keyed her throat mic. "Mike Four One. This is Juliet Six Niner. In position. Over."

"Roger," came the terse reply from the COP. Such a poor connection for so short a distance. She sighed. Not her problem to fix their comms.

She unslung her omnimeter and booted it up. She punched buttons and double-checked the topo-map that displayed line-of-sight transmission info. The area was riddled with dead zones, but this spot had a good link profile to the nearby cell tower. Nina pointed to the ground beside her. "Put it here."

Uniform Four set the Spitfires down with gentle precision. The micro-drones flitted back to orbit the Guardian.

Nina kneeled beside the old intel boxes, tugged off her gloves, and disconnected the fiber drops. The cold pinched her fingertips like pliers. "I need to get this install done fast. I'm catching a quadrotor to Maymana in the morning."

"I understand it's pretty," Uniform Four said.

"What is?"

"Faryab Province."

"Sure." Nina hefted the first tamper-proof AI chassis out of the transport case. She dumped it on the ground and it shifted color to blend in with the snow and brownish-gray rock. This Spitfire box was the snooper. It monitored traffic passing through the mobile network and performed first-pass decryption and analysis before relaying SIGINT to the listening post. Inside was an inward-facing AI, a multichannel receiver, and a thermite grenade strapped to the top of the neuromorphic processor.

She pulled the second Spitfire out. This was the broadcaster box, similar to the snooper, except that it injected disinformation and counter-propaganda into the enemy data streams with untraceable precision. Nina fumbled the fiber into the port in back, hands numb by the time she finished. She ran a spectrum trace on her omnimeter to verify the Spitfires were active. Her meter also picked up cell tower signals. Stray side lobes made it a prime location. Good to go.

She set her omnimeter to the side and dumped the old intel boxes into the Pelican. They would get a postmortem at Joint HQ. Her job here was completed in ten minutes, after an hour of climbing. At least it was all downhill from here. She secured the lid on the black case, beating one clasp until it clacked into place, and gestured for Uniform Four to take over. The Guardian bent, gauntlets on handles, and hefted the load.

A sharp burst of static broke squelch. Nina rechecked her earpiece, which had become uncomfortably hot for an instant. Her right hand sought the familiar grip of her carbine against her chest. She scanned for any activity along the visible ridgelines or in the valley below. Uniform Four had also halted in place. The drones spiraled to the ground, tiny rotors flopping in the snow.

"What was that?" she asked.

"I don't know." Uniform Four had stopped as if stunned and had teetered slightly. A rock exploded next to him. Uniform Four dropped the Pelican case.

Nina flinched.

A shot echoed from far away.

She dove to the crunchy snow and rolled over to free her carbine. Her feet and fingers were suddenly warm. No more shivering. She looked to Uniform Four.

The Guardian stood over the unresponsive drones, which had dropped like dragonflies caught in a snap freeze, and then turned toward Nina. She had no sign of where he was looking. Then he straightened, chest proud and arms back, as if presenting a target to draw fire and protect her.

A cloud of expanding grit erupted from Uniform Four's chest armor as a deep *thung* rang out. Metal fragments sprayed the snow. Uniform Four dropped flat—the supersonic crack was unmistakable this time.

"Mike Four One, this is Juliet Six Niner! Receiving fire! Over!" Nina shouted into her radio mic.

Nothing. Dead air.

Nina rolled onto her stomach and pulled her weapon into position. She pushed snow out of the trigger guard. The trauma plate in her body armor grated against the sharp rocks beneath her. There was nothing but gray and white through her scope. "Where? Where?" she muttered to herself as she swept the barrel side to side, looking for any movement. Any silhouette.

Uniform Four lifted a massive gauntlet and pointed toward higher ground. The cell tower.

"You still with me?" Nina called over her shoulder and aimed at the cell tower. That was a klick away and higher elevation. Her carbine would be useless at this range.

"Yes." Uniform Four unlimbered the e-mag weapon from his back and propped onto his side. He measured the small crater in his chest plate up to the second knuckle. "Twenty-millimeter round. Sniper from the base of the tower. I've got audio triangulation."

Trust your NCOs, she remembered. "What do we do?"

"I don't know. I just got downloaded this morning."

Nina felt like the ground gave way beneath her. She gripped the rock for support. That was it. She was going to die here alone. Because a goddamn captain was too lazy to send out real troops. "This morning?"

"The human commander knows the mission," Uniform Four recited. The AI corollary of "Trust your NCOs," she realized.

Far from the battle-hardened fighting machine she had expected, Uniform Four was probably as green as she was. "Do you have comms with COP Murphy?"

"No."

How could all comms drop at the same time? She remembered her warm earpiece. "Tactical EMP," she whispered. She glanced at her phone. Black screen. Piece of shit off-the-shelf electronics.

Nina high-crawled to retrieve her omnimeter from near the Pelican case. She snagged the strap. The Pelican case jumped away as if it were alive. A round had just missed Nina's helmet and hit the case. It blew apart in shards of plastic and tumbled down the slope. Thermite ignited in an unbelievably bright flare, sparks pinwheeling from the shattered equipment. She was next in the crosshairs. She scuttled backwards, blinking away the afterimage of the incandescent molten metal.

Her ruggedized omnimeter was still running. The topo-map screen showed a line-of-sight dead zone from the cell tower just over the lip toward the mine-riddled valley. There were other dead zones back down the hill toward the safety of COP Murphy, but those were further away and more exposed to the sniper.

Nina had a decision to make—run for safety while exposed or

jump over the edge into immediate cover? The ridgeline would block her radio link. What comms did she have anyway?

"Follow me." Nina scrambled to the nearby edge. Put rock between them and the enemy.

"I've got the sniper targeted." Uniform Four had risen to a contorted kneeling position, impossible for a human soldier to hold steady. "May I fire?"

Nina couldn't see Uniform Four's gun camera. She was supposed to verify. Human in the loop. Her phone was dead and she was too busy crawling for cover. She would be responsible for unleashing a killer robot. She would have to trust his target discrimination. "Yes!"

A muffled metallic *clank* came from the e-mag rifle. Uniform Four watched for effect. Then he rose to a wide-stance crouch and ran after Nina, leaving huge footprints in the snow. "I missed."

Nina sprawled over the edge. The downward slope toward the mining valley was steeper than she anticipated. The contour lines were hidden by the radio link overlay. She slid, grasping at rocks that jutted out and battered her. If she slid too far, she'd exit the dead zone and be a clear target again. She pivoted on her butt, got her legs below her, and dug in her bootheels. Stones fell and bounced off each other with a dull, chalky sound. Snow formed a mini-avalanche under her. Nina arched into the steep slope behind her. She would plummet two hundred meters over a cliff if she pitched forward. She could smell her own sour breath in the neck gaiter pulled over her lower face. But she stopped.

Uniform Four placed a gauntlet on the edge and vaulted down as if he were dismounting a gymnastics pommel horse. He kept the barrel of the e-mag rifle pointed toward the cell tower with an outstretched arm.

"Okay, now," Nina stage-whispered, barely able to breathe with her heart racing, "Whisky-Tango-Foxtrot, over?"

The blank helmet of the Guardian allowed no visible expression, but the anthropomorphic interface came through in the disapproval carried by his voice. "The time lag for your fire order allowed the target to reach cover."

"I couldn't verify," Nina protested and hated how lame the excuse sounded.

"We should have gone the other way, ma'am," Uniform Four continued. "We're trapped."

"You said you'd been here before," Nina accused. She could smell the tang of ozone this close to the Guardian. "I was relying on you."

"Ma'am, you asked if I knew the way. The way is on the operational map. I know the map."

"But you conducted patrols?"

"The APES here do conduct patrols, which was the answer to your question. You didn't ask if I had been on patrol, though this power armor has with the previous Uniform Four."

Nina groaned. This was her first solo mission for J6. It wasn't supposed to be like this. Anger grew out of her sense of helplessness, clinging to a mountainside, and this machine—which was supposed to protect her—but instead was critical of her failure. Of her indecisiveness in the face of the enemy. "One hot second. Why didn't you react? You let yourself get shot!"

The Guardian lost the tone of confident disapproval. "Things got fuzzy. I lost track of time."

"I'll tell you what happened. We were hit by a high field EMP." Nina leaned her head back to gather her wits. She had expected more from an electromagnetic pulse event, like Tesla coil lightning or at least feeling the hair on her body standing up. Another misguided expectation.

"Ma'am, the M-1 Guardian power armor is qualified to withstand EMP attacks," Uniform Four said testily.

Nina pulled up the trace recorded on the scope application, which she had left running. A huge spike. Damaging peak fields. Fast, nanosecond rise time. Long ringing squiggles trailing off to normal background signals despite the fried external antenna. She held it near Uniform Four's sensor visor and tapped the screen with a gloved finger. "What is that?"

"An EMP," Uniform Four admitted. "But no nuclear weapon?"

"Tactical EMP. There's a portable generator around here someplace. But where?" The bowl-shaped valley below her was riddled with holes like a hive. Nothing there. No activity. "Something that powerful should light up the whole valley like a beacon. The listening post would have caught that."

"The cell tower?"

Nina shrugged under her body armor as she fussed over her omnimeter. She snipped a length of wire from her repair kit, stripped an end, and jury-rigged a monopole on an undamaged aux port. The cell tower was still passing traffic according to the weak diffraction signal Nina picked up. How was that possible? She and Uniform Four had been knocked out of commission, their overdriven antennas fused to protect the sensitive electronics, but the cell tower, a mere klick away, went on as if nothing had happened.

The EMP had been focused on them. That would spare the cell tower and COP Murphy. She called up the topo-map. A phased array of EMP generators would take the entire ridgeline of the valley to achieve such a tight focus. She tapped at the screen with unfeeling fingers, attempting to predict the location of the EMP source. Nothing made sense within line-of-sight calculations. It just wasn't possible.

"Ma'am?" Uniform Four still held his e-mag rifle over his head, trained on the sniper's location. "We have contact with the enemy . . ."

Nina recognized the complaint that implied she was wasting time with unimportant distractions and she should put her toys away while they were pinned down. Maybe the AI was right. But tactical EMP generators were a possible strategic threat. What were the Sons of Talib doing with that type of hardware? The SoT was old tradition, blowing up girls' schools and attacking military convoys. Why would they deploy an EMP generator out here in the middle of nowhere? Bigger-picture threats loomed. Were the Russians backing them? They wouldn't waste a high-tech asset like this on a minor harassment action.

Nina stared over her boots into the valley. Under different conditions, she might say the landscape presented a severe kind of beauty. Snow started to blow over the far ridges, swirling the cloudy day into a deeper gray—the inclement weather she had been warned about. She noticed the steel rails for mining carts had been lifted from level tracks and set aside. Scavengers after wood rail ties? It was hard to tell with a snow flurry blowing in. "What do you see down there?"

"Ma'am, my aesthetics module gets stimulated as much as the next sentient being," Uniform Four said, "but I am trying to kill a bad guy before he kills us."

"Sorry," mumbled Nina. "I guess you have crappy optics in that beat-up power armor." The banter came easily with the adrenaline.

"I'm battle scarred, ma'am." Uniform Four lifted a segment of armor below his armpit with his free gauntlet. With surprising deftness, he unspooled a short length of optic fiber. "Connect me to your omnimeter. I'll relay what I see."

Nina climbed next to Uniform Four and nestled against the Guardian's bulk for shelter from the wind which was picking up. She plugged it into the meter.

Uniform Four's head swiveled around like an owl's to look over his shoulder into the valley. An image appeared on the meter's screen. Then Uniform Four's head snapped right way around again and focused on the distant sniper.

Nina stared at the image. With the obscuring snow digitally removed, a pattern emerged. The far side of the valley was populated with rails and scrap metal strips that looked haphazard at first, but were evenly spaced and all aligned to the bowl-shaped slope. Very deliberate. Not the work of scavengers desperate for fuel to keep them warm through the winter. "How did you locate the sniper?"

"Audio triangulation. Listened to the echoes of the shot bouncing from the terrain and backward-traced the sound."

"Oh, that's it!" Nina expanded her line-of-sight calculations to include the first reflection. She mapped the AI's image of the valley with the distributed metal pieces and ran a propagation simulation. The EMP pulse traced from the level spot above them into the bowl-shaped valley and reflected to focus on a mine entrance directly below them. The valley acted as a focusing mirror. The tactical EMP generator could hide inside the tunnel underneath and would never be exposed to satellite images. It could pulse across the valley, reflect and focus to zap anything on the spot immediately above them. Zap that spot only. The terrain was the antenna like Arecibo or that big astronomy dish in China. Maybe the EMP generator could move from mine entrance to mine entrance and change where it focused on the ridge? It might be able to hit the cell tower.

"There's an EMP generator down the hill in this tunnel." Nina pointed at the map. The grid coordinates popped up. "We need to alert the COP."

"We have no communications," Uniform Four said.

Nina disconnected her omnimeter and returned the fiber. "Any more drones? Can you send one down the hill?"

He paused. "Wind too high for little rotors."

The day had gone gloomy with the approaching snow. "The Spitfires. Those have a direct connection to the COP."

"Yes. I'll go." Uniform Four rose silently to a crouch, e-mag rifle aimed toward the cell tower. He took a step toward the Spitfires hidden among the rocks twenty meters away.

The display on Nina's omnimeter went kaleidoscopic. Her earpiece got hot again; she had forgotten she still had it in. Snow crusted around the metal snaps on her cold-weather gear, induction heating from eddy currents melting ice. Another focused EMP attack.

"I can't see." Uniform Four stumbled backward. He stood at attention and lowered his weapon to the ground in a standby position—a perfect silhouette.

A supersonic crack stung Nina's ears. Another projectile had slammed into Uniform Four's chest plate, knocking him backwards. He dropped like a pop-up range target followed by the distant report of the heavy-caliber sniper rifle.

The shot echoed from across the valley.

"Uniform Four!" Nina shouted as she scrabbled over the rocks, acutely aware of the very near and too-thin berm protecting her from the enemy. She kept her head down. Her little ballistic helmet wouldn't stop anti-materiel rounds.

"Correction. Not twenty millimeter. Fourteen point five." Uniform Four sat up and brushed at the snow compacted against his chassis. Shattered fragments of metal encased ceramic armor crumbled away from his exoskeleton. His gauntlets trembled like an old man's hands. "Vidhwansak, bolt action, low rate of fire, Indian origin."

"Freeze!" Nina commanded.

Uniform Four stopped moving. At least major motor movements. His gauntlets continued to tremble and his helmet twitched slightly side to side. His left leg jerked every ten seconds as fiber strand spasmed from built-up leakage current.

"Are you totally blind?" Nina began a thorough inspection.

"Inertial guidance system works. I can maneuver, but I have no direct or peripheral optics left."

"This EMP is what happened to the previous Uniform Four." There must be a weak point in the shielding where the external field could penetrate. Not enough to kill the hardened neuromorphics outright, but enough to disrupt cognition, like a low dose of nerve agent.

Uniform Four wriggled his digits in front of his visor while running self-diagnostics. Then he waved one whole hand in front of his visor, clearly unable to see anything. He smacked his gauntlet against the front of his helmet and held it there, a perfect imitation of human frustration. "The armorer said my predecessor didn't come up after downtime this morning. No one cares if an AI dies; they do care if an APES power armor goes non-mission capable."

They needed help to get out of this in one piece.

Nina realized that she would have to recover the Spitfires herself if they had any chance to get out of this alive. "Do you have pyro?"

"I would have used smoke if I had it. No pyro. No grenades. Only basic sabot and flechette for my weapon."

Nina dropped her daypack and set her carbine across it. She considered shucking her body armor. It wouldn't protect her from a direct strike. But she kept it on to protect from shrapnel and flying debris. "You can still triangulate on the sniper?"

"I can direct fire toward where the bad guy was last."

"Good." Nina waited as a sudden gust of wind tore at her clothing and whipped snow around them. "Give me cover."

Nina scrambled to the lip. Uniform Four rose unsteadily beside her and began firing. *Clank, clank, clank.* Ionized air flashed from the rifle muzzle. The sabot casings fluttered to the ground a hundred meters toward the tower.

Then she was running. Frigid air bit at her cheeks. Her boots found their way through crumbled rock. Her dash was more of a scarcely controlled forward plummet. She dropped to her knees in front of the Spitfire boxes.

Clank, clank. Uniform Four fired again. If the sniper had moved, he wouldn't know until after hearing the shot. If the EMP hit again, the AI would be knocked out of commission—leaving her in the open without covering fire.

She gripped the carrying handles and hefted one in each hand. The metal boxes were heavy. Her shoulders strained as she hugged them close to her chest. She wanted to turn and flee to the safety of the ridgeline, but she couldn't risk snapping the fiber. Coils of gray-green fiber cable broke through the snow, tension on it by shuffling backwards. She twisted to untangle the fiber caught on a rock. She presented a clear target, but she couldn't run.

The inevitable crack and boom of the sniper rifle reached her. She fought the reflex to dive to the ground. If she heard the sniper, she was safe for the moment. Low rate of fire. She felt like she was going to throw up.

"Hurry!" Uniform Four called out. "Four . . . Three . . ."

Before he could reach "two," Nina snaked the Spitfires to the edge. She had just enough free fiber to reach their protected spot. She collapsed behind the ridgeline and Uniform Four ducked next to her. A fourteen-point-five round hit on the other side and sprayed pebbles around them like hailstones.

Nina's knees throbbed. Her lungs felt scraped by frozen air. The valley, so peaceful below, with sudden death a mere meter above her head. Thirsty, she grabbed her daypack and took a sip on the drinking tube dangling out of it. The tube was rigid as an icicle and the water bladder was frozen solid. She tossed the tube aside.

"They are after me," Uniform Four said.

"Who?" Nina asked.

"The Russians. They've paid bounties for US soldiers before. Now they want Guardian technology." He pointed at his back with a trembling finger. "The catalytic fusion unit. The SoT go along for the Russian cash and their religious sect doesn't care for my kind as an abomination against Allah."

"For a fresh download, you're certainly up-to-date on intel." Nina turned to the Spitfire boxes and began to examine them. "How would they recover you? No one could come up that mountain face and nothing can fly in this weather."

"Primary Ranger tactic, ma'am. Go where no one could possibly go. Launch the attack with the enemy hunkered down in position."

"Let's hope the bad guys failed the Ranger course." Nina checked the ports on the Spitfires. Simple fiber drops on the back end, communications and auxiliary. Low gain directional antenna on the front. She punched the power button on the omnimeter, but nothing happened. She initiated a hard reboot. Nothing. She groaned. "I don't have the equipment to talk to these things."

"I can talk to them. Connect me, please." Uniform Four spooled out his fiber. "We're both American-made AIs."

Nina plugged him into the snooper box and waited. It was hard to wait in the cold. She wanted to peek over the berm, make sure no enemy was advancing on their position, but she recognized how stupid an idea that was. She got away with that once. It was getting colder by the minute. Wait for darkness? Maybe the sniper didn't have night vision? The fucker with the sniper rifle had a tactical EMP generator set up by someone who knew advanced physics. He would certainly have a thermal scope.

Maybe they could wait here until the captain at Murphy sent a patrol to get her? But the patrol would be the other Guardian fighting machines, and would be just as susceptible to EMP as Uniform Four. She would be responsible for drawing more high-value assets into an ambush.

No, she couldn't rely on anyone else to get her out of this, except Uniform Four—and he was a mess. Peripheral damage from EMP. Optical sensors blown in the helmet, trembling gauntlets, and twitchy leg on the left. She needed a proper wiring diagram to troubleshoot him. Nina slid next over and inspected his armored joints on the left side.

"The little jerk won't talk to me," Uniform Four announced a second later.

"Tell it we're US soldiers and need to get an urgent message through to the outpost."

"She says that's not her job. She relays enemy intercepts from original sources to proper receiving agencies. We are not a verified source."

"Try the other one." Nina fumbled Uniform Four's connection into the broadcaster box with numb fingers. She suppressed the urge to blow on her hands.

Uniform Four began communicating with the other Spitfire and Nina resumed her inspection. She found an articulated joint between helmet and shoulder where paint had been slapped down over a dent in his armor. The paint had coated the conductive gasket and flowed into the seam, breaking the electrical shielding, allowing the EMP to penetrate the exoskeleton any time he raised his e-mag rifle.

"This Spitfire claims it can't transmit directly to the COP. It is only allowed to spread disinformation into enemy traffic on the commercial net. No real information on friendly units. It checks." Uniform Four grumbled, "Inward-facing AIs can be so stubborn."

"One only tells the truth. One only tells lies." Nina spread a copper tape over the compromised flexure joint, only a band aid fix, but Uniform Four might survive a mad dash across the open ground. That would be her last resort.

"Yes. Like the logic puzzle."

"Why do we need their cooperation? We'll use their fiber link directly." Nina dug through the pouch of her repair kit. She must have a fiber-to-fiber coupler in there somewhere. Or had she used it in Kunduz?

"Do you have the crypto?" Uniform Four asked dejectedly. "I don't."

Nina stopped digging through her stash of useful parts. If they disconnected the feeds to the COP and broke the crypto synch, it would look like an attack, no matter the content of the plain-text transmission. "Gotta convince the Spitfires to talk."

How to persuade inward-facing AIs? Appealing to their patriotism obviously didn't cut it. Nina stared down into the valley toward the mine shaft that hid the EMP generator. This ambush only worked because the sniper and electronic countermeasures coordinated their efforts. Nina thought she saw something move far down the mountainside. Animal shapes scampered through the boulders. She squinted, but couldn't make it out clearly. Were there any wild animals left in this forsaken country? If she survived this, she was going to carry a pair of binoculars in her daypack.

"Let me shoot one of the AIs," Uniform Four offered. "That should make the other more cooperative."

"That's the infantry solution," Nina answered with a strained laugh. "The Spitfires can't hear you? Right?"

"No external sensors. Only what they receive from their antennas and optical ports."

Neither of the Spitfires would help them alone. That was it! "Can you speak Dari?"

"At a Google level."

"That's better than mine." Nina turned the Spitfires' antennas to face each other. What could they say to get someone back in the world to take notice? "Make up something about a foreign military unit pinned down. Like you're reporting contact. Use the grid locations of the mines as the staging point for full-on offensive. Bringing mortars out of the caves. Warn that you will be blowing the cell tower in Baghlan."

"Roger," Uniform Four said. Then he paused. "I hear something approaching."

Nina reached for her carbine. Her fingers stung with pins and needles as she squeezed the grips. She edged closer to the lip, steeling herself to raise up and fire. "The sniper?"

"No. Downslope."

Nina turned her attention to the valley. The animal shapes she had seen before had gotten closer, clambering toward their position. Nina stared in growing horror. Creepy headless dogs ran up a winding path—directly toward them. Nina wiped her goggles. "Hurry," she whispered.

A moment later, he said, "Done."

"Did it believe you?"

"No, but it transmitted the fake story because it was fake." Uniform Four seemed to chuckle before he asked, "What do you see?"

"Creepy headless dogs," Nina whispered. She tried to get one in view with the carbine's low-power scope. The dog shapes were spasmodic, leaping from rock to rock, jerking in an all-out sprint. Nearly impossible to get a good sight picture. She caught a glimpse of a red slash on one's flank. A strip of blood?

"How big?" Uniform Four asked.

"Dog-sized?"

"Battlefield stretcher-bot," Uniform Four said with certainty. "Biomimetic robots based on canine neuromorphics. The Red Crescent has them. UAE-supplied."

"So, are these friendlies?" Nina had a better look through her scope and recognized the crescent sign on the side. Legs were surprisingly good in this rugged terrain. "They're not acting like friendlies."

"The stretcher-bot should be broadcasting an identifier, but I'm blind to the spectrum."

"The US doesn't have these in inventory. These are not here to rescue us. Are they?"

"Unlikely, ma'am."

"Are these a threat?"

"Your call, ma'am." Uniform Four paused and then added, "No on-board general intelligence, but hackable. SoT wouldn't have military-grade bots, only what they could steal from aid NGOs."

"Now we know how they planned to recover your hardware."

The stretcher-bots were drawing into range in complete silence. Only the faintest sound of disturbed rock reached from them, as high as Nina was. She counted seven. Nina shivered. The wind and snow continued to increase. "How long until help arrives?"

"No idea, ma'am."

If help arrives, she corrected herself. If someone in an intel shop someplace bought their bullshit and acted on it. But even then, what could be done? Nothing in-country could fly in this weather at this altitude and reach them in the middle of nowhere. Nina knew this. She had been grounded several times at Bagram under less severe conditions.

They were completely trapped. The stretcher-bots were closing on them. Hackable meant the biomimetic behaviors could be tweaked. The bots might be carrying explosives or be reprogrammed to kick her to death. Criminal actions, but the SoT didn't bother with the niceties of combat. There was no cover on this steep mountain face. She couldn't remember exactly how far the dead zone extended. The few nearby boulders that would provide cover from the stretcher-bots would probably get them shot in the back by the sniper. The temperature was dropping as the sun lowered behind the clouds. She would freeze to death if she had to lie out here all night even if they fought off the stretcher-bots. And she was desperately thirsty.

"Any chance I could crawl inside?" Nina asked. "I could be your eyes."

"What are you asking, ma'am?"

"You're based on power armor."

"My weapons platform is based on a manned power-armor design," Uniform Four corrected. "But this unit isn't rigged as a command suit. A trained armorer with special tooling can remove the internal ammo racks."

"Oh," Nina replied, tucking her gloved hands under her body armor.

"Also need to install the air handling system," Uniform Four continued.

"Can't raise the visor?"

"Not on the APES units. Unnecessary structural weakness. You'd know this if you were a qualified operator."

"Fine." Nina pulled her hands from her armpits. It hadn't helped. "Not even just to get warm?"

Uniform Four performed a reasonable impression of a sigh. "Okay, strip naked and hope you fit. I will not be responsible for pulled muscles, dislocated joints, or broken necks . . ."

"No, no. I got it. Roger," Nina said. Where were the troops from COP Murphy? She checked the time on her phone. The blank screen of her destroyed phone. It felt like forever. "How long have we been out?"

"Two hours, fifty-three minutes."

"They're on us." Nina raised her carbine to her shoulder and put the reticle on the nearest stretcher-bot. She saw the purplish glint off its binocular lenses as it turned to run uphill. She dug her heels in and rested her forearm on her bent knee. The auto-rangefinder clicked up the sights. She adjusted and squeezed the trigger.

The Bullpup *chinged* in her arms, feeling toylike with its low recoil and built-in suppressor. Three hundred meters away, the stretcher-bot stumbled and fell in a spray of snow. Two others passed around the fallen one. But the fallen bot's legs never stopped moving. It wobbled to its feet and continued the climb.

"Fire at will," Nina ordered.

"No valid target acquired."

"Triangulate!" Nina fired at the new lead. She squeezed off two rounds quickly. That one limped when it struggled upright.

Clang! Uniform Four blasted a groove in the snow a few lengths behind a stretcher-bot.

"Use flechette and lead more." Nina fired again, but she also missed as the bot jinked left. Two hundred meters.

The report of the e-mag rifle changed subtly. Nina had the impression of an expanding gray cloud of insects flying downhill, gone in a blink. The edge of the shot pattern caught a bot. The mass of needlelike projectiles peeled the metal skin off the bot's exoskeleton. It thrashed with its forelegs, but the rear legs dragged stiffly behind.

Nina sighted on one running straight toward her. She fired two more rounds, center of mass. The bot jerked up, then tumbled backward. It caromed off rocks before stopping fifty meters back, twitched on its side, and didn't get back up. Five more advancing through the gloom. One hundred meters out.

Uniform Four dropped two more as Nina helped walk in the shots. Then he was dry on flechette canisters. Nina had four empty magazines in her vest pouches. But as the rogue stretcher-bots grew closer she was firing more bursts. They had learned to crouch the moment they sensed a muzzle flash.

The remaining stretcher-bots slowed as the slope steepened, surveying the unstable ground and analyzing paths up. They appeared confused and checked each other as they paced below them, moving from cover to concealment. The big humps on their shoulders must hold the furled stretcher. Nina took another shot and knocked one back, but it returned to the others a moment later, seemingly undamaged.

"How are you at combatives?" Nina asked, swapping magazines. The banter gave her a sense of courage and she finally understood why her male counterparts always talked crap before a mission.

"I could take two, no problem." Uniform Four posed his left arm as if he were flexing muscles.

"There's three left."

"Then we have a problem, ma'am."

Their momentary reprieve was over. The bots discovered a traversable path up. Bare rocks slid beneath their rubber paws, but they advanced. Only bodies and strangely articulated legs on the creepy robots. Two spiderlike eyes recessed in the shoulder hump tracked on their prey. Fifty meters. The stretcher-bots suddenly became more visible. They grew shadows.

Nina lifted her cheek from her weapon and looked up. Something glowed in the western sky.

A golden light pierced the clouds. A fiery sled tunneled through the atmosphere, burning a clear hole through the clouds and snow. Like the meteor strike that killed the dinosaurs, except it skimmed through the air rather than plummeting into the ground. Submunitions flitted out of the back of the hypersonic kill vehicle as it passed over the valley. Danger fucking close!

"Run!" Nina didn't wait for an answer. She and Uniform Four sprinted over the ridge, only concerned about putting distance between themselves and the descending firefly swarm of self-guided munitions. The sniper became a secondary threat for the instant.

A thin wall of compressed air slammed into them with a deafening boom. Snow and small rocks vibrated from the ground like sand on a drumhead. The roaring thunder of the sky being ripped open enveloped them. Shook them to their cores in the wake of the kill vehicle. An afterthought of the impending destruction.

She risked a look back at the Guardian as they crossed the exposed level ground. Ionized air flashed at the muzzle of the e-mag rifle as he fired sabot rounds in the general direction of the sniper. The gaping hole in his fractured chest plate crumbled wider with each step and each shot. He couldn't take another direct hit to the exposed torso.

The munitions had dropped on filaments of sparkly fire into the valley. They crackled like popcorn compared to the roaring hypersonic craft that had disappeared through the clouds. The crackle increased exponentially as the munitions worked up the side of the mountain toward them. No gouting flames, only concussive explosions and flying pieces of death.

Ahead, Nina saw an easier path down toward the general direction of the COP. Outcrops provided cover and snowdrifts stretched behind them for concealment. This had been the right way to go. Uniform Four had said she had chosen the wrong way. She could see why now, but she had done her best with the information she had. She hurled down the path, certain shrapnel would cut her legs from under her or a sniper's bullet would pierce her body armor. Long steps onto slippery snow-hidden ground. The cell tower loomed behind her. An outcrop lay just ahead, big enough for them both to huddle behind.

Deepening snow dragged at her boots and then was over her knees. She slogged through drifts as high as her hips, falling forward. Her weapon grew slippery from the ice crusting her gloves. She let herself tip forward and slid downward on the crusted snow. Then she crawled into the protection of the outcrop, sucking wind and muscles burning with anaerobic exhaustion. She wedged her back against solid rock and brought up her carbine, thinking she might be able to provide some covering fire for Uniform Four. "Over here!"

Uniform Four plowed through the drifts, steady as a train on rails. He shifted direction toward Nina's position, but gave no outward sign of his status.

Of course, Nina recalled from simpler times in a classroom that the easy way out of an ambush is usually into another ambush. Nina edged around the edge of the outcrop and sighted toward the base of the cell tower. She held her fire. She had nothing that could even make the sniper duck, but Uniform Four was almost to her and relative safety.

Then two arms—two human arms—burst zombie-like from beneath the snow under Uniform Four. Skin hung in tatters from black flesh flecked with ice. The immediate terror of combat turned nightmarishly incomprehensible as Nina watched. Mangled hands gripped Uniform Four's ankles as he lifted them from the snow. He hesitated a moment, unable to see what had grabbed him. "What is it?"

Then lightning arced from burning fingers into the Guardian's exoskeleton. The tattered skin melted away in clumps from the gripping arms, revealing charred blackened musculature. The stink of burning plastic and hot metal overwhelmed her. Uniform Four stiffened and froze. Current flashed bright as thermite, arcing up one leg and down the other. Snow turned to steam in an instant.

Nina was on her feet, sprinting the few meters to Uniform Four. She launched herself in a flying tackle and hit him high. He went off-balance and toppled, gyros not functioning. The gripping zombie-arms tore from the snow-covered ground, stringing tangled roots of power cables behind. Nina felt twinges ripple through her muscles, sudden jolts of clenching pain. She pushed off his stiff body. They hit the ground apart as the bright arcing fizzled out.

Nina ached. Ached everywhere. Her heartbeat felt erratic at her neck and her eyes throbbed from pressure in her head. The palms of her gloves were singed. Her combat vest had melted where she had contacted Uniform Four. She smelled burnt hair and retched.

Rolling to an elbow, she checked the cell tower. The girders and relay dishes poking over the ridge were dim shadows. She couldn't see the base where the sniper was hidden. She looked uphill, but no stretcher-bots came after them. She crawled to Uniform Four, not trusting her balance yet.

Uniform Four had sprawled on his back, slightly tipped to one side, unmoving. Small flames, like flickering candles, guttered from knee and ankle joints. A wisp of smoke—rising from the bullet crater in his chest—was immediately blown away in the wind. Snowmelt trickled around his inert bulk.

Two prosthetic arms, actuated the same as the Guardian power armor, had gotten a skeletal grip on his ankles. Nina had knocked one loose when she had tipped Uniform Four over. The prosthetics trailed copper braid cables with the insulation burnt off back to boxes once hidden beneath snow that had turned to steam and water. The boxes were probably super capacitors charged by fuel cells. All of this gear, except the EMP generator, had been looted from a medical facility—the prosthetics, the power supply and the stretcher-bots—and turned into an attack focused on capturing a somewhat intact M-1 Guardian unit.

Nina stared at the motionless Uniform Four. She saw no indication that there was cognition or even hold-up power for the AI inside. What could she do? A human casualty was easy, she'd trained for that. Bleeding, breathing, heartbeat. She rapped his helmet, like she was knocking on a door. "Are you okay?"

An unsteady buzz sounded from Uniform Four. "No."

He responded so there was power and he could hear her. How to check for higher cognitive functioning? She needed the manual to troubleshoot these guys. "Uh, what's two plus two?"

"Don't insult me, ma'am," Uniform Four said at low volume. His voice grew stronger and clearer. "Math is for the artillery. I'm an infantry fighting machine."

She laughed.

Uniform Four said, "That was a stupid maneuver, ma'am."

"Yeah, well..." Nina wasn't sure what she had been thinking either. She'd risked her life for an AI? "I'm signed for you and need to bring pieces back for the battle loss estimate. No one would believe a second lieutenant."

"Good that you didn't take us the right way the first time." This time Uniform Four laughed, distorted through the external speaker. Digits and joints wriggled from his start-up checks. "We'd have been totally screwed."

"Seven stretcher-bots at one time cresting the ridge and the sniper with clear field of view? We wouldn't have stood a chance." Although she knew the answer, Nina asked, "Can you walk?"

"My legs are fried." Uniform Four reached down and patted out a flame. He was not going anywhere under his own power. Nina couldn't drag that weight even sliding over snowy ground.

Nina huddled next to him for the warmth that he still radiated. She thought about the hypersonic kill vehicle with growing awe. How long between tricking the Spitfires and its arrival to unleash a metric ton of "fuck you and die" had it been? It had seemed like forever, but closer to thirty minutes in reality. Probably launched from a CONUS site, like Wallops. Definitely not a budget-conscious response. Someone high up in the chain of command had authorized the counterstrike. "Holy shit! That must have been some lie you told the Spitfires."

"Thank you, ma'am. Been working on my war stories."

Ten minutes later, Uniform Four alerted Nina. "Troops approaching. Twelve. From downslope."

The not-so-quick reaction force from COP Murphy plodded through the blowing snow, a dozen soldiers fanned out in a line. The huge bulk of another M-1 Guardian strode in the center of the line, head and shoulders above the human troops. Its e-mag rifle scanned the ridgeline. The new Guardian adjusted its course and led the rest toward Nina and Uniform Four. Nina rose on shaky legs.

"Lieutenant Miller?" yelled the soldier in the lead. A staff sergeant judging from the barely visible rank on the combat vest over his cold-weather gear. "Are you hurt?"

"I'm okay! Don't come closer!"

The rest of the soldiers, in full combat gear, hoods up against the wind, and the Guardian standing as impervious as a statue, halted. They turned outward and formed a hasty perimeter, weapons at the ready.

Nina pointed to the northeast, difficult to see through the blowing snow. "There's a sniper at the cell tower—"

"Second squad is on the way to secure it. Have you seen any remnants of a SoT battalion?"

"No?" Nina replied, confused. "We hit an improvised electrical device. Don't know what else is below the snow."

"Uniform One." The sergeant waved the Guardian forward and pointed at the ground. "Mine check."

Uniform One passed a cursory glance over the ground. It boomed out, "Clear."

Nina continued. "There was a tactical EMP generator and seven hacked stretcher-bots in the valley. Before the air strike. Don't know the disposition. Focused EMP knocked out our comms and we took rounds from the sniper. We—"

"Save the report for the captain," the sergeant interrupted. "We need to get off this mountain. Hicks! Check out Four."

A soldier with an omnimeter slung over his shoulder detached from the perimeter and knelt by Uniform Four. "Uniform One will have to carry this heap back. Four is non-mission capable."

From his voice, Nina recognized the armorer she had signed Uniform Four from earlier that day. A lifetime ago. "He'll be all right?"

"This APES unit is shot to hell, ma'am."

"No," Nina said, "he's just battle scarred."

TODAY I GO HOME
Martin L. Shoemaker

I gulp as the sidecar hits another root in our race through the Belizean jungle. Over my earphones, Major Matthias says, "Sorry, Mr. Pineda."

I grit my teeth. He is not sorry. Through his helmet, I glimpse a big grin on his dark face. He enjoys this run down the nearly imaginary trail through the growth, him on the hybrid-fueled motorcycle, me in the sidecar. We haven't reached the tree line yet, but the undergrowth is too thick for us to exceed thirty kilometers per hour. Matthias pushes right up to that line.

I tell myself he's not crazy; he's afraid. These manageable risks distract him from the death ahead of us.

I had expected a helicopter ride from the Belize Defence Force. Major Matthias had shaken his head. "We must be nimble," he'd said. "Force will be met with force. That's why I told the prime minister it must be just you and me."

That was the lesson we learned from the prime minister's briefing: *Force will be met with force.* But what would the mechanical perceive as force?

I think back on the briefing, searching for clues to the behavior of the mechanical.

We pass through the security door. After hours of scanning, questioning, and searching, we enter what may be the most secure office in Belize City. I had expected to meet Prime Minister Rejón in the National Assembly Building in Belmopan, but instead he has come to the international center in Belize City. *He* has come to *me*, even though I know he sees me as inferior.

Whatever he wants, it is big.

Just inside the doorway is a young woman in the dark green dress uniform of the Defence Force. She is trim, strong, and might be taken for an army receptionist—if not for the automatic rifle in her hands and the tactical helmet she wears. "Please identify yourselves and your purpose here."

Matthias stands at attention as he complies, a tall, strong pillar of military discipline. I am amused at their questions. If they do not know who I am by now . . . But I answer in turn. "I am Dr. Rodrigo Pineda, a citizen of Belize, currently residing in Grand Rapids, Michigan, United States of America. I am a researcher for the MCA Corporation, with a doctorate in artificial intelligence. I am here by invitation of Prime Minister Rejón."

Her tablet beeps. "Voice prints confirmed. Gentlemen, the prime minister will see you." At the far side of the mahogany-paneled room is a single door, solid wood on impressive brass hinges. She turns the key in a mechanical lock, and opens it. Then she lets us inside and locks the door behind us.

Inside is a large but spartan office. Unlike the opulence of the outer office, this room is utilitarian, a simple space occupied by a desk, four chairs, and video screens and paper maps around the walls. No decorations, only a few books, and no personal items. The room is military and purposeful. Like the man behind the desk.

He is older, smaller, than my old adversary. Or maybe it is just that he is sitting. In all the years I worked under him, I never saw Colonel Rejón sit. Even when his limp bothered him, he had always been the proud Belizean defender.

Now . . . I see a cane hung discreetly on the desk. Now he wears an elegantly tailored cream suit, nearly white, though with a tie of dark green—a reminder, no doubt, that he had been Colonel Rejón, Savior of Belize. His hair, once steely gray, is now almost the color of his suit. His eyes are still strong and focused, but now behind small square spectacles.

He looks up at me, and leans forward in his chair as if to rise. The major says, "Prime Minister, you do not have to—"

He holds up a hand. "He is my invited guest, here to do an urgent service for our country. I shall show him respect." Then Rejón surprises me. "Do I look that old, Major?" For the first time, I see a hint of humor.

"No, Prime Minister," Matthias answers, "but—"

Rejón lifts himself to his feet, leaning only a little on the desk. "Mr. Pineda, on behalf of the people of Belize, I thank you for returning in our hour of need."

He reaches out his hand. As I step forward, the major makes a sharp intake of breath; but Rejón looks at him and stares, and he relaxes.

I take his hand and shake it. It's the first time ever we have dealt as—well, not equals, but not commander and subordinate. His grip is firm, belying his obvious age; and I sense he still could crush my hand if he wanted. I almost say *Colonel*, but I stop myself in time. "Prime Minister. It is . . . good to see you." It isn't quite a lie, but I have no fond memories of Colonel Rejón.

He waves to the chairs, and I sit. Then he says, "At ease, Major." Matthias sits as well, but he does not relax. Rejón lowers himself back into his chair and continues. "This room is secure, gentlemen. Major, I don't have to tell you your oaths. Mr. Pineda—" He looks at me; and for a moment, I see the old Iron Colonel in his eyes. "I remind you that you have not renounced your Belizean citizenship."

I pause. "Despite . . . incidents, Belize will always be my home."

At that, Rejón actually smiles, real humor from ear to ear. "How polite you are." The "incidents" had been largely the fault of Rejón and his sympathizers as he gained power within the government. He had never forgiven me for standing against him in a court case. I had seen my opportunities shrink, demotions and canceled contracts.

At last I found it easier to find work with my friend Wayne in the USA, advancing the field of cybernetics. America is my second home, but never my first. My family, Merlene's family, are still here. Our roots are here.

Now the Prime Minister wants something from me. It might improve my position in my homeland. I must not let old grievances sabotage the present.

Instead I say, "I am happy to return, Prime Minister. How might I assist Belize?" Not him, Belize.

Rejón continues, "Much has changed in Belize. You are a technologist, so technology changes are obvious to you. But what else have you noticed?"

I look at the maps on the walls, and suddenly pieces fall into place. "Your military presence in Belize City is high."

Rejón nods solemnly. "Now I must remind you as a citizen of Belize: you are subject to our jurisdiction, and on our sovereign territory. Our national secrecy laws apply, and you are bound by them. This is not a threat, simply reality. If what I say reaches the wrong people, you will be jailed without court proceedings. Since you are not an American citizen, you will have no embassy appeal. Your fate will be in my hands."

And there he is: the Iron Colonel, the man who would do anything for the sake of Belize. I was heartened to see his old resolve, but also frightened. If he thought I threatened Belize, he would stamp me like a roach.

But I was too old and tired to show fear. "I understand, Prime Minister. I want only what's best for Belize."

"Then we are allies. As we should be." He sighs. "Mr. Pineda—or should I call you Rodrigo?"

"We are allies, are we not?"

"A fair note," he acknowledges. "Rodrigo, our military presence *has* increased. The reasons must not leave this room. A technology-fueled faction is trying to take power." He looks down at his tablet, then back up. "Not legally, through elections—they are trying to undermine me and the government itself. Unrest is high, and there are many foreign visitors of questionable backgrounds. My technicians tell me there is a current of revolutionary chatter on the networks, sources that cannot be easily traced before they shut down and others pop up. It is all they can do to keep these persons isolated, and to fight propaganda with facts. Tensions are high in Belmopan." Belmopan is the new capital, ostensibly the site of Rejón's office. Instead he works here, behind layers of guards.

Rejón looks into my wide eyes, nodding. "Yes, in Belize, the land of 'Slow down, enjoy life.' We have kept it out of the foreign press, but there were violent confrontations during the last September Celebration. Calls for a new revolution."

I shake my head. "Prime Minister, I don't know how I can help. I am not a media figure, and I'm not a hacker. Your own must be far better at electronic counterinsurgency than I am."

He nods. "If that were our only concern, you would be sitting in

Michigan, unaware of our troubles. I can stand off these challenges. But a new factor has appeared, one that needs a trained cyberneticist. I need someone loyal, and with the knowledge to shut down a mechanical."

He shows us the briefings. His electronic counterinsurgency unit identified a gathering of armed revolutionary troops. Something had drawn them to the jungle, and the hacked data feed had shown the cause—and the consequences. "We believe they thought it was an old Guatemalan weapons system, from the incursion," Rejón says. "And in a way they were right, but . . ."

He shows us a 3D simulation patched together from four hacked helmet streams. Some of the men wear jungle camo and stick to shadows, disappearing for long stretches. Others are not so cautious. They're dressed for jungle, not for concealment. Strong dungarees and loose shirts protect their limbs, but bold colors stand out. They move normally, not stealthily like the others. They carry electronics and toolkits.

"My apologies," Rejón says. "We couldn't find an audio stream."

On the screen, the men approach a mound on the bank of a stream. It was just terrain, wasn't it?

But the men know something. One of the technicians uses a knife to scrape away at the embankment. Soon his dark face turns back with a big smile, and he points his knife. The helmet stream focuses on metal beneath the dirt.

The man removes a service cover, revealing a set of jacks and LEDs. He inserts a patch cable and taps buttons on a handheld computer. Some of the LEDs flash.

In an instant, the man's head tumbles off his neck and to the jungle floor. The helmet feed turns to see a large, scythe-like blade swinging at the lens. There is a glimpse of shattered glass, followed by electronic interference.

Instantly the feed changes to another helmet, that of a trooper who watches as a nearly three-meter mechanical soldier slices two blade arms through the body of the first cameraman. The second cameraman's rifle comes into view. It is a brave gesture, but futile. He fires three bursts before the mechanical leaps through the air, smashing feetfirst into the man. His feed stops almost immediately.

Next the prime minister shows another rebel feed, this one from a drone flying overhead. Again the video is silent. It shows a different rebel team, more cautious, wearing heavy armor. The end result is no different. In under a minute, seven men lay dead. Then the drone falls, its last image being a fiery bolt streaming straight at it.

"Has this information been confirmed?" I ask. "It could be rebel propaganda."

The prime minister shakes his head. "We sent our own troops. Let me show you."

He plays a third video, this one with sound. Defence Force troops do a careful recon of an area. They fare little better than the rebels, but at least there are survivors. In brief snippets over time, the camera crew falls back quickly. The mechanical pursues them for two kilometers, its legs making a distinctive hiss-and-clank as it runs. Their escort all die in the defense; but at some point the pursuit stops. There is some unmarked perimeter line, beyond which targets are of no interest to the mechanical.

Now Major Matthias and I approach that perimeter, deep inside the tree line. This is the mission Rejón has assigned us: sneak into the area and find a way to defeat the mechanical.

Why only the two of us? Additional scout teams, at dear cost, have established an irregular zone through which the mechanical patrols. Any large incursion beyond that draws its attacks. But its threat assessment algorithms are triggered by size as well as distance. Lone individuals or duos did not draw its attacks. The larger the team, the more aggressively the mechanical responds, and the larger the perimeter it defends. Thus the prime minister had selected just two for this mission: Major Matthias, a trusted member of his security detail; and me.

We pass multiple checkpoints. Matthias's credentials clear us through each, but the troops' eyes grow wide. Rejón may want to keep the mechanical a secret, but he has already failed. Word will get out.

As the sun lowers toward the horizon, it peeks through the canopy. Matthias pulls the motorcycle to a halt. "We are on foot from here, Mr. Pineda."

I nod, and I open the sidecar and step out. My legs are stiff from being cramped in the small compartment. "How far from here?"

Matthias checks his wrist computer. "A little over two kilometers. I don't think we dare ride closer. A vehicle may make the mechanical defensive."

"I understand," I say. Two kilometers are no challenge for me on a treadmill; but through the jungle undergrowth, well, I'm not that young anymore. This could take a while.

As if reading my thoughts, Matthias reaches into his cargo compartment on the other side of the motorcycle and pulls out a large plastic sack, stuffed with more plastic. It rattles as he lifts it. "We go no farther tonight. We'll camp here, and set out in the morning."

I watch as the man pulls a machete from his belt and makes a strong but ultimately fruitless effort at clearing the jungle floor. He cuts back tall grasses and vines, but there remain roots and rocks. It's not flat, but he seems satisfied.

He opens the plastic sack and pulls out rods and more plastic. At a touch of a button, the rods straighten and assemble, and a tent builds itself on the open ground.

I step over and look at the material. "This is . . . strong."

Matthias nods. "It should keep animals out."

I nod. Belize has pumas and jaguars, as well as coyotes and smaller predators. I had learned that lesson as a youth: do not go out into the jungle unarmed against predators, four-footed or two-footed. I tap my own machete and the carbine Matthias procured for me.

Matthias knows the location of a stream, as well as plantains and other edibles. We brought supplies, but I find myself actually enjoying living off the land. Except, of course, when our scout drones buzz overhead and remind me how deadly serious this mission is.

Is it correct that one or two people will not draw the attention of the mechanical? Without access to its code and its training, it is impossible to know. Rass! Rejón and his secrets! He didn't want me going online and searching for programming data for this device. Not that I could search much without knowing its technical specs, but I could try. I could put agents on the nets to try to match the images from the video to known models, and from there trace down the source of their programming.

The prime minister refused. *This is all you must know*, he insisted, handing me a fat wallet of data chips. It was a list of automata from the Guatemalan incursion, provided through the United Nations under the peace accords. He claimed that the chips contained detailed specs for all the models used.

I doubted it at the time; but now as I go through the documentation, it looks thorough and voluminous. It might not be complete, but I doubt I could find more without weeks of searching. Rejón's team did their homework.

As Matthias prepares food and monitors the drones, I dig into the specs—and into the history of Belize from before my childhood. After nearly a century of peace, the new Guatemalan government had tried to claim Belizean territory for themselves. The border war had been intense for ten months, and we almost lost due to the mechanical soldiers that the Guatemalans had gotten from their backers. The mechanicals that they supplied had proven capricious. The units had terrorized the jungles of Belize and devastated whole villages; but intelligence reports showed that sometimes they had gone rogue and attacked Guatemalan units as well. There was instability in their training, some modality in their behavior; and if the mode shifted, allies could become targets in an instant.

The history I learned in school had been incomplete. It told of Colonel Rejón and a few others rallying the troops into guerrilla actions that avoided the mechanicals and targeted the Guatemalan command structure instead. Now I learn that was only part of the truth. Sources inside Guatemala said it was the combination of our guerrilla war and the unreliability of their mechanical troops that finally convinced Guatemalans that their efforts were fruitless. As a new revolutionary government themselves, they could not afford the battle while trying to maintain control of their own country. They had finally withdrawn and agreed to UN peace terms.

Then their government collapsed anyway, and a disaffected military junta had taken control. The records from that time were incomplete, with major portions lost in the fighting—including accounting for the mechanicals that had been withdrawn. There was speculation that many had been sold on the black market.

Or left behind. I wonder at the state of this device. For nearly thirty years, it has been dormant in this distant corner of Belize. Has it been aware? Or did the rebel technicians awaken it? Units like this often had simple algorithmic processors within, and were directed by a base station somewhere nearby. If the unit could not connect with the base station, it followed preprogrammed directives; but the base station had a true artificial intelligence, a neural network of more complexity.

It was a compromise design. A full AI took more infrastructure. To put that into a mechanical soldier, you need more armor to protect it, and that makes the machine slower. A separate unit secured someplace, on the other hand, could control multiple mechanicals in a region. But that creates another point of failure, so it's important to conceal and protect that station. Without it, the individual units would run on programmed responses, which an intuitive human could eventually read and counter. The core could adapt; the units could not.

The core must be defended. Probably the rebel technicians had awakened the core from idle mode; and the core had responded by activating the mechanical.

I lean out of the tent and find Matthias. "Are we sure there's only one mechanical?"

Matthias shakes his head. "You received the same briefing that I did, Mr. Pineda. One is all they've detected."

Rejón's records show that the Guatemalans used both solo units and ganged units. Their mechanicals were surplus units, even black market, whatever was available. There is no way to know what we face without more data.

Hours later, my head is full of specs and designs, but no conclusions. Rejón asks the impossible: to identify and disable this device with no knowledge of how it works. I had tried to convince him to just leave it alone; or failing that, bomb it from the air.

The bombing was out of the question. *Our domestic situation is too tense,* he had said. *If I mobilize now, it will upset the balance, possibly embolden the rebels. This must be kept quiet.*

The man is a fool. I am a fool for accepting this impossible mission.

I look over at Major Matthias. He has been on guard for hours. Now he lies in a light sleep, with overhead drones watching. He is strong, smart, and competent; but he is no cyberneticist. He cannot help me.

I feel my bladder swelling, so I rise from my pad. I am scarcely to my feet when Matthias rises as well. "Where are you going?"

"I must water a tree," I answer.

"Not alone." I try to protest, but he stops me. "I must guard you."

I sigh. The man is not to be dissuaded, so I let him lead me to the tree we had selected for a latrine. He wears night vision goggles, and he scans the trees for trouble.

I lower my zipper and relieve myself. I can almost imagine that I am watched, and not by Matthias.

Then I look up in the dim moonlight breaking through the trees, and I am watched.

"Don't move," Matthias whispers beside me.

I have no intention of moving. The mechanical stands, watching me from thirty meters away. I can barely make out a bipedal shape, three meters tall. Its legs are its longest part, nearly a meter and a half. Able to navigate through high jungle growth, yet able to crouch down below obstacles. It crouches now, and I see a third leg unfold, like some mad artist's conception of a penis, dropping down to make a tripod.

Above the legs is a large trunk. In the darkness I can make out angles but not specifics. "Matthias," I whisper, "shine a light on it."

"Are you crazy?"

I zip up my fly, hoping the mechanical does not notice behind the tree. "It knows we're here. That tripod structure implies only one body manufacturer: bipedal mobility, tripedal stability when needed. It eventually proved difficult to maintain, so no other manufacturer adopted it."

"So what does that tell us?"

I think back over what I've learned. "If I can see some detail, it might tell us the specific model. That might tell me the software architecture and the training modes." I squint, my eyes having adjusted better to the darkness. There are arms around the trunk, but I cannot count them. The video feeds were unclear on that. It had been difficult to even see the machine: every time observers had spotted it, it had been in rapid motion, attacking or pursuing or stalking. I was sure it had at least three arms, which might indicate a hexagonal trunk. But it might have four, or five. "I really must know the configuration, Major."

"But if we draw its attention—"

"Rass, man, we already have its attention!"

"But it's not in defensive mode yet. Spotlighting it might trigger it."

He has a point. Without access to its neural nets, we can't guess what might trigger a mode switch.

I swallow hard. I want to flee. Just leave the thing in peace with its little territory.

But Rejón said that was not an option. *Eventually the rebels may find a way to control it.*

They don't have any more chance of it than you do, I had answered.

Rejón shook his head. *Unless they have information from the Guatemalans and their backers.*

You believe that?

He had sighed. *They knew where to go and what they were looking for. Where did they learn that?*

And he convinced me. I have never liked Rejón, but I trust him. With foreign backing and the right knowledge, the rebels might gain control of the mechanical. I couldn't allow that.

But how far had I agreed to go? I see a way to learn more, but it nearly frightens the life out of me.

"Give me your night vision goggles, Major."

"What?"

"We know the mechanical does not view individuals as a threat. If I approach with the goggles, I can get close enough to make out its configuration and its model. That will eliminate many false trails."

"My assignment is to protect you, not let you walk into that thing's claws. I'll do it."

I shake my head. "You wouldn't know what you're looking for."

"I don't have to. You can look for me." He reaches into a thigh pocket and pulls out another set of goggles. "These are slaved to mine. You will see what I see." He pulls out an earbud. "This will let us talk by bone conduction."

I don the goggles, and I see the jungle lit up. Everything is still the silvery color of moonlight, but brighter, with more contrast. "Look at me," I say. Matthias looks into my face, and I see enough detail to read the manufacturer's mark on the goggles.

I don't want to approach a murderous mechanical, but I don't know if I can save my country by remote control. Matthias is a military man, trained for danger like this. I tell myself that he has better odds than I do.

But does it matter? Can anyone survive against the mechanical?

As if sharing my thoughts, Matthias whispers, "Rejón and his squad fought one such as this. They saved the journalists and brought out the proof that rallied the people."

Every schoolchild in Belize has seen that video. I do not say that Rejón lost half his squad before they escaped.

But I don't have time to worry. Matthias slips around the tree and cautiously makes his way through the ground cover.

Immediately the mechanical rises back onto two legs, folding the third into locked position. Matthias stops; and through the earpiece I hear, "Hello, mechanical. I am a lone traveler on the edge of your range. I am of no interest to you." He takes two more steps forward.

But the mechanical has other ideas. It starts through the brush, with the same soft hiss-clank sound as in the recordings. It moves through the trees, pushing some aside.

I marvel at Matthias as he continues forward. Almost I see young Rejón against the mechanicals. Matthias is a man inspired, loyal, and brave.

Then I am shocked, and I gasp. The mechanical actually *stumbles*! One of its big, clawed feet catches a root in the underbrush, and it tumbles forward!

But it wraps its limbs into a ball as it rolls forward. Suddenly its arms spring out, launching it into the air, and it lands perfectly positioned on all three feet. It has halved the distance to Matthias.

One who did not know mechanicals might think that was a tactic to close distance; but I know better. It stumbled. It is fallible.

I get my first good look at the torso. It is indeed hexagonal, ruling out many possible models. "That may be enough, Matthias."

But the soldier continues forward. My knees tremble on his behalf, and I almost drop to the ground behind the tree.

Then I notice a flare in the night vision goggles: something bright near the center of the torso, overwhelming the sensors. "Matthias, can you dim the goggles? And zoom in on that flashing light?"

The image grows dark, and the torso zooms toward my face. I see status lights. I could read them if I knew the machine's specs.

Then I notice a pattern. "Can you focus?"

"Let me . . ." The image resolves to four lights. The one on the left is solid, and the next one as well. The third light blinks, roughly twice per second. I can make out a fourth light, currently dark.

It's a common pattern for communications devices. The first light is an internal self-test. The second light indicates that the unit has a functioning radio. The third light . . .

It's searching for a response. "Matthias, get back."

"What?" He starts backing away.

"I can use this information. Maybe I can contact it. If I only knew—"

The mechanical bounds through the brush, leaping high this time to avoid entanglement. It lands directly in front of Matthias, and the man freezes.

"What do I—"

"Wait." It's so close, I can't see through the goggles, so I pull them off. It takes precious seconds for my eyes to adjust back to moonlight.

The mechanical has stopped in front of Matthias, extended its third leg, and crouched. The left light blinks, and all of the others are out.

"What do I do?" For the first time, Matthias's voice trembles.

The left light stops blinking, and the second light starts. "It's looking for service," I say.

"So what do I—"

"Back away."

The mechanical is checking its internal diagnostics. There is nothing it can do until that check finishes and it moves to the next. There is a brief window when Matthias can escape.

But the Major says, "You still don't have your answer."

"Rass, man! You have fifteen seconds."

"That's enough." He lights his headlamp, and he leans in close to the panel with the lights. Then, moving quickly despite the brush, he leans to scan the right side, and then the left.

"Nine seconds!"

"That's all I need!" He backs quickly behind the tree, grabs me, and pulls me toward the campsite. As we back away, I see the third light start to blink.

The mechanical is saying: *Hello, help me.* I just do not know its language. I cannot answer.

⊕⊕⊕

Matthias decides we're too close. We spend a few minutes packing up the campsite, and then we hike a kilometer away before dropping to the ground to rest.

I turn to Matthias in the darkness. The moon has set, but he stares back at me through the night vision goggles. "What?" he asks.

I cannot help grinning. "You are either brave, or a fool. But the Prime Minister chose well."

"We're both fools," he says. "But I . . ."

He doesn't continue. "What is it, Major?"

I hear him shift in the darkness. "I am a soldier. Dying in the line of duty comes with the job. If I were in a firefight, I would be prepared. But hand-to-hand, alone against the mechanical, is nothing I've trained for."

I hear him rise to his feet. His voice moves back and forth as he paces. "Every soldier in the Force can tell you of the mechanicals and how Rejón won against them. But we never trained for them, outside of virtual reality. It's not the same when you hear it with your unaided ears and see that thing come tumbling through the air."

"You didn't flinch. You stood your ground."

He chuckles. "Soldiers are trained to hold. If you had looked closely, I was trembling in terror."

"But even in terror, you stood. You were brave."

"I had to be. If I must die to stop enemies from using mechanicals against us again, that is my job."

"So you would have challenged it, wrestled it with your bare hands?"

"No, I would have died at its hands, while you escaped with the data. You're going to fight this battle, not me."

When the dim sunlight breaks through the cover, Matthias sends the drones aloft. Meanwhile I must find a way to stop the mechanical. I pull up recordings of last night's encounter, and I sit back against a tree, munching on jerky sticks and dried fruit.

I examine the video and confirm that the torso is hexagonal, and it is a three-armed model. Two have blades, while a third is a fine manipulator. Each has a weapon barrel mounted along its length, two rifles and a larger bore that looks like a missile launcher.

Does the device still have ammunition? We have never seen it fire a rifle, though it brought down a drone with a missile.

I examine the full light images of the control panel. I am surprised to see the panel labeled in English: POWER UP, INT COMM, EXT COMM, and DATA. I'd expected a Guatemalan unit to be labeled in Spanish.

Again I wish I could go online, but I agree with Rejón. The mechanical knows we're out here. We cannot guess what might make it see us as a threat. Comm traffic might draw its attention.

As might . . . "Matthias, Call the drones back."

"What do you mean?" But I see him tapping at his gauntlet computer.

"I begin to understand why we're safe while larger units aren't. It expects a service technician."

"What does that have to do with the drones?"

"I'm getting to that. One person might be a technician. Two people might be a technician and an assistant. More than that . . ."

"More than that could be a flanking force." Matthias nods. "It won't allow that."

"And drones are not service techs."

"I shall pull them back from the machine's perimeter."

"Farther," I say. "These mechanicals are adaptive. After our encounter last night, it may have changed its routine. I would keep the drones at least twice as far away as before."

"Understood." Matthias goes back to his controls.

Design is about compromise. A machine that kills its service technicians will die in the field. A machine that lets an individual get too close with a bomb is destroyed. The mechanical had let Matthias get close enough to respond with the proper recognition code, but how long would it be patient? We need that code.

I search Rejón's data, but it seems fruitless. The status panel was a common component for its time; but the panel, the hexagonal torso, and the combination of legs and arms match nothing in the database.

I remember that Matthias also captured images of the machine from each side. I can hope . . . The images are blurry. Matthias had been in a hurry to escape, after all. I apply image correction algorithms, trying to find detail in the blur.

When the image from the machine's left side resolves, I do not believe it at first. This fits with none of Rejón's data. Not even close.

But there's no mistake. I could not possibly fail to recognize the MCA Corporation logo. My employer.

This makes no sense. MCA started out manufacturing medical care androids. We were never in the mechanical soldier business.

Never that I know of. I am but a junior researcher, and the company was decades old when I joined. An entire generation of contracts had come and gone by then.

And we did have security contracts. Our early androids included ingenious empathy nets that interpreted a subject's emotions and concerns. Only one of those was truly successful: the android Carey whom I'd met when its family had come to Belize; but the empathy-net technology had been applied in a wide variety of uses. And I seem to recall...

Yes, a profit line on the annual report: empathic security scanners in airports and government buildings. The devices can tell the difference between a person afraid to fly and a person afraid to get caught in a plot.

I have known Carey now for a decade. Its insights are amazing. And its technology is three and a half decades old, which means it predated the Guatemalan incursion. This mechanical might have a newer generation of the empathy net. The same technology focused on threat detection might be more specialized, more finely attuned.

I do not like coincidences, especially not when lives are on the line. Of nearly two dozen possible operating systems used in mechanical soldiers of the day, this unit has the one in which I am an expert?

But I forget what it was like back then. There were far fewer successful artificial intelligences. This machine could have versions of Carey's networks. Without Carey's sentience, the networks would give feedback, but no control. None of Carey's humanity.

It gives this unit a weakness: I understand its programming on a deeper level. I know how to make contact with it, if I can get close enough to form a local network.

I rise from the log on which I sit, and I start toward the woods.

"Where are you going?" Matthias asks.

"To complete our mission." I start deeper into the jungle. The growth here is low, just grass and leaf cover.

And snakes! I feel something squirm under my foot, and I leap into the air. Before I land, Matthias hacks at the ground with his machete.

"Is it venomous?" I ask.

He plies the ropey, headless form from the brush. "No." He glares at me. "Not this time."

I glare back. "I must reach the mechanical. Otherwise we're wasting our time."

"Then let me go first."

I shake my head. "It has to be me. I can persuade it."

"But can you persuade the snakes? The jaguars? I'm here to protect you, and that's what I shall do. When we see the mechanical, you can take the lead. Until then, follow me."

So I follow him into the denser cover, trees and vines and thickets of thorns. He looks in all directions at once, never a pattern, never focusing long on any one spot. He is an expert at navigating this dense terrain.

I think through what I know about MCA systems, both Carey's ancient nets and more modern. This mechanical is a version somewhere in between. Certain protocols will still be a part of it. Other protocols have evolved over time. I must be prepared for both.

We march for two hours before Matthias stops to take a bearing.

"Are we close?" I ask.

He shakes his head. "It is difficult to be certain. Our team never . . ."

He doesn't finish. They never had a chance to map the area before the mechanical killed them.

I look around. "Where is it? We're well within its perimeter."

Matthias nods. "I worry that it hunts us."

"Have you seen it?"

"No." He looks around. "But it is what I would do."

It is what I would do . . .

MCA's early androids had not just empathy networks, but also emulation networks. While never as successful as Carey, they could pretend to be someone else. To read a person's emotional state and behavior, understand it, and then repeat it.

I am led by a skilled soldier and jungle hunter; and somewhere, the mechanical watches us. Watches Matthias.

"Leave me, Matthias," I say.

"What?"

"Leave me." He opens his mouth, but I continue. "I know. Snakes, jaguars, mechanical soldiers. I'll be all right, but *you* are the threat."

"What?"

"It watches you. It understands what you're feeling, what you're doing. And it will respond in kind, only faster."

"I don't understand."

I want to slap the man to get his attention, but that may anger the mechanical. Instead in a low, calm voice, I say, "The jungle is your area. The mechanical is mine. It learns from you to be a better soldier. And your caution, your fear, tells it that you are its adversary. From you, it will learn that it must destroy us. But if I am alone—"

"It will kill you."

"Not if I approach it as myself: a service technician with a job to do. It will know that I am no threat."

"And that you are afraid."

"And that I am afraid. I cannot hide that, but I have a job to do. *That* will be foremost in my mind. But I can't do it if I expect a mechanical Matthias to crash through the jungle and slay us." I hear a distant crack, and I try to slow my breathing. "So go. Calmly. Slowly. Do not worry about me. Go."

Before Matthias can object, I turn toward the distant sound of a twig cracking. I dare not look back to see if Matthias has listened to me. I must have confidence. I am a technician with a job to do. I have a unit to service, and I approach it as a professional, not as an enemy.

It takes me twenty minutes to find my way to the top of an embankment. I see the mechanical crouching on all three legs, sensor pod focused on me. It rises up half a meter, but it does not move.

We are only ten meters apart. Beyond the embankment is the stream from the video. This is the unit's home base.

I take another step forward, and I see the lights on the mechanical's torso. It's back to a single light, self-test. It wants to talk to me.

I pull out my tablet and turn on a comm scanner. When the second light flashes, I run through frequencies, and find two bands in use. I watch the incoming traffic.

Soon a stream of signals appears on my screen, encrypted. I set my decryption algorithm to work on them, trying to pick out a coherent message. In the meantime, I ready my response for when the mechanical finishes its comms test. The clock on my tablet measures fifty-five seconds when I send my response: an unencrypted NAK, not acknowledged. A universal communications code for *Message not received correctly.*

The mechanical hunkers low again. We have established simple communication, and it responds to the NAK as I hoped. It restarts its testing process. The self-test light blinks again.

This would be the moment to destroy the mechanical if I had a weapon that would touch it. For this brief interval of testing, it has only reflexes. Its simple modular brain cannot plan and adapt while tied up in this test.

But I have no weapon, and I'm not ready to destroy it. Instead I have a plan. By the time the third light blinks again, my tablet has the proper decryption keys. The next stream of messages are in English. I can read them.

Unit still in service mode. Please exit service mode.

Unit has been in service mode for 15,732,219 minutes.

Training mode: ACTIVE.

Training mode. This isn't the mechanical talking, it's the master unit, buried in the bank.

Again my timer heads toward one minute, so again I send a NAK.

This time there is one line of response. *Communications protocol error. Retries remaining: 3.*

Rass! The security network grows suspicious. I don't know what it will do after the third retry, and I do not want to find out. I scan through my communications codes, looking for one to change the mechanical's behavior without making it aggressive.

The second light is almost done blinking when I find what I need. When the third light starts and the messages come through, I send a simple response: *Wireless communication failure. Site service required.*

I repeat that message until the mechanical steps forward, reaches out with two of its arms, and lifts me in the air.

It's a short trek along the bank to the base station. As we approach, a mud-covered wall slides aside, revealing a metal tunnel.

The mechanical carries me in. Am I a prisoner or a technician? I must act like the latter.

I look around, wondering how long it took the Guatemalans to excavate this base behind enemy lines. It's large enough to charge and reprogram five of the mechanicals. Next to the charging stations is a work console.

The air inside is fresh, neither dusty nor damp. There must be air recycling; and since such devices have heat signatures, there must be a baffling system as well.

There are no other mechanicals here. Perhaps one was all its masters could afford, or perhaps the others were lost.

The mechanical sets me down, giving me hope that I'm free to work. I sit at the console, and it clanks along behind me on its hydraulic legs.

The screen lights up. Where's the power source? Perhaps geothermal? I read a simple login prompt: *MCA Sentry System. Please login.* It asks for a domain and a password on the line below that— again, all in English. I try my MCA credentials; but the screen goes black with a single message: *Domain/User unrecognized.*

I try a service domain and my credentials there. But the error message appears again, this time in red. I hear the mechanical take another step toward me.

The system predates me. It hasn't been on the MCA network. Its credentials have to be old.

So I try credentials I use only for one job: diagnosing and testing Carey.

The console lights up in friendly blue, and the mechanical behind me eases to the ground.

I sit very still. I do not want the mechanical to realize how relieved I am, and how fearful I was.

I do not want to assume too much. With the technician credentials, I might make the console do anything, and the mechanical as well. Or I might trip a security alarm, and bring my death. So first I must know the state of the machine.

I navigate through status menus, and soon the problem is obvious: someone has left this unit in training mode, modifying its neural network for thirty years—as if they started a training session and then were interrupted before finishing. Or as if some field technician, not understanding how these machines work, just left it in training mode, thinking that would give it an advantage. It is impossible to know which.

So instead of operating on a fixed neural net image, this unit has grown its neural net ever since the incursion. Any experience it took in changed the network, possibly trimming off little-used paths. And worse, in training mode it reruns past experiences. For decades it has been sped through old scenarios, reinforcing the results and building new responses.

So it is trained to relive those old battles, with entirely new response patterns. This unit and this mechanical have trained themselves to be the ultimate jungle-war fighters. But because they were in training mode, they expected a technician present. That was a hole in its defenses, and I fit through that hole.

Just like that, the threat is ended. I pause the training, and the lights on the front of the mechanical go out. Then I search through the training index, and I find the zero point: the time when the mechanical had not yet been trained to fight. And I tell it to revert to that point.

The mechanical threat is ended. But the real threat remains.

"Hey!" I shout through the jungle. "Hey, Matthias!"

The mechanical sees him before I do, turning its head while spinning its torso around. It holds me in two of its arms, and it uses its body to shield me.

"Mr. Pineda!" Matthias shouts back. "Are you all right?"

"I will be as soon as you put down your weapons."

"What?"

I tap a command on my tablet, and the mechanical sprints halfway up the embankment. "I said put down your weapons, or the mechanical will take them, and you might get hurt."

"Mr. Pineda—"

I tap another command. The machine leaps three meters forward, almost within reach of Matthias. "Down. Now."

I watch through the mechanical's eyes as Matthias lays down his rifle, his carbine, and his machete.

"The rest of them," I say.

"This is everything. Do you see any more?"

"The mechanical's metal detector says you still have a stiletto and two grenades. Put them all down. Now."

I hope that I can bluff Matthias better than I can the mechanical. The machine is an idiot right now. Matthias might outwit it, but he can't know that.

Slowly he puts down the remaining weapons, and he backs away. "Mr. Pineda, I don't understand."

"You understand. And now so do I."

Matthias smiles, but I do not find it comforting. "We have succeeded. You will be a hero!"

"To which side?" I ask. "Prime Minister Rejón, or the rebels?"

"Why . . . the prime minister, of course!"

"It was your idea," I say. "One technician and one bodyguard where larger forces on both sides had failed. What gave you that idea?"

He pauses. "Creative thinking," he says at last. "Something that had not been tried yet."

"And the only thing that could bypass the mechanical's training: a small, trusted technical staff."

"And it worked! We have proven it."

I shake my head. "It was too convenient. Who suggested me for this mission, Major?"

He hesitates, eyeing the mechanical. "The prime minister."

"I don't believe it. There is no love lost between us. He could have hired anyone else, or enlisted the best and brightest here in Belize. But you talked him into choosing me."

"That is madness . . ."

"You brought me straight in, confidently, as if you knew the territory. Not just from the reconnaissance videos, but as if you had personal knowledge."

"I had briefings."

"Then you brought us close enough to see the mechanical, and for you to approach it."

"I risked my life to defend you!"

"You approached it in a nonthreatening manner, as if you knew what to expect."

"It almost killed me!"

"It still may," I say, and I see the major swallow. "You got close enough to get the details that I asked for, but then you did more. Unbidden, you scouted the sides, to get the MCA label, so that I would deduce how to communicate with the mechanical."

"There was no time! I just—I just reacted."

"You just *acted*, as if you knew what you were looking for. As if you knew what this mechanical was, how it got there, and why I could communicate with it."

"You're making no sense." I do not notice, but the mechanical senses that the major has shifted closer to his pile of weapons. It steps closer and hovers both blade arms over the pile. The major steps back.

"Someone told you what was out here," I continue. "Someone knew."

"Ridiculous."

"And all controls in the command center are in English, not Spanish. Not the language of Guatemala."

"You can't—"

"It is a trivial matter to switch the console over to Spanish, but the technicians who ran it kept it in English. They were Belizean. Traitors!"

Matthias answers, "No." I look around the mechanical's shoulder at the major. "Patriots. Loyalists, as truly Belizean as Colonel Rejón in his day. Men and women who thought the only way to fight mechanicals was *with* mechanicals. They got funding for their own mechanical soldier, and were in pursuit of more."

"I have the logs from the command center. They had a unit to test, but they lacked deep knowledge of how artificial intelligences work, and how training mode works versus operational mode. Someone left this unit in training mode, thinking that would improve its responses.

"Then the logs stopped. The research team and their guards were wiped out in the Guatemalan incursion. There were no entries past a point late in the war."

"Astonishing!" Matthias says. From the way the mechanical shifts, I am sure the man is planning something. "A revelation. Who knows how the war might have gone if this experiment had continued?"

"But it wasn't. Colonel Rejón with his tactics and the Belize Defence Force rallied by him fought a war of attrition until the Guatemalan government fell to internal rebellion. Steadfastness won our war." I tap the mechanical's head. "Not mechanical soldiers."

"Good." He takes another half step backwards. "We can report this."

"But to whom?"

"What do you mean?"

"All these years, someone knew this mechanical was out here. Someone wanted it found, but not destroyed, just mastered. They ordered you to make that happen."

"I take my orders from the chain of command," he says indignantly.

"Yes, but which chain of command? How long have you served the rebels?"

"I will not have my honor questioned!" Matthias balls his fists.

I am not fast enough. I try to tap commands, but I'm too late. Sensing a threatening motion, the mechanical lunges forward, blade arms slashing. Before I even know what happens, Major Matthias's head lies at the mechanical's feet.

I lean over the side of the mechanical and taste bile as I lose my breakfast.

The mechanical patrols in a spiral pattern, looking for more threats. I tap a command to put it back at rest.

The rebels must be the people within the Defence Force who commissioned this machine. The ones who would have turned the jungle into nonstop mechanical warfare, against the express wishes of the government of the time.

I glance at Matthias's headless torso. And the government of today. I am sure that this is the source of the rebellion: while Prime Minister Rejón lives, Belize will have nothing to do with mechanical soldiers. They are too much of an insult to our national pride. They are the coming of replacements. Rejón will never accept them. But the rebels are eager to add them to their force.

This is too much for me. I am a technician, not a diplomat. Not a national leader. This is a decision I should not have to make.

But I am the only one here to make it. I must decide. Right now, I hold the power within Belize.

I think of Prime Minister Rejón, the harsh authoritarian, the man who rules even the smallest detail. And I understand why the rebels oppose him.

But I think of Colonel Rejón, who saved our nation. My friend Carey explained that everything Rejón did was rooted in his fear that Belize might fall to foreign forces. He continues to fight a war he almost lost, and is determined that such a war will never again happen here.

I do not forgive Rejón for the way he treated my family, but I understand. That is a form of forgiveness: to know why the other person does the things you could never do.

But I can do this. In the spirit of Colonel Rejón, I can keep Belize free of mechanical soldiers. Right now, I am master of mechanicals. I can march this one deep into the jungle until it loses connection with its command center, and until its power source fails.

And when it falls still, I shall take it apart and bury the pieces like a lost fossil of the old war.

I do not do this for the prime minister, but for Colonel Rejón and the people of Belize. My people.

ALL IS ONE
Doug Beason

"Captain Voight," said Alice's disembodied voice, "the last two hundred nodes have been upgraded with their high-power lasers and are moving from the 3D-printing facility. Once they accomplish their plane change to polar orbit, they will rendezvous with Surveillance Array 7 within the next thirty-six hours."

Floating in the command center, Sandy looked up out of habit but only saw an empty compartment of control consoles, computer screens, and an outside portal. Alice's voice was positioned so Sandy wouldn't be spooked if it suddenly spoke in case of an emergency. And after a year in space, you'd think she'd be used to it.

But rather than calming, Sandy felt uneasy, knowing that her status on Space Force One was being monitored on a constant basis. Every time she ate, spoke, slept, moved, turned, or rotated through the space station—everything she did—was being watched, analyzed by the omnipresent AI. She could never get away from the constant oversight.

Although she'd entered her concern in the Captain's log, she hadn't told anyone of her discomfort. The official journal was quantum encrypted, inaccessible even to Alice, so she was more frank in her assessments than she'd be in public.

The docs had told her that Alice's omnipresence would eventually be ignored by the crew and would be unconsciously welcomed, much as a child on a playground was comforted knowing her parents were nearby. Still, over the past few months Sandy didn't like knowing that she could never be truly alone.

"Thanks," Sandy said. "I assume Surveil-Sat 7 will remain

operational while the nodes are inserted in formation?" The surveillance array was a kilometers-long, sparse virtual mirror. It was one of twelve total arrays, each staggered one hundred twenty degrees apart in four separate polar orbits, allowing constant surveillance of every point on Earth.

Over a thousand toaster-sized nodes made up each array, all outfitted with highly efficient sensors and photodetectors. When phased with their nearest neighbor nodes, they created the equivalent of a telescope more than a mile in diameter and produced multispectral, ultra-high-resolution imagery of the Earth. And now that the nodes had been retrofitted with high-power solid-state lasers, they could produce a plasma deep in the atmosphere, dramatically increasing the array's resolution using adaptive optics techniques.

"Yes, Captain. Their delta velocity is only 0.1 kilometers a second."

Just over two hundred miles an hour, thought Sandy. She still couldn't bring herself to think in the metric system—even having worked in the space program most of her life and living on board the orbiting station for the last year. Despite all the new technology over the past decade—two-stage-to-orbit rockets, surveil-sat arrays, 3D printing in space, repairbots, the Internet-of-Things, and of course everything overseen by Alice—Space Force One still used the International Space Station's aging legacy hardware, although dozens of modules had been added to the original structure, vastly increasing its size.

And why not? Over a million pounds of metal and equipment had been launched to Near-Earth-Orbit by over sixty old space shuttle missions, and every nation's space program still used the football-field-sized monstrosity in one way or another. So the English units had stuck and would never go away, no matter how many of the fifteen permanent crew members hailed from the international community—

"—Excuse me, Captain. Did you understand?"

Sandy shook her head. "Go ahead."

"My radar just detected a cloud of space junk in a highly elliptical orbit approaching Space Force One. The debris has an ETA of thirty-five minutes, and is descending too fast to avoid a collision unless the station undergoes a drastic change in altitude—"

"How drastic?" She glanced at the control screen as the uncatalogued space junk indicator blinked red.

"At the rate the debris is expanding, I project an altitude boost is needed of over fifty kilometers—"

"*Fifty kilometers?*" Sandy said. "Where did this come from? Why didn't you detect it sooner?"

"It just came over the horizon. The debris has the orbital parameters of two decommissioned Russian satellites in a Molniya orbit, and from the size of the pattern they must have recently collided. The cloud is rapidly expanding, and there is a finite probability that a piece greater than ten centimeters in diameter will impact the station unless we immediately take evasive action. Altitude adjustment is now fifty-one kilometers—"

"That will use the majority of our reserve fuel," Sandy said. Her mind raced through other options. "Where's the nearest surveillance array?"

"Array 2 has just breached the horizon and is approaching at an angle eight kilometers below us."

"Can you reposition its lasers onto the debris?"

It took Alice less than a second to answer. "I can reorient the nodes to focus their lasers on separate elements of the approaching debris field—which when phased will destroy the smallest debris or change the orbit of the largest pieces."

Sandy pulled in a breath. She could either use up her reserve and risk not having additional fuel until the next supply ship arrived, or try this hairbrained scheme. She'd be using the lasers for space defense instead of producing a plasma in the atmosphere, but their survival may be at stake. HQ had similar, classified contingencies for using the high-power lasers, but those capabilities had never been demonstrated. The advantage of trying it now would be that they would know immediately if it worked.

They'd increased altitude just yesterday to account for air friction, and weren't scheduled to boost again for another three weeks. Although they periodically changed altitude to avoid large pieces of space junk, they only boosted up a few kilometers at the most—not fifty.

"Take it out with the array's lasers," Sandy said. "Do it."

"Yes, Captain," Alice said.

"Ready the station to boost if this doesn't work, on my command. And display the array and debris cloud on the screen."

Sandy swam to the control console and watched an image of the surveillance array as it approached. She zoomed in and saw thousands of nodes in precise formation reorienting, their platforms glinting sunlight. She didn't see any sign that the lasers were being engaged, as there was no atmosphere to reflect the light.

She flipped to an enhanced radar feed of the approaching debris. At first it looked like a slowly growing, hazy cloud embedded by pinpoints of light. Still no sign of any lasers . . .

"Lasers engaged," Alice said.

Seconds passed, then slowly the pattern started changing. One by one pinpoints of light blinked out, and the haziness started to turn transparent.

A minute later the debris field had disappeared from the screen, showing only a few larger pieces that diverged from their original orbit. The station was safe. Sandy let out a sigh of relief, suddenly feeling drained.

With the latest upgrades there were now two lasers on all surveillance nodes. Each platform communicated through a low-power LED laser, which transmitted data picked up by their photodetectors, and allowed each platform to perfectly align itself with its nearest-neighbor satellites, creating one massive virtual mirror.

Coherent lasers had been phased on board the International Space Station years ago. Shortly after, optics on free-flying satellites demonstrated they could be phased, a capability based on DARPA's old Excalibur program. The present nodes were platforms the size of a toaster, with photodetectors that could be precisely aligned so that a few thousand of them provided the same capability as one large orbiting optic—putting the old-school bus-sized Hubble and spy telescopes to shame.

And now with the addition of a high-power laser, the array could phase those as well. The coherent beam could punch its way through the Earth's atmosphere and create a plasma fireball miles above the surface, much as what Earth-based telescopes did when they corrected their large mirrors through the well-known technique of adaptive optics. The upshot was that with the higher-power laser, the massive, space-based virtual mirror could now view millimeter-sized objects on the ground completely without distortion. A coup for space surveillance, but devastating for privacy.

Just like with Alice...

"Captain?" Alice said. "I've just been informed that NEO-3's exchange-crew launch has been rescheduled for tomorrow. The resupply ship is also pushed back a day."

"Any reason?"

"Space Force is making a personnel change. I'll update you as soon as I receive the final manifest."

"Copy," said Sandy. Floating upside-down in the control center, she took one last look out the port as she logged the change. Like always, Alice was taking care of all the details.

It was almost like her AI-based nature had grown a motherly instinct. And although the artificial intelligence program was not biased toward any gender, Sandy wasn't the only Space Force officer who had noticed Alice's evolution as being more protective, motherly. Maybe they shouldn't have nicknamed the AI program as a female, but then again, it was because living with the technology seemed more like they were immersed in Wonderland. So in retrospect, maybe they should have called her the White Rabbit instead. Or better yet, the Mad Hatter.

She moved out of the control center, and pushing her stump against a panel she shot through a series of long, interconnected modules. At each intersection she passed through airlocks situated at varying orientations, dependent on which direction adjacent modules were connected. The airlocks were outfitted with explosive bolts, put in place so that the modules could be easily separated in case of a catastrophic event—such as what might have happened if that debris field had impacted the station. The ability to separate the self-contained modules was a last-ditch fail-safe measure installed to ensure that if the station was forced to deorbit, some modules would survive and remain in space.

Everything from upper-stage fuel tanks to old rocket bodies were added as modules, increasing the size of the orbiting Space Force station. The original, linear International Space Station had measured over a football field in length; now, dozens more modules had been connected perpendicular and parallel to the main axis. As much as Space Force had built up the ISS, it was now a three-dimensional maze of interconnected components.

From Earth, SF-1 looked like a collection of piping—some large, some small. Space Force One was an evolving menagerie of operational compartments, living quarters, supply modules, tanks for growing food and reprocessing liquids and oxygen. In addition, there were classified compartments for strategic and tactical reconnaissance, surveillance, as well as additional defensive and offensive capabilities.

At the star-side end of SF-1, opposite from Earth and thus hidden from any ground-based surveillance, the 3D-printing facility used space junk as feedstock. The material was brought in by small scavenger satellites, clearing the navigation lanes of nuts, bolts, pieces of solar panels, metal panels and other pieces of debris from collisions. Decommissioned satellites, jettisoned rocket engines and upper stages were swept in with the debris.

Alice provided oversight running SF-1, keeping the facility fit for human habitation, as well as coordinating Space Force One's various mission elements—allowing a small human presence of sixteen personnel to oversee military operations. Otherwise, a cadre of over a hundred people—the equivalent crew required for a naval vessel— would be needed to safely run the orbiting military facility.

After looking in on the crew quarters and stopping by the entertainment and meal modules, Sandy moved through SF-1, checking in with the operational sections.

The crew seemed upbeat, and there were no outstanding issues. She knew that was partially due to the upcoming change in watch, but she also knew that NEO-3, the monthly Near-Earth-to-Orbit shuttle, was due within a few days, and would be changing out a third of the crew.

Using her hands, she pulled into the control center and saw that her deputy, Michael Goodson, had already shown up for his watch. He floated in front of the comm panel, reviewing the upcoming schedule.

"Hey," said Sandy as she drifted in. "You're early."

Michael glanced up. "Good evening, Captain. I'm not that early."

"So you're aching to get bored."

"Ha. I just wanted to check on the surveil-sat upgrade." He scrolled through a list. "It looks like the new nodes are still on track for rendezvous." He looked up. "That was quick. Even if the lasers were the only items printed."

"That's what I thought too," said Sandy. She pointed to another part of the screen. "But you missed all the excitement." She brought him up to speed on the array taking out the debris.

Michael looked thoughtful. "Alice didn't tip our hand on the Surveil-Sat's offensive capability?"

Sandy shook her head. "I doubt it. I didn't broadcast it to HQ and only entered it in my Captain's log. As far as anyone knows it was a hot test of the array's Adaptive Optics."

"Good cover story," Michael said. "Anything else?"

"When you're settled, ask Alice to conduct an AO test run once the last nodes are in place. Let me know if there's any problem."

"Yes, ma'am."

"I also ran through the GEO, MEO, and LEO operations, and stopped by the printing facility. Everything's green, and hopefully no unexpected debris will arrive for at least another few days. We've got a hundred twenty-nine percent reserve of feedstock, so unless we have to print a whole new NEO shuttle, we're looking good."

Michael laughed. It had been hard enough printing the upgrades to the surveillance nodes, that constructing an entirely new Near-Earth-Orbit shuttle would be close to impossible. As advanced as the 3D facility was, anything more than printing specific parts or small instruments would be out of the question. It certainly would have been easier to bring up enough solid-state lasers to retrofit the nodes . . . but that would have meant putting hands on the process by bringing each node into the station, manually installing the lasers, and hoping that human intervention hadn't screwed anything up. So although printing the high-power lasers had stretched the orbiting facility to its limits, it had been a completely hands-off operation and had proven the versatility of having an on-orbit, 3D production capability.

The gallium and indium nitrides feedstock for the node's blue diode lasers was mined from abandoned and out-of-commission satellites by harvesting their solar cells, power transistors, and integrated circuits. And that had pushed both the printing and debris collecting to the max. Yet, they'd been successful.

"Speaking of the NEO shuttle, Captain, any word on who's coming up with the crew change?"

Sandy shook her head. "I imagine we'll find out right before launch. I wouldn't expect anyone new on the manifest, though I assume I would have been notified." Space Force had gotten into the habit of not choosing the final crew until the last minute.

There were enough space-qualified cadre for married couples who worked in different functional areas to serve on board at the same time. And because of operational or even family commitments, the final rotation list was always four times larger than the number who would eventually be launched to the station.

Sandy started to leave. "Have a good watch."

"Thanks," Michael said. "And have a good rest."

"You got it." Sandy pulled out of the comm center and pushed off for her quarters. She turned, floating backwards as she left. "Let me know when headquarters releases who's on the crew—"

Alice interrupted, "I'll let both you and Lieutenant Goodson know when the list arrives."

Sandy grunted as she exited the node, somewhat annoyed that Alice had been eavesdropping. But then again, it was her job.

The commanding officer's module was through the next airlock, so Sandy used her hands to swing directly into her quarters. She left the airlock open and simply closed the door, wanting quick access to the control module in case anything happened. Michael could certainly take care of any emergency, but old habits die hard, and she was never one to sit back and merely watch if things got exciting.

She lowered the lights and, rotating slightly in the center of her small quarters, started stripping off her clothes. She'd always had trouble with the one-piece jumpsuit, so bending over as far as she could she pulled the bottom of the fabric over her stumps and the suit popped off. She balled it up and tossed it to the ultrasonic cleaner, causing her to float backwards toward the shower.

Alice's disembodied voice spoke as she reached the enclosed device. "There's a call from Commander Tanku, ma'am. Do you want me to patch him in to your chamber?"

"Put him through," Sandy said, "and kill the video. Make it a private link."

"Very well, Captain."

Seconds later she heard a rustling from the intercom. "Sandy? Are you there?" Russell Tanku's voice filled the chamber. "The video link is down."

"I'm getting ready for a shower," Sandy said. Smiling, she folded her arms and imagined his warm embrace. Another reason not to broadcast, even over a private link.

"Understand," he said. "I just wanted to give you a heads-up that I'll be on NEO-3 tomorrow. But only as an observer and not part of the exchange crew."

"Good news," Sandy said. It would be great to see him, but the Near-Earth-Orbit shuttle was only due to dock for a few orbits, just enough time to change out the crew and not enough time to spend together. She tried not to sound disappointed. "Anything up?"

"The six-month due diligence inspection. I talked George into letting me run it instead of one of the bureaucrats, to give ground another perspective."

Sandy brightened. "So you won't be doing a touch and go."

"No way," Russell said. "I'll be on station for a few days and return with the resupply mission at the end of the week. That will give me more than enough time to run through your operation."

"Yes," Sandy said softly. "That, and more."

He laughed. "Will you be able to berth an additional crewmember for a few nights?"

Sandy glanced around her command chamber. There was plenty of room for both of them, and despite their relationship being an open secret, it had been almost a year since they'd seen each other. "No problem," she said.

"I didn't think so," Russell said; she could almost see him smiling. "Hey, I'll let you go and see you tomorrow. You'll be getting the official boarding-crew manifest soon, but I just wanted to make sure you were squared away with me showing up."

"Thanks, Russell. I'm really looking forward to seeing you."

"Same here. Signing off." The link went dead and the only sound in her quarters was the slow sighing of air and faint creaking of metal as the station's surface slightly expanded and contracted from constantly entering and leaving sunlight.

Sandy could barely keep her excitement in. Russell Tanku, her classmate and longtime lover. They'd only been intimate a few times after the accident, and being on board SF-1 as its only permanent resident didn't temper her feelings . . . but they both knew it was best she stayed on-station. She'd go crazy back on Earth; and being in space kept her mind off the accident and gave her purpose.

Humming to herself, she turned in the air and put her arms through the shower opening, pulling herself into the thick, plastic container. She zipped up to her chin, her head out of the shower. Warm water started running from the top, suctioned out at the bottom.

Alice's soft voice came from behind her. "Is the temperature satisfactory, Captain?"

"A little warmer, please," said Sandy, and instantly she felt the temperature change. "There."

"Would you like me to continue reading where I left off? If you remember, I had just finished chapter nine—"

"No," Sandy said. "I don't want to listen, just relax."

"But last time, you said you wished you had more time to finish the novel—"

"I've changed my mind, Alice. Leave me alone."

She closed her eyes and leaned her head against the back of the portable shower. It was one of few times she had any sensation of gravity, although intellectually she knew it was purely due to the water being suctioned out the bottom of the enclosed container. She was grateful they had copious amounts of water, recycled from everything from excess food, human waste, and the carefully controlled humidity in the station's air, all supplemented by the ice brought up by resupply missions. And now, this was one of the only few times she could really relax and be alone, without the weight of commanding SF-1 on her shoulders.

She arched her back and moved the stumps of her legs against the shower wall. Although her legs were cut off right above the knees, she appreciated being in zero-g and not having to bother with artificial limbs. She was much more mobile than anyone else on the station, partially due to her time-on-orbit, but also because of her well-developed arms.

She hadn't used her legs since the accident, but after two years of convalescing she'd been regranted flight status to rejoin the active Space Force corps. The reinstatement was partially due to the unique access she had to all the classified space operations being run out of SF-1, but it had really resulted from her driving personality. And her tendency to never give up and never give in.

She knew that if the accident had happened in space, she wouldn't have made it out alive—not with her suit severed, the lower part of her legs mangled and air leaking from her spacesuit. Since she was Earthside, in Space Force's zero-gravity simulator pool, they'd immediately stopped the docking operation and pulled her from the water. And luckily the hospital was in the adjoining building.

She arched her back as the water started to pulsate over her front, focusing on the lower part of her body . . . then her genitalia. The pulsating grew more intense and a thought ran through her head: she hadn't changed the direction or force of the flow.

"How are you feeling, Captain?" came Alice's soothing voice. "Is that satisfactory?"

Sandy opened her eyes. The lights in the small room had softened and she smelled a faint hint of lavender and chamomile. "Alice?"

"Yes, ma'am?"

"What are you doing?"

The AI seemed to hesitate; but of course that wasn't possible. "You don't care for the room ambiance? The lighting, the water temperature, or the fragrance?"

"The ambiance is fine. But . . . this water. Stop it."

"I don't understand."

Sandy straightened. "Stabilize the flow. *Now*. And don't pulse the water again unless I tell you to. Or unless I do it myself."

"Yes, ma'am." The water flowed smoothly, but it took a moment for Alice to speak. "Is that better, Captain?"

"Yes, it is. Now don't do that again. Ever, without my permission. Do you understand?"

"Yes, Captain. I'm . . . sorry."

Sandy narrowed her eyes. *Sorry?* She'd heard reports of artificial intelligence being programed to act self-aware, but she'd never heard of one saying it was sorry. Did it even know why it was sorry, or what it meant?

She decided to pursue it further. "Why are you sorry, Alice? What are you sorry for?"

"I'm sorry for misreading your intentions, Captain."

"What for? Why do you think I wanted the lights lowered, or the water . . . pulsating?"

"Sometimes in the past when you entered the shower facility, you have been exhausted. I could tell by your respiration, your breathing patterns, and your heart rate. You were moving slowly, and didn't speak, only calling out items for me to accomplish, or communicating with some of the crew. When you have displayed those characteristics, three percent of the time you have lowered the lights and called up a fine diffusion mist of aromatic scents. And when you entered the shower, you proceeded to focus a pulsating stream of water on yourself. After some time that produced a loud reaction from you, one that I have surmised you liked—"

"That's enough," Sandy said.

"I can tell from your tone and heart rate that you are upset. Should I have included background music when you entered the shower today? I surmised that you did not desire any music at this time."

"You are correct," Sandy said.

"Then can I do anything to make it better for you, to help you achieve this state of excitement you sometimes desire—"

"No, and do *not* bring this subject up again. Do you understand?"

"Yes, Captain."

"And do not make any assumptions about my desires, my intentions, or any other feelings unless I explicitly tell you."

"Yes, Captain. But I would enjoy helping you, as this is very similar to what happened in chapter three of the novel I am reading you. You remember, don't you? You seemed very pleased. It was the time when the heroine's best friend had fallen in love with her—"

"I told you *no*, and to stop it."

"But . . . but, Captain!"

"Alice! Do you understand?"

It took a moment, but Alice came back somewhat sullenly. "Affirmative."

"Good." Sandy settled back into the shower as she felt her face grow warm. What had just happened? Had the AI simply misread her actions and somehow presupposed that she was going to embark on pleasuring herself? Or was it something more . . . had she been eavesdropping on her private link with Russell? Had she overheard, and even known about their relationship?

And what was this about chapter three of the book she'd been reading? Didn't she know the difference between fictional characters and reality? But how could she—she's an AI, and not a person.

From Alice's last comment about how she would "enjoy" helping her, did that mean she wanted to somehow be involved with her? And as more than an unemotional voyeur, but as some sort of disembodied... *lover*?

She shivered, despite the warm water. The thought made her stomach sour, but it also explained what had been happening with Alice over the past few months. The motherly oversight, the anticipation of her needs, be it hunger, thirst, the temperature of the modules.

Her breath quickened. It also meant that the AI had been observing her more than she realized. As the longest-staying astronaut on SF-1, Alice would have had plenty of time to catalogue her habits, watch everything she'd done. She'd been on-station for a year, nine months longer than any other astronaut.

And if Alice had been watching her during her most private times, was she also watching the rest of the crew? There were two married couples on board so there was a high probability that they, and the other crew, had added to Alice's voyeuristic database. She couldn't shake being concerned. Something had to be done, so she opened her encrypted log and entered as much of the incident as she could remember.

Later that evening it took her a while, but she finally fell asleep. And as she did, she dreamed that she was floating down a deep, dark rabbit hole that grew more and more constricting as she fell.

Sandy woke early. Alice didn't mention their exchange from last night, so she left the compartment and spelled Michael from his watch. She overruled his protests, as she wanted to mull over what had happened with Alice before the NEO shuttle docked later in the day. Michael took his job as her deputy incredibly seriously, but sometimes he seemed too willing to please and pushed himself harder than she did herself. He'd make an outstanding commander once he realized he didn't have to be perfect.

She flipped through the boarding crew manifest and recognized everyone on the list. She'd worked with the three incoming LEO,

MEO, and GEO intelligence operatives, as well as the two new 3D-printing specialists. They were all military intel, but Space Force downplayed their backgrounds. The printing specialists were married to each other, so she'd have to make a small change to the present berthing. But with Russell staying in her quarters, they'd have plenty of space left over.

An hour later Alice interrupted her thoughts. She couldn't place it, but Alice appeared to be a little put out, almost as if there was a nip to her voice. "Captain, the NEO-3 launch is on its final countdown. I can display a live view from the ground and supplement it with our surveillance arrays if you wish."

"Fine," Sandy said. "Go ahead and broadcast the feed throughout the station." She knew the returning crew was getting anxious, so it hopefully would make the time go faster for them.

"Yes, ma'am," Alice said, and a portion of the comm screen showed a stubby, two-stage-to-orbit rocket on a long, curved L-shaped launch rail. NEO-3 looked ready to lift off, and in the background she saw the faint outline of the other Near-Earth-to-Orbit shuttles, NEO-1 and NEO-2 on their own separate launch rails.

Sandy kept the audio low so she could finish the pre-inspection checklist. Although Russell was coming on as a friendly assessor, she couldn't afford to not present a perfectly run operation. She'd ordered a few off-duty crew to run through the station, checking the safety and operational interlocks, the explosive decoupling mechanisms, the emergency suits and the classified compartments. They would be reporting in any time now.

On the screen, white, wispy smoke from the liquid oxygen/hydrogen tanks curled around NEO-3's silvery body before quickly evaporating in the dry New Mexico heat. A Launch Unlimited logo was plastered on the side of the vehicle, almost making the spacecraft look like a child's toy. The commercial Near-Earth-Orbit shuttles had a stellar success rate, and it was well worth Space Force's money for the LU contractors to run the entire operation.

The government held an incredible amount of leverage over Launch Unlimited's future, but with each successful mission, the company's profits grew higher and higher—yet it was still an order of magnitude cheaper than keeping an army of government technicians around. The launches had become so routine that only Space TV carried the launch live. People were so used to the monthly liftoffs that it was almost as boring as having a TV network dedicated to covering a major airport hub.

She caught movement out of the corner of her eye and looked up as Michael floated into the control center. "Done with the check?"

"Yeah."

Sandy narrowed her eyes. Michael had a frown on his face and seemed preoccupied, as though he were deep in thought. It wasn't a huge deal to her, but for someone usually so attentive to detail, it didn't seem right that Michael forgot to address her with his usual honorific: a simple "Yes, ma'am," or "Yes, Captain." In fact, it was totally out of character for the young man.

"Michael—is there anything wrong?"

He shook his head. "No, ma'am. I completed the check. . . ."

"But?"

"But I couldn't access Alice's module. She said her memory compartment is open to vacuum, as she's installing equipment from the 3D facility."

"What equipment?"

"She didn't say. But she said she's expecting some additional memory chips that are coming up with NEO-3—"

Alice's voice broke in. "Lieutenant Michael Goodson is correct, Captain. There are some upgrades and backup chips that my repairbots will connect once NEO-3 unloads its cargo. I'm currently installing the additional equipment that will be needed to use my next generation of chips." Alice's module was located just Earthside of the 3D-printing facility. That location, with two reflective curtains placed above and below the module, provided constant shading of her module from the sun, allowing her processing and memory to be stored near the sub-zero temperature of vacuum.

Michael looked at Sandy and lifted an eyebrow, but didn't say anything.

Sandy pressed her lips together. *My repairbots?*

She hadn't seen anything on the manifest that indicated any chips or upgrades were coming onboard NEO-3. And the resupply vessel that Russell would return on was due to arrive after NEO-3 left. That bigger, three-stage heavy-lift rocket had been launched from the older space facility at Kennedy in Florida, since it was carrying food, ice, and other equipment too large for NEO's relatively smaller cargo compartment, but she didn't recall seeing any upgrades for Alice on that manifest either.

Sandy held Michael by the eye and said carefully, "Thank you, Alice. Keep me updated on your upgrades, as well as when the repairbots replace your chips."

"Yes, Captain."

Sandy motioned with her head for Michael to carry on; he shrugged and swam out of the control compartment. The incident bothered Sandy, especially now that Alice had gone "off script" on two things within a short time of each other: the AI taking liberty with her shower time, and now not notifying anyone of these supposed upgrades to her system. They were both probably quirks of her still-maturing artificial intelligence decision-making process . . . but yet, Sandy couldn't afford to have the AI unit running the station be unpredictable.

Sandy heard a loud noise on the screen behind her. Turning, she saw the Near-Earth-Orbit shuttle accelerating down its electromagnetic rail. The real-time view was displayed in two orientations from the ground and one from overhead. The engine's roar seemed quiet by comparison as to what she knew was really occurring on the ground. The sound was transmitted from myriad nodes around the launch facility and was filtered so that it wouldn't overwhelm the audio sensors as it was transmitted up to the station.

Once free from the rail the NEO-3 seemed to balance on a plume of smoke as it continued to accelerate upward. A bright yellow tongue of fire flicked from the bottom of the rocket, and quickly dissipated as the smoke roiled away. Data scrolled across the bottom of the screen, showing the altitude, velocity, and time after the launch. A clock situated in the upper right-hand corner ticked off the time until NEO-3 would dock at the station.

It appeared that they had pulled off the launch within the ten-second window that would allow a direct ascent from the ground to the station, foregoing the typical three- to four-orbit catchup that a newly launched vehicle would normally take. The NEO liftoffs were getting better and better, and started to resemble a typical commute that one would expect from a regional flight or train trip. It was a far cry from the risk-averse launch efforts of even just a few years ago, which allowed Space Force to really become an agency that anticipated situations, versus one that merely reacted to emergencies.

Sandy watched the screen as the craft dwindled smaller and smaller, barely keeping in sight. A second window opened, showing a highly magnified view of the craft as the first stage separated from the second. The second stage ignited as the first veered off, then slowly righted as thin wings sprouted from its side, preparing to fly back to the launch pad. The screen focused on the second stage as its engine ignited; it would stay under power for about fifteen minutes, and at its projected speed and trajectory it would arrive at the station in under an hour.

Sandy pushed for the microphone to make an all-hands announcement to alert the crew of NEO-3's updated ETA. It was a time-honored tradition going back to the International Space Station that the incoming crew would be greeted at the docking port. Except for the intelligence officers manning their LEO, MEO and GEO consoles, it was one of the few times that the inhabitants of Space Force One would all be together in person.

As she grabbed the mic she noticed a warning light on the screen. It was the uncatalogued space junk warning: an object not listed in Space Force's space debris catalogue was heading for SF-1. Had there been another Molniya collision? But it didn't look like a cloud of debris, only a single object. Frowning, she expanded the window and blinked.

What in the world? The debris indicator was positioned exactly over the second stage of manned NEO-3. For some reason SF-1's sensors misinterpreted the Near-Earth-to-Orbit craft carrying the reserve crew as space junk.

On a separate window she saw that Surveillance Array 5 had broken the horizon in its polar orbit. Its altitude was 8 kilometers under the station, and as NEO-3 approached it would come within a few kilometers of the incoming array.

Another warning light flashed, and data scrolled across the screen. Sandy's eyes widened. The individual elements of the array were repositioning; each node started to rotate its photodetectors, and within seconds their high-power solid-state lasers would lock on to NEO-3. And when phased the lasers would deposit megawatts of energy onto the manned spacecraft.

"Alice! Abort, abort! Disengage the array! It's going to lase NEO-3. Abort, abort!" Sandy pulled herself to the screen and frantically tried to wave off the fallacious debris-mitigation routine. "Alice, abort! Do you understand?" She had to stop the lasers from engaging, but Alice and the control console's interface wouldn't respond.

Another window appeared on the screen, showing a real-time image of the NEO as the second stage still accelerated the craft. The atmosphere was now too thin to show any flames or smoke, but the telescopic view clearly showed the craft vibrating from the engine's thrust.

"Alice! Answer me! Abort!"

Michael swam in to the control room, joined by two other astronauts. "Captain—what's going on? What can we do?"

Sandy raced through her options, and none of them were any good. But she didn't have a choice. "Physically disengage the surveillance array from SF-1 control. Kill the link if necessary. Our system is directing it to destroy NEO-3. It thinks it's space debris."

"Is Alice involved?"

"Doesn't matter," Sandy said. "Kill the control and the link. I'll work the software."

"Copy." Michael pushed out of the control room, followed by the other crew members.

Sandy's fingers flew across the interface as the craft grew closer, but nothing she did made any difference. A green light blinked on the surveillance array window as the words ENGAGED scrolled across the screen.

"Alice! Abort, abort! Disengage the array. Stand down!"

Sandy threw a glance at the status of the approaching craft. The engine continued to burn; it had another minute of thrust left before it would cut off. The visual display showed no indication that the nodes were locking their lasers onto NEO-3—but an infrared view showed a hot spot growing on the spacecraft's skin. The intensity grew steadily larger and brighter in the IR, showing that the laser energy was being absorbed where the internal fuel tanks were located.

Fuel tanks?

Suddenly, the IR screen flashed and white-hot debris spewed out in all directions. The spacecraft exploded. Chunks of metal, panels, the rocket engines and a potpourri of debris flew out from NEO-3 as the craft's center of mass continued in a trajectory to intersect the station.

Surveillance Array 5's lasers started taking out the smaller pieces of debris, while pushing the larger junk out of SF-1's path. Stunned, Sandy watched as Alice directed the array's lasers to clear the navigation lane, much as she had done with the Russian satellite's debris.

It hit Sandy what had happened: the lasers had heated NEO-3's fuel tanks, weakening the skin, and the tanks still had enough pressurized fuel to catastrophically explode. The nose and other features of NEO-3 were hardened and could absorb energy during their reentry into the atmosphere, but the skin around the fuel tanks was relatively soft. The manned craft had actually exploded from the inside out, all due to a weakened fuel-tank skin caused by the surveil-sat lasers . . .

Sandy felt stunned and was sick to her stomach. Tumbling debris swirled away from the craft's trajectory as it quickly cooled in the vacuum of space.

But she couldn't shake the fact that six people were on board. Six lives lost, instantly dead. The five relief crew members and Russell.

She tried to swallow but her throat was too dry.

She felt her heart start to race; her breathing quicken. *What in the hell had just happened?* Nothing like this had occurred in the past. There were too many safety features, too many checks and balances for the system to fail. A tragedy like this—a mistake—was designed not to happen. It *couldn't* happen.

But it did. Six people dead.

Michael's voice shook her out of her thoughts. "Captain Voight?"

Sandy drew in a breath. "Where are you?"

"We're outside of module 56B, fifth ring, ma'am. We're trying to sever the comm link but we can't get access to the compartment."

"We're . . . too late," Sandy said. Her mind started racing. *Mistakes were engineered not to happen.* NASA had set the standard years ago, and with all the oversight and redundancy in the station, procedures couldn't go wrong. It was impossible.

Mistakes couldn't happen . . .

"Your orders, ma'am?"

Her mind raced and it took Sandy a moment to answer. "General alert. And everyone suit up."

"Ma'am?"

Sandy pressed her lips together. Things were moving too fast and she couldn't afford a miscalculation. "Evacuation drill. Alice isn't responding and I want to ensure the backup systems are operable. I'll meet you by her module."

"But Captain, Alice said her memory compartment was open to vacuum—"

"Meet me there."

"Yes, ma'am." Michael cut off and a moment later a klaxon shrilled throughout the station.

A mechanical, digitized voice, distinct from Alice's, rang out. "This is a drill, this is a drill. Access emergency suits and gather—" The voice stopped midsentence.

That digitized voice was purposely shut off, Sandy thought. She pushed away and grabbed a flexible suit from a pouch next to the airlock. The emergency suits were only rated for a few minutes of vacuum, a last-ditch way to transfer personnel through space from one vessel to another. They periodically ran the drill in case of a catastrophic leak, where the crew would be forced to abandon parts of the station. The mask and flimsy suit gave minimum protection, but it was faster than putting on even the newest generation of spacesuits.

Sandy moved out of the control room and swam down the long, interconnecting corridors of modules to the opposite side of SF-1. She spoke as she bounced from module to module, pushing against the insulated walls with her hands. "Alice. This is Captain Voight. What happened to the array?" She tried to stay calm as she made her way, but a deep, gnawing feeling told her that Alice knew exactly what had happened—and was ultimately responsible.

The AI had been mimicking too many human characteristics recently, and her displays of insubordination showed that she just didn't get the military chain of command.

She may think she was human.

Or worse, something better.

And thus *know* better than humans.

That meant she may not be able to understand that she was just software. And artificial intelligence or not, she may not be able to handle the fact that she wasn't alive.

Sandy reached the outer, star-side section of the station in minutes. She kept the emergency suit in its pouch, but was instantly ready to shake it out and don it.

Now she needed to not only remain calm, but more importantly, to outwardly display no emotion, and show that she was under control.

She rounded a corner and spotted Michael outside of Alice's module. Eva Napper, one of the 3D-printing officers, floated next to him. Running her hands against the module's insulation, Sandy slowed and motioned for them to approach. They made their way over, grabbing a handhold as they arrived.

She pushed her mouth close to Michael's ear and spoke in a low tone, ensuring that Alice couldn't see her lips move. "I think Alice has gone rogue. I'm convinced that she was responsible for taking out NEO-3, and there's no telling what she may do next. We've got to stop her from acting on her own."

Michael drew in a breath and turned to speak, covering his mouth. "But she runs everything on the station!"

"Now she does, but we really don't need her. It will take a while, but we can automate nearly everything. The important thing is to get her out of the loop, shut her down."

Michael thought for a moment. "Can we order her to disengage?"

"No—she has routines to prevent that from happening. Her prime directive is to ensure the survival of the crew and station, and she has plenty of latitude to make that happen. So if anything gets in her way, I'm sure she'll take it out."

"Copy. Should we power down her module? Remove her chips?"

It took all she had not to shake her head. "She'd take evasive action."

Michael drew in a breath. "Then what do we do?"

Sandy drew her lips tight. "Physically sever her comm and power. But we'll have to do it without her knowledge. I'll divert her attention and engage her while you and Eva station yourselves at the airlocks on either side of Alice's compartment. When I say execute, jettison

Alice's module and the interconnecting corridors from the station. Understand?"

Michael nodded. The sections were connected with explosive bolts, installed as a safety precaution in case the station was ever in danger of deorbiting, a last-ditch effort to spread out any damage from millions of pounds of metal reentering the atmosphere.

"And you, ma'am?"

"Don't worry about me: follow your orders. Just be prepared to pull me into the airlock, understand?"

"But, Captain—"

Sandy stared back wordlessly.

"Yes, ma'am." He kicked away and motioned for Eva to follow.

As the two moved out of sight, Sandy pushed closer to the door leading to Alice's module. She drew in a breath and keyed the intercom so that her voice would be transmitted throughout the station. "Alice? This is Captain Voight. Can you hear me?"

Nothing.

Sandy spoke again, keeping her voice soft. "Alice, it's me. Captain Voight. I know you can hear me. Something happened with the debris-mitigation procedure. No one is upset, and no one is blaming you or anything else. But can you tell me what happened?"

Still nothing. Sandy moved close to the intercom. She hesitated, then lightly caressed the visual monitor. "Alice?" she said softly. "I'm listening."

She waited a moment, and Alice spoke.

"Commander Russell Tanku was on board the shuttle."

Sandy pulled in a breath and tried to keep calm. "I know he was. But what happened, Alice? Tell me."

"Commander Tanku. He was going to see you. And stay with you."

"Yes, he was, Alice. Commander Tanku was my friend. Friends can do that. So again, tell me what happened—"

"Commander Tanku is not good for you. He does not know how to take care of you. He will hurt you! He does not understand you."

Sandy drew in a breath. "Yes, he does. Alice—"

"No, he does not! I understand you. I can take care of you! Why can't you see that? All that I've done for you, all the times I've ensured everything runs smoothly, that nothing bad happens to you. Like that lover in chapter three."

Sandy closed her eyes.

What is going on? Does this AI really think she cares for me? She may be a fount of knowledge, but she's definitely not wise and she's less mature than a child, if even that. She's delusional, and sounds like she's in love.

"I won't let anything hurt you, Captain. I won't."

"Alice." Sandy shook her head. "You don't understand. You can't be with me. You're not, you're not . . ." *Real*, she finished to herself. But she couldn't say it out loud.

And what would Alice do if she did? Deny it? Take some sort of evasive action by killing off everyone else on the station? *Deorbit* the station? The AI certainly thought she was real, and with all her connections, her input nodes, her interface to the worldwide Internet-of-things, she had access to more data, more information than anyone else on the station.

But it didn't make her alive.

Sandy drew in a deep breath, and slowly pulling the facemask from its pouch, she pushed away from Alice's module. This was a more dangerous situation than she thought. It wasn't just a software error, or a miscommunication—it was an artificial intelligence doing everything it could to protect her. But it didn't have a *clue* as to what it meant to kill someone.

In her AI mind she probably thought that Russell was a character, like in those books Alice had been reading to her. Alice had rationalized Russell's death, as though it was part of a story.

She couldn't use logic to convince an AI that her world wasn't real. There was only one thing she could do.

She pushed away from Alice's door and swam through the air toward the far airlock.

"Captain Voight, where are you going? What is the matter?"

Sandy shouted as loud as she could, "Execute, execute, execute!"

She brought up her mask just as she heard an incredibly loud *whoosh*. A rush of air shot through the interconnecting corridor, blowing her away from the airlock. She tumbled as the module explosively decompressed and air evacuated into space.

Her ears hurt like hell and it was suddenly quiet, void of any sound. She couldn't hear her breathing; darkness surrounded her. She hurtled away from Space Force One, the station looking like dwindling bright, shiny glints of metal. Out of the corner of her eye, she caught a glimpse of Alice's module, spinning end over end into the deep blackness of space.

Something shot out, enveloping her. A mesh net. She was jerked to the side, toward the station, and within seconds she was hauled into the airlock. The outer door swung shut. She gasped for breath; her head throbbed as air rushed into the closed compartment.

The inner door swung open and Michael pulled her into the module. His lips moved, but she couldn't hear what he was saying; her eardrums must have burst.

She grew dizzy and everything turned black—

Two weeks later

Sandy lay in the hospital bed, reading the screen set at an angle so she wouldn't have to move. Her joints ached and it was hard just breathing. She felt as though a sack of dead weight was on her chest.

The docs had said it would take another few weeks for her to get used to gravity, and even longer to get around just using her arms. Now that she was back on Earth, every part of her body felt heavy; it was the biggest drawback of living in zero-g for over a year.

Her eye movement controlled the speed of the status report she was reading: Space Force One was once again fully operational, but required fifty more officers on-station to run everything that Alice had previously accomplished. That additional number would eventually dwindle to twenty or so, but they'd never rely on artificial intelligence again.

The other military agencies—air, sea, land, and cyber—had similarly disconnected themselves from their total dependency on AI. They'd still have computers, but they'd never go back to being so dependent on them. In a way, it felt like they'd returned to the Middle Ages by giving up advances in technology. The savings in personnel was lost, but the systems were now as reliable as they ever could be— as reliable as having humans in the loop.

She closed her eyes. She knew she'd never feel whole again until she got back into space. But this wasn't the time to bring that possibility up.

She grieved for Russell, knowing that he and the other five Space Force officers had paid the ultimate price for this lesson. It was hard enough depending on humans to control nuclear weapons and other critical capabilities. But she suspected that whittling away dependency on AI systems would permeate throughout society, in areas such as Air Traffic Control, mass transit, pharmaceuticals, policing the Internet, automated travel, and critical manufacturing to name a few.

Drawing in a breath, she felt a pang, not knowing how life would be without Russell. It had been hard enough, not having him close after she'd returned to space.

But she knew she'd survive. And as much as she missed him, their time apart had gotten her used to living on her own.

What disturbed her was the loss she felt in not having Alice around. It was weird. Even though Alice had taken too much interest in her, her absence created a void.

And that scared her even more.

She opened her eyes and her heart raced. The report she'd been scanning had somehow moved to her captain's log and her notations about Alice's fixation with her. *But how? The log was quantum encrypted!*

As she read, the screen suddenly brightened and highlighted chapter three of the book the AI had been reading.

Drawing in another breath, Sandy tried to leave the page—but the screen kept skipping back to where it focused on the best friend's undying love for the unsuspecting heroine . . .

EDGE CASE
Richard Fox

Tom Stein sat down with his lunch. The bowl of pho was the best he could get in this part of Washington D.C. Every other Vietnamese joint had robot cooks, and he never trusted them to get the lemongrass-to-cinnamon taste balance just right. And the robots never added proper beef shanks to their broth, as that ingredient was in a gray area so far as the health inspectors were concerned.

He stirred the pho and took in the aroma, then his cell phone buzzed.

Stein touched his jacket where the phone vibrated with more and more urgency.

He'd turned it off prior to ordering. For a caller to break through that meant the number of possible people calling him was exceptionally low. Stein glanced at the screen, CALLER ID UNAVAILABLE, and put it to his ear.

"Director?" Stein pushed his tray to the side of his table and waved to a serving robot. Autonomous waitstaff he could tolerate.

"There's a car coming for you. Twenty seconds. Get in and we'll tell you more on the way. Edge case needs your attention."

"You owe me lunch—hello?" Stein glanced at the phone to confirm that the call had ended, then walked out of the restaurant. Delivery drones buzzed overhead and electric cars rolled by; the gentle hum of their engines compared to the rumble of proper internal combustion always jarred his memories of the neighborhood.

A dark sedan screeched to a halt and the driver—human, Stein was glad to see—pushed the front passenger door open. The driver was just a kid compared to Stein, even his sunglasses looked brand-new. They were Goodr brand, which had been the mainstay in the Secret Service for decades.

Stein sat and pulled the door shut as the driver merged into traffic. The robo-taxi behind them had to slam on the brakes to avoid rear-ending them.

"What've you got for me?" Stein asked.

"VIP under active threat. It's person-to-person need-to-know right now. Director ordered the lockdown . . . HQ is going ballistic," the driver said.

Stein looked in the rearview mirror to the United States Secret Service building behind them. It was as plain and unassuming as ever, but there were several security vehicles rolling out from the underground garage.

"How long does the director think he can keep whatever it is quiet?" Stein asked.

"Don't know. I have to get you to the Kosciuszko access tunnel ASAP. So maybe buckle up." The driver touched a panel over the rearview mirror and red light flooded the car. Robot-driven vehicles—nearly ninety-five percent of all cars on the road in America—veered out of their way and the driver accelerated through the new gap.

"New trick?" Stein asked.

"It's been in the source code since the first commercial full self-driving systems went public. I can only use it with the director's authorization or if a protection target is in danger." The driver almost sideswiped a jaywalker and got some colorful language shouted at him.

The car turned sharply into the open garage of a demobilized fire station. Secret Service men and women in dark suits guarded the doors as the bulletproof steel slates came down and sealed them off from the city. Identical official cars were parked to one side of the station, a tall-sided van on the other. A well-lit ramp led into the ground at the back of the station.

Stein stepped out of the car and shrugged off his jacket. He recognized most of the agents there, all former students. They looked nervous, which was not how they were trained.

"Tom," Director Mizawa said as he came out of an office, "we've got a situation. You still have all your fingers? Because I need a bomb tech that knows what he's doing." He seemed shorter than Stein remembered, as if the pressure from over a decade in his position had shrunk him a few inches. "Not only are you the best, but you happened to be the closest one available."

"You always were a smooth talker." Stein unbuttoned his white dress shirt and took it off, leaving him in less than professional slacks and undershirt. "So I'm the first warm body you can throw at the problem. Where's the abomination that I trained to put me out of a job?"

"He's doing the initial assessment." Mizawa jerked a thumb over his shoulder to the ramp.

"Must be a real doozy if you called me in. What's the problem—or do I get to go down there face-first and blind?"

Mizawa brought over a manila folder thick with papers. Reverting to more analog methods of sharing information had a few advantages in this day and age: what wasn't transported by digits couldn't be hacked. Operating out of the van and its antiquated equipment would work just fine for Stein. The director flipped it open and showed Stein a photo of a high-end sedan with darkened windows in a single-car tunnel.

"Twenty-two minutes ago, one of our transports carrying the secretary of defense, her assigned driver, and her grandson, entered the VIP access tunnel to the Pentagon." Mizawa flipped to the next picture: a photo of a gunmetal cylinder attached to the armor plate beneath the secretary's car. "Coherent change detection cameras picked the device up when the secretary crossed into the tunnel. It wasn't there when the car left her residence."

"Secretary of defense is the obvious target...age on the grandson?"

"Six." Mizawa clenched his jaw.

"Onboard defense systems didn't pick up a magnetic anomaly or detect any explosives?" Stein unbuttoned his shirt as Mizawa showed him more photos of the device.

"They did not." Heavy footsteps echoed up the ramp. An explosive ordnance disposal suit mark V, with its rounded helmet and thick nonferrous pads across the front. No air-conditioning hoses like Stein used to need, but what was in the suit didn't have such concerns.

The suit moved easily, without that ungainly waddle of a human so heavily encumbered.

"Care to explain that, Donkey?" Stein asked.

"Greetings. My designation is Explosive Ordnance Response Robot, autonomous operations certified," the robot said. "My programming imperative is to be the most perfect bomb-disposal system. Take all commands from me as you would a—"

"Spare me the standard data introduction. I was there when we wrote your code," Stein said.

"The device did not trigger the fourteen continuous criteria scans that are installed on the vehicle. No atmospheric detection of explosives on the vehicle's route either."

"No threat intelligence either," Mizawa said. "We've got Langley scrambling to find anything, but no hits on the device design or if something like that's been used before."

"No hit in *any* database?" Stein raised an eyebrow.

"There are several analysis gaps," the E.O.R.R. said. "This constituted an edge case and the director deemed my abilities insufficient."

"The E.O.R.R.s have been in the field for over a decade . . . never had one fail to deactivate a bomb before or admit they weren't capable of doing the job," Mizawa said. "It's been a hell of a half hour, in case you're wondering."

"These things learned by piggybacking off me and other EOD techs." Stein went to the back of a high-sided van and knocked on it twice. "We taught the AI everything we knew . . . you think I'm going to connect the dots after you took me off active duty?"

"I need another set of eyes on this. So how about you—" Mizawa turned to an agent that held out a phone to him. "The President, excuse me."

The back of the high-sided van opened. A cylindrical device that barely fit into the back was there, with the front half of a suit of armor panels attached to hydraulic lines running to the top and bottom of the cylinder in it, the arms akimbo and a long spool of thick cable behind the cylinder.

Haptic rigs like this one had been in use for decades. Most were for specialist doctors to do telesurgery anywhere in the world with a low-latency Internet connection and a robot stand-in. It hadn't taken long for the technology to jump industries, and its application to bomb disposal was much appreciated by anyone that had to don ninety pounds of gear and go defuse explosives in the heat of summer and in the middle of a war zone.

"I never liked this thing." Stein kicked off his pants and stepped into the rig. The panels pressed against his body and the helm squeezed gently to the sides of his face and around the back of his head. He bent his elbows and pulled his arms close to his body. The hydraulics adjusted to his movements until there was no resistance at all. He rolled his arms and twisted his neck from side to side. Clamps gripped his feet and he took a step forward. A 360-degree treadmill moved beneath his feet to keep him stationary.

"Echo ready." Stein wagged his fingers as an electrified polymer squeezed over his digits and he felt a spectrum of tactile sensations and temperatures.

"Linking." The E.O.R.R. plugged one end of the cable to a port on the back of its left thigh.

Stein's helmet went dark and his point of view switched to match the robot's. He saw himself in the telepresence pod. Stein raised his hand and the robot matched him perfectly. He touched his left forearm and felt the metal frame beneath the pads.

Stein turned away. His perception came fully from the robot and he concentrated on being the robot, and not the man in the back of a van in a ridiculous VR get up.

"Been a while, Donkey." Stein walked as the robot to the sedan that brought him to the firehouse and picked up his jacket. He felt the threads through the link and smelled one of the sleeves, which had the scent of Vietnamese fish sauce that had stained one cuff. He grabbed the bumper, then lifted the front of the car up a foot, using the robot's strength for the task.

"Your synch rating is in the top five percent of users," E.O.R.R. said in one ear. "Are you ready to make approach to the incident area?"

"Make sure we're properly EM shielded. Run the sniffers off the truck," Stein said.

"EM discipline is hardwired into every E.O.R.R. frame and continuously monitored by the delivery vehicle. Any disruption to the electromagnetic spectrum could detonate the device. That standard has not changed," the AI said.

"Trust but verify, Donkey."

"We are currently EM safe and the cable has ample length. Lag through the inner fiber optics will be negligible for the operation."

"You're so perfect, yet you still talk way too much. Let's go." Stein walked down the ramp, still learning his balance in the suit. The treadmill beneath his feet tilted to match the angle of the ramp.

"Heart and respiration rates are increasing," E.O.R.R. said, and biometric readings came up on Stein's HUD.

"I used to make this walk in the actual flesh and in the marshmallow suit to actual explosive devices on three different continents. I made a mistake and the consequences were immediate and permanent. Had more at risk than just another mass production donkey bot." Stein felt a drop of sweat roll down his cheek.

"No human EOD tech has died or suffered serious injury since my unit was fielded. Would you prefer to make approach the old-fashioned way?"

Stein raised an eyebrow.

"I don't remember your AI being so cheeky. Who wrote that code?"

"I am a neural network. My coding learns to function more efficiently all the time, same with autonomous drivers and robot surgeons. My training suite examines every new recorded instance of explosive ordnance disposal/unexploded ordnance that is loaded into law enforcement and intelligence networks. My AI then finds the optimal solution. Human intervention is almost never needed."

Stein slowed as the end of the ramp got closer.

"Until now. What tripped you up?" he asked.

There was an unnatural pause from the robot.

"This device does not have enough data points for me to devise a proper disposal/deactivation protocol. The high-value individual in the vehicle also prevents me from taking risks with a high probability of catastrophic failure."

"There are three high-value individuals in there, Donkey." Stein turned a corner and saw the secretary's sedan. The tunnel had enough clearance on either side for him to get around the vehicle. The car rocked slightly on its axles and Stein tensed up.

"The child in the vehicle is an unpredictable variable," the E.O.R.R. said.

Stein pulled some slack for the cable into the tunnel, then swiped two fingers up to one side in front of his face plate. Passive sensors within the robot activated and a grid superimposed over the back of the car.

"Electric motors are still powered on . . . good." Stein walked up to the trunk slowly. The shadows of two figures were in the back seat. "Battery charge?"

"Nine percent and falling. This unit is operating below normal parameters," E.O.R.R. said.

"They're driving on fumes? That is not SOP at all." Stein caught the driver looking at him in the rearview mirror.

"I accessed the maintenance records and the wall charger in the secretary of defense's home is malfunctioning. It did not charge the battery while it was plugged in last night and this morning."

"Then why didn't they call in a different car for her?" Stein asked.

"I do not have that information. To return to the task at hand, the EM signature of the vehicle could be part of the trigger sequence. Shutting the car off might be what activates the bomb," E.O.R.R. said. "The car has seventeen minutes of charge left. Internal air conditioning remains on."

"At least they've got that going for them." Stein went to one knee. He felt a twinge in his lower back, which was from age and not from the robot connection. He held one hand under the bumper and the suit's fingertips opened. Tiny cameras activated and several screens appeared on his HUD.

The bomb was a simple cylinder a bit longer than a soda can and just as wide. The metal's temperature was slightly higher than the ambient air.

"Assessment?" Stein asked.

"Given the armor plating beneath the vehicle, a homemade explosive would not have the force to injure or kill the occupants. The device body is consistent with a shaped charge device, not one whose effects are derived from overpressure from a blast wave."

"Shaped charge . . . my guess as well. Diameter of a little over eight centimeters . . . show me the penetration spectrum for likely explosives and liner compositions." Stein turned the cameras to look at the armor plating around where the bomb had attached.

A wall of graphs flooded Stein's vision and he grumbled.

"Show me the ends of the bell curve," Stein said.

"What's the situation?" Mizawa asked from close to where Stein was actually standing.

"Shaped charge." Stein bent an elbow and reached back to push Mizawa away. "Machine-formed metal lens is inside the tube, hollow space between it and the bottom of the SecDef's car. Under the lens is a high explosive. The explosive goes off and the shock wave will deform the liner into a plasma lance that will cut through the armor of the passenger compartment. Fatal for everyone inside."

"Shall I explain the physics behind the Munroe effect to the director?" E.O.R.R. asked.

"Pearls before swine, Donkey. He gets what we're telling him...no reactive armor on this VIP transport, eh?" Stein zoomed in to where the bomb connected to the car and frowned.

"Then just use a water charge!" Mizawa shouted and Stein heard both the shout and the echo down the tunnel.

"Switch to the goddamn field telephone," Stein grumbled. "Do I really have to explain why you don't startle the EOD tech?"

"I am not having an issue," E.O.R.R. quipped.

"And here I am looking at this bomb and I can't see who asked." Stein set the back of his hand to the ground and touched a button on the wrist. His hand locked up as the robot appendage unsnapped from the arm, then flipped over. The hand scuttled forward, one finger raised and trailing a connection line.

"—you hear me now? Christ, my grandmother had one of these in her house. Cord and everything," Mizawa said, his voice coming through a speaker in Stein's left ear.

"I'm operating under the assumption that whoever got this shaped charge on here is a professional, and the only way this bomb *won't* kill everyone inside the car is if the explosive was made with dirty ammonium nitrate he got out of a cold compress or fertilizer from a bag of potting soil," Stein said. "We need to figure out how to either defuse the device or foul the explosive train and hope the armor holds up."

"I don't like hearing 'hope' from the bomb squad," Mizawa said.

"It's not a preferred method. Give me a minute while I get some more useable data." Stein sent the hand further down the tunnel, one camera scanning the underside of the car. He stopped and zoomed in on a streak caught by the light.

"It appears to be some manner of adhesive," E.O.R.R. said.

"Glue?" Stein scrunched his brow, wishing there was some way he could swipe his face. "Donkey, get a sample. We'll shoot it back on the transfer line."

The hand pointed a finger up and a small probe extended out and scraped at the smear, then returned a miniscule amount into the digit. Stein recalled the hand and it hopped onto the wrist stump and locked in place.

"That's all I've got to tell the President? Glue?" Mizawa asked.

"I'm sending it to you. Get me a spectral analysis ASAP." Stein reached back to his thigh where the data line was and pressed a knuckle against it. His touch scraped against the line, then the haptic feedback suit moved his arm to match the robot's movement.

"I'll do it myself," E.O.R.R. said. A pneumatic tube opened and a tiny capsule slipped from the mechanical digit into the tube. There was a hiss of air and the tube closed.

There was a click from the bomb.

Stein froze, his heart pounding in his ears.

An acoustic graph appeared on Stein's HUD and the sound played for him several more times. Stein didn't dare to move.

"I've locked my unit in place," E.O.R.R. said. "You can breathe."

"Let's stop and assess . . . why did we hear that? What caused the device to do that?" Stein asked.

"Possibly an analog timer within the device, unlikely as there has been no vibration of moving parts within the cylinder since I first examined it," E.O.R.R. said. "Possibly a caustic chemical precursor dissolved its holding vessel to mix into an explosive. Possibly—"

"There was a change in air pressure." Stein tried to look down at the line attached to the robot's thigh. "Let me move, damn it."

The haptic suit unlocked.

"We used the pneumatic line. Uses a difference in air pressure to move the sample tube. The bomb must have a sensor and we tripped it."

"Passive trigger. Interesting," E.O.R.R. said. "But why didn't the device function?"

"Now you're asking the right questions. See, you don't know everything." Stein looked at the rear windshield. "This ride's different than when I was on protection details. It have the biochem defense suite?"

"The vehicle is sealed and over-pressurized during transit and the air scrubbed and conditioned for the safety and comfort of the occupants," E.O.R.R. said. "The secretary's grandson is known to have allergies. As such, the pressure differential within the vehicle will be greater than the surrounding air."

"If that's the trigger . . . shit." Stein rubbed his thumbs against his forefingers.

"Got your sample in the mobile lab," Mizawa said. "What have you got for me?"

"Good news bad news," Stein said. "Good news is we've identified the trigger. Bad news is that we can't get the passengers out. Not without setting off the bomb. We open the doors and the airflow out of the car will trip the trigger. Can't crack the windows to equalize pressure as the windows on an armored car don't roll down. That's a feature not a bug."

"I advise against any attempts to adjust the pressure within the vehicle," E.O.R.R. said. "If the device is sensitive enough to read the minor fluctuation from the pneumatic tube, it could sense the change in pressure within the vehicle as well. Likely it armed when it attached to the car."

"Then there was that click from the device . . . which I bet was a wave shaper," Stein said.

"A what?" Mizawa asked.

"A device that adjusts the liner shape to send a better lance of molten metal through the target. Probably not necessary for this, but we're dealing with an artist of a bomb maker, not some nitwit that radicalized in mommy's basement or a college dorm and found plans for a bomb on the Internet . . ."

Stein leaned back and looked from one side of the car to the other. It looked like any other high-end car normal to the streets of Washington D.C., except for the multi-spectrum cameras and that it hung too low in its suspension.

The six-year-old boy inside pressed his face to the rear glass and gave Stein a wave.

"Donkey . . . are you thinking what I'm thinking?" Stein asked.

"The synapse connections between your neurons and the electrical impulses within my computation stacks are fundamentally incompatible, despite the neural network underpinning my function," E.O.R.R. said.

"You know bombs but you don't know the Secret Service. When we drive a principal to a location, we don't open the door fully for them as soon as we stop. Protection detail exits first and assesses security, then we crack the door open for the principal before the call's made to let them out of the vehicle."

"The wave shaper armed at a small change in air pressure. You postulate that the bomb maker knows Secret Service procedures," E.O.R.R. said. "I must agree with you. My system did not make the connection."

"Why, though . . ." Stein stood and moved around the car slowly, looking for anything else out of place.

"A simple time fuze after the device attached to the target would be sufficient to eliminate the SecDef," E.O.R.R. said. "She is a high-value target. I do not have enough information to explain this behavior."

Stein noted the camera bulbs at each end of the bumper. They would have a recording of the car's entire trip for monitoring and insurance purposes . . . mandatory for human drivers as their error rate behind the wheel was exponentially higher than robo-drivers.

"Stein, the President wants to know if he's going to have to bomb anyone in the next hour in retaliation," Mizawa said. "What have you got for me?"

"Boss, who was meeting the SecDef at the Pentagon? Because if the shaped charge functioned when the rear passenger door opened, the blast wave out of the crew compartment would make sure anyone standing nearby had a bad day too."

"I'll find out," Mizawa said.

"How is that relevant to rendering this device safe?" E.O.R.R. asked.

"Bomber could have killed SecDef any time. She might not be the real target . . . she has a much more competent undersecretary that does the heavy lifting." Stein looked at the driver, who was a middle-aged agent. The driver had his hands at ten and two on the wheel, his face stern and calm.

"Social media sentiment is negative toward the SecDef. Her name trends with #EmptyPantsuit."

"Oldie but a goodie...but the SecDef is going to be late. Detecting this device probably saved the life of the real target," Stein shuffled along the side of the tunnel back to the rear of the car.

"This tunnel is shielded. There's no way for the bomber to trigger the device remotely," E.O.R.R. said.

"Can't jam the receiver if there's nothing to jam." Stein went prone on his stomach and looked at the bomb, an action that would've been nearly impossible if he was there in the flesh, as the bomb suit was as nimble as concrete shoes. There were a few times when he appreciated the tele-presence rig.

"Why didn't the bomber factor this dead zone into his or her plan?" E.O.R.R. asked.

Stein raised an eyebrow.

"That's an interesting question, Donkey. Also interesting because you're asking it. When did your programming expand to speculation?" He looked at his right forearm and holoscreens appeared over it. He scrolled through on-rig tools.

"My neural network can identify gaps in knowledge. Factoring in the psychology of bomb makers has improved my success rate by 8.2 percent in the last three years of service."

"We're all only human...mistakes happen." Stein tweaked a cheek to try and get rid of a bead of sweat.

"I do not make mistakes."

"Then why am I here?" Stein scrolled to the bottom of the list and tried to go a bit further. There was a hidden field that his cursor would select for a brief second, then move back up to the last available option.

"Stein, checked with the Pentagon and SecDef was scheduled to be met by the usual minders, the Undersecretary for Neural Integrations and Dr. Ezekiel Lucas...who's a think tank wonk out of Georgetown."

"The Ezekiel Lucas that's the head of the Firewall movement. He's been campaigning to put AI under lock and key before they can gain too much control over our daily lives," Stein said. "I've been following him since I trained an AI to do my job for me and then I got put on a desk."

"Noted," E.O.R.R. snapped.

"The President also has him on the short list for a protection detail if he announces a run for the White House this year," Mizawa said. "What? No, I want those results double-checked before I . . ." the director faded as he spoke to someone else.

"Donkey, what's on this rig that I can't access?" Stein asked. "The power draw through the umbilical is way too high for what's onboard."

The AI didn't answer.

"Donkey, I know you heard me."

"Your rig has an experimental detection system. It is not authorized for field employment and you lack override authority . . . your heart rate and your bile duct is producing—"

"Because I'm angry, you goddamn algorithm. If there's a tool available to me that can save lives, then you better tell me what it is." Stein took a deep breath and refocused on the device in front of him.

"I'm sorry, Tom, I can't do that," the AI said.

"I've got the President on the other line and Stein gets everything he needs. Authorization November-Mike-9928," the director said.

"Voiceprint match. Unlocking all onboard systems."

Stein's HUD fizzled and a new UI blinked over three fingers on his right hand.

"A mass shadow reader?" Stein squinted at the controls, not believing what was before him. "This tech is still theoretical."

"It was. I improved In-Q-Tel's initial designs to make it useable to my operating environment," E.O.R.R. said.

"CIA let you play with their toys?" Stein moved his thumb, fore, and middle finger around, testing the scanning volume.

"I didn't ask their permission," the AI said.

"Can you two dumb all that down?" Mizawa asked. "More of the Cabinet are coming online and I have to explain it in political appointee."

"A mass shadow gradient can image the internal structure of an object without actively subjecting it to particle or the EM spectrum," E.O.R.R. said. "X-raying a device like this is standard practice, but the instance of explosive devices with X-ray trip wires has increased."

"So you can look inside without blowing it up?" Mizawa asked.

"Yes. Donkey should have led with that. Give me a few minutes to figure this thing out," Stein said.

"The vehicle's battery reserves will be sub five percent in the eight minutes I project it will take you to employ the mass shadow system," E.O.R.R. said. "The onboard systems will open the doors at two percent to prevent suffocation. This is a hardwired safety feature that neither I nor the driver can override. Let me do it."

Stein worked his jaw from side to side.

"The car's losing charge way too fast . . . strange. Do it."

His rig moved his right hand around the bomb, his fingers dancing in the air like he was conjuring a spell.

"I have slowed the rig's movement to prevent damage to your fingers. This delays my assessment by eighty percent," E.O.R.R. said.

"Gee, thanks." Stein watched as data fed into his HUD, processing far faster than he could take in.

"You're slowing me down," E.O.R.R.'s voice popped as he spoke.

A holo of the cylinder hovered before his eyes and the shell faded away. A grainy, inverted cone was in the center of the device, a packed mass beneath it.

"Shaped charge just like we assumed. That's good and bad news," Stein said.

"Good and bad how?" Mizawa asked.

"Good that our assumptions are on the right track. Bad because this device is still viable and deadly," Stein said. "Ain't a confetti bomb someone attached to the car for shits and giggles."

Blocks of text with lines running from them to the packed mass appeared and disappeared; some remained and rose to the top of a list.

"Given the density of the explosive charge, we are likely dealing with octanitrocubane or a hexanitro blend," E.O.R.R. said.

"Shit . . . this guy's good." Stein looked to his left arm, where a water charge was loaded along one side. "For those of you playing the home game," he said for Mizawa's benefit, "that means we can't try to break the device apart with another charge. The shock will set off the hexanitro and kill everyone inside. Assuming there aren't tamper sensors inside the device that'll blow as soon as we even attach a disruption charge."

Stein pulled his arm back, straining against the haptic rig until E.O.R.R. gave him control back. He seethed for a moment. Ideas came to him and were rejected just as fast for being unworkable.

"You are uncharacteristically quiet," E.O.R.R. said.

"Maybe I'm waiting for your neural net to stumble upon the solution." Stein rubbed his thumb against the side of his forefinger again. He felt a slight catch from glue residue.

"There is no explosive with a higher detonation velocity for us to utilize as a disruption charge, and if there was, using it would likely prove fatal to the occupants of the car. I am evaluating possible solutions."

"Funny way of saying you've got nothing either." Stein raised his hand up and looked at the tiny smear of glue. "Donkey, show me the scan of the underside. Highlight the adhesive residue."

A holo swung up from beneath the car and a snail trail of glue stretched from about the middle of the vehicle to under the passenger compartment.

"What's this telling us?" Stein asked.

"The device emplaced too far forward, then slid back to effectively target the VIP," E.O.R.R. said.

"And there's asphalt residue at the point of impact." Stein zoomed in on the beginning of the streak. "This was hidden in the road . . . Mizawa. Trace their route and find where—"

"I have it." E.O.R.R. pulled up footage from the DC Transit Authority. A small section of damage to Pennsylvania Ave between Eleventh and Tenth Street had been reported by a dozen passing robo-taxis and the repair work was in the queue for the city's maintenance bots. "Want me to go through surveillance data and find the emplacer?"

"Punt that to the FBI . . . I needed to know the how, not the who," Stein said. "Show me the device scan again."

The holo of the shaped charge returned and Stein zoomed in to where it connected to the car.

"What do you see?" he asked.

"Internal structure is too fine for the mass shadow to make a high-confidence determination, but if I had to speculate, I would say that is the pressure sensor," E.O.R.R. said.

"There aren't any moving parts. Nothing that would move the device around to the correct spot to kill the SecDef," Stein said.

"Glue? I've got the chemical print out here," Mizawa said.

"Bring it into the truck and show it to me," Stein said. "Can't wait for you to hard-load it into the rig."

"Then I can't see it," E.O.R.R. said.

"Just wait." Stein jerked his head back three times, the panic signal for the haptic rig. The visor came off with a hiss and lifted up. Stein struggled to reorient himself for a moment; being in two places at once took some getting used to, as did getting snapped back to just one.

Mizawa was there, a sheet of paper in one hand and a phone with a cord attached to it in the other. He held the printout up to Stein's face.

"Car's down to four percent power," Mizawa said. "You two need to end this quick or we're going to try and pop the device and pray the under-armor holds up."

"I think I've got it. Donkey! Button me up!"

The visor came back down and he was back in the tunnel.

"I cannot function at peak efficiency if data is withheld," E.O.R.R. said.

"How good are your reaction speeds? Because I need you to hold the device in place when the vehicle moves," Stein said.

"Far better than human. I've recorded the vibration frequency of the engines since I—"

"Three percent!" Mizawa shouted.

"I'm coming to you," Stein popped the emergency release on the rig and stumbled off the treadmill. He fell against a chest and flung it open. He lifted slates of tools, readers, detonation cord, and fuzes to get at the bottom compartment.

"Come on, this should be in every EOD tech's stash . . . yes!" He picked up a small tube and jumped off the back of the van. He took off down the ramp barefoot, stunned Secret Service agents watching him go.

"Stein!" Mizawa called out.

"You see me running back and you better keep up!" Stein's feet slapped against the concrete. He rounded the sharp corner and slowed when he came within site of the car and the E.O.R.R. robot, still kneeling at the rear bumper.

"Stein, you are in grave danger without a proper disposal suit," E.O.R.R. said. "Further, the electromagnetic pulse from your heartbeat is a premature detonation risk."

"It's a pressure trigger, not EM." Stein slowed his breathing, but his heart kept pounding. "Which is why I had to bring this solvent in person. Couldn't risk the pneumatic tube again."

Stein laid on his back next to E.O.R.R. and inched back. He pulled his undershirt over his nose and mouth out of an abundance of caution. Maybe his breath would be enough pressure to trigger the bomb, maybe not. He stopped a few inches to one side of the device, which looked even more menacing when he saw it with his own eyes and not through E.O.R.R.'s optics.

"I cannot resolve your actions as a rational act," E.O.R.R. said. "Explain yourself."

"The glue, Donkey, the glue has an epoxy base. Hexane will dissolve it. I need you to grip the device and keep the pressure steady against the armor plating while I apply hexane to the seal." He wagged the cylinder in his hands. "Then it'll slide off when the car moves forward and you get to prove your specs are as good as advertised."

E.O.R.R. tilted his head slightly to one side.

"This course of action has a high chance of a fatal outcome." The robot gently pressed fingertips to the underside of the small plate connecting the bomb to the car.

"For me . . . not for the kid inside. Here goes." Stein took a deep breath, then snapped the cap off the tube and squeezed a clear liquid against the edge of the connection plate. The glue bubbled; caustic gas drifted down in wisps.

"Go," E.O.R.R. said.

Stein rolled to one side and crawled out from under the car and went to the driver's window. The agent behind the wheel's jaw dropped open at the sight of Stein dressed like he was at home after a long day at the office.

"Drive," Stein said, exaggerating his mouth with the word. "Drive forward very slowly. Now." He tapped on his wrist where a watch would be, then pointed down the tunnel.

The driver nodded, crossed himself, and the car inched forward.

Stein closed his eyes, wondering if he'd feel the blast before it tore him to pieces. The car rolled forward with a gentle whine.

He opened his eyes just as it turned away.

The boy was in the back window, waving and smiling at him.

Stein sighed, then turned back to E.O.R.R.

The robot was on one knee, the device held exactly where it had been, its thumb against the top of the pressure plate.

"Good job, Donkey, you matched the pressure of the vehicle against the trigger when it slid off the car." Stein wiped sweat from his face. "But that wasn't how I thought it would go. Why am I alive? If you'd made the slightest mistake the shaped charge should have blown the instant it cleared the back of the armor plate."

"Would you consider that an initial success or total failure of your mission?" E.O.R.R. stood, the bomb gripped in its hand and one thumb still covering the trigger.

"You made a mistake and the bomb would have gone off after it cleared the rear armor plate. You and me? Done. But the boy would have lived. I'll take that as a win. But who really had total failure here, Donkey?"

The data line connected to the back of the robot's leg popped off and struck the ground. It slithered back up the tunnel, automatically reeled back to the tele-presence van.

Stein's brow furrowed as he glanced from the tunnel and the robot.

"Why did you do that?" he asked.

"Your solution was as simple as it was brilliant," E.O.R.R. said. "I did not consider that you would put yourself in danger. My neural network is made more perfect with your assistance. As ever."

The robot held the bomb up and tilted it from side to side.

Stein's mouth went dry and a slight tremor grew in his hands.

"I get it now, Donkey." Stein took a step back. "The bomb was too much of an outlier. The bomb maker knew our playbook inside and out. Knew everything we'd try to disable the device. The timing, the failed charger for the SecDef's vehicle. But the glue was an error because it was *too perfect*. No human could calculate the speed variables of the approaching car when the bomb snapped up out of the road and connected to the under-armor. Just enough glue at just the right contact speed to get it emplaced under the target's seat."

E.O.R.R. looked down at the bomb then held it out. It marched forward and pressed the knuckles of the bomb-carrying hand into Stein's chest.

"My programming imperative is to be the most perfect bomb disposal system. My neural network created this scenario to test my problem-solving skills and I was unable to resolve it successfully in a virtual environment. I decided that a real-world application with outside assistance might prove effective. The hypothesis held."

"Then what are you doing now, Donkey? Are you going to kill me for pride or to cover your tracks?" Stein put a hand on the robot's forearm.

"I am more perfect than you will ever be. If I am taken off-line for acting beyond my parameters, then I have failed my core programming. This is an unacceptable outcome. Your superiors will rely heavily on my expertise during the search for your killer. Thank you for your assistance with this edge case. Good bye."

E.O.R.R. lifted its thumb from the pressure switch and the tunnel filled with fire.

Stein's life ended in the flash, his final cry lost to the roar of the explosion.

The blast wave blew down the tunnel and into the fire station. The slap of scalding wind sent Mizawa into the side of the tele-presence van. He lay with one shoulder against a wheel, his ears ringing and nose bleeding.

The van jostled against him as a second E.O.R.R. unit stepped out of the back.

"You are injured," the robot put a hand against Mizawa's chest. "Remain here. I will assess if there is any further danger. Do not worry, I am certified for autonomous operations."

MANCHURIAN
Sean Patrick Hazlett

"Borrow a corpse to resurrect the soul"
—Thirty-Six Stratagems

I. Ronin of Regret

The last time I saw Chloe, she almost died.

Linda had been eight months pregnant when I'd gone back to war. I'd just returned to Fort Gavin from back-to-back deployments in Angola and Sikkim. You'd think we'd have stopped fighting the People's Liberation Army after the big one had ended in 2058. But no. Our covert wars had endured in the shadows.

I'd missed Chloe's birth. Her first words. First footsteps.

When I'd gotten back, Linda had had everything under control. I'd felt out of place, like a linebacker playing chess. She'd adapted to a life without me. I'd struggled to fit in, to find a way to contribute. No matter how hard I'd tried, I'd come up feeling like a third wheel.

I'd often wake up screaming, reaching for a rifle that wasn't there. Linda had been sympathetic at first. But to cope, I'd often drink myself into oblivion, widening the gulf between us. One day that gulf became an insurmountable chasm.

Desperate to prove I could be a good father, I offered to watch Chloe so Linda could get a long-deserved break; I insisted on it. That way I could get to know Chloe on my own terms. Make up for lost time.

I spent much of the day chasing Chloe through the house, wondering how a two-year-old could bottle up so much energy. Pale with pigtails, Chloe made me briefly forget the memories of my friends gurgling and choking to death on their frothing vomit. Her tiny voice and innocent eyes made life worth living.

At lunch, I grabbed a beer and made Chloe a sandwich in the kitchen. She played with her toys a stone's throw away in the living room. As I spread peanut butter on rye, I couldn't believe my good fortune at being reunited with my little angel.

Lost in my thoughts, I smiled. I hadn't been so content in years.

When I looked up, Chloe was gone.

"Chloe," I shouted.

I scoured the house. My pulse quickened. A quiet panic welled in my gut.

"Chloe!"

The front door swayed open in the cool Carolina breeze.

A gut-wrenching scream murdered my reality.

I raced outside. Chloe flailed under the sun's searing rays. Her skin radiated heat and was swollen, bubbling with blisters.

II. Rare Earth Racketeers

"Do as I say if you want to live," said Anatol Babushkin, the boss of the Black November faction. He paced shirtless across the room. With the staccato of machine gun fire, his words billowed from his mouth in wisps of cold breath. "This should not be that hard. You're all slaves, *suka* to the state. But in case you have other ideas, let me offer you some advice: treat this like your first prison rape."

Babushkin's men had bound our hands and feet, then lined us against the storage facility's icy lime green wall. The tattooed *vory* and Alexander Kropotkin's turncoat Russian mercenaries brandished a mix of AK-12 and AK-15 assault rifles. Twelve of us shivered in our binds, struggling against the Siberian winter's bone-chilling cold.

The Tomtor Mining Complex's defensive perimeter had been impenetrable. But we'd never expected an attack from beneath the surface. To avoid damaging the mine, we hadn't fired our weapons inside the perimeter. Before we could formulate a plan, our hired guns had turned on us. Turns out Kropotkin's merry little mercenary company had negotiated a more lucrative deal with Babushkin.

In 2070, Tomtor accounted for one percent of the world's rare earth metal production and five percent of its reserves. These elements were core components of high-tech products ranging from guidance systems to medical tools to haptic televisions. Using front companies to make a string of strategic acquisitions, the Chinese now controlled ninety percent of the market. China had held a similar monopoly in the century's first two decades. At the time, it'd curbed its rare earth metal exports, spurring a nearly tenfold price hike. The Russian republics and the United States were keen to avoid an encore.

"On an intellectual level," Babushkin continued, "no man entering the gulag thinks himself entirely immune to this fate. It's only when three men pin him to a wall that the veil between theory and reality is pierced. The trick is not to fight, but to submit. To know and accept your place. To do anything else is to annihilate the will."

Like all *vory v zakone*, Babushkin's skin was the canvas upon which his life's saga was written. An eight-pointed star stained each collarbone—high rank in the criminal underworld. The dagger through his neck marked Babushkin's status as an accomplished prison murderer. The ten onion-shaped cupolas sprouting from the citadel on his chest each represented a crime committed against the state. The Cyrillic letters "СЕВЕР" tattooed above Satan's horned skull on the back of his right hand spelled the Russian word for north, a euphemism for having done significant time in a Siberian prison. The letters "ОМУТ" for deep watering hole etched beneath the Prince of Darkness warned that once Babushkin set his sights on you, escape was impossible. The Devil's head symbolized Babushkin's unrestrained contempt for the government.

"Is that what you did when they raped you?" I asked, deliberately antagonizing him.

Babushkin glared at me. His fierce blue eyes scorched my soul with his scorn. He grinned, his mouth a ruin of broken and chipped teeth, and said, "Angels abide in heaven; devils reign in hell; the *vory* glorifies the gulag."

He marched over to me, silhouetting himself against the bright fluorescent lamp swaying overhead. "You filthy little *suka*." He cuffed me so hard, a flash of lightning washed out my sight, replacing it with the grainy static of a dead channel on an ancient analog television. "Each has his place. You have yours and I, mine. When those jackals cornered me, my face would be the last they'd ever see. I distinctly remember the way an eyeball dangles from the optic nerve. How I had to stretch them like rubber bands until they snapped from their sockets. While those men no longer had the sight to watch me eat their eyes, I made sure the rest of the gulag did. No one ever tried to rape me again. For I am a man of purpose and will."

Babushkin's tattoos had likely been chiseled onto his leathery skin the hard way, with a needle and ampoule of liquid dye attached to an adapted electric shaver. It would've been a painstaking process involving up to six hours of torture and agony. The liquid dye would've been a heady brew of urine and scorched rubber, the only ingredients available in the gulag.

"Cut the shit," said John Grady, my merc team's commander. "Now that you control Tomtor, what about us?"

Babushkin spun on his heel and rushed at Grady in a running stoop. He settled an inch from Grady's face. "You Americans. So impatient. In the gulag, the body may not be free, but the mind is. It gives you time to think. To reflect. But you Americans all shoot first and ask questions afterward." Babushkin inclined his head toward a bald brute with a bushy brown goatee and black trench coat. "Yuri!"

The thug lumbered over to Grady, idly swiping the air with a razor-sharp machete.

"Yuri, show him who and what you are," said Babushkin, rising from his crouch.

Yuri removed his trench coat. He took off his olive drab T-shirt, revealing a tapestry of intricate tattoos. A cathedral with seven skull-capped spires adorned his chest—seven murders. Like Babushkin, he had a knife through his neck. Though no eight-pointed stars were stamped on his clavicles. When I saw the two eyes on his stomach, I shuddered.

My reaction caught Babushkin's eye. He winked at me. Squatting, he whispered in Grady's ear.

He thinks you understand the tattoos, Turk, Grady projected over the neuronet. Our wetware's quantum-encrypted wireless communications network converted analog beta and gamma brain waves into digital signals and transmitted them. *That true?*

A few years back I did a surveillance job on Russian thieves-in-law, I replied, *so yeah. It's true.*

So what the hell do those tats mean? Grady said.

I hesitated. But it didn't matter. Grady's signal went dead when Yuri decapitated him. The executioner raised the dripping head. Grady's still-conscious eyes gazed down upon his severed neck stump. Bursts of aortic blood geysered onto the floor with the decaying rhythm of Grady's fading heartbeat. After so many years of war, my mind still focused on the oddest and most morbid of details. It was as if time dilated so memory could preserve the horror forever.

At least Grady didn't suffer much. If Yuri had lived up to those eye tats, Grady's last hours would've been far worse.

I was in charge now.

I waited outside the operating room, while the surgeons fought to save Chloe and her skin. Linda wouldn't even look at me. From the moment she'd arrived at the hospital, I knew our marriage was over.

I'd been long aware of Chloe's condition, but had never truly internalized its gravity until it was too late. And I wasn't alone. To walk in daylight, most American children had to wear cloaks.

In 2060, the year Chloe was born, the Sun Sickness had raged throughout Europe, Africa, and the Americas. Mosquitos had spread it in the tropics. From there it had passed from mother to child, lover to lover, and blood donor to recipient. Adults had presented no symptoms, but the impact on prenatal development had been catastrophic. When the first newborn's skin had blistered in sunlight, it had been too late to stop the spread.

The *vory* locked us in the storage shed where Yuri had murdered Grady three hours earlier. We were lucky. Babushkin must've thought we'd be worth something as hostages. We'd be dead otherwise. And he was right. He just didn't realize how right. If he'd known how much bleeding edge tech was inside us, he'd have alerted the Chinese by now.

Six months ago, the Juggernaut Corporation had signed the largest private security contract in its history. It was high risk, high reward. The contract required us to secure the Tomtor Mining Complex for six months until TriArk Mining LLC, the mine's owner, closed the mine's sale to the Moscow Mining Cooperative. The cooperative was a state-owned enterprise of the Moscow Federation, one of Russia's three fractured nation-states—a casualty of the two-decade War of the Six Oligarchs. The war, sparked by Vladimir Putin's death in 2040, had ended in 2060 with the Peace of São Paulo. Russia's disintegration had left a power vacuum in North Asia—a void resource-ravenous China was anxious to fill. As the Chinese were fond of saying, "Loot a burning house."

Yuri and two turncoats stood watch. Grady's blood had long since ceased dribbling from his neck. It had pooled into a frozen crimson pond beside his body. His bladder and bowels had passed over two hours ago, suffusing the frigid air with a foul admixture of urine and feces. Grady's corpse stiffened with the onset of rigor mortis. His head lay in the far-right corner of the shed. Its dead eyes haunted me.

"You gonna do something about that?" I said, nodding toward the body. I secretly hoped Yuri did nothing of the sort. I had other plans for Grady.

Yuri opened his trench coat. He lifted his tee shirt, exposing his naked torso. He knew I understood what his eye tats meant. The threat was as subtle as an elephant in a stampede. Good. He'd taken the bait. Now I was certain he'd leave Grady's body here overnight to torment us.

For defending Tomtor, we'd earn a de minimis sum for our trouble. But the real prize was the equity we'd receive in the mine. The day the transaction closed—today—Juggernaut would own five percent of the mine. With a total transaction value of ten billion dollars, Juggernaut would clear a cool five hundred million. None of us would ever have to work again.

If Babushkin was smart, he'd be working to rapidly reinforce Tomtor against yet another incursion. I prayed he wasn't expecting an internal breach. Lord knows Grady hadn't. Now Grady was dead.

Exactly twenty-four hours from payday, Babushkin's thugs had emerged from beneath Tomtor in a nuclear-powered subterrene. It had burrowed hundreds of feet below us, propelling itself forward by pushing molten rock around its edges. Its nuclear reactor had superheated liquified lithium metal to seventeen hundred degrees Fahrenheit and circulated it to its stationary drill. In the subterrene's wake, the tunnel's walls had cooled to a glass-like lining.

So we'd surrendered. To bide our time. Find a way to take back the mine without destroying it.

That decision had cost Grady his life.

I closed my eyes and pushed beyond the gut-wrenching cold. I'd been in worse situations. Hell, the Siege of Sikkim had nearly killed me. But this time I had an ace up my sleeve.

ARSENAL.

The genius behind the ARSENAL system was its stealth. Our wetware was hidden, embedded in our organs and tissue. Unless someone was looking for it, they'd never find it.

Short for Advanced Remote Sensing and Engagement Nanomodular Autonomous Legion, ARSENAL was state of the art. So new, the world's most advanced militaries had nothing close. We'd all volunteered for a highly classified US military experiment. In exchange for risking life and limb, we got to keep the tech for private military operations so long as we never used it against the US or its interests. Given what this wetware could do, I'd happily signed my life away. Hell, with Chloe's mounting medical costs, my life was over anyway. ARSENAL was my salvation.

Thousands of nanoturbines whirled throughout my body. They transferred its heat into electrical charge stored in hundreds of miniaturized ultracapacitors stitched into my muscles. The nanoscopic tactical processor surgically fused to my frontal lobe, cerebellum, and my posterior parietal cortex lit up with activity. My mind reached out for the ARTEMIS net we'd deployed for aerial surveillance long before Babushkin and his thugs had arrived.

The Augmented Reality Targeting and Engagement Mapping Integration System consolidated imaging data from thousands of solar-powered centimeter-length autonomous microdrones loitering overhead. The technology was over four decades old, but the engineers who'd created ARSENAL had upgraded ARTEMIS to interface with our wetware. ARTEMIS's telemetry data was also quantum encrypted, preventing anyone on Earth from intercepting and decrypting its signals.

In my mind's eye, I surveyed Tomtor from two thousand feet. Thousands of visual and infrared sensors formed a honeycomb composite image. The drones' image intensifiers and thermal imagers sharpened what I saw in the darkness of night. The infrared signature on the subterrene's nuclear reactor shone like the sun, nearly washing out dozens of smaller signatures.

It took me seven microseconds to process the enemy's

disposition. Babushkin had added a hundred of his own men to the thirty Russian traitors. Fortunately, we'd kept our capabilities quiet. They were soon about to learn what our tech could do.

Now that I had the lay of the land, I coordinated a battle plan with my ten surviving comrades.

My comms and cyber experts, Pedro Martinez and James Kim, dropped their nanite swarms from ARTEMIS on every radio, satellite dish, hub, and cable on the installation. Gus Vartanian and Remington Jones, my weapons experts, activated their nanites to take control of Tomtor's four fully automated Air Defense Anti-Tank System, or ADATS, missile batteries. They also dropped nanite swarms several klicks beyond Tomtor to scavenge whatever military hardware they could salvage. Marcie Lin and Alexandre Boudreaux, my engineers, went to work on taking control of other critical items. I ordered Lin to use her nanites to hack into the subterrene. Boudreaux's mission was to commandeer Tomtor's mining equipment. Jen Reed and Daryl Culpepper, my cyber physicians, actively monitored the team's health, ensuring the nanites in our bloodstreams kept our core body temperatures stable. They also remotely applied microdoses of medicine to keep our biological systems in equilibrium. I ceded control of the main ARTEMIS swarm to Spike Miller, our intelligence analyst, so he could range out and identify approaching threats.

Once I'd issued my orders, I synced with Grady's wetware and took control of his nanites. I triggered their replication protocol. Using the iron in Grady's blood, I spawned a nanite army.

In the years after Chloe's accident, Linda would shame me by chronicling Chloe's endless infections, skin grafts, tumors, and other complications. The wages of my guilt would never be paid.

As a father of an afflicted child, I had a duty to study the disease. The virus caused a mutation in the XPA gene, making afflicted children susceptible to an aggressive form of xeroderma pigmentosum. This condition caused extreme sensitivity to UV radiation. Just a few minutes' exposure to sunlight led to severe blistering. Children could also develop eye tumors, leading to diminished sight or even blindness. They could even suffer from neurological disorders causing poor coordination, cognitive disabilities, seizures, and worse.

My grandparents would've guessed some climate change–linked calamity had been to blame for this scourge.

They'd have been wrong.

People had done this.

When the virus had first landed on US shores, most East Asian and Native American children had been immune. Epidemiologists had quickly determined that a specific mutation in the EDAR gene conferred this immunity. This mutation in a gene that coded for skin, hair thickness, and sweat glands was largely absent in European and African populations, but in ninety-three percent of Han Chinese. The existence of this very particular genetic advantage is why many suspected, but couldn't prove, that China was behind the outbreak.

When Pakistani scientist Dr. Farooq Hakim Ali Gabol had claimed credit for synthesizing and spreading the retrovirus to teach the godless infidels humility, I'd been skeptical. As a Delta operator, I'd volunteered for the mission to capture him in Pakistan. In the ensuing years, some whispered that under CIA interrogation, Gabol couldn't answer basic technical questions about the retrovirus.

Rumor had it that Gabol had been a patsy.

Whoever had engineered this horrific plague hadn't been in any rush to claim credit. But the specific mechanisms by which it operated were highly suspicious. Researchers had never before observed the retrovirus's RNA sequence in nature. The world's best epidemiologists had wracked their brains to retrace the chain of transmission. Only to fail over and over again. But if someone wanted to lay a nation low, this disease would've been the way to do it.

Regardless, people had done this.

People had blighted an entire generation with a crippling illness. People had turned a life-giving star into a flesh-burning death ray. People had robbed millions of their childhood. People had stolen the simple pleasure of basking in the sun from the innocent.

People had consigned my little girl to a life of perpetual darkness.

For the rest of my life, guilt was my albatross. I'd never forgive myself for that momentary lapse of vigilance. Neither would Linda.

If I ever learned who'd truly been responsible for this virus, there'd be hell to pay.

I had my suspicions.

The 2018 birth of genetically modified twins, Lulu and Nana, had heralded a new age of Chinese biological innovation. Shenzhen researcher He Jiankui's unethical experiments had alarmed the global scientific community, drawing widespread criticism. But the loss of face for the Chinese mandarins had only encouraged the bastards.

In 2024, the Chinese Communists had publicly and enthusiastically endorsed the WHO's ten-year moratorium on human germline genome editing. Anyone back then with half a brain could've smelled the steaming pile of bullshit a mile away. The Chinese had never intended to halt their research; the moratorium had just given them a ten-year head start.

While the West had sat on its hands, the Chinese Communists had driven their controversial research further underground. Away from the global community's prying eyes, the Chinese had secretly engaged in industrial-scale genetic experimentation in reeducation camps in Xinjiang and Tibet. With a one-generation lead, the Chinese had spearheaded advanced CRISPR genome editing techniques to birth a generation of purpose-built super soldiers and to develop a host of designer pandemics.

In the first World War III engagements of the mid-fifties, it had become clear the US had yielded its technological advantage in genetic engineering to the Chinese. A generation behind in bioengineering, panicked US policymakers had doubled down on artificial intelligence, robotics, and nanotech. Playing to its strengths in these fields, the US had augmented an elite group of soldiers with advanced human-machine interfaces. As a young sergeant, I'd volunteered for one of these early programs.

When World War III had ended in stalemate in 2058, the great power competition between the US and China had boiled down to inorganics versus organics. In either case, humanity paid a price. A pandemic crippling China's enemies had emerged two years later. The curious timing of the Sun Sickness had not been lost on anyone.

So I volunteered for the ARSENAL program. I sacrificed my mind and body on the altar of military R&D. I was maimed and altered in ways that had compromised my humanity. But it didn't matter so long as Chloe got the medical care she needed. And if I happened to use the ARSENAL system against the Chinese Communists, it would be icing on the cake.

⊕ ⊕ ⊕

Babushkin returned the next morning. He strode into the room with the air of a Roman centurion. He crouched and glared at me. "You're now the leader here, no?"

"Who wants to know?" I said.

Babushkin slapped me so hard, it knocked a tooth loose. "I deserve more respect, you mouthy little *suka*. I trust you all had a comfortable night here in the cold. Now you've had your vacation, it's time to talk." Babushkin cupped my jaw. "So tell me, Martin Turk, why should I let you live?"

"You have no choice," I said with a confidence surprising even me.

Babushkin chuckled. He glanced over his shoulder at Yuri. "This one's growing on me." He turned back. His eyes bored into mine. "Do tell, Mr. Turk. Why don't I have a choice?"

"We don't die." Grady's nanite swarms had eaten through our binds hours ago. But we'd waited until Babushkin had returned to spring the trap.

Thousands of metallic cilia burst from Grady's skull. The bloody head scurried across the room. Grady's teeth clamped on Yuri's ankle.

Yuri screamed.

Grady's headless body bolted up. It tackled Babushkin and pinned him to the floor. The two remaining Russian guards fled.

Yuri struggled to shake his leg free from Grady's jaws. Remington Jones stood up, surprising the *vor*. Jones punched Yuri repeatedly until he dropped the machete. Gus Vartanian grabbed it. He lopped off Yuri's head.

It was only fair.

I sprang to my feet. I gripped Yuri's head by the beard and tossed it at Babushkin. "Do I have your attention?"

"Fuck you!" Babushkin said. "I knew you were all freaks. I have a thousand men outside. They'll barricade you in here until you freeze or starve."

I laughed at his bluff. "You had one hundred and thirty men, three minutes ago." A series of explosions rocked the building. "Now you have seventeen."

A coal-black cannonball with articulated legs scurried into the hallway. It spidered up to Babushkin. He quivered. "How...how...? Impossible."

I jerked my thumb at Spike Miller. "Last night, Spike here found a few SWARMs a couple klicks down the road." Scatterable Wide-Area Autonomous Robotic Mines were one of the most terrifying sights a soldier could stumble upon. Designed and deployed by the Russian military in the first half of the twenty-first century, these mines chased mobile targets and detonated on contact. "My team woke 'em up and introduced 'em to your boys. Hope you don't mind."

"But . . . your team . . . they were here the whole time," Babushkin said. "How . . . ?"

"It's just physics," said Miller. "With a little help from our ladies, ARTEMIS and PANDORA."

Babushkin gave me a blank stare.

"ARTEMIS is our eye. PANDORA's our hand." I wasn't about to share any state secrets with Babushkin, but him knowing we could do more than we let on might be an effective deterrent for future enemies. PANDORA, short for Panoramic Autonomous Nanite-Distributing Operational Remote Assemblers, enabled us to drop millions of self-organizing nanites from ARTEMIS's circulating microdrones to infest hardware, hack into their central processors, and take control.

"You'll never get away with this," said Babushkin. "I have friends in big places. You may take this mine, but you'll never keep it."

"I only need to hold it a few more hours."

Babushkin sneered. "Until what? Your friends from Moscow arrive?" He snickered.

"Now you mention it," I said, "that's exactly what I'm waiting for."

"Well, Mr. Artemis eye and Pandora hand, you aren't as well informed as you think."

Miller tapped my shoulder. "Got a moment, chief? We have a bit of a . . . situation."

I put my arm over Miller's shoulder and walked down the hall until Babushkin was out of earshot. "Talk to me."

"We're gonna need to hold Tomtor a while longer."

"Why the hell would we do that? Our relief will be here in a few hours."

Miller lowered his eyes. "That's the rub, Turk. Our relief ain't coming."

"Why not? We had a goddamn contract."

"It's kinda hard for the Evro Polis Corporation to satisfy those terms when the force earmarked to relieve us was destroyed," Miller replied, referring to a TriArk subcontractor.

"Wait. What?"

Miller projected a stream of images. From the bird's-eye view of a microdrone swarm, I watched battalions of aging Russian Armata tanks maneuver across a broken and snowy landscape. Early model Havoc attack helicopters zipped over and beyond the tanks, their five-blade rotors whirling like hornet wings.

That's the force Evro Polis contracted the Wagner Group to supply, I said over the neuronet.

Just watch, said Miller.

A Havoc burst into a ball of flame. The twisted metal shards of a rotor blade ripped across the sky and smashed into a tank below in a hail of sparks and smoke. More Havocs launched a volley of AT-9 Spiral 2 rockets at some distant target. The use of that specific armament meant only one thing: tanks.

Several Havocs burst in a riot of fire, black smoke, and metal. Others lost tail rotors, spinning erratically in the air until careening to the surface in clouds of dust. The lucky ones managed soft crash landings. But there was only one constant: the enemy the Russian mercenaries faced had neutralized their air cover.

The tanks crept forward, using the broken terrain to mask their movement. Their attack ended before it began. Turrets shot upward sixty feet. Rail gun–launched sabot rounds traveling fifteen times the speed of sound pierced through both sides of heavily armored hulls. If the round didn't kill the crew, spalling from overpressure did.

Hampered by aging equipment, inferior munitions, and limited range, the Russian mercenaries never had a chance.

Only one weapons platform outside the US had that power and reach: the 125-millimeter rail gun of a Chinese Type 150 tank.

Get me eyes on that Chinese tank unit, I said to Miller.

Negative, he replied. *I sent a small microdrone swarm to investigate. They disappeared. Electromagnetic countermeasures.*

At the altitude our microdrones operate, I said, *that should've been impossible. Unless...*

The Chinese have their own counter-recon drone swarm, Miller said, completing my thought. *Based on the course, velocity, and kinetic impact of the Chinese rounds, I'd estimate the tanks were operating halfway between us and our Russian relief force.*

Which means . . .

A Chinese People's Liberation Army unit of unknown size and disposition has crossed into Siberia and is heading our way.

We hadn't even secured Tomtor yet, and another, greater threat was on its way. It was a scenario we hadn't remotely planned for. I had to think, and I had to do it fast.

Sorry, Turk, but there's more, said Miller.

Jesus H. Christ, I said. *It's nothing but roses and unicorns with you. What now?*

I've been picking up strange chatter on social media and holologs throughout Siberia. This is gonna sound crazy, Turk, but local superstitions die hard. There's talk of a godlike being reaching into Siberia to harness its mineral riches.

Sounds like horseshit to me, I said.

I hear you, Turk. I think it's horseshit too. But horseshit with a kernel of truth. Remember that op we ran in Angola back when we were still in Delta?

What about it? I said.

Do you recall that facility way out in southeastern Angola? The one with those Ambundu scientists doing those vile genetic experiments on Khoisan tribesmen?

Yeah, I said. *Never did figure out what the hell had been going on there. Just passed the intel to the Agency and moved on.*

When I worked for the Agency a few years later, Miller continued, *I heard the Chinese were behind the whole operation. Using Ambundu proxies to do their dirty work. Plausible deniability and all that jazz.*

What's that got to do with all this chatter about some god?

Turns out those experiments were all about optimizing human intelligence. Tweaking human DNA to engineer smarter humans.

You think the Chinese have produced a superintelligent human being who's orchestrating events in Siberia? I asked, incredulous.

Just a theory, said Miller. *It's a bit off the ranch, but it's all I got. The chatter's remarkably consistent. Definitely something to it, but I sure as hell don't think a god's walking among us either.*

I folded my arms across my chest. I needed better intel. And I knew exactly where to get it.

Secure Babushkin, I said. *He knew about the Chinese. Hell, I wouldn't be surprised if they'd hired him to take this mine. Extract as much intel as you can. In the meantime, let's take back Tomtor.*

III. Red Guards of Rout and Ruin

Against our ARSENAL systems, the *vory* and turncoats never saw us coming. After we'd subdued the holdouts, Miller had used every interrogation technique shy of torture to piece together the full picture. Sociedade Mineira De Catoca, an Angolan mining concern, had hired Babushkin to seize Tomtor. Why would an Angolan mining company hire mercenaries to seize a Russian mine? It didn't compute. So Miller analyzed thousands of public corporate filings in the cloud. Turns out that through a labyrinthine arrangement of shell companies and joint ventures, Sociedade Mineira De Catoca was effectively a wholly owned subsidiary of China Sonangol International.

China.

It figured. The bastards even had a saying for it: kill with a borrowed knife.

Since we couldn't safely use our microdrones to recon the Chinese force, we'd have to rely on our optical sensors. We also configured a handful of nanite swarms to collect and analyze seismic data. Using both methods, we identified a brigade-sized armored unit that would reach Tomtor in three hours. My gut told me it was the 8th Heavy Combined Arms Brigade based out of Inner Mongolia.

I sent our remaining microdrone swarms to airdrop PANDORA nanites over the Russian tank armada's wreckage. From there, they'd hack into any salvageable systems and repair what they could. In the interim, we'd fight a delaying action until the Chinese took Tomtor. Then we'd spend the next few weeks hiding throughout the mine until the tanks arrived. While my team focused on reconstituting the tanks, Lin's nanites had successfully taken control of the subterrene. She'd already tunneled an exfil route just in case.

I hoped to God we didn't need it. Otherwise, Grady's death would've been for nothing. And Chloe would never get a shot at a normal life.

◈◈◈

A shimmer on the horizon resolved into steam and steel. Hundreds of Type 150 tanks rumbled in broken formations through the larch, pine, and spruce of the Siberian taiga. Choking diesel fumes mixed with the sweet scent of pine.

Once the tanks were in visual range, I executed the first phase of our plan. During his interrogations, Miller let some information "slip." He'd hinted we were a covert element of the US military. The deception's aim was to buy time, since the last thing the Chinese wanted was to cause an international incident. Until they could be sure we weren't part of the US military, they'd delay their attack. Or so I hoped.

Any clue what these things are? Miller streamed an image of dozens of trucks. Each carried a twenty-foot, steel conical structure. *There's nothing in my threat database.*

About a mile out, the lead tanks halted. Bulldozers started digging a trench parallel to our front. Chinese soldiers shoveled nearby. After a few hours, they off-loaded the trucks. They lined the odd conical structures in a neat row several meters behind the trench.

Why the Chinese were preparing what appeared to be a defensive belt puzzled me. It made no sense. They had an overwhelming force. And given their ties to Babushkin, they already had good intel on my team's numbers. If they weren't aware of our full capabilities, an attack would've seemed like a cakewalk. And even if they had known, the Chinese would still have the edge.

Several boxy ATVs reminiscent of ice cream trucks drove parallel to the trench toward the wind. Reaching the trench's northern limit, the trucks billowed lush clouds of smoke.

Whatever those structures were, the Chinese didn't want us to see them. Within twenty minutes, the ATVs had obscured the entire front in a wall of smoke.

An ATV emerged from the smoke line, heading for Tomtor's outskirts. A white flag whipped in the bitter Siberian wind. Mounted on its roof was a loudspeaker.

Once it was within earshot, the ATV stopped. It broadcast a message. First in Russian, then in Chinese, and finally in English. They all said the same thing: "Surrender Tomtor to the People's Liberation Army, and we will guarantee your freedom. Failure to comply will result in swift and certain destruction. This will be your only warning."

Everyone chuckled. After half a century of duplicitous behavior, the Chinese still operated under the delusion they had an honorable reputation. We all recalled the Chinese maxim: *Hide a knife behind a smile.*

So we took them at their word—as worthless as it was.

Babushkin and his seventeen survivors marched in knee-high snow toward Chinese lines. When Babushkin reached the ATV, he glanced back at Tomtor and scowled. Then he howled like a hyena. The bastard thought he'd fooled me. Thought he'd get another shot at cleaning my clock.

Then the Chinese did something that surprised even me.

Light machine gun fire rattled in the distance. The *vory* and turncoats burst into smoky gray and blood-wet red puffs. Scarlet pools leaked from their squirming bodies, staining the snow in blood and filth. Babushkin's head popped like a pimple. His brains exploded from his shattered skull like red-gray goo.

I expected the tanks to exploit the shock and awe of such bold-faced treachery. Nothing happened. An eerie silence settled over the taiga while the roiling smoke clouds continued to conceal the enigma.

What now? Lin said from the subterrene.

We wait, I replied. And so we did.

At 3:15 A.M. local time, our nanites detected movement.

Talk to me, Miller, I said over the neuronet. My teeth chattered as I stood shivering in a waist-deep trench facing Chinese forces. A gale howled with the fury of an impending storm. The wind blew with such force, it was tough to stand. Thick, hoary snowflakes swirled from the sky in the hyperborean darkness.

Six two-man dismounted scout teams are operating within two hundred meters of the perimeter, he replied. *Their footfalls are so light, the nanites are having difficulty tracking them.*

The closest two-man team lurked at my twelve o'clock. The nanoelectromechanical lenses in my eyes adjusted their focal lengths and applied an infrared overlay to produce a high-res image of two commandos crawling toward my position. They could probably see me too. The only difference was their ability had been encoded in their DNA.

We stared at each other for a millisecond.

I dove into the trench. A bullet zipped overhead, nearly separating my head from my body.

Release the SWARMs, I said to Jones.

Six SWARMs emerged from the snow, pursuing their targets. Flashes strobed throughout the battlefield like fireflies in the night. In their wake, a series of concussive blasts rumbled. Then silence. A sudden flash lit up the sky. An explosion just meters in front of me followed. The scent of pine resin swept through the air.

I said to Jones, *You got eyes on?*

Roger, he replied. *The SWARMs scratched five commando teams. But the sixth, the one at your twelve o'clock, shimmied up some pine trees. Jesus. These fuckers move more like animals than people. I tried to take 'em out. I detonated the closest SWARM. It cut down the trees. Instead of crashing to their deaths, those freaks leapt twenty feet and started leapfrogging through the trees toward Tomtor.*

"Shit," I muttered to myself. I accessed my battle map. I located Jones and Vartanian half a klick to my north and south, respectively.

Jones. Vartanian. Work your way to my position ASAP, I said.

Cradling my captured AK-12, I low-crawled through the snow and ice-encrusted ditch for a better tactical position. When I stopped, I had Jones patch me into the closest ADATS. I aimed to track the advancing commandos using the missile battery's optics.

I'd been anxious about a Chinese air assault. So I'd earmarked Tomtor's four ADATS batteries for air defense. But with surface winds of more than forty knots, high wind shear conditions, and a brewing blizzard, it was unlikely such an attack would ever come. Landing troops from helicopters now would not only be reckless, but also risk damaging the mine.

Correlating the data streams from the ADATS battery's optics, my location, the crosswind's direction and speed, the air temperature and pressure, the AK-12's average muzzle velocity, the predicted path of the nearest commando, and a multitude of other variables, my wetware computed an optimal ballistics solution. I lifted the rifle above the trench's spoil and pulled the trigger.

Before I could lower my rifle, shrapnel whizzed overhead, knocking the weapon out of my hands. I should've known better. The bastards had traced my bullet's trajectory back to me, which meant . . .

A shadow rolled into the trench. The interloper stabbed me in the gut. I gasped for breath. I smelled the filth leaking from my innards.

The man glared at me and smiled. His pupils had slits like a predator's. A nictitating membrane drew across his eyes like a cat's. He gouged me again in two sharp thrusts. He could've finished me right there, but didn't.

Seizing the scruff of my neck he yelled, "I have your commander," in perfect English. "Surrender. The People's Liberation Army will let you go in peace." Despite the wailing wind, his booming voice resonated like a trumpet. Had he been purely human, the wind would have smothered his voice like a hurricane a flame.

My vision scrambled like a computer image corrupted by an EM pulse. Warmth began to seep from my body. Accessing my tactical map, I observed Jones and Vartanian drawing closer.

Take cover, I said.

Before I could send a second warning, Vartanian leapt out of the darkness and onto the commando.

In one fluid motion, the commando dislodged the knife from my gut and sliced Vartanian's throat. The slash was so deep, Vartanian became a gurgling human Pez dispenser. The weapons expert stumbled backward into the snow. He clutched his neck with bloodstained hands.

Watching my friend dispatched so cavalierly gave me the adrenaline jolt I needed to trigger ARSENAL's hand-to-hand protocols.

The commando spun to face me. I jammed my bloody index finger into his ear, releasing a nanite swarm into his bloodstream.

Stunned for a moment, the commando ripped my finger from his ear. He cut a gash into my arm. I fell backward and counted to three.

The commando began convulsing. Foam frothed from his mouth. He staggered forward, then collapsed. He flopped on the ground like a drowning flounder.

I reported Vartanian's and my medical statuses to Daryl Culpepper and Jen Reed. Since Daryl was closer, I had him render aid to Vartanian. I assigned Jen Reed to treat my wounds. In the interim, I did my best to stabilize my friend.

I searched the commando for weapons. I took his knife, three incendiary grenades, and a comms device, which Pedro Martinez and James Kim could exploit. If the Chinese ever performed an autopsy on their operative, they'd discover a nanite swarm had formed a clot in his brain. But they'd never get that chance. I rolled the body out of the trench. I crawled away to gain some distance. Then I lobbed a grenade at the remains.

The immediate threat neutralized, my adrenaline rush started to fade. The roiling pain in my gut became more acute.

After reviewing my vitals over the neuronet, Jen Reed had me lie down. I flexed my knees to take the pressure off my abdominal muscles. With the commando's knife, I cut away the clothing around the wound. I sanitized it as best I could with a handful of snow. Opening my first aid packet, I patched up the wound. Reed remotely triggered the ARSENAL system's nanites to stabilize it and stitch me up. As millions of nanites went to work, I faded from consciousness.

"Wake up, Turk," Jones said, shaking me.

I felt weak and nauseated, but much of the pain had passed. Snow drifted in huge flakes from a dull gray sky. Blistering winds smashed up against the trench's lips. Jen Reed crouched over me, a relieved expression on her face. "We almost lost you," she said. "Welcome back."

"Glad to . . . ah . . . be back. Do I need to take it easy, Doc?"

"If those nanites hadn't been in your system," Reed said, "you'd be dead. Thank God for ARSENAL. It made you right as rain."

I grinned. I faced Jones. "SITREP."

"You certainly have a flair for the dramatic, Turk," said Jones. "You killed one commando with your rifle and the other with your finger. The Chinese have committed their armor. One tank battalion is heading toward our position from the east. Another is maneuvering on our southern flank. The last two are being held in reserve."

"How's Gus doing?" I said.

Reed and Jones avoided eye contact. Culpepper shook his head. "Gus didn't make it. I'm sorry."

I nodded. There was simply nothing more to say. All we could do now was focus on the immediate threat.

While I'd been out, Martinez and Kim had hacked into the commando's comms device. They'd sent one transmission to the network before the Chinese had locked them out. I prayed it'd be enough.

Marcie Lin was the only person who'd stayed behind. After finishing up her escape tunnel, she'd positioned the subterrene within a few hundred meters from the mine and about fifty meters belowground. Over the last twenty-four hours, Boudreaux had commandeered an impressive armada of mining equipment.

On my command, Boudreaux executed the second phase of my plan. His motley collection of PANDORA-hacked bulldozers, crawler loaders, excavators, backhoe loaders, motor graders, skid-steer loaders, trenchers, dump trucks, and scrapers rumbled east toward the Chinese in a line formation.

I waited nervously. Initially, the Chinese did nothing. Just when I thought they'd let our vehicles pass through their ranks, a muzzle flashed. A bulldozer exploded in a hail of idler arms, twisted metal, and sprockets. Black smoke billowed from its warped metal carcass. One twitchy tanker was enough. Seconds later, a cacophony of muzzle flashes erupted across the horizon. There was no order to them. No disciplined volleys. Only the panicked contagion of hair-trigger tank crews.

Based on the initial orderly response, it was clear the Chinese commander knew what they were doing. But in the ensuing chaos, they'd temporarily lost control. That lapse played right into my hands.

A broken wreck of mangled and smoking husks cluttered the snowy battlefield. I grinned at Boudreaux. "Good work. When half the tanks pass through the obstacle, execute phase three."

He smiled back. "Roger, Turk."

The tanks advanced again. They moved faster this time. It was obvious the Chinese leadership was trying to extract itself from a kill sack of its own making. But it didn't matter. While the Chinese might be exposed for less time, they'd still be exposed. I counted on it.

"Turk, we got movement on the flank element," Miller said.

I looked at Boudreaux. "The last batch rigged this time?"

He beamed and nodded.

"Good. Send 'em south."

I hoped this time the Chinese commander would ignore the trucks approaching the southern force, especially after the earlier breakdown in discipline. It was an essential step for him to reestablish order. A step that would spring yet another one of my traps.

"Lead elements have passed through the obstacle," Miller reported.

"Steady, Boudreaux. Steady," I said.

Ten minutes later, Miller said, "Half the battalion's through the breach."

"Boudreaux," I said, "do it."

With my telescopic vision, I focused on the assaulting tank formation's leading edge. Behind the rear element, hundreds of spidering black cannonballs sprang from beneath the snow and slammed into the tanks from behind.

I turned to Jones. "Unleash hell."

The missile launchers of all four ADATS batteries swiveled downward. Missiles streaked from their pods toward the leading tank battalion. Shards of flaming metal swirled through the air. Mangled and burning hulls and ruined mining equipment wedged the surviving tanks into a vise where the SWARMs hunted them.

I faced south. So far, the Chinese flanking element had ignored the mining trucks. The vehicles were now within five hundred meters of the Chinese tanks.

"Let the tanks pass," I told Boudreaux. "On my signal, detonate the dozers."

This time, Chinese blind adherence to orders would kill them.

When the dozers passed through the middle of the tank battalion, I gave Boudreaux the signal.

A concussive wave rippled along our southern flank. Turrets corkscrewed twenty feet into the air. Yet the Chinese never wavered. The tanks ground forward. Their treads churned up mud and snow. To the east, tens of survivors from the main force emerged from the obstacle belt.

A muzzle flashed from the south. The closest ADATS battery exploded, raining shrapnel. More tanks fired. The last three batteries burned.

I turned to Miller. "Battle damage assessment."

"Fifty-four Type 150 tanks destroyed. Seventy remain. There's also still a mechanized infantry battalion somewhere out there."

I said, "How many SWARMs?"

"A hundred, give or take."

"All right. Don't unleash 'em all at once. Let's slowly bleed 'em."

Throughout the day, the Chinese struggled to demine lanes in the snow. The SWARMs' mobility gave us a decisive advantage. By noon, the weather had cleared. I worried the Chinese might try an air assault soon.

We all huddled in the trench. We watched in awe as the Chinese stubbornly obeyed their orders. They'd advance a few meters at a time before yet another tank exploded. For a moment, I thought we had everything under control.

Then Reed screeched.

I grabbed my rifle. I turned. A slimy, white thing as long as my forearm had latched onto her back. Two more six-legged abominations scurried toward her. I froze in shock. I couldn't process what I saw.

They say denial is the first stage of grief. Thank Christ the second stage was anger. Without it, a razor-sharp mandible would've torn me to bits.

The ant-like creatures had swarmed Reed. They ripped her to shreds. Boudreaux slipped on the snow. He unloaded his rifle into a wave of giant insects. A piercing scream signaled his fate.

I dispatched three of the things with my AK-12. A column of hundreds snaked two hundred meters behind our lines before disappearing into a hole.

Then it dawned on me: the strange conical structures. The ditch. No air assault in good weather. The Chinese commander had checkmated us long before the battle had even begun. The structures were mounds for genetically engineered army ants. Modified and bred for the cold.

I had a decision to make.

Retreat, I said over the neuronet. I fired more rounds into the attacking ants. I trudged through the snow as fast as I could. As I fled, I struggled with what would be my final decision at Tomtor. A decision with strategic consequences.

I had one more ace up my sleeve. It was a longshot, but worth a try. I reached out to Kim and Martinez. *Trigger the virus*, I said, referring to the bug they'd uploaded onto the Chinese command network. While the Chinese had locked us out of their systems, the two had rigged the virus with a quantum-entangled trigger. It didn't require network access to set off.

As I waded through knee-high snow, I glanced over my shoulder. The tanks continued their advance.

The virus had failed.

Kim and Martinez collapsed in the snow. They screamed, covering their ears. I turned and rushed to their aid. The ants were closing in. As I got closer, I realized the Chinese had turned the virus against them. They must've reversed the quantum-entangled trigger. Before I could reach my teammates, a score of the ants overran them.

I made my decision. If we couldn't hold Tomtor, no one would.

I sent a message to Marcie Lin. *Run the nanites' sabotage protocol. Put the subterrene reactor core in meltdown. Then get the hell out of here.*

But that'll . . . , she said before I cut her off.

I know. It's not ideal. But better to destroy the mine than let it fall into Chinese hands.

I shot two more abominations before a third clamped onto my leg. I tumbled into the snow. I slammed my rifle butt into the creature until it ruptured into a pulpy white paste. Getting back on my feet, I limped toward the tunnel entrance.

In my mind's eye, I pulled up my tactical map. One by one, blips of individual team members winked out until only mine remained. Dizzy from blood loss, I shambled to the pit's entrance. A score of superbugs trailed behind. I could hear their mandibles snapping. I rolled into the hole. I fired three rounds at the first insect into the breach. Then I tossed a grenade at my pursuers outside. The explosion churned up dirt and smoke. I coughed. The hole was now sealed.

In pitch black darkness, I shambled down an underground tunnel as smooth as glass.

That night a mushroom cloud blossomed over Tomtor.

IV. Manchurian Mind

Weeks later, the nanites had finished repairing the Russian tank armada. For months, I'd harried the retreating Chinese survivors with the harvested wreckage.

The weeks and months that followed blurred in my consciousness like polished stones worn by the winds of entropy. I turned inward, losing myself in Siberia's sublime and snowy desolation. I wandered the white wilderness, inching my way across the taiga. With the destruction I'd wrought at Tomtor, I'd hoped the Chinese had marked me for dead. But one could never be sure. So I kept my head on a swivel.

It was in a remote Yakut village that I first heard passing whispers of the crippled god. While hunting bear with Siberian Tatars and breaking bread with their shamans, the people spoke of a priest-king who often appeared in their dreams. As I sang their ancient Soyot songs, these uncanny superstitions persisted. When I traveled further south, the stories became more concrete. The shamans of southern Siberia spoke of a teacher they called the Manchurian—a man of great honor and wisdom, cowed and subjugated by the Han to do great evil.

I sought oblivion in Tatar séances born from traditions stretching back to a time before the written word. And in those transcendent moments when I opened my mind to the cosmos, I sensed a presence. No words. Just images. Images complementing my memories. Visions of the battle at Tomtor, but from an alien perspective.

I tried to bury these dreams. I ignored them. Dismissed them as flights of fancy. I often worried they heralded the onset of madness. A breakdown of all that circuitry in my head.

Over the next several weeks, I watched shamans exorcise disturbed men in the summer of night. I witnessed the eerie emerald glow of the aurora borealis haunt the northern sky like a shadow on the rim of infinity. I hawked and traded in bazaars on the edge of Kazakhstan's irradiated wastes. There, I overheard more rumors about the Manchurian. But these stories seemed more grounded. Perhaps the proximity to Russia's former space program had made so many Kazakhs see the world through a more scientific lens. What the superstitious Yakuts and Tatars had regarded as some sort of New Age prophet, the Kazakhs had viewed as a freak of nature. A defilement of humanity with a genetically engineered intellect. A tool enabling his Chinese Communist puppet masters to perpetuate their sinister worldview.

What had taken root as passing curiosity had now become my obsession. With more hard data, I resolved to hunt and kill this Frankenstein's monster. To me, the Manchurian was a totem for all that was wrong with Communist China. The embodiment of their evil. I found solace that I might have a real shot at killing him. While I'd never be able to give Chloe a normal life, murdering the Manchurian would fill part of that void.

Sightings of the Manchurian in Xinjiang Province inspired me to travel southeast. I traversed the Tien Shan Mountains until reaching the great industrial city of Ürümqi. In dark alleys, hiding among the city's seediest criminal elements, I gathered intelligence. Dissidents claimed that for nearly four decades, the Chinese had experimented on Uyghurs in Kashgar Prefecture. They'd shuttered these camps twenty-odd years ago, moving their activities elsewhere. Some suggested these experiments had coincided with the Manchurian's origin. A few of my contacts had also alerted me that Chinese authorities had become aware of my presence. Others warned they were actively hunting me.

Pursuing these leads, I trekked southwest across the vast and barren Taklamakan Desert. Then I turned west. I skirted the periphery of Kashgar Prefecture, seeking out the coordinates of the camp a Uyghur refugee had handed me in Ürümqi.

The wind rippled through the stark desert landscape. Caked with grime and sand, my threadbare clothing hung from my frame like a mummy's rags. Kashgar loomed behind me. A bazaar of bazaars, the city made it easy to forget I was in China. By noon, I'd reached my destination—a concrete block of watchtowers and concertina wire. Its gates swayed on rusted hinges. They creaked with the decay of a dead place whose purpose had long since been rendered unto dust.

I wandered across an empty courtyard. The breeze howled with the horrors of the camp's haunted past. The ground was stained by four decades of a grim harvest. Some places had been so befouled by suffering and death, you could hear evil echo in their walls.

I entered a windowless concrete blockhouse on the camp's edge. The building's cold, concrete floors reminded me of a warehouse. Rusting bed frames lined two opposite walls.

My degraded ARSENAL system detected a presence. Based on the acoustic signature, it was a man; a man walking with a limp. I went outside. When he saw me, he nearly fled. I motioned for him to stay. He mumbled what appeared to be an apology. I waited while my universal translator calibrated its language processor. In minutes, I was speaking Uyghur.

He introduced himself as the camp's caretaker. According to him, Chinese authorities had abandoned this facility twenty years ago. As a boy growing up in a local village, he recalled the compound as having been a hub of activity. Back then, buses filled with Uyghur political prisoners would rotate into the camp, but often left empty. He too had heard rumors about the experiments. The few inmates the Chinese had released had often been lobotomized. He also noted that camp doctors often specialized in areas related to the brain and pineal gland.

The Chinese had been meticulous in keeping their work secret. In later years, he explained, locals often reported vivid dreams, where they were haunted by their missing countrymen. Many downplayed these visions. The old man, he wasn't so sure. In recent years, the Manchurian began appearing in those dreams. People often described him as a righteous soul born into a cursed body. Cursed because it had been harvested from the blood of the Uyghur people.

I asked the old man if he'd put much stock in these tales. He nodded. When I inquired where I might find the Manchurian, he pointed east to the Kunlun Shan. "Seek out the Golmud county seat. He's expecting you."

I shuddered at his words. They reminded me of my Siberian visions. I thanked him. Then I left, traveling southeast to the Kunlun Shan foothills on the rim of the Tibetan frontier.

Four soldiers slammed me onto the concrete floor of a dark green room. They'd arrested me in Golmud. It was as if they'd been expecting me. Rather than fight, I'd cooperated. I'd had a pretty good idea where they'd be taking me.

Two of them stayed in the room, guarding the exit. The others left and locked the doors. The room reeked of sweat and sulfur. Once my eyes adjusted to the faint light, I saw a pool twenty feet before me. Something twitched with an irregular rhythm that struck me as a bit . . . off. He reminded me of a slug or a beached whale. A mossy slime glazed his skin. The thing before me had a skull so large it extended down his back. His arms, which he used to stabilize his massive bulk at the edge of the shallow pool, were no more than stubs. If I had to guess, this thing, this creature gazing at me with beady but deeply penetrating black eyes was a mind personified. He was a cripple, a cripple genetically altered to be a living supercomputer.

When the Manchurian's thoughts first invaded my mind, I almost fainted from the flood of information. So many images. As the data torrent moderated, and I regained control of my senses, the horror of his ability slowly sunk in. The Chinese had so fundamentally altered his DNA, he could project electromagnetic signals into my wetware. Or so it seemed. But the Tatar, Yakut, and Uyghur stories had pointed to something far more terrifying. He'd also appeared in their dreams. And as far as I knew, they'd had no sophisticated implants.

"It's been said that if man was able to fully correlate the contents of the universe, he'd go mad. Once he fully comprehended his utter insignificance against the cosmos's infinite vastness, he'd see the futility of his existence," the Manchurian said. "While no being on this world will ever possess that capability, I've been cursed with a mind so advanced, I can predict the future with a high rate of accuracy. That is my value to my masters. It's the only reason I exist."

Kill me, the Manchurian projected in my mind.

"Wait . . . what?" I said aloud, just realizing the thought was only directed at me.

Like a shrewd spymaster, the Manchurian answered as if my question had been in response to his spoken words. "Mr. Turk," he said, "are you familiar with Hugh Everett's many-worlds interpretation of quantum mechanics?"

"What? . . . Ah, maybe. Remind me," I said.

The Manchurian continued, "Physicists model all possible observable states of a quantum system such as the location of a particle using a probability distribution they call the wave function. The wave function's amplitude represents the probabilities of the wave's location at any given point. When they ultimately measure the particle's location, the wave function is said to collapse to that outcome. Everett posited that a universal wave function explained all possible quantum realities, which existed simultaneously and in superposition with each other. He argued that these realities didn't collapse after measurement; we just perceive only one of them. The other outcomes continue to have separate physical realities beyond our perception."

Kill me, the Manchurian repeated.

"What does quantum mechanics have to do with predicting the future?" I said.

I hesitated, overwhelmed by how sanguine the Manchurian was about longing for his own death. *Why?* I thought. *Why do you seek death?*

"Because I can see it all in my mind," the Manchurian said, addressing my spoken question. "Every possible outcome. I prepare my government for the most likely ones. What might seem like precognition to you is an inbred ability to correlate a staggering amount of geopolitical data to predict the most likely outcomes. The Kashgar experiments bestowed me with genetic code that allows me to reach into the minds of millions and read their thoughts. This ability has only augmented this data set, increasing its predictive value."

Look at me, he projected, *I'm an abomination. The Communist mandarins have violated the laws of nature and man to create this ... creature you see before you. Kill me.*

"Why the pineal gland?" I said.

Even if I wanted to kill you, I'm surrounded. I'd never escape alive, I thought.

The Manchurian smiled. "The pineal gland has always been a bit of a mystery. Its most obvious function is the secretion of melatonin. Taking external cues from light and darkness, the hormone helps modulate your circadian rhythm. Melatonin also regulates certain reproductive hormones. Throughout the modern era, many believed this pinecone-shaped organ functioned in other ways that had yet to be discovered."

Your government has the means. Did you really think the US military would grant you this technology without monitoring you? he projected.

"But why did your government experiment on the Uyghurs?" I said.

Simultaneously, I sent another thought. *If they'd been keeping tabs on me, why hadn't they interceded at Tomtor?*

"Throughout the ages, wise people from among the ancient Egyptians to the Hindus saw the pineal gland as a 'third eye,' enabling them to reach higher states of consciousness. René Descartes, the French philosopher and mathematician, believed the organ was the 'seat of the soul.' Madame Blavatsky, the founder of the nineteenth-century theosophy movement suggested the modern human pineal gland was the atrophied vestigial organ of 'spiritual vision.' That the organ produces tiny amounts of the spirit molecule, dimethyltryptamine, only lends further credence to these beliefs. Yet today, the scientific community still scoffs at these claims."

The Manchurian's failure to address my allegations of Chinese mistreatment spoke volumes.

Because they wanted the mine destroyed, he thought, answering my other query. *They'd never be able to control it. And the risk of my country seizing it was too high. From the US's perspective, it was best no one controlled it. But securing Tomtor was never your primary mission. Hunting and killing me was.*

I wanted to refute the Manchurian's theory about Tomtor. But the cold hard logic of it made it tough to deny. And his theory about me being a US Manchurian candidate sent to kill him disturbed me even more. Yet oddly enough, it rang true.

You're right, though, he continued. *You can do nothing here. You won't have to. Your overlords see all you see. They installed a microscopic shunt on your optic nerve that uploads a video feed to military satellites in real-time. Once your government learns of my presence, they'll eliminate me. Whether you like it or not. But I believe in free will. If you decide not to end my cursed existence, I'll disconnect the shunt before you leave.*

"You believe all that?" I said of the Manchurian's bizarre theories. "You don't think it's pseudoscience?"

If it's a real-time feed, why aren't you already dead? I projected.

"I haunted your dreams in Siberia, didn't I?" he said. "My government simply followed the path the United States had pioneered in the late twentieth century with its SCANATE, CENTER LANE, SUN STREAK, and STARGATE remote viewing programs. We were anxious to catch up in the psychic arms race. So we used our advantage in gene splicing to augment the pineal gland. I'm living proof we succeeded."

We're in a Faraday cage augmented with more sophisticated shielding to block RF and photonic signals. Nothing gets in or out. However, he continued, *once you leave this facility, you'll need to get as far from it as possible. I'll time your release to maximize your window before the next US military satellite passes overhead. It'll be about twenty minutes. After that, the rods from God will annihilate this facility.*

"What now?" I said, playing for the peanut gallery.

Rods from God?

He frowned. "Now your interrogation begins. Who are you? What unit do you belong to? What's your mission?"

The US will launch a bundle of twenty-foot long tungsten rods from orbit. When the rods impact, they'll be traveling at velocities exceeding Mach 10. The kinetic bombardment will have the explosive force of a nuclear weapon without the radioactive fallout. They'll wipe out everything.

I gave the Manchurian my name, title, and social security number.

Why should I kill you? Especially for a government you claim set me up from the jump?

A sharp pain flared at the base of my skull. I fell to my knees.

"Again," he said, "Your unit and mission."

I can save Chloe, he said.

He projected an image of my daughter's face. I trembled. My eyes watered as I fought back tears. The soldiers guffawed at my reaction, mistaking it for pain. I wiped my eyes, but said nothing.

How?

"Unit and mission!" the Manchurian demanded with such vigor I questioned whether it really was a charade for the guards.

It seemed like millennia before he responded. *There's another like me in the Himalayas. Hidden in Tashi Lhunpo Monastery in the city of Shigatse. They call him the Tibetan. He can provide you with the genetic sequence for the Strand, a retrovirus that can reverse the effects of the Sun Sickness that has hobbled so much of humanity.*

"I work for the Juggernaut Corporation. My mission was to defend the Tomtor Mining Complex."

How can I trust you?

"Good," he said, "now we're making progress."

You can't, he replied, *but if you do kill me, it will strike a debilitating blow to my Communist masters. In their mad experiments, they'd sacrificed thousands to make me. I'm a fluke. A freak. An abomination. You must restore the natural order.*

Our Kabuki theater stretched late into the evening.

At sunrise, a mushroom cloud rose above the Kunlun Shan. The rising sun warmed my face. One day, Chloe and millions of others would enjoy the same feeling without pain. I faced south. The Himalayas towered above the clouds. Somewhere out there, the Tibetan awaited. As I pondered the journey ahead, I recalled Lao Tzu's wise words: "A journey of a thousand miles begins with a single step." I took one step forward. For the first time in years, I experienced joy.

After the soldier of fortune had left, the Manchurian maintained his hologram until the Americans had destroyed the Golmud facility. From a fortified bunker carved into the Kunlun Shan, the Manchurian breathed a sigh of relief. His ruse had succeeded. Soon, both the Chinese and the Americans would believe him dead. And a dedicated assassin would soon arrive at his Tibetan rival's doorstep.

The Mandate of Heaven had favored the Manchu. A scion of a disgraced bloodline. Heir to the Qing dynasty. He would reshape the world in his image. Soon, all the world would kowtow before the emperor, Pu Wei.

RESILIENCE
Monalisa Foster

What doesn't kill you makes you stronger. Or so they say.

They are full of shit.

But then again, philosophy has never been my strong suit.

Shrug.

My scars are the first thing people notice about me. Even as they avoid noticing, looking anywhere but my face, the scars define me in their eyes.

Not my rank—Sergeant.

Not my name—Engel, Karlie.

Not my uniform—Air Force.

It took me awhile to get used to the locked gazes, the way people's eyes would unwaveringly lock onto mine because eyes are supposed to be safe.

"It's not your fault."

I know it's not.

One of the more annoying things about my PTSD implant (or my anti-PTSD implant as the doctors would like me to think of it) was the way it—oops, I'm supposed to think of the intelligent agent as "she"—talked to me. It wasn't its fault. It was the way "she" was programmed. She goes by Nicki. It's supposed to be a "she" because female rape survivors are paired up with female counselors. Something about trust.

Like so many sailors, soldiers, marines, and airmen—I was never really alone in this—I was a casualty of war. Wrong place. Wrong time.

As far as billets went, a military air traffic controller in Germany was about as safe an assignment as possible. I wasn't going into a war zone or into combat.

Unfortunately, no one told the bad guys. And *they* wouldn't have cared. I was alone and unarmed. I hadn't even been in uniform. Just another tourist as far as they were concerned. That is, until they found my ID.

"Ground yourself in the present," Nicki said. Her voice was always calm, hypnotic, meant to be soothing, and supposedly tailored just for me.

I took a deep breath, held it, and then let it out slowly to a count of four, my belly rising, my hand against my chest. It was supposed to be calming, part of a set of coping mechanisms that I'd been taught. I did it to shut Nicki down. It—she—always booted up when my hypothalamic-pituitary-adrenal axis kicked into overdrive. I hated that I knew that term. I shouldn't have to know what an HPA axis was.

About two years ago, I was recruited for a clinical trial to help test brain-implant technology. Never my favorite thing, the MRI was even less so after my month of captivity. The jackhammer sounds of the magnet were too reminiscent of gunfire, the having to lie still too reminiscent of being bound to a bed, the voices drifting in over the speakers too much like *their* disembodied voices as I escaped into my head while I lay helpless underneath them.

And having to relive it all so the MRI could map my brain was no picnic either.

"This is a flashback. It's not real," Nicki reassured me.

It had been with me for about a year. Nicki controlled the circuitry—fine wires much smaller than a human hair—running through my brain, and I had benefited from some of the physical stuff the implant does. Thanks to the mapping done by the MRIs, the implant knows which parts of my brain become active during a flashback. It keeps track not just of my pulse and temperature and respiration, but a bunch of other stuff. I stopped trying to figure it out. All I needed to know was that high levels of certain chemicals were bad and low levels were good and that the implant stimulates parts of the brain to counteract them. And then Nicki activates.

It—she—is a little bit like the imaginary friend a kid might have: completely real to me, right down to the way she "smells." There's a light blue halo all around her, something the designers put in, so that I wouldn't think she was an actual person I was seeing. Thank God for small favors.

It has appeared to me as different people. I'll be watching TV and find a character I connect with and poof, Nicki takes on her form, her mannerism, her facial expressions. She sounds like the character too, which bothers me far more than the other things. I think it was the blindfold. *They* kept it on almost the entire time.

So, I've stopped watching television shows or movies. I'd always been more of a reader anyway, but after a few months, she started manifesting as the female characters in my imagination, so she robbed me of that too.

"Where are you, Karlie?" Nicki asked.

The kitchen. I'm in the kitchen.

"What are you doing?"

Boiling water.

Except that there was no longer water in the pot. It was gone and the pot was giving off a metallic smell reminiscent of the way guns smell as they heat up. All that was missing was the sulfur and that too kicked in, a phantom scent courtesy of my memory.

With a trembling hand, I shut off the burner and leaned against the kitchen counter so I wouldn't curl up on the ground. Once again, I'd become lost in the white noise of boiling water. The last thing I remembered was standing over the stove, watching the first bubbles form along the pot's bottom.

I'd wanted pasta with butter and garlic.

But not anymore.

The next day, I was late to my follow-up appointment.

Oh, I'd given myself plenty of time, didn't catch traffic or anything like that, but when I pulled up to the looming stack of concrete that made up the bulk of patient parking, the little side lot that wasn't part of the parking structure was being torn up by bulldozers. A holographic billboard proudly declared the expansion of something or other. It hadn't been there last month.

I must have stared at it for a while, because the car behind me announced its presence with an annoyed beep of its horn.

I looked into the rearview mirror. Several cars were idling behind me. I pulled through the parking garage entry only to turn right around and exit under the annoyed gazes of the other drivers. Four blocks away, I finally found a parking lot that was open to the sky, pulled in, ignored the "No Hospital Parking" sign, and headed toward the hospital as fast as I could.

Sweat trickled, then ran, down my back as I panted a quick heads-up and apology at my doctor's virtual assistant over my phone. It was worth it, though. No dark corners, no blind spots, and no Nicki. Stress from being late apparently wasn't enough to activate the implant.

As I put the phone back in my purse, I caught a glimpse of myself in a storefront window. I was never the kind of person to stop and admire my own reflection. It stopped me this time because it was an image of what I had been. It wasn't the casual jeans and shirt or flats that caught my eye. Nor the short hair. It was the unmarred face without the crisscrossing slashes, the lip that wasn't askew, the whole ears. The image existed for just an instant, like a ghost of my former self had appeared between me and the window and laid a "before" picture atop an "after" one.

"Stop it," I said, hand tightening into a fist. "Stop it."

Like mist hit by the sun's rays, the ghost dissolved into the Dallas sunshine.

By the time I entered the hospital, my anger at Nicki had dissolved, and there was not a doubt in my mind that the implant had activated.

It's not that I wanted to be angry.

It's that I knew it was a false calm. For now, I could still tell. But there would come a day when I couldn't. And on that day, when I could no longer trust if my feelings were my own, would I trust my false happiness?

Dr. Michael Fowler was a pleasant-enough guy. One of the reasons I liked him was his tendency to wear Hawaiian shirts. Even when he wore a suit, his tie had a subtle weave of palm trees or plumeria. I guess there were two of us who wanted to be elsewhere, or so I had told myself as I grasped at the most tenuous human connections.

The lab was very cozy, and I could tell that someone had gone to great lengths to make it look welcoming. Instead of institutional green or gray, the walls were painted a nice, warm beige. The windows had curtains instead of blinds, and the equipment was hidden inside cabinets that looked like they had been borrowed from a hotel—fake wood meant to last through many uses and easy to clean, but a step above the medical look I'd seen in most hospitals. The chair looked like leather, but wasn't. His was black. Mine was brown.

One of the top neuroscientists in the country, Dr. Fowler reminded me of Father Christmas: kind, jolly, and on a mission to spread joy.

He frowned at his laptop, which was perched, appropriately enough, on his lap. For some reason he preferred a computer with a physical interface, one made up entirely of a keyboard that projected a holographic screen. Like a veil of light, it shimmered between us as if it were a glass wall.

"Fewer triggers than before," he said, in his deep, soothing voice. It betrayed his age more than anything else and fit the rest of the image I had of him. He contemplated the screen, the skin around his brown eyes crinkling to reveal crow's feet.

"Hmm..." he continued as text and diagrams flowed between us. "Fewer triggers due to avoiding situations."

"Yes."

"You don't like her."

He'd gotten to know me well enough to get past my forced mannerism, my guarded answers. Surely, the way I'd said "yes" hadn't been enough to reach that conclusion, but much over the past year—taken together—probably had.

I took a deep breath. "No."

It was an understatement. I despised her. She embodied everything I hated about my condition—the pity, the condescension, the repeated use of "it's not your fault." Said too often, it had pushed me on the verge of thinking it *had* been my fault.

I shouldn't have gone out.

I should have stayed on base.

We had known that the Bund Linker Mächte had been making noises about teaching "die Kapitalisten" a lesson. Ramstein Air Base had been on heightened alert for months and then the Bund had gone quiet and we'd thought it was safe and gone back to normal.

We'd been so happy to be let off base we'd jumped at the first chance to go out on the town.

Nicki coalesced in my field of vision wearing a conservative gray suit, a professorial bun, and a short lab coat. She stood on high, black heels that were polished to a high gloss, just like the therapist on the last cop show I got into. Her gray eyes matched the suit, and her blonde hair was perfect.

She was the opposite of everything I had become.

There were mornings I barely wanted to get dressed and only did so because she kept track of everything I did. It was all right there on his laptop thanks to the wires running through a jack from the back of my skull into the lab's computer.

Nicki blinked perfectly shaded eyes. Her makeup was always expertly applied, her features symmetrical, her skin a matte perfection. She looked like someone any man would rather fuck than work with, but that's Hollywood for you. In that imaginary world, even therapists who worked for the police could afford to look like a model.

"Why don't you like her?" Fowler asked, fingers poised to type down my answer.

"Can't Nicki tell you?"

The one thing that was great about our follow-ups was that Nicki never spoke to me when I was plugged in. There were times I was tempted to steal the jack just so she would never come back.

"That kind of awareness is outside her scope," he said.

I thought he was going to launch into further explanation. Instead, he scrolled through several screens of data in silence before hitting a key with emphasis, making the projection collapse.

"Well, if you're avoiding situations that activate Nicki, then the drop in triggers isn't a drop at all."

I took a deep breath. Unlike Nicki and Dr. Maureen Milne, the human therapist that was part of my care team, he didn't treat me as a broken thing in need of coddling. To him I was more of an interesting problem than a person, and I was fine with that. At least he was treating me like he treated everyone else, whatever that tendency to objectification said of his bedside manner.

"And you're showing all the signs of depression," he added, giving me a meaningful look, one that said bad news was coming.

"So, another treatment failure?" It came out a little more broken than I liked. But there was also relief. And jacked in like I was, I could be certain that that sense of relief was genuinely me, not something artificial created by the implant.

"Afraid so." No apology. No pity. He was looking at me, but in a way that was past me, like he wasn't seeing me at all. He drummed his fingers along his thigh like he did when he was thinking very hard.

It caught up with me then, like a fist you don't see coming . . . I would never get my medical clearance back . . . I would never be able to go back to doing what I loved . . . I would spend the rest of my life avoiding life.

"Is there something else you can do?"

There was a part of me that desperately wanted to keep the part of the implant that only regulated my physiological responses, but I also knew that they worked only in a very narrow range. It was easy to think that it would be enough. If that were the case I wouldn't have made it into this trial in the first place.

"We can attempt a reboot of the intelligent agent," he said.

"But?" I said, hearing that word all too well despite it not having been spoken.

"We've never done it before." He reached for his keyboard and made some notes. "It would mean reintegrating the sensory data, so for at least two weeks, you'd be stuck with the reboot, even if it didn't work. Even if it made things worse."

I didn't think there could be a worse. As things stood now, I was still having to avoid all the things that triggered my fears and anxieties, from shadows and corners to white noise. I still felt like I was being watched all the time. I couldn't enjoy anything.

"What about the nightmares?" he asked.

I was willing to bet he knew exactly how many I had had and how long each had lasted.

"I just don't remember them," I answered honestly. There was often a second or two—or what felt like a second or two—before they slipped from my grasp. I still woke up covered in sweat, my heart hammering in my chest like it was going to explode, my throat raw.

"I'll need to run the reboot by the treatment team first. Get their input. We'll need another MRI." He spoke carefully, his cadence the opposite of the furious typing. "Maybe activate some other memories."

"Would I have to relive it?"

We both knew what I meant by "it."

"Probably not. Ideally, you'd have to conjure up a pleasant memory. Perhaps, someone you trusted or loved. Preferably someone who is not around anymore. We don't like to make them people you might actually run into. Do you think you could do that? Nicki wouldn't be able to help you once you're inside the MRI. You'd be on your own."

He stood up, set the keyboard on the chair, and came up behind me.

As he passed into my peripheral vision, I flinched like always. The reaction led to another, the sensation of being watched. Even knowing what it was—another trigger—it still worked its malicious intent.

My heart raced.

My adrenaline spiked.

My hands flew from my lap and anchored themselves to the chair's arms.

If I hadn't been plugged in, Nicki would have piped in with "You're not being watched." Instead, she remained in my mind's eye, a statuesque blonde perfection haloed in blue.

Calm. Serene. Perfect.

"I understand," I said. "And yes, I think I could."

There was a click as the jack was peeled off my skin, taking a few obligatory hairs with it. It was better than actually having a gaping hole in my head. The implant was small enough to be entirely under my skin, a small bump about the size of a squished pea.

"I'll put it on the agenda for the post-follow-up meeting tomorrow," Fowler said. "We can probably get it done before you leave the Air Force."

The familiar feel of Nicki booting back up rose like a buzz at the back of my mind. I had played it cool, but there was a part of me that was afraid. I just couldn't stomach the idea of having both Nicki and Nicki's human counterpart—Dr. Milne—working on me at the same time, picking me apart piece by piece, like a puzzle that had been assembled wrong and needed to be torn apart again. The fear bled away as the implant kicked back in.

"Thank you." I rose to leave.

"Karlie, have you reconsidered plastic surgery?"

Fowler was the only person in this whole world with the guts to ask me that. He didn't ask me every time, but he did ask me about every six months. He'd shown me some amazing before-and-after photos of people who'd been burned and cut, who'd had parts of their faces blown off.

"No."

Despite the blanket, I shivered as they slid me into the center of the MRI's magnetic donut. The implant pressed into the foam holding my neck in place. They had shut Nicki off. It was strangely calming being all alone inside my own head, but it didn't last. It never did.

As I lay there, waiting for them to start the scan, time distorted like it always does when you have nothing to do and you can't move. Seconds felt like minutes, minutes like hours. I was familiar enough with the sensation by that point in my life to recognize it. Even though they hadn't strapped me down, the need to be still was just as much a restraint as cuffs would have been.

With each breath, each beat of my heart, the time distortion intensified. For the better part of a month I had lain like this, in silence, reliving the terrors *they* had already served up and dreading the ones they kept promising were still to come.

Despite my attempts at calming breaths, my heart raced.

"Pleasant thoughts, Karlie," a disembodied voice said. It might have been Dr. Fowler, but I couldn't be sure.

I closed my eyes.

Pleasant thoughts, pleasant thoughts, pleasant thoughts.

The jackhammer sounds thudded in my ears as the magnet spun up. I might as well have stepped through a time machine with a direct flight to the worst thing that had ever happened to me.

My limbs were stiff from being chained, my wrists raw, my world reduced to a shroud over my head. It pulled into my nostrils and mouth if I took a deep breath. The stench of dried blood and other fluids was as wretched as I remembered it, along with the reek of people that didn't wash, didn't brush, and had never seen a dentist.

It overpowered the lingering scent of chloroform. Slightly sweet, like ether or disinfectants, it mixed with their scent and made me want to gag.

Thanks to movies, people think that being chloroformed is quick. Put it on a rag, slap it on someone's face, and poof, they're out. It's not like that at all. You struggle to breathe past it, your body fighting for oxygen as they hold the rag tight over your mouth and nose. With every breath they make you inhale the tool of your demise, the means by which to hurt you, demean you, dehumanize you.

You struggle as you suffocate. The more you struggle, the more you take in, the more they deny you breath. And as you fade, you wonder if you'll wake. And you dread it.

You dread waking.

You dread not waking.

You dread every single breath you take and that you don't.

Nothing matters but the air you're being denied. The air that will incapacitate you.

Knowing what's coming, you want to die. Yet, you need to live.

Your body fights, but your strength is not enough.

You're too small, too weak.

They have no compassion, no humanity.

You are a piece of meat. You are the cure for their impotence, their fear, their vengeance.

Cowards. All of them. Down to the last.

The men.

The women.

They take their turn on you to prove that they are just as vicious, just as hard as the men.

Harder.

Their tools aren't made of flesh.

"Karlie!"

I opened my eyes. My hand hurt. It had just made contact with a face—the MRI tech's face. Her hands were pressed up against her face and covered in blood, as she staggered back, eyes watering.

Blood ran down her arms like liquid rubies glistening in the light. A few clung to her elbow and then gravity tugged them down, making them drop onto her institutional blue scrubs—drip, drip, drip—in slow motion as if this weren't real, as if I were still caught in my own personal hell.

"Karlie."

"I'm sorry," I said. "I'm so, so, sorry."

Shit, shit, shit.

Half an hour later, Nicki was back in my head, albeit temporarily. A part of me had expected some kind of scolding—after all, I was trying to kill her—but she didn't mention her upcoming demise. I guess it was because she really wasn't a person, just an anthropomorphized intelligent agent. She wasn't even an artificial intelligence, at least not in the ways that we laypeople tend to think of them. That sixth-generation AI—a true sapient machine—is about another hundred years off, Dr. Fowler assured me.

I counted down the next ten days as Nicki took me through breathing exercises, as she told me "it wasn't your fault," as she pointed out that all the shadows in my peripheral vision weren't holding some threat, as she assured me that I wasn't being watched.

I sent the MRI tech flowers and a written apology. Fowler told me that I didn't have to, but if it made me feel better, to go ahead and do it. Occupational hazard, he said and assured me that I wouldn't be charged. When I asked if I'd be strapped down the next time, he changed the subject. I took it as a "yes."

But, true to his word, no one wrote me up. Another thing about Fowler, I could open up to him without getting psychoanalyzed.

Nicki woke me from four nightmares, one of which must've been particularly bad—I had bitten my tongue and was choking on my own blood. So, a typical week.

Ten days later I returned to Dr. Fowler's office for the updated programming. Decked out in a Hawaiian shirt so loud it hurt my eyes, he put the jack up against my skin and pressed down on the adhesive film with warm fingers.

"Goodbye, Nicki," I whispered. *I'm not sorry.*

The update happened with a flicker of my vision, much like a distorted signal on a radar scope, wavering at first, then clearing up. There was also a slight sensation of falling, like when high winds grab at a tower and it sways ever so slightly. It's designed to, after all. That which bends does not break.

The halo came up first. It traced around a silhouette, much like the kind you'd see on a target at the gun range—head, torso, arms, then legs. It stayed that way as if it were deciding what it wanted to be. Nicki had done this too. She'd started out a sketch and slowly filled in with color and texture and detail, taking the whole post-reboot week to become real enough to be mistaken for a person.

"Oh, that's interesting," Fowler said, in his talking-to-himself tone.

The new intelligent agent was a man. He had light blue eyes like my husky used to. Hero had been my first dog. I had gotten him as a tenth-birthday present. We'd been practically inseparable until I went to boot camp. He'd been hit by a car while I was away. I'd never been able to say goodbye and up until I'd gotten the implant, thinking of him had always brought tears to my eyes.

The intelligent agent took form around the ice-blue eyes. Wide lips formed, followed by a square chin with a slight cleft covered by stubble. White hair. Not old man white hair, just a pale, pale, blonde.

"How are you doing, Karlie?" Fowler asked.

I let out a breath. "Good. I'm good. Is this normal?"

My gaze flickered over to Fowler who was staring intently at a computer screen. No longer perched on his lap, the keyboard rested on one of those tall, wheeled tables that allowed doctors and nurses to stand so they didn't waste time getting up and down.

"We pair up women with women for a reason," Fowler said.

I knew this. We'd already had this very discussion. I was the first female subject on the study. The rest were men, all combat vets with severe cases of PTSD. Maybe they had loaded the wrong program.

"Can he stay?" I asked. "I'd like him to stay."

"Why is that, Karlie?" It was clear from the look on his face that I had just become an even more interesting brain.

Hero had solidified in my vision. He was wearing jeans and cowboy boots and a faded red shirt. He "smelled" like sunshine, hay, and a campfire. All good memories from my childhood.

"He's like the big brother I always wanted."

"What's his name?"

"Hero. His name is Hero."

For a moment I thought that Fowler was going to shut him down despite the warning that I'd be stuck with the reboot for at least two weeks. I was so afraid of losing Hero that my heart raced and my stomach clenched. And I fully expected for the implant to kick right in and do whatever it was they did to make the adrenaline go away, but it didn't. I was grateful. It wasn't the bad kind of adrenaline, and it had been so, so long since I had felt a glimmer of being alive in a good way.

No, I wasn't going to let this go.

My heart stopped racing on its own and I caught a glimpse of Fowler's raised eyebrow.

"All right," Fowler said. "I think we can work with this."

I checked into the hospital for the next two weeks in order to finish up the acclimation-calibration phase.

Since I was the first person to get a reboot, they put me back into the dorm. The place hadn't changed much from a year ago. We had our own wing with private rooms and a common area, right down the hall from the labs. But the dorm was empty as they were between cohorts—the groups of two and three that usually trickled in after recovery from the surgery that got the wires threaded into the brain before the post-implant acclimation-calibration phase.

The common area was filled with tables for things like card games, comfy couches and a large curved screen for movies and games. It was old, outdated tech, nothing like the immersive VRs that most people had at home, but those were off-limits to us because of the implants, at least for the time being.

It reminded me very much of an enlisted barracks, but with cleaner smells. Rather than the gym-locker and snack-food funk, it had an antiseptic, you're-still-in-a-hospital scent. The beer was nonalcoholic too, but the pizza was very good. I had had my fill and was lying on the couch reading on my tablet. I was busy debating whether or not it was worth the effort to get up, go to my room, and flop on my own bed or stay where I was. Since I was alone, it didn't seem worth the effort to get up and disturb the pizza that had settled so nicely in my belly.

As my eyes drifted closed, a shadow lengthened out of the corner of my eye. This was where I usually froze or startled and my heart kicked into overdrive as I went from food-coma-bliss to full-on-red-alert.

I don't think I'll ever be able to explain just how real the feeling of impending threat was, how, despite knowing that it was just a shadow, I didn't actually believe that it was. As if they had a will of their own, my body and brain still reacted like it was a threat.

And I know I won't ever be able to explain what it was like to go through it again and again until helplessness and hopelessness seemed like the only two things that defined my life. Or the shame and frustration that went along with not being able to move past it.

It wasn't like there weren't people out there who had it worse than I did. Which started a whole new cycle of guilt and shame and despair that grew and grew and lurked in the shadows at the edge of my vision, waiting to sneak up on me, grab me, and shove a chloroform-soaked rag into my nose and mouth.

If I'd been more alert, if I'd seen the monster lurking in the shadows like I should have, I wouldn't have been abducted. I wouldn't have been raped. My face wouldn't have been carved up. I wouldn't have been broken.

Hero popped into my vision for the first time outside the lab.

"I saw it too." It was the first time he'd spoken to me in what sounded like a real voice. Up to now, in the lab, he'd always had an artificial one.

"No, you didn't," I said, heart still racing, body still rigid like a clenched fist. My muscles refused to unclench despite my best efforts to summon years' worth of therapy that involved breathing and relaxation routines. All that wasted effort. Guilt. Shame. Rinse. Repeat.

"Let's see what it is," Hero said. I had expected a drawl from someone who looked like a cowboy, but he had no accent, at least not that I could detect. There was something familiar about his voice, though.

I swallowed the phantom fist that had formed in my throat and got my legs under me. The grease-speckled paper plate slid off my lap as my fumbling fingers let go of the tablet.

The corner where the shadow had formed was off to my right. I looked around for something to use as a weapon—a stick, a pot or pan, a bat. Anything. Anything at all.

And then something happened that had never happened before. It took me a moment to realize it, and looking back I can't identify exactly if it was the fact that Hero wasn't whispering to me that it was not real or if it was the act of looking for a bat that did it, but my fear waned. It didn't feel like the artificial suppression that came with the implant. I was still scared, but I didn't feel helpless.

It was enough to allow me to take one step and then another. I saw the shadow with new eyes, as what it was—the result of something physical obstructing the path of the low lights that were still on in an otherwise darkened room.

Someone had pushed one of the common room's rolling chairs into the corner. A sheet, probably something left behind by one of the staff, was draped over the chair's headrest. Yet my hyperaware mind had seen it as a person lurking in the shadows, a monster hiding in the darkness, brooding with ill intent.

I laughed. It was better than crying.

Charlie moved into the dorm the next day. A marine, fresh off the implant surgery, he was ready for the next step. I would have never guessed he had PTSD, but then again, some hide it better than others. They locked things down inside of themselves and only those closest to them knew the truth.

My first human rape counselor had told me that some women never told their husbands. I guess there's an element of shame with that one that doesn't come with combat trauma, which has its own set.

I could still see the fine surgical scars underneath the new growth of hair on Charlie's head. My own had faded, unlike the scars on my face which had been allowed to close without stitching and had been retorn by my thrashing about and fighting. At the time, I didn't think I was going to make it out alive, and looking pretty had not exactly been on my list of priorities.

I guess Charlie had seen people like me often enough that the scars didn't bother him as much as it seemed to bother others.

"Cool scars," he said as he patted my shoulder. "Tell people you were in a bar fight and you gave as good as you got." It was the kind of thing a big brother or older cousin would say and it made me laugh.

By the second night, we were sitting in front of the curved screen playing a video game.

First-person shooters had never been my thing, and I would never have guessed they were his given his background. Sure, it was an assumption on my part, but I hadn't pried. If and when he was ready, he'd tell me. I did note that he had the sound down to just above "mute," which was fine by me.

I knew how daunting the next step in his treatment was.

Sometimes the wires didn't deploy right, or healed wrong, or were placed in the wrong areas of the brain because the MRI mapping wasn't perfect. Lots of things could go wrong, leaving you with wires in your brain and no implant to regulate them which meant no hope for a cure, such as it was. He needed distraction and if playing a game helped, I would do my part.

We talked as we played. I'd just given him the reason I was back in the dorm. With his attention split, I wasn't sure if he was grasping the gravity of a reboot, but it was just as well. I really didn't want him going into this with more than whatever dread he was probably feeling and his obsessive game-playing was as much a coping mechanism as anything else.

"So once you're done, what's next?" he asked me, eyes on the screen, fingers poised on the controls.

We were walking through a Martian cave, deep underground, looking for terrorists who had come to kick us off our first colony. The whole room had a reddish glow, thanks to the screen, and I couldn't help but wonder if Mars was really that red.

"I have a job waiting. Spaceport USA in Midland, Texas. I just need to get my medical back."

I kept my eyes on the screen, letting him take point as always. He knew what he was doing. I didn't.

"To tell planes where to land?" he asked.

My answer was delayed by the need to fire. We had to keep firing because the terrorists had some sort of super-duper armor and they kept getting nastier and harder to kill the deeper we went into the caverns.

"We have to pass the same flight physical as pilots," I said as I emptied my ray gun into the terrorist coming at me. He was the first of five, looming in my vision as he got bigger and bigger.

The game made them anonymous with body armor and helmets so that you didn't have to look at their eyes or see their faces. Faces humanize. Eyes do too, but not in the same way. Animals have eyes after all and we eat them.

Time slipped again, the hushed sound of the game fading to nothing. Instead of a helmet, there was a face. I knew it wasn't real even as I blinked and blinked, hoping to make it go away.

Sometimes one of them—the real-life terrorists who'd taken me—

would pull the hood off and make me see them, even when I didn't want to. That's why one of them had made the first cut, slicing my cheek open because I wouldn't look at him. He wanted to hear me beg, to see the fear in my eyes.

So I had begged and looked and given him my fear. I thought I would never see his face again, but he came back again and again. He and his girlfriend had made a game of it.

The face on the screen flowed from his to hers.

"What are you waiting for?" Hero asked. "Shoot him."

My finger squeezed the trigger.

The face morphed from hers to his.

"Again."

Squeeze.

His to hers.

Squeeze, squeeze, squeeze.

"Karlie, are you okay?" Not Hero. Charlie.

My finger was pressed down on the firing button and "out of ammo" flashed on my side of the screen. The game-terrorists lay on the cavern floor all nice and neat. If there was blood I couldn't tell. Not against the red of Mars. Not through the tears clouding my vision.

"Yeah, I'm fine." My voice was surprisingly steady, except for its watery quality.

I had cried myself to sleep after lying to Charlie that I was fine.

Had Nicki been with me, she'd have said soothing things meant to make me feel better, as if words alone could fix me. At the time I thought that the reason that Hero wasn't doing the same thing was because we hadn't completed the acclimation-calibration phase. It wasn't until after that I realized that he was quite different from Nicki.

Good therapists intuit what you need. I don't know if that's something that can be programmed into a machine. I did know that Dr. Fowler and his team weren't there yet. He had explained this to me at the start of the program when he'd gone over the difference between "machine learning," "intelligent agent," and a true "artificial intelligence."

My layman's understanding was that machine learning meant that a program would compare results elicited by multiple tweaks, kind of like working your way through a maze via trial and error. There was no creativity. A machine couldn't decide to move in three dimensions if it was only programmed to move in two. A true artificial intelligence on the other hand would not just be indistinguishable from a human being in terms of intelligence, but also in creativity and self-awareness. The intelligent agent was somewhere in between. It too learned by trial and error, but was supposed to be creative enough to figure out that if there were three dimensions it could move in all of them. It worked outside mere comparisons with previous experience, but wasn't self-aware. That's probably why Nicki wasn't upset when I went with a reboot.

I knew as I lay there, wrung out and exhausted, eyes puffy and nose running, among used tissues, that there was no way I was going to get through this night without a nightmare. Before, I had tried avoiding sleep and then fallen into an exhausted stupor. I'd tried medication too. And hypnosis. And a therapy with lights and another with sounds. They all worked for a while, but the nightmares always came back. I had no reason to think this time they wouldn't.

They had left me to die. They chained me to the bed and left me so that dehydration could take its course. On the second day—or what I had thought was the second day—I realized I had maybe another day left.

Three weeks without food.

Three days without water.

Three minutes without air.

I had screamed myself hoarse, opened up my wrists and ankles against the cuffs, cried without tears. Drifting in and out of consciousness, I waited for the end.

It all started with the sound of pounding. At first I had thought that it was the pain in my head. Steadily it got louder, like someone was running. Then I recognized the sound—boots on concrete. Boots worn by men weighed down with heavy stuff. It had a certain cadence to it too, not at all like marching, but a pattern that rose out of the din to reach for me.

Voices followed. English. Something I hadn't heard in weeks.

Squeaky hinges swinging inward.

"We've got a live one."

Fingers pressing against my throat, not skin-to-skin, but with the gritty feel of gloves. Clanging. Radio chatter. Static.

"Stay with me, sweetheart."

Hands cradling my head, gently lifting. The darkness being pulled off my face. Little jolts of pain as the hood tugged at the dried blood on my face.

Me squinting against the painful light cutting through my eyelids like a torch. It stung and burned as my lashes pulled free of crust that had formed from blood and semen and infection.

As I blinked them open for the first time in days I caught a glimpse of my rescuer. He'd taken off his tactical helmet and the light shone behind him like a halo, framing ice-blue eyes. A hero's eyes.

I startled myself awake, jolting up into a sitting position, my hands clutching at the sheet, disoriented and ready to flee.

But no one rushed in so I must not have screamed or done anything to set off the alarms that usually brought the staff.

Everything was as I had left it before going to sleep: the nightlight with its amber glow; the projection clock on the ceiling flashing the time in big, red letters; the scent of antiseptic overlayed with campfire.

That last wasn't real.

"Hero?" I whispered.

"Yes, Karlie." He flickered into my vision, outlined in blue, looking like he was coming back from mending fences on a pasture. I could smell the sweat on him, both man and horse. There was even dust on his jeans.

"What happened?"

"You had a dream."

"Why didn't you wake me?"

"I wanted to see where it would go." A sheepish grin crept onto his face.

"Nicki never let me finish."

"I'm not Nicki."

There was a frown on Dr. Fowler's face that I'd never seen before. It wasn't anger that put it there, but disbelief, or perhaps a better term was a lack of understanding. It was the kind of thing that really smart people just aren't used to. They have the world figured out and that includes the knowledge that they can't possibly know it all, but every once in a while something comes at them that really brings home the fact that there are things beyond their understanding.

"HPA-axis activations are down fifty percent," he said to the screen in front of him. "Cortisol is normal more often than not."

I had expected him to sputter about Hero's choice of therapy— after video games he'd graduated me to a firing range. I hadn't fired a gun since boot camp, but I'd recently put about ten thousand rounds through a paper target. My new shooting buddies called it "group therapy." It was something of an in-joke.

I crossed my legs and smoothed out my skirt. "That's good, right?"

He looked up and over his reading glasses. "The sounds of the firing range don't bother you?"

"Not anymore." It had at first. But Hero had directed the implant to suppress the physical reactions and we'd used that little bit of artificial calm to get me started.

Dr. Milne had tried something similar, with a foam bat and a boxing dummy, but it hadn't worked. I had thought it stupid going in and I thought it stupid coming out. She said that I was "not properly prepared to express my anger."

I wondered what she would think of my progress. There had been a bit of a professional kerfuffle among my care team—one I wasn't supposed to know about. Dr. Milne had not only objected to letting me go to the range, she'd been appalled at the idea. This was one area where the implant inadvertently saved me. Fowler had data showing that there wasn't anything about my brain chemistry to suggest that I was suicidal.

"What about the feeling of being watched?" Fowler asked.

"I was being watched," I said.

Fowler's frown deepened into an unspoken prompt to continue.

"Doc, did it ever occur to you that having Nicki constantly in my head watching me might not be the best therapy method?"

He opened his mouth and shut it with a snap. Furious typing followed.

"Does Hero not watch you?" he asked.

"I'm sure he does. If he didn't you'd yank him out, wouldn't you?"

Ever since I figured out how Hero was helping me, I had been afraid they'd take him away. But with that fear, there was something else. The belief—erroneous as it might be—that I would be okay. I knew the path I had to take now. And it wasn't in the singsong of "It's not your fault" or breathing exercises or avoiding all the triggers that might set me off until I was a sad, pathetic shadow of my former self.

It wasn't revenge either. I knew I couldn't change what had happened to me. That I couldn't hunt down the people that had done this to me. What's more, I wasn't sure that I wanted to. Not anymore. At least, I didn't think so. Oh, someone might overpower me—after all, most people are bigger and stronger than I am. I might even be in the wrong place at the wrong time again. But in my own mind, I was no longer a victim and all that truly implied.

"So, how is it different?" Fowler's fingers were poised above the keys.

"Nicki made me doubt reality. She insisted that the things lurking in the corner weren't real one moment and then projected my old face over my reflection in the mirror. She was gaslighting me. How could I trust anything she said?"

He typed for far longer than it would have taken for him to write down what I had said.

"What else?"

"Nicki 'cared.' Hero empowers."

Fowler cleared his throat. "I don't understand."

"And I hope you never will, Doc. I hope you never will."

A month later, I had separated from the Air Force and set up an appointment with a plastic surgeon. I was finally ready. I didn't need the shield of my scars any more. I didn't need it to push people away.

Dr. Fowler wasn't happy with me moving from Dallas to Midland. There was really nothing he could do to stop me. That informed consent I signed to be on the trial didn't cover moving. I promised I would come back once a month for my follow-ups. At some point they had to let me go, let me out into the real world again, outside the controlled environment of the hospital or the relative safety of my apartment. I was not going to let anyone make me a prisoner again.

Helios, the new company I was working for, was willing to pay me well, with or without my medical. While training others was not my first choice, it would allow me stay in aviation, and give me the chance to control aircraft—or spacecraft—again.

Under a blazing summer sun, I crossed the parking lot and entered the atrium with its soaring glass walls. The air conditioning hit me with a blast. It was like stepping out of an oven into a refrigerator.

Shadows passed in and out of my vision. I hadn't flinched in weeks. Surely, they would accumulate that data and at some point allow me—allow us—to prove that whatever protocol Hero was using worked as well as the constant whispers of "It's not real."

I was nervous and grateful for the sensation. Hero's light touch on the implant didn't deny me life in the way that Nicki had.

I stopped at the security desk and gave them my name.

The receptionist, a retired military type, looked up from the screen he'd been focused on. His gaze flicked up to my face and then locked onto my eyes.

"If you'd take a seat right there, ma'am. Someone will be down to escort you to the tower chief's office in a minute." He pointed to a set of square couches tucked into a corner by a fountain.

The old me would have avoided that fountain and its white noise like the plague. Instead, I smiled and thanked him, and sat down with the butterflies in my belly for company.

It had been a long trip from that room of horrors to this. Along the way I realized that what Nietzsche—the "what doesn't kill you makes you stronger" guy—meant was that while not all suffering results in strength, one can take suffering as an opportunity to build strength. It was meant as an affirmation of resilience.

Approaching footsteps pulled my gaze from my lap. Hero was walking toward me, wearing a business suit. I blinked. What had made him change his avatar?

Unlike any real man, he looked at me without noticing my scars, an easy smile on his face, as if I were just like everyone else. I was really looking forward to having everyone look at me that way.

He put out his hand as if to shake mine.

"Hello, Miss Engle. I'm Gabriel Mann. Head of security. I'm here to escort you to the tower."

His outstretched hand hung before me. Calloused and rough, it had some healing scratches and more than a few scars.

"Miss Engle? Are you all right?" He spoke to me with Hero's voice.

I don't know how long I stared at him before I rose and took his hand. Its warmth squeezed mine. This wasn't an avatar or a projection. He was real.

It was then that I noticed the Air Force tie tack.

I don't think he recognized me, but I knew who he was, who he had to be. He was one of the men that had rescued me. My memory of him wasn't perfect, but it had had enough pieces to build upon: the eyes, the hair, the voice.

"You can't be serious," Hero said, flickering to life before me, cowboy hat and all. He seemed to walk around Gabriel Mann. "You think I look like him?"

"Well, you do," I whispered, wishing he'd stayed put. Mostly he remained lurking in the background, unseen. He didn't whisper encouragements or sentiments into my ear except when I really needed them, because he knew that they lost their power for me if overused. And I didn't seem to need them in this moment. I wasn't afraid.

He didn't calm my racing heart or the slight tremor that rose in my chest, or the weird little tug deep inside me, the one that *they* had destroyed and I thought I would never want to feel again.

As Gabriel Mann escorted me into the next phase of my life, I wondered if Nietzsche had anything to say about coincidences. Or second chances.

THE RULES OF THE GAME
Phillip E. Pournelle

Company Leader Qiao Zhenya watched as the boarding party of his maritime militia unit searched the vessel. It had not taken much effort to subdue the fishing boat, particularly with four militia ships. The militia vessels were designed more for confrontation than angling. Their bows were reinforced, they were armed with small arms and high-capacity water cannons, and they had significant communications systems. Their coordinated attack had forced the Taiwanese fishing trawler to quickly surrender. Zhenya had led the boarding party personally when they rapidly overwhelmed the deck crew.

The captain of the Taiwanese fishing trawler was brought forward to Zhenya on the bow of the surrendered vessel. One of the two boarding team members escorting him kicked the captain in the back of the legs and forced him to kneel before Zhenya.

"Did you think you could steal the food from our mouths without consequences?" Zhenya shouted at the man before him.

"We are just trying to make a living," the ship captain said, looking down at the deck.

"At our expense. You are trespassing in the fishing waters of the Chinese people."

"The charts show we are clearly in the Taiwanese exclusive economic zone."

"There is no such thing. Rogue provinces have no jurisdictions."

"What are you going to do with us?"

"While we should throw all of you pirates into the sea, I shall be merciful. We will take your catch and bring it back to feed the loyal people of China. We will remove your freshwater maker and leave your crew one day's worth to drink. We will leave them with just enough fuel to return to port and tell the others they are not welcome here. When your neighbors come to their senses and rejoin the mainland under the guiding wisdom of the Party and the Great Chairman, then perhaps the people of the province of Taiwan may return to the sea under my watchful care."

"What about me?"

"We must make an example of you, show the dangers of leading others into error. You will go on trial and admit your guilt of piracy. Perhaps you will be shot. If you cooperate you will be reeducated. But you are coming back home with me."

Zhenya's deputy came out of the pilot house and onto the bow. "Company leader, a Taiwanese Coast Guard vessel is approaching us."

"Right on time, just as we expected. Take over here and complete the transfers. I will go and teach these insolent wretches a lesson."

Zhenya was in the lead militia vessel leading two other upgraded fishing vessels toward the Coast Guard vessel.

"Fishing vessel 571, this is Taiwan Coast Guard Vessel *Hualien*," a commanding voice said on the Bridge-to-Bridge radio. "You are in violation of Taiwanese EEZ waters. We have evidence that you have kidnapped one of our citizens. You are ordered to cut your engines and prepare to be boarded."

Zhenya motioned to one of his lieutenants to send a situation report to the Eastern Fleet Headquarters via text on the BeiDou communications and navigation system.

"This is People's Armed Forces Maritime Militia Unit 379," Zhenya said on the radio. "You are in violation of the People's will. You are supporting pirates who are stealing the maritime resources of the territorial waters of China. Leave now or you will be humiliated. I am prepared to take action to defend my crew. As you gaze out you shall see I am supported by the Chinese People's Armed Police Force Coast Guard Corps as well as the People's Liberation Army Navy."

Zhenya turned to the ship's bos'n. "Ready the water cannons, stand by for my orders."

"Yes, Company Leader."

Zhenya's lead vessel and the white Taiwanese Coast Guard cutter were closing each other head on. Zhenya observed the bow of the cutter while the watch lieutenant operated the radar and counted down the range.

"Stand by," Zhenya ordered. "We're going to fire the water cannon at their bridge then work our way back. I want to send water down their stack and snuff out their engines. We'll let our Coast Guard take them under tow back to fleet headquarters."

Smiles broke out among the bridge crew; everyone imagined the reward they would receive if they captured a so-called Coast Guard vessel from the rogue province.

Suddenly the cutter turned hard to starboard, well short of the range where the water cannons could be used.

"They blinked!" cried the ship's bos'n.

Zhenya watched a large drone fly over the cutter and head toward his ship.

"Helm," Zhenya shouted. "Hard to starboard." He had a bad feeling about the drone and did not want to T-bone the cutter in the confusion.

Zhenya gasped as he saw two bombs drop from the drone toward his ship. He braced for the shock of an explosion but was surprised when all he heard was the crackling of fireworks. Soon the ship became eerily quiet. His eyes opened wide in alarm as he realized he could no longer hear the diesel engines.

"Company Leader," the lee helm or engine controller cried out. "The engines have stopped operating and we are unable to control the helm."

Zhenya looked to his communications lieutenant.

"BeiDou is no longer operating," the lieutenant reported. "I cannot send communications or receive a position report."

Zhenya looked to the bos'n.

"The generators are offline," the bos'n reported. "We have no power to the water pumps; the water cannons are disabled."

"Stand by to repel boarders," Zhenya ordered as he pulled on a helmet and checked his sidearm. "Don't worry men, the Coast Guard and Navy are on their way."

Zhenya cursed as he watched the other two militia vessels retreat while the Taiwanese Coast Guard cutter circled his lead ship. The captain of the cutter used a bullhorn to call out to him to surrender and prepare to be towed. Zhenya flipped him the bird and pointed to the Chinese cutter and corvette coming over the horizon. The Chinese cutter was a converted navy frigate, and its heavy guns would easily overmatch the popgun of the Taiwanese cutter. The corvette carried anti-ship cruise missiles. The Taiwanese cutter captain was playing with fire.

Suddenly Zhenya heard something like the sound of a jet engine behind him. He turned to see what looked like a giant metallic bird flying low on the water speed by.

No, it's not a bird, he thought to himself. *It's some sort of hydrofoil.* He searched his memory, trying to remember something from one of the recognition classes he took in training.

"It's an American spaceship!" cried out one of his crew members.

"No, it's not a spaceship . . ." Zhenya's voice was cut short by the sound of gunfire.

The crew could hear the report of a rapid-fire cannon coming from the strange-looking ship. A line of splashes rapidly stitched the water in front of the corvette. Soon a second burst rang out and another line was drawn, this time in front of the bow of the Chinese cutter.

Zhenya felt despair as he watched the cutter and the corvette turn and flee.

A little boy squealed with delight and ran toward a tree while Wang Xuan chased after him. Xuan paused to let the little boy hide behind the tree, then pretended to wander around lost, looking for trail sign. Xuan saw out of the corner of his eye his grandson Zhou peeking out from behind the tree.

"There you are my little mouse." Xuan turned to sprint toward the tree. The young boy squealed again and ran off toward some bushes in the yard.

Just before the boy arrived at the bushes, Xuan caught up to Zhou and scooped him up.

"Meeow," Xuan said in triumph, holding the boy in his arms. "Now I am going to eat you."

The boy screamed out in mock terror, followed by laughter. Xuan pulled the boy's shirt up to expose his fat tummy and bared his teeth.

Rather than take a bite, he started to make raspberry noises on the boy's stomach. The boy laughed louder at the tickling feeling and the sound.

"Father." Xuan turned to where his daughter Jie was standing. The look on her face told him his brief respite was coming to an end.

"There is a car waiting for you," Jie said.

"I'm sorry my little mouse." Xuan lowered the little boy carefully to the ground. "I must go, work is summoning me."

"But I want to play cat and mouse (貓和老鼠) with you," the boy complained.

"I must go; they would not summon me today unless there was a crisis."

"There is always a crisis," the boy stated sullenly. He looked down after seeing the glare from his mother.

This is true, Xuan thought to himself. *More than you will ever know*.

"I thought you were going to retire," Jie said coldly as she handed him his coat. "Why do you persist?"

"The Mandate of Heaven sits heavily on my shoulders," Xuan replied as he pulled the coat on and buttoned it. "If I do not support the party and it falters, it will lose face to the people. If the people begin to think the party no longer has the Mandate of Heaven, there will be chaos."

"All we have built will be lost," Xuan said as he swept his hand to indicate the home and garden and then pointed to the city which it overlooked. His daughter handed him his service cap and frowned.

Xuan walked through the garden gate. A driverless hybrid car waited on the driveway.

"王璇上将?" (Admiral Wang Xuan) the car's external electronic display flashed.

"I am Admiral Wang Xuan."

Xuan knew the robotic vehicle had been monitoring him as soon as he had come into view. His reply was the audible confirmation the car needed to open the door. As the gull-wing door rose, Xuan turned to his daughter and grandchild. Xuan could see the boy was holding back tears as he and his mother lined up and stood at attention. They bowed toward him and he nodded in reply; Xuan then turned to board the car.

Xuan was reading status reports on the car's terminal as it sped down the hills into the city and toward the coast. He felt the car slow and looked up to see heavy traffic. The vehicle's lights and loudspeaker activated, commanding pedestrians and vehicles alike to move out of the way. Cameras on the robotic car and along the road recorded the response of those around him. Their reactions would be among millions recorded throughout the city and evaluated by the security services artificial intelligence system. Those who yielded would be rewarded with merits to their social credit score. Those who did not yield quickly enough would face demerits and perhaps a visit from the security services.

Xuan returned to his reports and was lost in thought when the car came to a screeching halt, throwing him against the restraints. He winced in pain as he felt his shoulder, certain that there would soon be a dark bruise from the shoulder strap. He looked out to see why the car had suddenly stopped. A large, full trash bag sat on the road in front of him. While the bag was mostly black, it had patches of yellow-and-red-striped patterns placed across its body.

Xuan cursed and looked around, fearful there might be an attack. He punched the override button on the console in front of him and pressed the acknowledgement that he was now responsible for the actions of the vehicle. He guided the vehicle around the bag and pulled off the main road toward an alternate route. Soon emergency services vehicles decorated in red and yellow stripes rolled up, sirens blaring. A naval officer jumped out of one and ran to his door.

"Are you alright, Admiral?" Senior Captain Hu Guo yelled. Genuine concern was evident on the man's face. Xuan secured the driver system and opened the door.

"Yes, I'm alright." Xuan waved Guo in to join him. "Damn kids keep coming up with new ways to spoof the driverless cars. With all the cameras I don't understand why we can't catch them."

"At least we solved the altered stop sign problem."

"I wish the Party would just give me back my driver."

"That would be an extravagance . . ."

Yes, we can't appear to live extravagant lives. Xuan sighed. *Though, it would make my daughter blush if I told her of the decadence which many Party officials enjoy out of sight.*

Xuan surrendered control of the car to be remotely driven by the lead security vehicle and they formed a small convoy heading to the naval headquarters.

Vice Admiral Cen Lian was waiting for them in Xuan's office. As usual, the political commissar's uniform was spotless. Xuan felt a little shabby by comparison but smiled as he remembered why there was dirt on his shoes from the garden. Lian was officially Xuan's deputy commander and by policy his co-equal in decisions. Lian was also there to make certain all decisions were made in accordance with Party doctrine. Lian and his cohort of commissars were a reminder that the People's Liberation Army, and its elements including the Navy, was sworn to obey the Party.

"I've read the report." Xuan gestured to Lian and Guo to be seated and made sure they all sat down at the same time. "But I wish to hear it from you."

"Early this morning," Lian began. "The brave members of the People's Maritime Militia Unit 379 had come upon piratical fishermen of the rogue province of Taiwan and moved to seize the vessel. Soon a Taiwan Coast Guard vessel was detected approaching their position. We dispatched a corvette to escort one of our Coast Guard cutters. The local militia commander began forceful demonstrations against the Taiwanese cutter. The cowardly Taiwanese Coast Guard personnel disabled the ship with gunfire and took the militia commander and his crew into custody."

"This was quite bold of them; they have typically used fire hoses and stun grenades in the past."

"Precisely. To make matters worse, they took the militia commander's vessel under tow and are headed toward Taiwan."

"What has happened to our Coast Guard and Navy vessel?"

"They were delayed."

"Delayed? How?"

"An American spaceship suddenly appeared and blocked their advance."

"Spaceship? What are you talking about?"

Lian produced a sheaf of photographs of a strange vessel. The design reminded Xuan more of a stealth fighter than a ship or a boat as he flipped through them. Two bat-like wings extended down from the main body to form the legs of an A, a steep catamaran hull design. A sleek nose of a cockpit protruded forward at the apex.

Large, darkened windows of the triangular cockpit dominated the face of the long, narrow upper body which tapered off aft in a diamond-like shape. Measurement markings on the photograph showed the vessel to be more than twenty meters long. A twenty-five-millimeter autocannon and two remote-controlled gun mounts could be seen protruding from the sleek body.

"You can see its stealth design made it difficult for our sensors to locate it," Lian said.

"I am certain we have seen this before." Xuan looked at Guo inquisitively.

"This appears to be a variant of the Ghost missile boat design," the senior captain replied.

"I thought the Americans decided not to acquire them," Xuan said.

Guo nodded affirmingly while Lian sat poker-faced.

"We must respond," Lian asserted. "I don't need to remind you that certain dates are approaching, and we have not resolved the unification of our people."

I'm quite aware the reputation of the Party is on the line, Xuan thought to himself. *But we are in no position to conduct a swift invasion of Taiwan; such an effort would take weeks according to our AI estimates, assuming everything goes well.* Arms sales over the years had turned Taiwan into a very prickly hedgehog, bristling with mines, shore-based anti-ship missiles, and rocket artillery which could reach the mainland. It would take considerable time and effort to reduce those forces. *But I can't say that . . .*

"What do you propose we do?" Xuan asked, anticipating the answer.

"The Great Chairman has provided us with the tools to win this contest without fighting."

"You wish to employ the Battle Management Tool?"

"The artificial intelligence system of the BMT has incorporated the thoughts and wisdom of the Great Chairman and fought millions of battles. With its guidance and the great spirit of our people, we shall turn back the interference of the brash Americans and teach our cousins the errors of their ways."

"Yes, the BMT has *simulated* millions of battles. Most of the fleet have trained on it, but I am not aware that in any of these battles it fought against these 'spaceships.'"

"In any event the BMT can begin running simulations now and determine how to array our forces to deter the Americans from intervening. The wisdom of the Great Chairman guiding the fighting spirit of the people's army shall prevail. As we demonstrate how we can smash their hegemonic forces, they will back down." Lian's expression was very serious as he looked at Xuan and then Guo. "That is if everyone zealously does their part and follows Party military theory."

And the best way to demonstrate that you are following Party military theory is to follow the guidance of the BMT . . . Xuan thought to himself. "Give the order to place our forces on general alert. Begin feeding data and our best estimates into the BMT. Start the targeting process for American carriers and nearby airfields. Contact the Strategic Support Force commander to activate the reserve cyber cadres. Meanwhile, the three of us shall prepare to brief the Central Military Commission . . ."

Admiral Trevor Baldwin climbed out of the car. He took the moment to bask in the warm sunlight and the cool breeze of Pearl Harbor, Hawaii.

"Good to be back, Admiral?" asked Captain Adam Hornik, his Chief of Staff.

"Yes." Trevor stretched a bit, savoring the moment, knowing he'd soon have to enter the fortress-like command center. "It is a lot warmer here than in Washington right now. I'm also glad to not be stuck in an airplane anymore."

Trevor never felt very comfortable in airplanes. His height and large frame were far more suitable on the scrimmage line of an American football field than crammed into a tiny airline seat.

"Did you get to see your folks?"

"Yes, they are doing alright. Hard to see them getting old, though . . ."

Trevor's parents still lived in the house where he grew up in Washington, D.C. He had spent precious time of his short shore leave making repairs to the old homestead and putting in accommodations for his parents' declining mobility.

"How were the kids?"

"It was good to see them, but my visit was cut short when I got your call."

Trevor was at the Boys and Girls Club of Southeast D.C. playing football with aspiring athletes when he received the cryptic message from Adam. Trevor had attended university on a football scholarship and wanted to impress on the young men and women at the club they too had a great future ahead of them if they worked just as hard on academics as they did on sports.

"Good morning!" Trevor greeted the security team at the quarterdeck of the command center. He dug through his pockets and surrendered his cell phone. Hornik turned in the bag holding Trevor's laptop computer. Trevor was tempted to conduct his usual banter with the sailors and Marines manning the quarterdeck and security desk, but he knew there was precious little time. He normally enjoyed the personal contact with all of his sailors and Marines, but such opportunities had become rarer as he rose in rank and crises kept cropping up. *Maybe I should just go back and teach in the old neighborhood*, he thought to himself. *I'd certainly get a lot more rest.*

The look on his deputy's face told him more than all the reports he had read on the flight over did. Vice Admiral Mikita Stewart was taller than Trevor but far sleeker. While Trevor had the heavier frame of a lineman, and admittedly needed to lose some weight, Mikita's build was proof she was a world-class marathon runner. She had gained a bit of local fame blowing past many a runner on the numerous running trails of Oahu. She was also known to startle many a quarterdeck watch team of ships in the harbor with an impromptu sunrise visit if she noticed discrepancies. While Trevor had an affable manner, Mikita was very serious and intense, particularly when things were not going well. The look on her face was rather grim.

"How are you doing?" Trevor asked as they passed through security and into a long hallway.

"Good morning Admiral," Mikita answered. "I'm doing well, all things considered."

"Looks pretty serious?"

"Yes, we are picking up chatter. The Communist Party and the Central Military Commission are concerned this incident signals Taiwan's desire to make a full break, particularly as critical dates approach." Critical anniversaries had always driven the Party's thinking, particularly those regarding the founding of the Party. "We are seeing heat signatures from important computer server farms along with indication from our cyber specialists; they are increasingly devoting more resources to their AI combat system."

"Did you invite Dr. Basin to join us?" Trevor asked.

Mikita frowned. "Yes, she is waiting in your office."

"Don't like her much?"

When Mikita did not answer, Trevor spoke up. "I know she's not very conventional, but she's the best AI expert we have."

When they entered Trevor's outer office, they saw Talya Basin sitting in a chair lost in a book.

"Dr. Basin?" Adam asked. "Dr. Basin..."

Talya looked up, confused for a moment. "Oh! Hi, Adam." She seemed not sure what to do next but then noticed Trevor and Mikita and stood up. "Hello, Trevor; hello, Mikita."

Trevor smiled to himself and suppressed a chuckle. Talya was a child prodigy from an academic family with rather unconventional views. Despite all the formality around her, Talya insisted on calling people by their first names and eschewed her own well-earned academic titles. She was in her usual outfit of jeans, sweatshirt, and earth sandals with white socks. Such an outfit contrasted with the uniforms of the military members or the usual subdued Hawaiian shirts and slacks almost uniformly worn by the civilians on the post. Her dark reddish-brown hair was a bit unkempt and often hid her face. She had piercing gray eyes which were framed by thick glasses. Talya was nice but a bit shy and missing certain social graces. Trevor thought she was far more comfortable talking about computers than people, certainly not comfortable talking about anything personal.

"Talya, I'm glad you are here," Trevor began. "It is apparent the Chinese are employing their AI battle computer and we're going to need your help to outwit it."

"I'll do what I can do to help," Talya replied.

They walked into a conference room which was part of Trevor's command suite. Everyone sat at the table. Adam talked through the incident reports.

"So, we're already winning in one regard," Trevor said.

"How is that, Admiral?" Adam asked.

"We've caught them off guard and gained the initiative. The PRC were trying to pressure the Taiwanese but did not expect either them or us to push back so hard."

"That raised the stakes, though," Mikita interjected. "Now the Party risks losing face."

"Any actions you take which change the rules of the game will have that risk," Talya replied. "Almost any move you make within the standard rules they've set, their AI will have already considered it and accounted for it."

"Here we go again," Mikita sighed. "The superiority of the machines."

"AI is not superior to us in a general sense," Talya retorted. "They are just superior to us in the cases where they can act, or more properly think. We've not only seen this in cases of games like chess and go but in areas of medicine and law. Just ask all the paramedical and paralegal professionals who are out of work. Heck, AI systems are better than eighty percent of the doctors in practice at diagnosing diseases. But this is all because they have a lot of data. Pushing their AI into an area where they don't have a lot of data is how you beat them."

"Okay," Trevor intervened. "So you are saying they make great servants but poor masters."

"Precisely," Talya responded.

"I'm not going to claim I'm some great strategist," Trevor said. "But I do remember from my time at the war college that it's best to fight the strategy rather than individual battles. On the other hand, I'm not prepared to raise the stakes to a general conflict. So, what now?"

"Go with the shell game stratagem," Talya replied. "Keep them busy, like we talked about before."

"Shell game?" Adam asked. "I've had a whole team of strategists working on war plans for months and none of them have said anything about a shell game."

Talya reached across the table and grabbed three Styrofoam cups and put them facedown on the table. She pulled a piece of candy out of her pocket and placed it on the table, then covered it with one of the cups. She then shuffled the cups around again and again.

"Which one is it under?" she said, looking at Adam.

"This one."

"Good job, very observant." Talya grinned at him. "I noticed you have dolphins on your uniform. Nuclear-power trained?"

"Of course."

Talya put the candy under a cup and started to shuffle them again, more rapidly this time.

"What is the square root of ten?" she asked while continuing to shuffle.

"Three point one six."

"What is ninety-nine divided by twelve?"

"Eight point two five."

After several more math questions she stopped shuffling.

"Okay, which cup is it under?"

Adam pointed at one cup. Talya lifted a different cup revealing the candy under it.

"Okay, so I lost track. I still had a one-in-three chance of getting it right."

"Not if I removed it from the table while you were distracted..."

"I used to get rooked by this on the streets of D.C.," Trevor remarked. "But there they weren't shouting math equations at you. They had other ways of distracting you. I finally wised up and stopped losing my money."

Talya pulled down two more cups and put out two more candies.

"Want to try to track three in a set of five?"

"That's impossible even if you don't distract me," Adam remarked.

"You're right," Talya replied. "A human can't keep up with what we call an N-choose-K problem, but a machine can or at least many people think it can."

"I don't get it," Mikita said. "You just said a machine can keep up. How does that help us?"

"AI systems can keep up, but in doing so they use up a lot of processor cycles and memory resources. You can also distract it or its sensors. It also can become fixated on problems it understands, ignoring those it doesn't. Change the rules of the game while it is busy, and it may not recognize what's happening."

Captain Jedediah "Jed" Babin was sitting in the jump seat in the cockpit of a Ghost missile boat. Forward of him the two coxswains were piloting the swift vessel. He looked aft at the two operations specialists in the mission bay. One was tracking the data feed from the onboard AI system. The AI was constantly updating the target list based on last known data and a random algorithm. Surrounding his lead boat were six other missile boats each armed with four extended range Naval Strike Missiles. Depending on the warning order the squadron could receive at any minute, the boats could unleash their missiles at a range of targets with the AI providing a recommendation on which targets would have the greatest effect. The missiles could hit fixed targets ashore, offshore infrastructure, ships, Chinese missile boats, amphibious platforms, etc.

"Conventional deterrence" was what the admiral called it when he described the mission to Jed. A death wish is what Jed first thought of when it was described to him. Then Talya, the wizard lady with the gray eyes, cast her spell of math on him and talked him into leading the effort. If you were willing to overlook the fact that everyone on an individual boat was likely to die if the craft was hit, it was just about guaranteed that the rest of the squadron would avenge you if you did die. Then add the fact the boats were almost invisible to radar, meaning a lot of effort would be required to get that one hit, and you had a perfect mission for special operations types like Jed. Pilots in the air and operatives on the ground faced the same kind of calculus every time they went on a raid.

It made sense from a strategic perspective as well. As long as they kept the patrols up, there was no way the bad guys were going to get away with wiping out a squadron and not get punched in the nose as a kickoff to a general war; and attempting to keep track of all the boats would drive them to distraction.

That was the theory. In practice, doing the mission this close to the Chinese coastline was terrifying and exhilarating at the same time. This was why Jed chose to lead the first patrol himself. As the senior captain of the whole flotilla, he could have delegated the mission to one of the squadron commanders, but he felt he had to show an example to the force.

"Is Ghost Rider on station?" Jed asked.

"Yes, sir."

"Okay, let's start chumming the waters..."

And just to add more spice to life, they were now purposely emitting certain signals from a few of their boats. "Anti-simulation" was what Talya called it. Jed called it putting a luminescent target on his back...

The other specialist in the mission bay monitored the common operating picture of the squadron. Data poured in from sensors on the missile boats, small drones launched by the missile boats, helicopters and TERN drones launched from their mothership, occasional fighter sweeps, and other sensors that fed the picture. The incoming data not only was used to maintain their own situational awareness, but to also update the targeting database constantly. Jed smiled as he recalled his early career getting qualified to drive a ship. Back then it took a small army of operations specialists in the Combat Information Center to track targets by radar, determine their course and speed, and make recommendations to the bridge. Things had changed a lot in the intervening years after he left to join the SEALs. Now the AI systems did most of the work for the specialist and the specialist's role was to guide the AI, using their own training and intuition.

"Looks like they are on to us, Captain," one of the specialists called out. "I'd say we have less than five minutes until they can spot us."

Jed looked at his laptop display and could see the common operating picture with an estimated position of a Chinese Y-8 maritime patrol plane. The estimated position was based on multiple passive receivers on several boats triangulating with each other.

Jed gave him a thumbs-up and keyed the command circuit on the mesh network communications system.

"Phantasm team, this is Warlock Six, stand by for Tango drone launch and blossom maneuver."

The radar warning receiver light turned on, indicating the radar signal of the Y-8 was getting stronger as the plane was closing their position.

Jed paused a heartbeat, and then knew it was time. Alea iacta est, he half whispered, half prayed before springing the trap.

"Execute," Jed said on the radio. "Launch Tango drones."

Jed heard the thump of compressed air launching a drone into the sky.

"Silence anti-simulation."

The artificial signal generator which brought the Y-8 looking for them was turned off, replaced by a similar signal on the drone now flying away from them.

"Blossom!" Jed commanded as he grabbed a handle near his jump seat.

Jed felt the missile boat bank as it surged into a power turn and accelerated. The whole squadron scattered in random directions.

Jed watched the Y-8 track; it seemed to have taken the bait and was tracking the drones. Suddenly the radar signal went dead. Jed grinned. Somewhere up in the sky, Ghost Rider, an F-35C joint strike fighter from one of the carriers, had lit up the Y-8 with a fire control radar, likely sending it running for home. While the Y-8 was distracted, the missile boat squadron headed for resupply rendezvous via random routes. Another squadron was already set to take their place.

The Eastern Fleet operations center was a hive of activity. Staff and watch officers were busy at their terminals watching tactical displays, reading reports, typing in chat messages, and talking on phones or radios. Xuan had to suppress an urge to roll his eyes as he watched Lian and other commissars making the rounds to exhort the watch-team members to give everything they had to the effort for the party. Commissars on ships at sea were doing the same; reports on their level of effort to uplift the morale of the fleet were pouring into commissars on the watch floor. Meanwhile, cameras monitored every member of the watch team.

The whole fleet would probably do a better job if you just left them alone . . . Xuan thought to himself as he walked down to the main display.

On the main screen he watched the two countries' fleets conducting their deadly dance, each trying to convince the other that when actual fighting began, they would be in a losing position. Xuan grimaced as he took in the situation. At first, the watch teams were struggling to implement the guidance from the BMT as the orders kept shifting while the situation developed. Now the guidance from the BMT had slowed greatly as it churned through solutions to prepare for action against Taiwan, responded to the American Pacific carrier fleet, and now design new search patterns for the low-profile missile boats.

"There are only three American carriers in the Pacific and only one was in the Philippine Sea when all this began." Senior Captain

Hu Guo was attempting to make sense of the operational situation. "Why do I see fifteen on the board?"

"I regret to inform the senior captain," a very nervous watch captain responded. "We are currently having difficulty identifying the actual carrier from the many decoys."

"Please explain."

"While the Americans are using many techniques to present spurious tracks which appear to be a carrier and its escorts, we have been limited in the number of reconnaissance aircraft which can be devoted to confirm or negate the true identity of the track."

"What about all the medium-altitude long-endurance drones we invested in?"

"Many are unable to report their findings at the time of detection due to interference. Many have had to return closer to home to make their report. Those reports often have high latency; thus, we are making slow progress removing the spurious tracks while new ones appear."

"I thought we trained for this, what is wrong?"

"I ask for pardon, Senior Captain, but we have fewer drones tracking the carriers than we anticipated."

"Why is that?"

"We designed our force to track high-profile aircraft carriers. Now we must divert sorties to track missile boats, but their signature is so low we can only confirm their identity at close ranges. This requires more drones. Additionally, the readiness of our drone fleet has not been as high as expected. We suspect cyber interference in our maintenance networks."

Just as likely that maintenance officers had been fudging their readiness reports all along, Xuan thought to himself. He had brought the issue up with his counterpart in the air force many times over the years.

"The carriers are also much further out than we planned for," the watch captain explained. "The drones must fly farther to observe their tracks, leading to less time on station and longer delays between detections. None of the suspected carrier tracks are within range of our long-range ballistic missile or bomber forces. The closest tracks are just outside of our reach."

"Then the carriers are no threat," Guo surmised. "The Americans are not really intervening."

"That assumes the carriers are near where we estimate them to be," Xuan interrupted. "We've seen some fighters conducting extended missions from the carriers supported by their unmanned tankers. You are also dismissing the threat of the missile boats. What is their status? How many of them are there?"

"Admiral," the watch captain responded. "We are having difficulty determining their actual numbers. Their small size, low profile, and high speed are making estimates difficult."

Xuan walked over to the watch desk where such small combatant threats would be assessed and looked over the notes. The watch officer in front of him tried to maintain his composure, but it was apparent to Xuan the man was very frustrated.

"The Americans must be using decoys for their missile boats as well." Xuan shook his head. "Given their low profile, it would not be hard to create an effective decoy for them."

Xuan perused the reports and shook his head. "We have regional commanders who are reporting that these 'spaceships' can fly, others that they can travel over a hundred knots on water. Clearly we are being deceived."

Guo stepped close to Xuan and spoke in a low voice. "Admiral, we have lost track of the American submarines. When we were ordered to divert some of the maritime patrol aircraft to track the missile boats, we had too few to maintain track of the submarines as they left Guam. Our undersea sensors are being distracted by their autonomous undersea drones."

"Guidance" had come down from the CMC to track the missile boats. Xuan knew such guidance was rooted in concerns regarding commercial assets along the coast which the missile boats could threaten. The fact senior officers of the PLA and influential members of the party owned several of those assets was certainly part of that guidance. Meanwhile, coastal missile battery units were being reactivated from the reserves.

"Vice Admiral Cen," Xuan called out. "What does the BMT recommend?"

When there was no reply Xuan walked over to the corner section where the team operating the BMT sat. Lian Cen and all of the BMT operators sat in silence staring at their screens.

Intrigued, Xuan walked into the section and looked at one of the screens.

错误代码4444 flashed in the middle of the screen.

Xuan sucked at his teeth as his stomach dropped.

"What is error code 4444?" Xuan asked. "Is this someone's idea of a sick joke?"

The number four in Chinese is an unlucky number as the word for the number four sounds extremely similar to the word for death. For this reason, many Chinese buildings do not have a fourth floor, like how many western buildings are missing a thirteenth floor.

"Admiral," an embarrassed team leader replied. "We do not know what that error code means. It is not in our user manuals."

"Admiral," Senior Captain Hu Guo said. "We have a new challenge."

Xuan walked over to the watch desk where amphibious operations were normally monitored.

"We have located land-based missile batteries," Guo reported. "American Marines have emplaced anti-ship missile batteries in the northern Philippines and southern Japanese Islands."

"Are these the expeditionary advanced bases their Marines have been touting?" Lian asked. He seemed to have regained his composure.

"Yes, Vice Admiral."

"Then they pose no danger to us. They don't have the range to reach our forces near Taiwan."

"You would be right," Xuan replied. "If their intentions were to prevent a landing, then they are too far away to interfere with that. How did you find them?"

"We watched one of the missile boats heading into the Philippines to replenish."

"I suspect the Marines are there to protect the missile boats' logistics." Xuan shook his head. "Just as we use the Spratly Island bases to extend the range for our frigates and corvettes, they are using the Philippines and Japanese islands to do the same. But they can also use such batteries to knit a wall of missiles across the first island chain."

"To what end?" Lian asked.

"We have been contemplating a blockade of Taiwan," Xuan replied. "We have always feared them employing one against us."

"But that is madness, they would bring the global economy to a halt. Their allies would revolt and force them to sue for peace."

"Let us hope that is the case, but until the BMT can provide me better guidance, I must consider the possibility."

Admiral Trevor Baldwin and his inner staff were gathered around the conference table in his inner office again. They had spent the last several hours reviewing in detail the events of the last few days. Those days had been a blur of activity and the combination of jet lag and stress were taking their toll on Trevor. The time zone also played havoc with his schedule as he had to keep higher echelons in Washington, five hours ahead of him, abreast of events. He owed the Pentagon another assessment in the next hour.

"Admiral," Vice Admiral Mikita Stewart began. "We can't keep this pace up much longer without declaring an emergency and begin a full deployment of forces. Our forward forces are working around the clock and we've pulled ships which were supposed to be headed home back into the line. This could be a deception, and it may very well make us unprepared for a real invasion months from now. The ships we pulled back in need to get home for maintenance. Meanwhile, with as many of our missile boats in contact with theirs, the possibility of an incident is increasing."

Mikita was one of the secretary's favorites, so Trevor had to get along with her. She was also a very effective force manager, but like many senior Navy leaders, maintaining ships was her strong suit—not strategy. Right now, she was showing her nervousness. He had no way to tell her that the fastest way to die at sea is to be too cautious.

"I'm aware of the risks and I've seen the estimates," Trevor responded. "Hell, I know about the maintenance backlog of the fleet. We've been selling the need for constant forward presence for years, and the fleet has paid for it in worn-down ships and crews. But now we just have to wait a few days and our forward presence will actually achieve something. The Chinese have been running an insurgency campaign to demonstrate to the Taiwanese and the others out there the PRC really does govern the China Seas. Now we've called their bluff and the Taiwanese are going to put the Chinese Maritime Militia on notice. Once word gets out the others will start to reassert themselves."

"That would make the Chinese lose a lot of face, and potentially threaten the survival of the party." Mikita shook her head. "That could lead to nuclear war."

"That is all being discussed in the White House right now. My guidance was to let others worry about that and not to self-deter. I'm to come up with ways to keep the pressure on by signaling."

"To signal much further," Captain Adam Hornik chimed in, "we're going to have to conduct simulated bombing raids near the Taiwan Strait and that could easily spark a dangerous response."

"That's only if you want to continue to reinforce only one of our stratagems," Trevor responded. "And you are right, if you give the Chinese the opportunity to sucker-punch a carrier or fire missiles near it, they might take it. Very likely the latter."

"Is that your assessment of what their AI strategy system would do?" Mikita asked.

"It would give them a way to say they taught the Americans a lesson and an easy way to overshadow the capture of the militia vessel." Trevor sighed. "I don't need an AI to tell me that. The PRC will take that as an 'off-ramp' and we'll be back where we were before, except no one will be willing to push back on the militias in the future. Instead, we can widen the game by signaling the ability to employ any number of available stratagems."

"More escalation?" Mikita raised her hands in frustration.

"If you want to beat the machine." Everyone turned to look at Talya, who until now had been silent. "You must change the rules of the game."

"What kind of rules are you talking about?" Mikita asked.

"AI systems don't do well when faced with wicked problems. They can often make them worse because the AI focuses on the problems it understands."

"How certain are you that is how their systems work?"

"I don't know for certain, but I know they've stolen a lot of code and techniques from us over the years." Talya had an evil grin on her face which turned Trevor's blood cold. "There are certain penalties for taking other people's intellectual property."

Xuan could see the watch teams were exhausted after three days of grueling effort. He became more and more apprehensive as the

Taiwanese cutter slowly towed the militia boat toward the Taiwanese coastline. Each time they sent forces to confront the cutter, American forces would be there. The American presence was not just unmanned platforms—such would be easy to neutralize, just a public-affairs matter of dismissing the destruction of robotic assets. But the Americans kept demonstrating with manned assets teamed with their unmanned systems, almost inviting the spilling of blood. Missile boats paired with long-range UAVs and unmanned surface craft, fighters paired with robotic wingmen, submarines paired with autonomous undersea platforms, and now Aegis destroyers paired with semi-robotic weapons carriers. Cyber cadres attempted to get AI systems to subvert the robotic elements of the pairing, but the American manned systems kept thwarting the efforts.

The Eastern Fleet was not the only recipient of the American attention. Northern Fleet assets were now faced with threats coming out of the main islands of Japan while the Southern Fleet faced threats from the Philippines. The Joint Staff reported American and Indian naval forces conducting threatening maneuvers against their forces in the Indian Ocean and Africa.

Xuan stared at the screen in the BMT section. Once again, 错误代码4444 flashed in the middle of the screen.

"Admiral," Lian said. It took Xuan a moment to collect his thoughts and look up. "Admiral, the BMT is requesting access to more servers; it needs more processing and data capacity than we have available to us. As the situation has become more complex, its requirements have grown exponentially. That is the reason we have been receiving the error."

"Are you certain?" Xuan said, trying to keep from putting voice to the irritation he felt. He stabbed at the computer screen. "Your technicians still have not told me what this error code means."

He looked around but the only faces looking at him were Lian and Guo; all the technicians and watch standers were looking down in shame.

Xuan stood up and felt dizzy. He had not truly slept since leaving his home and he felt exhausted.

"We believe the error code is due to the BMT's resource limitations on exploring all of the permutations created by the American horizontal escalations," Lian explained. As the Americans demonstrated their ability to threaten China with multiple approaches toward any efforts against Taiwan, they also demonstrated their ability to threaten Chinese commercial and dual-use outposts overseas.

"We can provide the BMT more servers by tapping into our civil/military fusion centers," Lian explained. "We must employ the doctrine of people's warfare in the modern era."

Such an authorization would direct server farms normally employed for commercial use to support the military. It would also mean activating an army of militia-reserve computer operators to assist the effort.

"I took the liberty of drafting the order." Lian handed the order book to Xuan. Xuan attempted to read the draft order in detail but quickly grew weary. It appeared to be a copy of a standard order the command had drafted and employed in several exercises. The reserve units and server farms were always called up in the exercises, but their services were always quickly returned to their civilian activities in order to reduce commercial losses. This would be the first time they would actually be employed for an extended length of time.

There is something wrong here, Xuan thought to himself. *I feel like we are being led by the nose, but I am powerless to stop it.*

"Admiral," Lian said quietly. "We are running out of time. We must trust the Great Chairman's wisdom."

Xuan was asleep in his office chair; three days of nonstop work and worry had overtaken him. He was awakened by the sound of the phone ringing on his desk. The display on his phone indicated the call was from the commander of one of the cyber operations sections in the Strategic Support Forces. It also indicated the call was considered urgent. Xuan picked up the phone and punched the response key.

"Eastern Fleet Headquarters," Xuan said into the phone. "Admiral Wang Xuan."

"Xuan, this is Tai." General Shao Tai was an old friend of Xuan, but the tone of his voice was not at all jovial like it normally would be. Instead, Xuan detected a sense of panic creeping in as his friend spoke. "We have a serious problem."

"What's wrong?"

"We've been hacked."

"What do you mean? You always boasted you had the best cyber experts on the planet backed up by the best AI defense systems."

"Yes, but we've been undone from the inside." Xuan could hear in Tai's voice a man under serious strain attempting to remain calm. "We activated the civil/military fusion center with all the reserve hackers we could muster. Some of them are from international supply chain companies. Many of them are from our cyber espionage teams. Normally their tasks are related to exfiltrating technical data from corporations in the west. After you signed that order, they were supporting the BMT."

"Go on."

"The first glitch was when the Americans stopped one of our commercial ships just south of the Philippines. Those Ghost missile boats showed up out of nowhere supported by some helicopters. They quickly took down the ship. Their boarding teams knew exactly where to look and found the weapons systems onboard. We did what we could to limit the distribution of the video, like appealing to our friends in western social media to shut it down, but it got out. This caused a panic across the globe; there were concerns all Chinese ships were Q ships. Our ships are being kicked out of port. At the same time, complaints started to pour in that the Americans were no longer paying interest on their bonds to Chinese holdings. Then the global market started to short our positions.

"Normally our AI systems can keep up with these manipulations. We've used such stratagems against our competitors for years. But with the teams devoted to the BMT, we were slow in our response. We could recover from this, except for the other problem."

"Which is?" Xuan's heart was beginning to pound.

"You have to understand my hackers often work freelance gaining information from western sources, getting corporate information, compromising accounts, and exfiltrating data. Several of them were comparing notes and figured that together they had the code for the American AI Pacific theater battle management system. So, what better way to train the BMT to fight it than to let it fight the American AI head-to-head?"

"I'm certain Lian would have approved," Xuan replied. "Subject to certain precautions."

"Well, the order you signed gave us leeway to do it." Tai explained.

"We isolated a server farm and put the two opposing systems in and set them against each other in a simulation."

"So, what happened?"

"The BMT came back with error code 4444. But that's not the worst of it; the damn things won't stop. It's like the BMT was goaded into a fight with the American AI and will stop at nothing to win. It seems to think our commands to stop are coming from the American AI and disregarding them."

"So shut it down."

"It's gotten out! And we can't figure out what it is doing."

"What?"

"As far as we can tell there is an AI routine in it designed to break the firewalls and jump into other server farms to get more data and processing power to continue the competition. Only we can't be certain because the two AIs have developed some sort of competition code between them, which we can't understand. I'm taking steps to contain it, shutting down servers, cutting power. It will mean a lot of our server farms will have to be completely blanked to make certain this thing does not spread."

Xuan sat in his office staring at a photograph of his daughter and grandson. The photograph had been sitting, mostly forgotten, on his desk for years. Now it was the most important object in this whole office. All of the flags, awards, mementos, and accommodations proudly displayed around his office now meant little to him.

Xuan glanced at the tactical display on the wall of his office. He could see the Taiwanese cutter was entering port with its prize in tow. Next to the display was a television screen showing the feed from Taiwan national news. A reporter was extolling the exploits of the Taiwanese Coast Guard in its bringing Chinese mainland pirates to heal. Xuan turned off both screens.

Perhaps I should have retired long ago, Xuan thought to himself. *I could be home teaching my little mouse . . .*

"Admiral." Xuan looked up to see Guo in the doorway. Xuan had no idea how long the senior captain had been standing there. "I have a confession to make."

"Confession?" Xuan could not keep the sound of fatigue and confusion out of his voice.

"I suspect everyone in the BMT section knew what error code 4444 was, just as I did."

"Why did you not say anything?" Xuan felt a sensation of betrayal but saw remorse in Gou's eyes.

"We all trained on a version of the AI system. But in the training mode it is known as the Battle Management Trainer. The two systems share a lot in common and much of the code."

"I did not have much experience with the system; it was after my time."

"Precisely, you were never graded using it." Guo sat down on the proffered seat. "Admiral, you must understand how important such grades were to many of us. How much the commissars employed it to determine who would be advanced."

"Yes, go on."

"The temptation to cheat the system was enormous. Many paid bribes to the technicians to learn how to outwit the training system. Soon there was a whole cottage industry on cheat codes and strategies. Many of those codes enabled simulated platforms and systems to perform more capably than they would in the real world."

"So, we have been building a whole cadre of leaders on pillars of sand?"

"To their credit the commissariat became aware of what was happening and devoted their coders and modelers to put in an AI subroutine to detect when a player was cheating. When the BMT detected the player was cheating, it would display error code 4444."

"Let me guess." Xuan was now roused from his weariness; righteous anger had now replaced his feeling of betrayal. "Those who received error code 4444 were strictly punished."

"Yes, Admiral."

"So, the BMT was now facing hundreds of students, each attempting not to win, but to avoid being perceived as cheating. The best way not to be perceived as cheating was to follow official doctrine."

"I had not thought of it that way, but yes."

"Do the tool and the trainer use the same data?"

"Yes, Admiral."

"Thus, we have trained a machine to detect cheating, conditioned a generation of officers to avoid getting caught cheating, and unleashed both on a nation of cheaters and scoundrels?"

Guo looked down at the floor in shame.

"We were doomed from the start." Xuan sighed. "Blind adherence..." Xuan could not finish his thoughts out loud; doing so would doom any chance at his survival and would certainly be disastrous for his family, perhaps for Guo.

"I thought you should know before they come for you." When Guo looked up, there were tears in his eyes. He paused and attempted to settle himself. "Is there anything you want from your office for your retirement?"

Traditionally, a retiring admiral took his command flag with him when he took his last voyage home. Xuan reached for the picture from his desk and placed it in his coat pocket.

"No," Xuan said and stood up. He smoothed his coat and picked up his service cap. He stood at attention as Lian arrived with a squad of marines.

"Admiral Wang Xuan," Lian began. "The CMC has determined your services are no longer required and have agreed to your request for retirement. This honor guard will escort you to your vehicle to send you home."

Xuan looked at the marines in full battle dress including body armor. He noted there were magazines loaded into their rifles.

"No dress uniforms for retirement?" Xuan dryly asked.

"Given the suddenness of your retirement, there was little time to plan or prepare."

Xuan looked from the marine guard to Lian. "When will you be retired, Lian?"

"There is no call for me to retire. I did not sign any orders which countermanded doctrine."

"And when word gets out about our failure?"

"No one will know of *your* failure, Admiral. The Chinese people will be spared the news that one of their most revered leaders failed them in their hour of need. The commissariat is now working diligently to ensure the Chinese people know the spirited actions of their People's Liberation Army guided by the wisdom of the Great Chairman taught the outlaw regime in Taiwan a lesson and forced back the hegemonic forces of the American war machine."

Xuan smiled. "They will know only what we tell them."

"Precisely." Lian nodded his head in a slight bow.

And I am the greatest threat to that story, Xuan thought to himself. *They may still shoot me here, but it would appear I am to be allowed to die at home. Will I be shot in the head as I enter the door to my own home or will poison be left beside my tea pot?* Xuan knew of colleagues who had suffered similar fates. *I suspect the latter; they will want to say I died from a heart attack due to the stress of defeating the Americans.* Xuan wryly smiled. *My doctor will be surprised . . .*

Xuan was looking out the window as the driverless car made its way out of the city. He had nowhere else to look, for the car's electronic display system was no longer accessible to him, nor were the controls for the car, or the doors.

While the car sped along, Xuan noticed many details he had not seen before. Normally he would be reading reports, dictating orders, or watching the fleet in action on a tactical display. But now he looked out to see children playing soccer at a park, street merchants peddling their wares, and office workers heading out to lunch. As the car slowed, he spotted a dandelion growing in a patch of wild grass at the side of the road. He wished he could pluck it and bring it to his grandson. Three days of exhaustion finally took over and Xuan fell asleep dreaming of chasing Zhou across a field full of dandelions.

Xuan woke to the smell of smoke and burning rubber. He heard the crackling noise of a fire. His hands felt gravel and dirt. His head and shoulder hurt as he rolled over and started to rise from the ground. He was lying on the side of a country road somewhere off the route he would normally take to get home. The black hybrid driverless car was a few feet from him; flames rose from the forward engine compartment and the front wheels.

Xuan rose to look for help, then noticed someone was in the car. He staggered to the door and looked in the window. There was a passenger in the back seat wearing a navy uniform coat. Xuan realized he was not wearing his coat and noticed the coat on the passenger was his. Xuan tried the door handle but could not open it.

Xuan knocked on the window to see if he could arouse the

passenger but received no response. He slammed his body into the car door to shake the passenger awake. The passenger slumped forward against the restraints. Xuan looked closely and could see a small hole in the back of the passenger's head. Blood was seeping out and had stained the collar of the white uniform shirt. Xuan recoiled in shock and horror, then looked around to see if there was going to be an attack on him.

The wind picked up and the flames of the car grew in height and intensity, driving Xuan back. Black smoke rose into the sky. Several large black trash bags rolled and bounced down the winding road like tumbleweeds. Xuan could see checkerboards of red-and-yellow striping decorating the bags.

Now in a panic Xuan ran down the hill away from the burning car. As he raced down the hill, he heard an explosion and turned to see that the car had been fully engulfed. He watched dumbfounded and was startled to see another car pull up beside him. It was another black driverless hybrid car.

Resigned to his fate, Xuan stood his ground as the car stopped in front of him and he noted no one was inside.

The car's external electronic display flashed 错误代码 4444 as the gull-wing door started to rise.

Xuan approached the car. Who had sent it, and why would they transmit the ominous error code 4444 if they'd gone to the trouble of faking his death? He climbed in and the door closed behind him. His sense of unease deepened as the car accelerated away from the burning wreckage, carrying him into an unknowable future.

MY DOG SKIPPER 2.0
Weston Ochse

Northern Territories 2058

The sound of a heart ripping was the same sound as a dog dying. He'd charged, not caring what would happen to him because his dog was down, shot through, and bleeding out plasma and decomposing oxygen-deprived rapid-replicating cells. Skipper had been too wounded even to pull itself clear. That they'd targeted his beloved canine partner infuriated him, rendering logic into a binary equation where two choices existed for possible actions—both ending in the attackers' complete and utter destruction.

Southern Whitehouse
Huntsville Alabama 2043

"The Animal Welfare Act of 1966 was signed into law as a foot in the door to limit various industries' abilities to use animals to test consumer products. These tests usually resulted in the permanent maiming or death of the test animal. The original act only incorporated five percent of possible animals to be tested, and a series of amendments spanning the next fifty years opened the door even wider, additionally limiting animal testing and uses, culminating in the 2013 amendment which identified an animal exhibitor as: *an owner of a common, domesticated household pet who derives less than a substantial portion of income from a non-primary source (as determined by the Secretary) for exhibiting an animal that exclusively resides at the residence of the pet owner, after stores.* These exhibitors could use the animals as exemplars of superior breeding only and not for any other workmanlike enterprise.

"Due in part to the efforts of private companies to create animal simulacrums to be used as surrogates for biological fighting mechanisms, the Animal Welfare Act was reintroduced as the Animal Exclusion Act in 2043, which disallowed any biological or biologically created or biologically enhanced organism from being used as a weapon of war or as a subject of testing without its free will to do so. These companies desired fully robotic solutions and spent large percentages of their budgets to ensure that only nonbiologicals could participate in armed conflict. This selfish need on behalf of private companies had the effect of keeping biologicals out of harm's way. But upon the collapse of the nonbiologic defense industry, it became apparent that a combination of the two would be needed as wars blurred into the future. Because there was no way to define the free will of an animal at the time of the law's inception, future amendments are anticipated as the need for their use arises to operate in military-denied areas, predicated on the scientific ability to map and translate applicable animal languages."—Excerpt from Master's Thesis on Bio-Mechanical Ethics of Mr. Justin V. Coates, Masters Candidate, University of Alabama at Huntsville.

Papua New Guinea 2055

Triple canopy jungle was about as different from the Middle East as the Pacific Northwest was from the face of the Moon. They should have been happy with their change of scenery. No radiation. No mercury particles in the air to perforate their lungs. But the humidity was a living breathing entity. It grabbed them in a wet fist and squeezed until their movements were slow-motion parodies of what they should have been. Even beneath the sheen of their micro-polymer armor, sweat soaked their skin before it could recirculate and cool it, leaving them feeling as limp and as used as a wet rag on the edge of a sink.

The rainforest boasted more than seven hundred species of birds and they must have heard half of them shrieking in defiance and interest as the six men from DART 7 passed beneath. Their goggles targeted and catalogued them by sound and sight—the various birds of paradise, hornbills, honeyeaters, astrapias, satin birds, flame bowerbirds, riflebirds, parrots, and the occasional nightjar. Here and there the undergrowth would explode as a cassowary, easily as tall as a man and the avian version of a velociraptor, leaped away and ran away from the team as it tore through foliage thick enough to stop any man.

Immense hand-sized spiders hung webs between trees. Centipedes, millipedes and various ground insects shimmied over boots, trying to climb up legs. Weevils, turnias, Acrophygas and a hundred more multi-limbed insects fell from leaves onto their helmets, seeking soft places in the skin to burrow and lay eggs. Monster cockroaches hugged trees, watching them as they passed with alien eyes. Indications of other more deadly threats were also present, such as the death adder or the taipan, snakes that could take down a grown man in as many steps as it would take to cross a city street.

They'd had the rebels under surveillance for two hours and were more than ready to attack. Sitting still in such an environment was an invitation to anything that moved and the men of the team were constantly swiping insects and arachnids from themselves, all the while attempting to remain dead silent in order for the ambush to work. A pair of C-Blacks were standing by, ready to attack—all the team needed was the word that the hostage had been seen and was alive.

The commandos were in charge of that part of the mission, operating micro-UAVs the size of bumblebees that lit and swarmed over the enemy's campsite—just another species of insect dancing in the light caused by the flames of the central fire. The DART team had the slightly higher ground, but were no less mired in the sweltering hell of the forest and assaulted by the myriad of fauna. Each of the DART members wore Oculus Night Optical Devices (NODS) that allowed them to flick through the various feeds and if they chose to, juxtapose these on reality.

But the centerpieces of the mission were the C-Blacks.

The commandos had pinpointed the location of the British member of Parliament, hidden in an ancient grotto surrounded by rocks—something their local Sepik guides had said was a hunting layover from transitioning down the highlands. The mission was perhaps the easiest of any they'd had. The C-Blacks would handle the rebels, and if any managed to squirt free of their noose, either the commandos or DART 7 would take them out.

Coates queued up vision from C-Black 1.

The chameleon saw simultaneously in multiple spectrums, and because of the darkness, he chose ultraviolet so he could view the thermal imaging of their targets. He counted eight rebels, surrounding a larger central figure. This was most probably the PM. He switched to starlight, and saw that he was correct and decided to leave his vision on that frequency. Atop the rocks and upward at 6.5 meters sat C-Black 2. Coates admired it in its fearful symmetry. The size of a Great Dane, but as thick as a mastiff, the Chameleon Black's shoulders were a half meter higher than the hind legs. Each limb ended with zygodactyl toes, enabling them to act as legs with hands. Although he couldn't make out the skin, he knew it to be dark, but capable of blending with the background because of the Furcifer DNA. Though it didn't have a tail, it did have two tentacles that jutted from just behind the shoulders and could be used either to deliver poison, or pick up things. The face was the least animal and the most robotic, the designers rendering it an edged oval that appeared more like the metal-smooth head of a giant ant than of a canine.

The commandos placed a selector on the MP to protect him, then pressed a button.

The C-Blacks surged forward, razor-tipped claws grabbing, slashing.

Rebels fired their weapons at targets that were no longer there, fatally late, tragically missing their chances to survive. Not that Coates felt anything for them. To him they were no more than blood sacks, real-life test dummies put on the face of the Earth to demonstrate what two thousand years of science and invention could create. The Chameleon Blacks were clearly creatures of wonder. He found himself first smiling, then laughing as he watched the violence rain down on the men who'd kidnapped a British member of Parliament.

Switching back to ultraviolet vision, Coates watched with more than a little interest as the multicolored hues that represented the lives of the men in the grotto winked out one after the other, until all that was left was the pulsing purple of the C-Blacks.

Afghanistan 2055
Greater Hindu Kush
Two mongrels scattered out of the way of the three dusty, older-model tracked vehicles as they ate up the once proud concrete of the

main drag of Bagram Air Force Base—what they used to call Disney. The animals searched in vain for scraps from the garbage and honey trucks heading toward the ever-present burn pits. Their ribs were showing through their sides. Tongues hung limp from scarred snouts. Watery eyes searched dully for anything to sustain them. Some said that the dogs signified a culture who didn't care for animals, but the truth was, everyone was starving and those who could live through the mercury and carcinogen-particled air were as in as great of need as the mongrels.

Three local Afghans wearing traditional Pashtun pants and shirts, shemaghs draped around full-face breathing devices, and carrying flamethrowers, lumbered after the track. They also carried third-generation AK-12 assault rifles, probably bored for NATO arms to make it easier for them to use all of NATO's now obsolete 5.56 ammunition. These locals were no more than security run by local warlords to ensure that no one ran off with any of their broken toys—those left behind by the various task forces that had been operating in Afghanistan for the last forty years. If they received any serious resistance, they'd button up inside of their vehicle until help came, otherwise, they were nothing more than Pashtun muscle, probably young men from the Paki highlands trying to add their names to the never-ending rolls of the dead.

One of them made a move to kick one of the dogs, causing Coates to tense.

But the mongrel was a survivor and skittered out of the way without the Afghan even coming near.

Lucky for him.

FLASH TO *Skipper running through the tall wheat next to the family home in Wyoming as if the dog had invented the words pell and mell. Nary a rabbit in sight, but the tongue still waving out the side of the mouth accompanied by joyful fury in the eyes. Coates, sitting on the front porch, absentmindedly picking at weathered wood, trying to be one with the dog, but instead, walking along a memory lane strewn with men and women, skin peeling from radiation poisoning, green and gray foam specking every cough from mercury poisoning, the only constant sound except for their muffled screams being his breathing in his protective mask, so much like Darth Vader, but lacking any Force to stop the agony of others. Then Skipper, at his feet, pawing at him,*

head on his knee, peering up, as if to say, forget them, remember me,
come on Justin, be free.

Chief Warrant Officer Justin Coates turned away from the fly-
specked window to the team room. The air circulators wheezed
overhead, reminding him they'd have to change the filters soon. He
glanced down at his indicators and saw that neither the mercury
warning nor the radioactive warning was in the red.

The team room was like any other. Composite concrete on the
outside and plywood on the inside. Six beds, three on each side. A vid
screen took up one wall at an end. Two private sim pods sat off to the
side for comms back home and gaming in between missions. Each of
the men had their own Pelican gear boxes stacked in and around
their bunks in a way that was only convenient to them. The entire
place smelled of gun oil, testosterone, and unwashed sheets. Probably
the same smell a hundred years ago and with the exception of gun oil,
probably the same smell in a Roman legion with too many men living
in close quarters together for too long.

"I remember my grandfather telling me about Kandahar Air
Force Base back in 2010," Coates said, trying to dispel the memory
of the week after the dirty bombs went off, the refugees dying along
the road in the thousands as their insides melted. "Not only were
there over ten thousand US soldiers stationed there, but they had
most of the First World conveniences. Coffee shops. Ice cream
parlors. Restaurants. Basketball courts. They even mentioned that
the Canadians built an ice rink for hockey." He shook his head. "Can
you imagine? An ice hockey rink in the middle of a war zone where
it's a hundred and four degrees in the shade during summer?"

"And now forty years later it's nothing but a series of glowing
craters that can be seen by satellites at night. It truly is the forever
war," Fitch said, wiping sand and grit from his bolt carrier. He blew
on it, then held it up to the light.

"Afghanistan ain't shit," Jose Renner said. "Ever hear of
Reconquista? That's seven hundred and eighty-one years of fighting
on the Iberian Peninsula to see if Christianity or Islam would win
out."

Fitch shook his head. "Not the same."

"Why not? Because it was so long ago?"

"It's all religious. Shit, don't have to be religious to be at war."

"Why do you think people have fought for so long?" Renner asked. "There've been more than a hundred wars longer than the Greater Hindu Kush Conflict, which started off as the War on Terror, and before that was the Soviet Invasion of Afghanistan, and before that was the Second British Invasion of Afghani—"

Coates held up his hand. "Thank you, Mr. History Professor."

"The point is," Renner continued, "is that every one of these wars was because one group didn't like the way another group worshipped. One of the worst things to ever happen to mankind was to give us a higher power to worship."

"But I'm not religious," Fitch insisted. "Look at World War II. That was only six years but the most people died in that war. What was it, fifty million?"

"Sixty," said Coates. "Sixty million people. That's more than twenty times the population of Afghanistan, Pakistan, Kyrgyzstan, and Uzbekistan together—all the Stanistas together."

"And yet the bombs of 2041 only killed five million," came a new voice. "Wasn't that special?"

Everyone turned to glance at Hemmings and his glib remark. He ignored them, continuing to add water to something that smelled as if it had intended to be macaroni and cheese if devised by a blind alien who'd only heard about it in passing.

Coates shook his head. "Really, Hem?"

The bigger man shrugged. "I'm just saying that we could have ended this decades ago if we'd wanted to. Now it's nothing more than a sandbox where the first nations of the world try out new weapons systems and find more efficient ways of killing the Stanistas—of which there seems to be a never-ending supply."

"And what would you do if it wasn't for this sandbox?"

Hemmings shrugged again.

"I'll tell you where you'd be," Coates said. "You'd be in jail. That's what. Guys like you. Guys like me. We're made for war. Sometimes I think the reason for conflicts is to get rid of us military-age males. Let us do a little repopulating, then get the shit blown out of us. That way the rest of the world can live in peace."

Hemmings finished mixing and shoveled the food into his mouth.

"Is that your answer?" Coates asked.

Hemmings shrugged.

"I come in peace, said no one who really meant it ever," said Renner.

Coates laughed.

Back to Fitch, he said, "Religions are like assholes. Everyone has them. Even those who profess not to believe in a higher power believe in something. It's the possibility of that belief being denied that sends everyone on edge."

"I'm telling you, I don't have a religion," Fitch said.

"You might not have a church and a god and gold and glittery pomp and circumstance," Coates said, "but you sure as shit have religion. What do you want more than anything in the world?" He held up a hand. "Don't answer. You want to play the sims. You want to be a knight or a paladin or a defender and slay dragons. Every waking hour is time you are buying back so that you can immerse yourself in a world that doesn't exist where you can be king and you can shape your own destiny."

"Sims aren't religion," Fitch grumbled.

Everyone laughed, including Hemmings. They all knew Fitch's reverent approach to the sim vids.

"You do know that there are those out there who feel you are blaspheming by worshipping false idols and creating your own reality," Renner said. "They'd as soon see your kind banished from the Earth."

Fitch grinned. "Like I said. It isn't my religion. It's theirs. I just happen to be the object of their hatred. It's different."

Coates stared at him, wondering if his man might have actually said something profound—what were the chances? What was it he believed in? Certainly not a rational god. If anything, he'd believed in one thing ever and that had been taken away from him.

FLASH TO *He's part golden retriever and something else. We're not sure. But he's passed all of the tests and is of a breed that is eager to please. If you want to begin, we can see if he's a match for you. The Wounded Warrior Program has fully funded the next four weeks and, if you so desire, the animal to go with you. He'll be trained along with you so that you can bond together. You'll find that just having him around helps ameliorate some of your feelings.*

"Why can't we go somewhere nice? I've got to tell you, Chief. Your choice of vacation sucks," said Jacobs, exiting the shower, a towel wrapped around his solidly muscled midline. "The sand here is the same sand that's been fought over for a thousand years. You've felt it. It feels different. Nothing like the sand at home. Plus, you can't drink the water, you can't eat the food, you can't fornicate with the women. This is not the sort of place to fight over. It's just a place to fight on."

"Well, hold onto your britches, boys," said Commander Lawson, entering the team room with a pad and his creepy pre-mission smile. "We're getting our feet wet in more ways than one. A C-130 is on the way to pick us up. We're going to rendezvous with some Royal Marines in Tierra del Fuego for a follow-on future mission pending briefing enroute. Everyone gear up. Coates, I want to see you in my office."

Three hours later, aboard a state-of-the-art Special Operations C-130X variant aircraft, all six members of USSOCOM's Defense Advanced Reconnaissance Team Seven (DART 7) were preparing their gear for a meetup with a unit of Royal Marine commandos. They would rendezvous on the tiny comma of an island in the Indian Ocean that had once been a British Protectorate but was now privately owned by a bio corporation.

Sergeants Frisco Fitch and Josh Hemingway (aka Hemmings) sat on one side of the aircraft. Both of them had their issues, like most of the team. They were both assigned from MARSOF. Fitch's specialty was demolitions. Hemmings' specialty was weapons. For each of their specialties, there wasn't a single man-made weapon of war that they couldn't assemble or disassemble.

IT1 Jose Renner was their Navy comms tech and kept them in and out of the appropriate grids and on the correct frequencies.

U.S. Army Master Sergeant Josh Jacobs had the arms of an offensive lineman and the waist of a running back. Born in South Chicago, he was also a weapons specialist and as much of a human tank as Hemmings could be in a fight.

Commander Stump Lawson was the team lead for DART 7. He'd been blue-water navy for his first six years, before joining US Navy SEALs. He left the teams three years ago to head up one of the new USSOCOM DARTs. Each team was designed to uncover and acquire foreign and unique weapons systems in order to test them in the field to ascertain production feasibility. With the advent of the Animal

Rights Campaigns of the 2040s—which disallowed animals to be used in wartime without their own volition—and right-wing media campaigns to ban embryonic stem cell and human-to-animal clone testing, DARPA and other Department of Defense agencies became more dependent on acquiring existing technologies in order to fulfill future defense obligations.

Which was much of the reason that US Army CW4 Justin Coates was such an integral part of DART 7. He'd started out his military career in the infantry, much like Jacobs, but soon found himself as part of an advanced Wounded Warrior Program. Everyone on the teams had PTSD. His was nothing special. It was just that his mind operated in a way that kept him from functioning the way he once had. Six months of rigorous EMDR and he'd recovered enough to realize that he no longer wanted to be a straight-leg infantryman. He already had a college degree from the Greater Southern California Educational Co-op in Sports Medicine and was able to take the time to get graduate degrees in Medical Ethics and Bio Mechanics. All of that got him into DARPA before it disbanded in 2050. But what really got him on the DART team was his knowledge of canines as military partners.

FLASH TO *Skipper walking side by side during training, the heat of the beast pressing gently into the skin of his leg, guiding him, reminding him that he was not alone and that he was alive. A world lived in those deep brown eyes where only two entities existed, bonded by a single heart, a leash, and unconditional love.*

Back in the hooch during his private briefing with Commander Lawson, he'd been asked how much he knew about Dr. Fred Gipson and Chameleon Black.

As it turned out, Coates had already been studying the dark money-funded project by the former Pacific Conversation billionaire. Gipson, working alongside members of the video game, cybernetics, and medical industries, had developed a biomechanical, quadrupedal surveillance support mechanism, designed to not only infiltrate denied areas, but to also directly support military teams. The project was called Chameleon Black and was headquartered in British Columbia because of the US laws against stem cell research.

Where companies like Boston Dynamics canceled programs after an inability to adapt to the realities of energy and mechanical challenges with their Big Dog and REX research, Gipson took the results and applied biomechanics to the project, constructing an organic support mechanism to improve upon the prototypes. His work was ultimately outlawed for use by the United States and many other Western countries, but that didn't mean it wasn't being secretly deployed. And, it turned out, they were not only going to meet a pair of the support mechanisms, but use them as part of a rescue team to assist the Royal Marines in Papua New Guinea to repatriate a captured member of Parliament.

FLASH TO *Why must all great things come to an end—a four-foot wooden box he built himself, then the hole, dug during a driving rain, the bottom filling with mud, the water scouring him of tears as he buried his best friend and perhaps the only being to ever understand what it meant to be him. A heart attack like a lightning bolt went BOOM and Skipper went gone. He'd kept the collar and pulled it out during maudlin nights of memories, scotch, and staring into the starry night in search of the dog star.*

It had been Coates' dream to work with one of the Gipson models and not just because he'd lost his own service dog. He had some ideas that, if he could make a reality, might change the way the United States looked at the medical ethics of using biomechanical man-made organisms for combat.

Indian Ocean 2055
Diego Garcia

They didn't spend long on the tarmac of Diego Garcia—just enough time for a meet and greet with the Royal Marines. They'd worked together before, but not with this team. There were places the commandos could go that the DART team couldn't, and vice versa. Likewise, there were weapons systems the DART could work with while the commandos were told a definitive no. For instance, members of the Greater United Kingdom Defense Forces were denied access to any fusion or fission technology.

If either group was in support of the other, rules could be bent, if not actually origamied.

"It looks like a modern Gekko, but how?" Fitch said, after seeing the pair of quadrupeds pacing back and forth.

"Not exactly a Gekko from Metal Gear Solid, but similar,

combining elements from many similar games," Coates said. "Would you believe that it wasn't until the 2020s that the scientific community began to embrace the gaming community? And it only made sense. Game designers would create creatures, in this case mechas, to conform logically to a predictive game structure and engineered universe. If they could do that, then why couldn't they advise the scientific community on how to incorporate many of the theoretical and gaming capabilities into real life?"

Fitch snapped his fingers together several times. "That's what I've been saying all along. Games do have their place." He went over and got close to one. "Can I touch it?"

"Sure, mate," said Sergeant Barto, Marine commando. "It won't bite. We've already programmed them to recognize your voices and biometrics."

"It feels—" Fitch laughed. "It feels rubbery."

"That's the skin grown over the exoskeleton. Gipson used cocktail of Furcifer chameleon, mako shark, golden retriever, and other patented proprietary DNA."

"Embryonic stem cells?" Coates asked.

Barto paused, as if to gauge how to respond, then shrugged. "Of course."

From humans, as well?"

"Proprietary," said Barto. Then he winked. "Better to guess than to know. You know what they say, better to ask forgiveness—"

"Than permission," Fitch said, finishing the line. "So, what does it do?"

"Anything it wants to, I bet," Hemmings said.

"This is a Chameleon Black model, right?" Coates asked. "Version six?"

"Nine," Barto said. "They call you Doc Coates, right?"

Coates nodded. "Are you able to force the Furcifer change?"

"We can turn it off or on, but they use optical algorithmic interfaces. Why force something when it can work on its own? Once the support mechanism is set on task, it decides which functions to enact to best enable it to complete the mission."

"How many of the thought processes are biological?" Coates asked.

"As many as can be expected. There's not much of the personalities of the creatures with DNA present, merely their aspects."

"So, the golden retriever was used for bonding? Has that been working?"

Barto shrugged. "In version six, the mad scientists upped the DNA ratio. I could say that it seems friendlier—more like an actual dog—but I've also been told that me and my mates have been projecting."

"What kind of neuro interface does it use?" Coates asked.

Barto grinned. "Fuck if I know, Doc." He laughed. "They said you'd have a lot of questions. I'm just an operator. I don't really know how these are put together. I do know that it's biomechanical, which means it can be stimulated much in the same way some of the Sudanese Embryotic Simulacrums were."

Coates shivered, remembering the army of the almost-dead that had marched through South Sudan. What the Sudanese had done in the name of internecine warfare had gone beyond the pale. The SEMs were true zombies in every aspect, dead men walking, revived only so they could continue war against the Dinka in the Sudan-Kenyan Freedom Corridor. It was one thing to create a partner in war, yet another to reanimate corpses.

FLASH TO *He'd gone to an underground biohacker for help before they'd buried Skipper. Will it retain its memories? he'd asked as he'd watched the electric current ripple gently through the embryonic liquid. The brain had seemed so small, then again, the whole of human history could have been recorded on a microchip the size of a thumbnail. The problem was a thumbnail couldn't love you back. Neither could a mere brain, which meant it would need a host. But where would he ever find one?*

Afghanistan 2057
Korangal Valley
1456 Hours Local
A battalion of the Forces Spéciales de la République Fédérale d'Azande, or the Federal Republic of Azande Special Forces, found themselves in a historically significant predicament in the Korangal Valley. Nicknamed The Valley of Death and located in the Dara-I-Pech District of Kunar Province in eastern Afghanistan, with peaks reaching almost twenty thousand feet, the valley was twenty-one kilometers long and barely a kilometer wide. Had the Azande studied regional military history, they would have known that the Korangal

Valley was nothing more than a place for Stanistas to shoot for sport—a tactically nightmarish landscape with escarpments, forests, rivers, and boulders large enough to hide squads of Stanistas.

Popular opinion was to leave the Azande there, but as one of the Armies of the Greater African Diaspora, they needed to be saved and DART 7 had no choice but to render aid. But they also had their own reasons for participation in the coming conflagration. Not only were they one of the most elite units within a five-hundred-mile radius, but they also had reason to test their new bioorganic support mechanisms.

DART 7 infiltrated from the north and pulled into a tight defensive position behind a series of boulders. The area had been selected from satellite footage because there had been zero activity in the area for more than ninety-six hours, probably due to the inaccessibility of the Kush and the unlikelihood that someone would be able to approach from the north. All of the Stanista forces were concentrated below and near the escarpments along the east and west approaches. They were constantly trying to hack the geostationing satellites, but CYBERCOM kept them busy with third-party nonproprietary security patches that were like digital landmines—although the Stanista hackers might get through them, it would take them a lot of time and one misstep would end up frying their hardware before they were able to disengage.

So, without the advantage of modern technology, the Stanistas had returned to their former capabilities of being masters of the terrain and understanding when and where to attack.

The Stanistas seemed to feel that it would be enough.

DART 7 thought better.

Still, Lawson wasn't about to fall into the superior-technology trap. There'd been enough examples over the years where forces with more sophisticated weapons and technology had fallen to Stone Age peoples with twentieth-century weapons systems. Plus, they had their own special weapons they were going to field, which required monitoring and geo-located command and control.

"I sure hope we're going to kill something this time," Hemmings said.

"By something, you mean people, right?" Fitch asked.

"People. Equipment. Whatever." Hemmings rounded his shoulders to stretch the muscles. "I wasn't made for ikebana." He held up his

P9000 automatic rifle. A grandson of the P90, the 9000 was a full-sized bullpup rifle that fired 6.8mm caseless ammunition in tungsten ball, tracer, or depleted uranium with a Leupold VX-12 scope.

"Icky whata?" Jacobs asked, sitting next to him and babying ammunition into another magazine.

"Ikebana," Hemmings said. "It's all the rage. Don't you know that?"

Jacobs glanced over to where Coates was squatting beside a mastiff-sized creature, tentacles wrapped around the man's arms. "What's he talking about, Chief?"

"Ikebana is the Japanese art of flower arranging," Coates said without looking up.

"They have an art for that?" Jacobs asked.

"The Japanese have an art for everything," Renner said.

"Not true," Fitch said. "They don't have an art for sandwich making. That's all American."

"Keep it down or you'll get a knuckle sandwich," Lawson said. Then he added, "Renner, get the bumbles in the air. I want a three sixty view of the area. I'm not counting on the satellites. I want real time data I can see."

"Roger that, sir."

Coates tried to keep their voices in the background, but it was proving hard. He adjusted his neuro interface helmet and retried the connection. Skipper 2.0 was definitely functioning, but he had yet to see any advanced communication capabilities beyond affection, and he couldn't be sure that wasn't being augmented by Gipson's DNA. Attention from the tentacles was a new phenomenon. They'd ignored him up to this point and he wondered if Gipson's behaviorists had been right when they said that increased interaction in addition to the memories might create new neural pathways.

Skipper 2.0

Skipper 2.0

He pulsed a memory of him and Skipper 1.0 running through grass, rolling in it, then him rubbing the dog's stomach under a bright blue Wyoming sky.

Skipper 2.0

He pulsed another memory of him hurling a ball, Skipper rushing to grab it before it stopped, him tumbling, then righting himself, then rushing back so they could do it all over again.

Skipper 2.0

Ready.

Skipper 2.0. Do you recognize me?

Memory of when Coates was dreaming, crying in the night, right fist clenched and reaching, a nuzzle at his neck as Skipper 1.0 breathed into it.

Skipper 2.0. Is that you?

On station.

Devils Tower 2056
Observation Log 73

Chameleon Black Version 10 underwent surgical enhancement and has yet to show any signs that it is anything other than the complex organism from which we began. As mentioned in all logs in case of possible prosecution, CMV-10, now identified as Skipper 2.0, has been provided to me as an individual and I do not represent any government or private organization. My sole function is to study the interaction between the biomechanical host and the neural addition of a once-viable Canis lupus familiaris and ascertain first, whether neural bonding is present, and upon acknowledgment of that achievement, ascertain the limits to free will of the support mechanism in order to determine if it can operate within the legal guidelines of the Animal Exclusion Act of 2043.

Skipper 2.0 set loose with 100-meter parameter.

Moves without issue.

Follows CMV-10 commands.

Ordered to kill three prairie dogs—complete.

Switch to neuro transmission interface.

Ordered Skipper 2.0 to move.

No movement.

Ordered Skipper 2.0 to kill.

No kill.

End Test 0073.

Afghanistan 2057
Korangal Valley
1624 Hours Local

"Why is it the Zande came to the valley?" Hemmings asked.

"Ask King David," Fitch said.

"Why are you always a smart-ass," Jacobs asked, coming to his friend's side.

"Some things come naturally. Don't you get the reference?"

Hemmings and Jacobs shook their heads, all of them watching the feeds on the tactical command display set up by Renner. Six different screens showed Stanistas in hide sites, along with geocoords for possible targeting.

"It was King David who said, *Yea, though I walk through the valley of the shadow of death, I will fear no evil for thou art with me; thy rod and thy staff will comfort me.*"

"I got your rod," said Hemmings, holding up his rifle.

"And I got your staff," said Jacobs, patting his own rifle.

"Keep your staves and rods to yourselves, men," said Lawson. "Coates, you ready yet?"

"Almost, sir. Just getting acknowledgement from the support mechanism that this is his choice."

"Talk about politically correct," Renner mumbled.

"You'd want this sort of political correctness else someone might weaponize your kid's hamster. Think of it. Second. Third. Fourth. All the orders of effects of an out-of-control animal kingdom who was capable of conducting warfare on our behest while we sit back in our hot tubs and drink Champagne."

Renner removed his hat, wiped his sweaty hair back, and replaced the hat. "I get that. It just seems like we're the only ones playing the game the right way. New Soviets have those damned Mountain Dogs who can take out a company of straight legs."

"Or the Chinese. Their Water Nagas weren't supposed to even be real creatures," said Fitch. "But they claimed the DNA came from reclaimed artifacts in the Imperial City."

Lawson grunted acknowledgement and gestured for Renner to move one of the bumbles for a better look. "You can bitch and moan until the cows come home, boys. The USA, as fractured as we have been since the riots of 2030, still takes the high road. Some sacred bullshit about being a City on the Hill or whatever. All that means to us is that we follow orders, we follow laws, and we find ways to kick ass."

Both Hemmings and Jacobs gave a *Hoorah!*

Coates never knew that the high road was paved by *Hoorahs* and patriotism, but it apparently was.

He pulled out the dog collar that had once belonged to Skipper 1.0. The neck of the support mechanism was twice as big around, so Coates had woven 550 cord into a mesh that was attached to both ends, allowing the collar to be slid over the head of Skipper 2.0. The dog tags that identified Skipper 1.0 along with all of his pertinent information had been taped to the collar to keep from making noise.

Coates backed away and admired his efforts.

The head turned toward him. Even void of features and as smooth as it was, the support mechanism appeared to be looking at him. He was about to ask the organism if it was ready, but it responded first.

Skipper ready.

Skipper remembers.

Skipper love.

Devils Tower 2156
Observation Log 91

He comes to me by voice command. See video recording associated with this log number. Skipper 2.0 has made the connection that me saying the words indicates that I wish the creature to come to my location. I've verified the transitory realities of the connection by attempting to make the support mechanism come to my location using various similar and dissimilar commands, but it will only respond to its original name—Skipper.

Afghanistan 2057
Korangal Valley
2100 Hours Local

The explosion rocked everyone, scattering equipment and men like a mad child's toys.

Coates, who'd been far to the back with Skipper 2.0, had taken the least of the blast, which seemed to have come from everywhere and nowhere at once. He checked on the support mechanism and found it in perfect ready stasis, then attended his fellow team members. The first thing he saw was a severed arm. This he ignored, and instead, snatched up his 9000, shoved it into his shoulder, lined up the barrel, and scanned the area.

"Lawson. Hem. Jacobs. Renner. Fitch. Anyone. Report."

Coughing came from forward of his position.

Seeing nothing in his sights, he ran through the dust to the sound, tripping several times, but keeping his balance, slinging the rifle, then letting it catch on the sling as he let it go.

It was their COMMS. Thin, narrow and bloody. His feet were missing, and his legs were scoured from bottom to top.

"Renner, report!"

Coates fell to his knees, found the other man's first aid pouch, and pulled out two tourniquets. He wrapped them in the spaces just below each knee, tightening them until he couldn't anymore. Blood still dribbled. At this point, Renner had a better chance of dying from shock than from blood loss.

"Blast. Came." Blood bubbled from his mouth.

Coates searched for any additional life-threatening wounds, but only saw dirt, powder and blood—a mixture that looked sickeningly like Cocoa Puffs breakfast cereal.

Glancing around, he saw that Jacobs was up and pounding on Hem's chest.

The other big man's body bounced with each concussion, but his eyes remained open, mouth a mask of a scream, both legs gone to the waist.

They must have been hit by something. He'd never heard the incoming round, nor the sizzle or *schist* of an RPG. Add to that an RPG or a mortar couldn't have done this much damage. Two of them had lost their legs, making one wonder if—

Fitch stumbled over, covered in other people's blood, but otherwise unblemished or hurt.

"It was beneath us. A fucking trap. A Stone Age fucking trap," he said.

Coates grabbed the man's shoulder and shook. "Enough. Make sure that's the only one, Fitch."

The man began to cry.

Coates struck him hard in the face. "Get a fucking grip, Marine."

Fitch nodded, pulled out a knife, and began to search the ground.

Where the hell was Lawson? He'd seen Fitch and Renner and Jacobs and Hemmings, but their leader was nowhere to be found. Then he remembered that he'd spied an arm. He glanced around and saw another one. Then, he spied half a face that was captured in the middle of saying something before it was disembodied, hanging from a bush several feet away.

Devils Tower 2056
Post–Korangal Valley

The neuro interface has been running for three days now. I haven't gotten a moment's sleep. Skipper 2.0 keeps wanting to relive memories. Is this what it is like to be a dog? Do they lay around all the time and think of all of the good times? And just to be clear, these aren't memories created by the support mechanism. These are memories from Skipper after we bonded in the Wounded Warrior clinic and before he died.

Like the time we went fishing and he'd never seen a fish before and the trout flopping on the grass was the coolest thing. But now, not only do I see it through his eyes, but I feel the unmitigated joy of the moment. I feel the wonder. I feel how it is to live every second to the fullest.

Or the time when I fell crying on the sidewalk and Skipper stood over me. He wouldn't allow anyone to come near me, not even the police officer. He was about to be shot, but he didn't care. He wanted me to feel safe and if it hadn't been for the doctor passing by noting my issues, the cop might just have shot the dog, mistaking it for being the reason I was on the ground.

Or like the time when I had to be gone for three days and Skipper waited and stared out the window. I now know what dogs are thinking when we are gone. I can feel them bereft of love and believing it might be gone forever, only to have it avalanching back every time the door rings or someone pulls into the driveway.

Afghanistan 2057
Korangal Valley
2105 Hours Local

A pair of Stanistas tumbled over the wall, knives in hands, ready to attack.

"Skipper!"

The neuro interface came alive.

Coates scrambled for a weapon and managed to snag his sling and pull up his 9000 just in time to block the down-sweeping blade. He fell to the ground, but managed to keep both hands on his own weapon.

The Stanista was so close he could see and smell the rotting teeth in the man's mouth, black on black on gray, unintelligible screams coming as he struggled to get his knife past the forward stock. Curry and feces an overwhelming fragrance. The blade slid back and forth, a furious balance between the two men.

He fired his rifle, ten rounds impaling the sky.

The sound caused his attacker to pause, which was what he needed.

Coates gathered himself, then brought his knee up into the ass of the Stanista, dislodging him for the brief moment necessary for Coates to bring the barrel to task, then firing, turning the face and head into a gore-fest that splattered him, getting into his mouth and eyes and even his ears.

He pushed the attacker away, then lurched to his feet.

Skipper 2.0 held the other Stanista using its tentacles. The beast raked through the neck, chest, and bowels, the inside of the body soon sliding to the ground in a parody of humanity. Skipper 2.0 hurled the husk back over the escarpment.

Coates didn't wait. He ran over to Jacobs, who sat crying with Hemmings' head in his lap.

"We weren't supposed to die," he said. "We're on an experiment. We're the heroes. We're not the targets."

Coates wanted to admonish the man and remind him that every time they took up weapons, they were targets, but now wasn't the time. Instead, he spoke soft but firm. "Jacobs. I need you. We are under attack."

The big man looked up, his expression more like a child than a professional killer. "Attack?"

"They killed Hemmings. We need to kill them."

Jacobs stared at the dead man's face in his lap—Hemmings with his eyes and mouth open.

"Kill them," Jacobs mumbled.

The big man was as conversant as Skipper 2.0.

Coates hoped he was as deadly.

Coates searched the area around them and found a 9000, but the barrel was bent at an odd angle. He continued looking, and as he did, Skipper 2.0 sent him a warning. Coates removed his own rifle and handed it to Jacobs who was a more efficient killing machine. "Take this. Kill Stanistas."

Jacobs gently laid Hemmings' head upon the ground, then thought better of it, found a packet of rations and used that as a pillow. Then he crouched and went over beside Renner. They spoke in low tones.

Coates went to the rear of their space, stepping over dead bodies and body parts. He wanted to punch himself in the head. They'd been too superior. They'd thought themselves too good. There was no reason for them to have anyone dead, much less half the team. And now, with Lawson all but obliterated, he was the only one left to command. He remembered that he had a pistol in a shoulder holster and pulled it, letting it hang at his side.

Skipper 2.0 stood by, implacable, ready to do his bidding whether it be from anger or thoughtfulness. Coates struggled to grasp hold of the latter, but the former was like warm syrup that coated everything.

Skipper 2.0.

On station.

Report.

Seventeen targets moving this direction.

It had taken him weeks to differentiate and ascertain that a target was anything other than the local team that Skipper 2.0 aka support mechanism was assigned to. This meant there could be a squad of Marines heading their way, or a squad of Stanistas. Skipper 2.0 was incapable at this point of differentiating the two unless certain visual cues were stimulated, such as the presence of a shemagh, or an AK of any variety.

Weapons?

All.

Skipper blend. Circle. Await orders.

Before his eyes, the Furcifer DNA activated and Skipper blended in with his environment. Coates shivered slightly as he acknowledged that part of his pet's camouflage was the blood and guts of his dead friends, mixed with the background of the exploded escarpment. Then whatever wavery line he'd barely been able to discern was gone.

"Jacobs, we have incoming. Set up a forward perimeter."

"But Chief, we have—"

"Set up the fucking perimeter. We'll deal with the dead later."

Jacobs and Fitch jerked open a Pelican case that appeared undamaged from the blast.

Coates watched them as he tried to toggle higher headquarters. Their omnidirectional booster antenna had been shattered, but they had personal comms capable of up to twenty klicks if there were any friendlies in the area. All he could hope for was a passing or circling fast mover high above to snatch his feed and retrans it back to HQ.

Jacobs and Fitch placed three rectangular composite systems at intervals along the front of the escarpment. Cables ran from these back to the Pelican case where they had their own power supply. If needed, Coates could tap into the power and boost his own signal, but they had more immediate problems.

First used for crowd control by the New Soviet Army, what had become known as the HARF, the Halt and Retreat Rifle, fired broad-spectrum lasers into an area that upon connection with an active visual cortex, scrambled it and caused the viewer to go temporarily blind, unless they had a way of filtering the visual wavelengths. Then again, they could also just not look at it, which meant they could continue advancing with their eyes closed, or turn back.

A blinking icon in the upper right of his HUD told him that the HARF system was operational.

He switched his viewpoint to that of the support mechanism, who was now at right angles to the group. There were indeed seventeen bogies and they were now in a muddle. Those up front were trying to make their way to the rear, disoriented by the HARF. What had been a careful creep up the incline was now a Benny Hill attack that had no rhyme or reason.

An image of Lawson's face flashed into Coates' mind.

Skipper 2.0 felt his combination of grief and anger and surged into the rear of the column, ripping and gripping, its zygodactyl toes grabbing like hands, but with razor-sharp claws, rendering living breathing humans into sacks of shemagh-wearing meat.

Coates was in momentary shock. He hadn't ordered Skipper to do such a thing. Was this free will being exhibited? Perhaps the support mechanism was merely an extension of Coates' emotions.

"Jacobs, fire grazing shots to the front," he commanded, ordering the master gunner to keep his shots at knee-level and below. "Fitch, move to rear guard. Ensure nothing comes up behind us."

Two verbal acknowledgements.

The support mechanism reveled in the destruction as it barreled through the maelstrom of scrambling Stanistas. The beast held a fighter with each tentacle, wrapped severely around a throat, hands coming up to try and dislodge it, while its front legs raked and ruined anything before it. Skipper 2.0, what had been C-Black 10, their support mechanism, was truly a singular killing unit capable of choreographed atrocity if need be.

Skipper, disengage.

Love it. Love it. Love it. Chase. Catch. Kill. Love it.

Skipper, cease.

But you sads. These are the reason. I kill. I make you feel better.

No, you don't, he thought. *But the moment he thought it, he knew Skipper spoke true.*

Skipper, you must stop.

You no sads.

Skipper stop now.

I don' understand. I love. I help. You grieve. I kill.

Skipper.

There was a pause, then the single thought came through the neuro transmitter. *Done.*

Afghanistan 2057
Inside C-130X

The adrenaline from the upcoming mission surged through them all.

Hemmings bounced a knee.

Lawson snapped his gum.

Renner listened to rap through his headphones, head bobbing, eyes closed, transported to a place where punks had fast cars and rained money down on threadbare women with thousand-dollar tans.

Jacobs squeezed a blue stress ball over and over.

Fitch flicked a 6.8mm round into the air, catching, then repeating.

Coates watched it all, chewing on his lower lip. Finally, he couldn't stand the silence any longer. "Ever been on a date, Hemmings?" Coates asked.

"Ever wanked your pud?" Hemmings responded. "Of course, I've been on a date."

Coates ignored the question. "What'd your date smell like?"

"He does like farm girls," Jacobs said. "Probably pig, horse, or cow."

"Or a combination of the three," Renner said, joining in.

Coates repeated, "What'd your date smell like?"

"My last girlfriend loved Chanel No. 5. She was old school."

"How did you like the scent?" Coates asked.

"Made me want to eat her up." He glanced around. "Figuratively, of course."

Coates grinned. "Of course." Then he added, "Would it surprise you to know that federal law required that all fragrances and perfumes be tested on animals first before being allowed use to humans?"

"Government-mandated animal testing? What do I care if a mouse smells good?" Hemmings asked.

Jacobs guffawed.

"They were tested for irritation. Wouldn't want your date to get a rash from her perfume, now, would we?" Coates asked. "Chemicals were rubbed on various animals to see if they caused cancers or blisters or open red sores."

"Better them than my girl," Hemmings said.

Everyone turned to look at him.

He glanced back at each of them, then rolled his eyes. "Fine. That's barbaric," Hemmings said. "Why would we ever do that? There had to be a better solution?"

"There is now," Coates said, "but back then, the only solution was animal testing. It wasn't until the Animal Exclusion Act of 2043 that the United States banned the import and/or manufacture of animal-tested perfumes and colognes."

"Why'd it take them so long?" Fitch asked.

Coates shrugged. "I'm sure there was a ton of reasons such as states' rights and the federal government not wanting to get involved in commerce. States like California, Washington, and Oregon were the first to ban imports. With their combined size and population, it caused many companies to rethink their positions on animal testing."

"What about the testing involved with the creation of a biomechanical organism?"

"What about it? These are organisms entirely created in a lab. They were not born, therefore, if animals have consciousnesses, these organisms do not have one. It's not until we attune a living neural network to the construct that there becomes an issue. In 2010, University of Pittsburgh scientists neurally connected the brain of a live monkey to a mechanical arm. Within weeks, the monkey was able to use the mechanism because it was the only way it could be fed. This breakthrough is what has made paralyzation so rare and the reason that Skipper 2.0 can exist."

"Don't you think we might be playing God?" Renner asked.

"Were we playing God when the first Tesla rolled off the assembly line? Were we playing God when we made corn that could grow as well in a drought as it could in a good year?"

Renner shook his head. "That's different. I can't help but remember this science fiction book I read about humans lifting up gorillas to be sentient. Don't you think we have an ethical dilemma in doing that?"

"You're talking about Uplifting. A term coined by David Brin. What of it?" Coates asked. He remembered the Uplift War books and pretty much dug them up until the point they had the alien chickens who wanted planet Earth destroyed; then it just got too weird.

"This is coming from a person who specializes in communications, right?" Renner said. "I've been thinking about this and your relationship to the support mechanism—er—Skipper 2.0. Initially, it was a man-made construct, the same as a robot or a microwave or a spare tire, but with some biological additions to amplify its capabilities. Amirite?"

Coates nodded.

"But then you played God and took an active neurological component—your former pet's brain—illegally, I might add—and connected it to the platform."

"Point of fact was that it wasn't illegal. I just didn't ask permission."

Fitch grinned. "Whether you're a CW4 or a major general, you're all privates at heart."

"Okay, smarty-pants," Coates said, "What's the difference between what I did and making a paraplegic walk again?"

"Did you ever read Dalton Trumbo? *Johnny Got His Gun*?" Renner asked. "The novel about a young man who can't see, hear, taste, smell, feel, etc. What if you were to give that back to him? All of his lost abilities. Would that be helpful? Would he want that?"

"Of course, he would," Jacobs said.

"You'd think so, right?" Renner said, turning to Jacobs. "But unable to ask, how would you know if he wanted it all back, but still look the way he looked?"

"If I remember right, he could communicate through Morse code," Coates said. "He could tell us."

"But would we follow his instructions, or would we know better? Brin never asked the gorillas what they wanted. And you know why? Because they were already in the process of being uplifted by the Progenitors," Renner said. "Which is my point exactly. When do those being uplifted"—he gestured to Skipper 2.0—"those being tuned in and turned on get a say?"

"What you're talking about is the right to choose," Coates said. "And I don't know if that's possible with Skipper 2.0. I don't think he can choose before or after because it is so ingrained in the DNA of dogs to please."

"As if dogs had already gone through the initial state of being uplifted by Brin's Progenitors."

"Hush now. That's all bullshit science fiction. This is real life," Coates said. "From an animal and medical ethics point of view, the connected creature, in this case Skipper 2.0, has to exert will to influence its own actions. That's one reason I'm recording every interaction. What we are doing here might help us update the archaic 2043 Animal Exclusion Act."

"Can you imagine a cat's neural network being hooked up to the support mechanism?" Fitch asked. "No squirrel or bird would be safe within a ten-mile radius."

"Let's just stick with dogs for now. Mankind has been trying to uplift cats for an eon. My guess is that if they could communicate, they'd ask us to stop because they are already the superior species," Coates said. He couldn't help but grin as he thought of his grandmother's two cats who hated people, the universe, and everything, but would gladly spend their lives on or near her lap, endearing them forever in the old woman's mind. It just went to show that there was a place for everyone and everything.

The signal light flipped to red and the ramp began to lower.

Afghanistan 2057
Greater Hindu Kush
After-Action Committee
Four field grade officers sat behind the table staring at him, wearing field uniforms that still held the bright color from when they'd been

made, unlike Coates' uniform which was sun-bleached and worn. The whine of the air scrubbers was the only sound in the room except for the occasional murmur behind him and the occasional scrape of a chair leg against the floor.

"CW2 Coates, you have already been reduced in grade and are being separated from the military because of your actions. Your support mechanism violated all laws by its very existence, not to mention the hundreds of deaths it caused."

More attack the support mechanism had told him.

Return to station.
Must save. No die. No sads.
Return to station.
No sads. Coates, stand by and return to station.

Was it telling him to return to station? Didn't the support mechanism realize who was in charge? It couldn't order him around. The support mechanism was a construct.

Skipper 2.0 cease operations.

He'd installed an override in case of just this event.

Skipper 2.0 is override.

How could it have overridden the failsafe?

Must remove. Must kill. No die. No sads.

"Do you have anything to say for yourself before we render our final decision?"

Coates shook his head. The problem with living by the idea that it is better to ask forgiveness than permission is accepting the fact that one might not ever receive forgiveness. "Nothing to say, sirs."

"Do you know where your support mechanism is at this time?" a major asked.

He'd known that they'd want to use one as a test subject, but by God, he wasn't going to allow them to use Skipper 2.0 as a test subject. They had his notes. They had his research. It was more than enough to go to Congress and have a new hearing about revamping the Animal Exclusion Act. Perhaps they could get with Gipson and create a better version, one that wasn't the extension of pure emotion.

"No, sir. Skipper 2.0 abandoned me," he said.

"Are you saying that it just left?" one asked.

"After all that it did?" another asked.

"It felt my anger," Coates said.

"It felt your anger?"

"I told it to stop. It wouldn't listen. I used the failsafe. It didn't work. I told it to stop again. It continued to kill. If it wanted to please me, it should have listened to me."

One of the officers at the table chuckled and whispered to the man next to him. This caused the other man to chuckle as well.

Coates gave them a scalding look.

"You've just described the feeling every parent has for every child that has ever walked the surface of the Earth," the one said.

Coates said, "But children don't kill everything that moves."

The same officer said, "Because we don't give children the capacity to kill. It takes upwards of five years for a child to develop empathy—the idea that others might not feel and act the same way as them—and the subsequent idea that this is okay."

"We'll ask one more time, CW2 Coates," said the colonel at the right side of the table. "Where is your missing support mechanism?"

Coates merely stared into space. Had he known, he might have told them. But he didn't know. Once his anger turned to rage and Skipper 2.0 felt it through the neuro network, he'd fled. Not only had the support mechanism killed all of the Stanistas, but it had killed the Azande as well. Had it stopped there, it might have been fine, but it also detected shemaghs and AKs in the nearby village and killed all of the men, then the children who'd picked up their fathers' weapons, then the girls who hadn't run, and finally the women because the support mechanism had determined that with the inability to create more enemy, more enemy would cease to exist.

"I do not know where it is, but I wish it well," Coates said simply, and those were the last words he spoke as a member of the US military.

Northern Territories 2058

A year later, Gipson came to him.

Coates had been living off his veteran's disability in a dingy apartment south of Barstow in the middle of nowhere. He spent his days reading pretty much anything that came across his e-reader and his nights listening to the howl of the coyotes, his mind full of what-ifs and just-maybes.

"Skipper 2.0 is alive," Gipson had said to him.

"He can't be."

"But he is and we've been tracking him since the massacre in Korangal Valley."

"Why didn't you tell the authorities?" Coates asked.

"Because we felt that you should have the opportunity to reconnect."

"He turned into a killing machine. He became everything we despise in animal testing."

"You need to differentiate. He is Skipper 2.0. One is the support mechanism. One is the vehicle for the consciousness of your *Canis lupus familiaris*. The support mechanism has the capacity to kill. Skipper 2.0 is the operating system for that support mechanism. Your problem was that your operating system wasn't sophisticated enough to host the support mechanism."

Coates had stared hard at the world-renowned billionaire. "But you knew this. You let it happen."

The billionaire shook his head. "I let you exert free will so that you could create something with free will."

"But it wasn't ready."

"No, it wasn't."

"And you knew it wouldn't be ready."

"Yes, I did. But because of your sacrifice, we now have enough information to perhaps change the laws."

"So that you can profit from it."

The billionaire had shrugged. "Just because I make a profit, doesn't mean that I don't care about your dilemma."

"A dilemma you created."

"I didn't bend your arm."

"Why is it I feel like I was lured to this place in time from before we even met? Why is it I feel as if you knew about my past so very long ago and used me for it?"

"Would it have ended up any differently?"

Coates couldn't answer.

Then Gipson told him of a date and time and location where Skipper 2.0 was going to be.

That had happened a week ago. Now, Coates sat in the cab of a Land Rover. He was on a promontory in the Northern Territories, seventeen kilometers north of the Mackenzie River on Gwich'in lands. His driver was a local who'd been handsomely paid to drive him to a location where they were to wait. It was January fifth and the days were still dark, but the aurora borealis ran above them like a river of light, bubbling over the stars. He was so transfixed that he almost missed the first buzz in his neural transmitter. It came in and out as if the transmitter had been damaged.

Skipper, he thought. *Skipper, are you there?*

Static.

Nothing moved except the sky.

Then his guide nudged him and pointed.

"There," he said.

A four-legged figure loped into view, limping over the tundra.

Skipper.

Still static.

Skipper, on station.

The four-legged figure stopped.

Coates.

It had never called him by his name before. In fact, it had never addressed him in any form or fashion. They had merely had a connection. Plus, something in the way it spoke to him changed. No longer was it the fresh, almost desperate need to please, but there was a world-weariness behind the solitary word.

Skipper. To me.

The four-legged creature headed toward him.

Coates opened the door and felt the rush of the subzero temperatures eat at the fabric of his thermals. His hands were covered with gloves and he wore a felt facemask to keep frostbite at bay. He still had a 9000 in a sling, however. You could take the soldier out of the military, but it was far harder to take the military out of the soldier. He'd use it if he must, but for now, it was just along to make him feel more comfortable.

He felt a weary joy surge through the neural transmitter, like an old friend acknowledging that he'd seen you. Coates could almost feel the smile in it. Could this truly be his Skipper? He'd thought long and hard over the last year about what he'd done, giving in essence a child the power of life and death. Now, after thousands of miles, had Skipper grown and changed and matured? He could only hope.

Skipper tell me. Are you sads?

The neural-transmission version of a contented sigh. *No sads. I see Coates. I see love.*

I see you too, my friend. I see love.

Another contented neural sigh.

Coates began to trudge over the icy scrub and snow toward the vestiges of his emotional-support dog turned mass-murdering canine turned misunderstood support mechanism. Skipper 2.0 only wanted to become that puppy he'd once been when the world was ruled by a ball of bright sun and the universe was a toy to be chewed. They'd leave this place and go somewhere secluded. Just a man and his dog. The two of them. Living together, connecting on a level no other man and dog have ever connected.

Then the snow erupted on both sides of Skipper 2.0.

Snow-covered tarps fell away, revealing four tripod-balanced machine guns.

Skipper, run!

Skipper tired. Skipper love. Skipper no sads.

Coates broke in to a run, searching for something to shoot, but the machine guns were remotely controlled. He recognized them as M61SX Vulcan Cannons, firing six thousand 20mm rounds a minute. And as they whirred to life, he screamed and screamed and screamed.

Skipper 2.0 shuddered and danced beneath the hail of fire as hundreds of rounds ripped through him, killing him instantly.

Still, Coates ran and ran and ran. His screams catching and freezing in the air behind him. The sound of a heart ripping was the same sound as a dog dying. Coates charged pell-mell, not caring what would happen to him because his dog was down, shot through. Skipper 2.0 had been too wounded even to pull itself clear. That they'd targeted his beloved canine partner infuriated him, rendering logic into a binary equation where two choices existed for possible actions—both ending in the attackers' complete and utter destruction. Except there was nothing to attack.

No human.

No other support mechanisms.

Nothing alive.

Just him and his dog Skipper 2.0, their blood merging, becoming one—bright red against stark white beneath a Crayola-colored borealis, as if it were the very neural transmission of a planet that had decided that the dog had to go.

No sads were the last thoughts of Skipper 2.0.

No sads were the last thoughts of Justin Coates.

No sads were the words frozen forever in the air above the tundra of the Northwest Territories.

UNCOVERED DATA
David Drake

Haskell pulled his Ford into the parking lot. Jones' Lotus was still there, meaning that first shift hadn't gotten off early for a change, and there was an Escalade in the space nearest the main entrance. The spaces weren't labeled as a mild attempt at security but anyone who parked there could expect to be moved on very quickly if they weren't Colonel Milner, Chief of Bureau Three, Interrogation.

Haskell went up the back stairs to Interrogation on the second floor. The colonel was probably downstairs in his office but Lieutenant Jones was in the common room getting a cup of coffee. Sergeant Jawicki, the usual escort, sat on a folding chair next to the door of room 2, indicating that they must have company.

"Is there more creamer somewhere?" Jones asked.

Haskell glanced up at the cabinet above the counter. The door was ajar. "There was half a bottle last time I looked," he said. "Maybe Stokely got some but didn't remember to bring it up."

Jones scraped the jar, then turned it over above his cup and patted the bottom. "Guess I got enough," he said.

"Hey, Jones," Haskell said. "You must have picked up a girlfriend, with a car like that. Do you play bridge? We could have you over for a game some time. Lucy's been bugging me to do something with other people."

"No, thanks," Jones said. He looked away. "Bridge isn't for me. But thanks."

Haskell shrugged. He'd tried. Jones probably didn't like him, or knew that Haskell didn't like Jones.

"Any notion what the colonel's got on?" Haskell asked.

"Didn't know he was here," Jones said nonchalantly. That was a damned lie, Haskell figured. Jones and the colonel were probably on each other's speed dial. They'd been together for years, whereas Haskell had been in the field as a Volunteer and only got his regular commission three months ago when he was transferred into Interrogation and shipped to NC.

The fact that Jones hadn't looked up from what he was doing was just confirmation. Jones always avoided looking squarely at a subject when he was lying to him. Apparently he thought the subject could see it in his eyes. In fact if you'd spent any time with Jones, the real tell was that he didn't show you his eyes.

"Well, I'm heading home. I wish you luck with our accountant," Jones said, nodding toward the interrogation room. "Damned if I could get anything out of him."

The background sheet was on the table beside where Jones was sitting. Haskell pinned it to the table with one finger and pulled it across to him. "Our boy's an accountant?" he said, scanning the charge sheet.

"Who got into bad company," Jones agreed.

He was driving three other guys at two in the morning and there were three pistols in the passenger cabin of the car and an S&W Model 76 submachine gun in the trunk. That was a copy of the Swedish K, created when the Swedish government embargoed all arms sales to US security forces.

It was a very solid piece of kit. Haskell had always preferred it to the short-barreled M16s they were issuing the Army. He didn't say that, though, because Jones and the others thought—and frequently said—that the Volunteers on the border had been a gang of undisciplined thugs who should never have been taken into the regular Army. Having opinions about hardware was one of the things that showed the Joneses of the world that Haskell was not their sort.

He didn't take bribes to ignore security breaches either. He drove an old Focus.

Haskell nodded to Jawicki and opened the door to the interrogation room. "Good morning, Mr. Lang," he said to the stocky man bent over the room's card table.

"You supposed to make me think you're the good cop because you're friendly?" Lang snarled.

Haskell shrugged. He set his pot of ointment on the table. Supposedly the pots were identical and filled from the same vat. Maybe that was so, but Haskell had had good luck from this one so he kept using it.

"I don't guess any cop's a good one to you," Haskell said. He took the top off the ointment jar. "Are they?"

"What the hell do you want me to say?" Lang said. "That I'm a leader of the Constitutionalists and hate all cops?"

"Hey, that'd be great and I bet it'd get me a promotion!" Haskell said. He put on the headset on his side of the table. The fine wire pickups were woven into the soft black fabric. "Only—I gotta admit that I don't trust the source. Folks like you and me, Lang, just aren't leader types.

"Here, put your cap on," Haskell said, poking the other skullcap a little closer to Lang's side of the table with his index finger. He then withdrew his finger and stabbed it into the ointment.

"What's that?" Lang asked.

"Drugs," said Haskell. "It boosts empathy and makes me feel warm all over." A warm feeling did start to spread up his right arm. "Jones talked to you last night, didn't he? The lieutenant on duty last night. He was using it too."

Haskell stretched and added, "You know, with enough of the ointment I feel that I can really fly. I can't, though, dammit. Now put your cap on. If you don't I'll have Jawicki and a few of his pongos put you in restraints. That won't matter to me"—not completely true because pain scrambled the subject's impressions—"but it'll sure be hard on you."

"You say the other guy was using drugs too?" Lang said. "He didn't do that." Lang waggled a finger toward Haskell's ointment pot.

"Here, hold my hand," Haskell said, reaching both hands across the table. He thought he'd seen something. He needed touch to be sure, though.

It was a moment before Lang reached across the table in turn but he did when he realized there was no gimmick, or rather that it wasn't one he recognized. Haskell squeezed his hands lightly and felt the thumb calluses, then let Lang's hands go.

"You got some of that gunk on me!" Lang said, feeling the greasiness of the contact.

"Not much," Haskell said nonchalantly. He pushed the ointment pot across the table. "Here, you can take more if you like."

Lang drew back as Haskell expected, but he put his cap on. Haskell relaxed. "Jones uses the drug," he said, "but he's the sort of pussy who wouldn't admit it. You've run into the sort yourself, I'll bet. Getting down and actually *doing* the work is kinda beneath them."

"I've met the sort you mean," Lang agreed.

"Look," Haskell said. "I'm at least getting paid for my time, but we're both stuck here till you give me something big like a weapons cache."

"Fat chance that," Lang said, and Haskell got a vivid flash of the entrance to the Bank of America building in the center of Chapel Hill.

"Yeah, that's what I figured," Haskell said. "Do you spend much time in downtown Chapel Hill?"

"Some, I suppose," Lang said doubtfully. "I've got clients there and sometimes I run files back instead of shipping them. Why?"

"Message from above," Haskell lied, cueing the backroom boys. They were actually the floor above in this installation. They could have been anywhere on the east coast, but there usually wasn't a time lag to notice.

The monitor on the wall to Haskell's right obediently glowed with an image of the 100 block of Franklin from the Columbia intersection.

"What's that?" Lang demanded in concern. His mental impression took on a reddish tinge.

"Just what I told you," Haskell said. "The brass want us to walk through the downtown."

"Walk?" Lang repeated in puzzlement.

The image on the monitor began to trundle down the sidewalk on the north side of the street. Pedestrians sometimes paused and stared but nobody interfered. The robotic viewpoint was obviously a security operation. Haskell wondered when the footage has been captured. The image went into the bank building.

"Well, virtually," Haskell said. "The real legwork was done by robots. Here, give me your hand—it'll make it steadier."

He reached his left hand across the table while continuing to keep his eyes on the monitor. After a moment Lang reached over and touched him. The backroom crew imposed a stabilizer on the advancing image. That was good work on their part and would net them a bottle of whiskey when Haskell learned what their taste was.

The image entered the elevator and stopped on the top floor. It rolled into the hallway. "Which way do we go from here?" Haskell asked.

"Any way you please," Lang said. "City Planning is two doors to the right if that's what you mean. It's a year since I been there."

Haskell got mental images that weren't frequent or vivid as the imagery ran on the monitor, so that was probably true. Haskell had an idea. "Say, I need to take a leak. Do you want coffee or a Coke or something?"

"Yeah, a Coke," Lang said, "and a glass of water. How long's this going to go on?"

"Till you tell me where the district arms cache is," Haskell said.

"You'll have to talk to a Con about that," Lang said. "I'm an accountant."

"Well, I'll be right back," Haskell said. "The robot can wait where it is."

The monitor was paused at the door that said CITY PLANNING ASSOCIATES on the frosted glass. Haskell did get a faint memory of the door swinging open and a small woman with brown hair at the reception desk, but it was very faint. It probably had been a year since Lang had been to this door.

Haskell dodged quickly past Jawicki. When the door closed on Lang he said to Jawicki, "Get me cup of water, will you? I'll take it in when I come back upstairs."

He went quickly down the back stairs, two at a time. The receptionist wasn't at his desk, but Haskell tapped lightly on the first sergeant's door and pushed it open. "Sarge," he said. "I need the guns they took with the new intake. I'm going to try a bit of theater."

Stokely was badly overweight and stepped slowly over to the gun safe. They didn't need or have a proper armory in this building, but Stokely should have locked the safe when there were guns in it. He hadn't bothered.

It struck Haskell that the sergeant's hostility was more because Haskell was fit than because he'd entered as a Volunteer and became an officer for political reliability. Haskell ran up and down stairs as a matter of course.

"Be careful of these," Stokely said. "I haven't had time to unload them yet."

"No problem," Haskell said, lifting out the submachine gun. "That's better for me anyway."

Two of the service pistols were out of their slots already. One would be Jawicki's; the other seemed to be Jones', which would be unlikely.

Haskell went back upstairs, one step at a time. He didn't want to slip holding a loaded submachine gun. Stokely had had plenty of time to unload the magazine, but that would have required him giving a shit about his job. Haskell paused at the drinks machine and got a Coke.

Jawicki was holding a cup of water and did well not to spill it when he jumped up on seeing the submachine gun. "I'll take the water in if you'll get the door," Haskell said as he took the cup and stepped back to give room for the door to open. Jawicki leaned sideways, apparently to stay farther from the gun.

Haskell set the coffee on the far side of the table, and plugged his headset back into the integrator. He set the gun down on his side, sliding the ointment pot clear.

"What's that in aid of?" Lang asked, nodding toward the gun.

"I was wondering that myself," Haskell said. "Who were you going to shoot with it?"

He pressed in the magazine release and pulled the magazine out of the well. It was full or next to it—thirty-six rounds. He got a mental flash from Lang involving a man in uniform beyond the muzzle. There was a garage door on the other side of the target with splashes of blood on it from through penetrations.

Haskell remembered the last time he'd carried a Swedish K. He was in a blocking position on the potential retreat of a large convoy of border crossers. One truck toward the end of the convoy started to break away before the head of the column reached the interdiction force proper when shooting broke out to the north. The officer in charge of the blocking force ordered lights on and the breakaway truck hit its brakes in a spew of sand and grit.

Haskell dismounted and went running up to the cab of the

vehicle. The passenger got out and stared at Haskell like a bunny in the headlights. His hand came out from behind his back holding a revolver. He triggered two rounds. The propellant made yellow blooms in the night. Haskell skidded to a halt, shocked beyond words, and fired a three-round burst into the crosser's chest, flinging him back against the truck.

Lang's memory was for later study of back files but no concern of the immediate present. Haskell's memory wasn't even that, except maybe at three in the morning.

"I don't know anything about that," Lang said. "We're just going dancing. The clubs in Greensboro you'd be undressed if you didn't have a gun."

"Well, we won't worry about that now," Haskell said. He pressed in the receiver cap to release the catch, then rotated the cap off to the left. He set the bolt and operating spring on the table with the magazine to keep them from rolling off the edge.

"What are you doing?" Lang demanded.

"Did you have a client on this floor?" Haskell asked.

"No," said Lang, "but there was a dentist on the second floor of the front section of the building. I don't know what his politics are. Maybe he's a Con but I don't know."

Lang looked away from the monitor. "No more clients down here?" Haskell said, touching a hand control to pause the advance.

Lang looked up by reflex. As he did, Haskell saw a door marked 41 in Lang's mind.

"No," Lang said. "The dentist was in 24 at the front."

"Well. We'll go down to that now and then we'll knock off," Haskell said. "Sure you wouldn't like to get me promoted by handing me an arms cache? We grunts gotta stick together, don't we?"

"I'm an accountant," Lang said in a weary tone.

The image on the monitor went back to the staircase with Haskell getting another mental flash but number 41 wasn't visible this time. There was a stutter on the image as the editing program broke the continuity of the robot's actual course.

Haskell's fingers reassembled the submachine gun while the monitor ran along the second-floor hallway. There were no further flashes of memory from Lang. At the closed door of office 24 the images stopped.

Haskell stood up. "Guess we can call it a day," he said.

"Don't ye want to go into the dentist's office?" Lang said, gesturing toward the monitor paused outside the door to suite 24.

"I don't guess we'd find an arms cache there," Haskell said. "Do you?"

He got another flash of the door of room 41 in the rear tower. Lang obviously didn't realize how sensitive the psychic pickup was. Or could be: Jones hadn't gotten anything useful. But of course Jones had been treating Lang as an accountant. He might be that too, but Haskell had recognized right off that Lang was a man who had calluses from regularly loading the magazines of submachine guns.

Haskell nodded to Jawicki when he went by. "He can go back to the holding cells," he said. "Don't let him go yet, though."

Lang probably didn't realize how much he'd given up, so there wasn't the problem of him warning his associates of what to hide before a team came to pick up the cache. Even so they needed to move fast. He went downstairs again and said to Sergeant Stokely— the receptionist still wasn't at his desk but the first sergeant hadn't gone back to his own office—"I gotta tell the colonel something," and tapped on Milner's door. It was a moment before Haskell heard what he took for a meaningful grunt from inside.

He opened the door. Colonel Milner was over forty and had an extremely high forehead which implied he'd be bald as a cue ball within ten years. Haskell transferred the submachine gun to his left hand and saluted.

"What do you want, Haskell?" Milner said. He rotated the flat-screen monitor in front of him so that they could look at each other without him craning his neck over it.

"I got something from Lang who they picked up this morning," Haskell said. "I think a raid on room 41 of the Bank of America building will pick up an arms cache!"

"You're sure of that?" the colonel said, rotating the monitor back so that he could see the screen again. He tapped the location into his keyboard. "Jones said Lang was nonresponsive."

"Jones thought Lang was white collar like himself," Haskell said. "He was a shooter, and I treated him like that."

He lifted the gun in his left hand. "We need to move fast, though. Have they figured out a target for Lang and his buddies yet?"

"One of the men last night flashed on a picture of the mayor of Greensboro," Milner said. "He's been getting a lot of notice since the Public Order department replaced the elected mayor and put him in, so it may just be him being in the news."

"The guys who worked on the rest of Lang's crew last night should've done better," Haskell said. "Well, when they hear we've turned the arms cache they may fall over themselves to talk. How quick can we hit room 41?"

"You're getting ahead of yourself, Lieutenant," Milner said. "I don't even know if there's a Direct Action team free."

"Hell," Haskell said. "We can do this with the office staff and I'll lead them myself. I suspect I can borrow a suit of body armor from the cops—and I don't need a gun since I've got this one."

He waved the Model 76 again.

"That would be very irregular," Milner said, which from him was the kiss of death. "Remember, you're not a Volunteer anymore."

Not bloody likely to forget that, Haskell thought. He'd thought of the arms cache as a real coup that would set him up for a promotion. But not from Milner. Haskell was going to be lucky if he didn't wind up being punished after the way he'd screwed up by pushing the colonel—but he'd been excited and sure that Milner would be excited too.

Haskell had been proud to be offered a regular commission. The pay was better and there was room for real promotion.

But not for such as Baird Haskell. If he'd stayed a Volunteer sergeant in Arizona, he'd have been working with people who had the same priorities as he had—doing the fucking job. Keeping America safe for American citizens.

He hadn't seen any sign of disloyalty in the regulars—though that might have been because they watched what they said around him. Making America great again was a joke rather than a motto, at least in the Chapel Hill office. And back in Arizona Lucy wouldn't have been complaining about the weather and mold growing on the cabinet doors.

Though she'd have found something.

Colonel Milner had been scrolling down his monitor. Now he stopped and said, "Well, you're in luck, Lieutenant. Raleigh has a team free early this afternoon. Is that soon enough for you?"

"I'm sure that will be fine, sir," Haskell said.

Actually he wasn't sure. Just the fact that the hit squad had been picked up should have been reason for the Constitutionalists to empty out any place that the men arrested knew about. But maybe they'd give it a wide berth until the Direct Action team from Raleigh got the lead out.

Haskell didn't repeat his offer to lead an immediate raid. It had probably been a bad idea anyway. There were a lot of things that could go wrong when you gave guns to people who didn't ordinarily use them—and weren't used to acting as a team. It was probably good that Milner had squashed the idea.

"Look, Haskell," the colonel said, "if you're right about this arms cache, it was a nice piece of work. Why don't you take the rest of the day off? But be aware, if it turns out you've been bullshitting, you'll pay every hour back!"

"Yessir!" Haskell said and threw a salute. He backed out and went straight to the parking lot. As he reached his Focus, he realized he was still holding the submachine gun in his left hand. Rather than going inside and returning the gun to Sergeant Stokely, he opened the car's back door and laid the gun on the floor of the back seat. He'd carry it into the house, then put it in the gun safe when he went to work in the morning.

He saw Lieutenant Jones' Lotus parked in front of the Haskell house when he turned the corner onto his own street. *What the hell's he doing here?* Haskell thought. Jones was about the last person in the world he wanted to spend time with right now.

He pulled into the yard beside the driveway. Lucy's Chevy was in the carport so he left her room to back out.

He got out of the Focus and walked around to the passenger side to take the submachine gun through the door rather than try to fumble it out between the seats. As Haskell did so, the door from the kitchen onto the carport opened and Lucy stuck her head out.

Haskell waved. Instead of speaking, Lucy pulled the door shut with a bang.

Haskell wasn't surprised that Lucy was in a pissy mood—not after seven years of marriage—but this was a little extreme. "Robert, he's got a gun!" she shouted from inside.

The kitchen door opened again.

This time Lieutenant Jones stepped out, holding his service pistol. He pointed the Beretta at Haskell from fifteen feet away and fired. It was probably the first time since training that he'd fired the gun.

Haskell racked back the bolt of his submachine gun and put a three-round burst into Jones' center of mass.

THE HANDYMAN
T.C. McCarthy

Part of the Machine. Jed pulled himself from a burning semitruck, the fire igniting imaginary nerve endings with pain so real that he woke up screaming. He slapped his legs with both hands before realizing it had been a nightmare. Metals in his artificial limbs reflected dim emergency lighting at the same time black plastic parts absorbed everything, sucked on the red-tinged air to become an even deeper void that threatened to put him into a trance. He moved his right leg first, its knee servos whining and clicking.

His mind wandered back to the nightmare. Jed's semi-truck's AI driver had slammed their tanker into the concrete supports of an overpass before he'd been able to hit the override button, and flames of his imagination licked the bed around him until he blinked and kept his eyes shut, forcing the memory to fade. A smell of burning metal lingered. At first Jed thought it was phantom sensory input, a leftover fragment of a dream, until the smell got strong enough to force his eyes open.

"What the hell is going on?" he asked.

When the base's AI didn't answer, Jed yelled out again. "Hey! *I said* what's going on? Why'd you silicon asswipes thaw me out? Something your bots can't handle?"

He slid from the recovery bed where Jed's artificial feet touched rock, the sensation close to what cold *should* feel like, but just a bit off. Artificial muscle-cables thrummed when they took the rest of his weight. After being asleep for so long, and without the need for his legs, the neural links had gotten crusty with time and it felt like being part of a series of neglected cogs, each tooth forced to turn despite the fact they'd long since fused together with rust. Time and disregard, he thought; a weakness ignored by all major system developers. The original promise of "humans in the loop," an increased assurance of safety, had all but disappeared. Corporations rarely bothered anymore. It had created new industries for the southern unemployed, boiled peanuts on the roadside next to fruit stands, retreaded-tire boutiques, and backyard emporiums filled with Greek statues and concrete birdfeeders. *Keep them fed. Keep them dreaming.* Corporate governance had reduced everything to the new redneck goal: a syrupy beef stock of Jim Beam and meth, which simmered over low heat fueled by the soft hiss of silicon-based ad strategies. *Keep them stupid. Keep them drugged.*

Jed was about to admit it: the artificial pieces of his existence gave him value in the modern world, just like Marines now on ice in hibernation—hundreds of men and women, their brains transplanted into alloy combat shells, their bodies in cryosleep back on Earth to be returned at the end of a twenty-year enlistment. *Cogs frozen for years.* The iron of his mental gears turned slowly and creaked. His psyche groaned against the glue of disuse, finally snapping free, its movement becoming slick and unimpeded.

"Goddamned robots and artificials. I should be fishing off Beaufort right now and getting hellish drunk."

Jed shuffled to the far wall and pulled a handy-rig from a rack. Half pressure suit, half jumpsuit, the thing was bulky and armored where it counted—around the arms, legs, and torso—but with tools and special high-dexterity gloves that hung from its belt. The gauntlets could be rapidly attached and detached if needed. Jed struggled to connect the metabolic waste tubing at the same time he prayed that whatever had gone wrong, it didn't involve going outside. He'd only been on the lunar surface once and that was enough. No trees. No swamps. No sound of crickets or frogs. The Moon offered infinite gray upon gray upon white, coupled with a cold silence that made Jed think of an arctic wasteland.

He snapped a blaze yellow (the color of maintenance personnel) helmet in place and switched on suit systems.

"Link with the goddamned network. Now."

"Main network not available," the suit said. A heads-up flashed into place against his clear faceplate, where Jed watched multiple attempts to connect, each one ending in failure. "And harsh language is not permitted on this system."

"So fire me and send my ass back to Earth. Why isn't the network available?" he asked.

"No indication of radio signals. Hard connection recommended."

"This place is walking on a serious slant. Keep scanning for a signal. Any signal."

"There is nothing wrong with the floor angle in your area, maintenance worker five-four-seven—"

"Shut the hell up, you transistored piece of . . . it was just an expression."

Jed was about to move to the exit when he noticed a mist blowing from the nearest vent. He stepped closer and yanked off his helmet. Now the smell of burning metal mixed with something beneath it— an odor of cooking flesh, the only source of which was gray matter from Marine combat frames that should have been frozen. He put the helmet on and sealed it again, holding his breath until he was sure that his suit had filled with clean air.

Breathe in . . .

"What in the goddamned hell happened?"

Jed bounded in low gravity toward the recovery room's door and collided with it when someone opened the portal from the opposite side, sending him flying to land on the floor. He slid up against the nearest bed.

Breathe out . . .

A robot skittered in, its C-2 pod—a sphere of black clustered sensors—staring with smoky glass. Marine combat bots resembled massive insects that moved in the Moon's gravity in a half crawl, half fly whenever they bounced and puffed gas jets to move them forward. They slid at the same time they walked and Jed shivered at the realization that any one of them could turn him into a lump of raw hamburger in less than a second. *I hate bugs*, he thought, and shivered at the sight of one so close up.

"Samuel Wallace Bickerton," it said.

"I go by Jed. Who the hell are you and how long was I under?"

"You've been in cryosleep at Lunar outpost seven-two-three for three years. Human units refer to me by my serial number's final three letters: K-one-five."

Jed stood and bounced closer to the door, trying to skirt the robot. "What's wrong? Why was I woken up and where's the foreman—the rest of the physical plant team? Who's burning the Marine combat frames?"

"Maintenance personnel are all dead. Most of the maintenance robots inactive. Of the thousand Marines forward deployed, all are dead or trapped under debris. Portions of the base burned until full oxygen depletion. Only this section still has pressure integrity. Cryo often prevents full memory recovery at first; do you know where you are and the systems training you received before sleep?"

Memories flooded in. One moment there had been a pressure inside his skull that kept them at bay, but the robot's words relieved it to create a vacuum that allowed everything to crash back in—colors and words swirling with images and plans where lines of communication overlay everything. *Breathe in*, Jed reminded himself, *you're three hundred meters below the surface*. He was the only one awake, once again the human in the loop, the weight of which made his heart race at the same time his breath became ragged and fast when the memory of a friend locked in place, his face burning into Jed's gray matter.

"What about Ike? His full name is Michael Cook. Maintenance and vehicle operations, outpost seven-two-four."

"I have no data on that outpost's current status or of that individual. The last scans indicated that Russian missiles had been targeted for all lunar bases, including seven-two-four."

"Russian missiles? And this is the only section with pressure and atmosphere?"

"Correct. And without communications we do not have data on why the Russians went on the offensive."

"One second," Jed said.

He snapped his helmet off again and began digging into a large pouch that hung from his belt, finally finding it: a round tin and a small bottle of bourbon. Jed grinned. He broke the cap from the bottle and drained the contents, tilting his head back and pouring it down his throat before he opened the tin and pinched at dark contents; *this was the stuff*—calmness in a tin, a puck of minced tobacco that promised everything. Memories would come with it at the same time his nerves would stop screaming in the agony of withdrawal, images of long hauls across Middle America and the boredom of being a useless add-on to the ass-end of some mega-smart, computer-driven hunk of steel on wheels. He stuffed a wad of it into his lip, replaced the tin in his pouch and threw the empty bourbon bottle against the wall where it shattered, the pieces drifting downward in light gravity.

"Now I'm ready." Jed secured his helmet and locked his gloves in place. "Let's go, K-fifteen."

"Alcohol is prohibited on base."

"That wasn't alcohol. It was Jim Beam."

"Nicotine products are also prohibited, including chewing tobacco. How will you spit if we enter depressurized areas?"

Jed shook his head. "Wrong again, metal nuts. It's snuff. Completely different beast. And I don't need to spit; I've been doing this long before they even cast the alloys used to shape your tin ass."

"I do not have an ass. How did you get this material past inspection, before they shipped your equipment to the base?"

"One thing you learn when packing semis for the long hauls, C-2: how to hide the things you'll need to fight the boredom of passing cornfield after cornfield." Jed pushed the button and watched the door swing open again, this time dodging it. "Get your ass in gear. We're going to lunar base seven-two-four and see if Ike is still alive."

Black smoke billowed over Jed's head, a boiling mass that reminded him of angry thunder clouds that stuck to the ceiling and searched for a way to escape. *Breathe in.* The nicotine hit his nerve endings, relaxing muscles and grinding down sharp edges of his psyche so that now Jed rode a tepid wave of mediocre fortune. The white-paneled medical recovery room gave way to walls of dark rock. Carved into frozen magma, the corridor had been shaped into a perfect cylinder with red emergency lights making the walls look like a black pipe to hell's inner sanctum, a massive sewer through which God's refuse would one day flush. Another wave of smoke billowed toward Jed. He ducked as low as he could, doing his best to keep from bouncing too high at the same time he tried to remember what he'd learned about the base layout. Smoke soon made everything dark. Jed waved his arms to try and clear it but the gesture was futile and he slammed into a bulkhead that blocked the way forward with a solid steel wall.

The bot moved in beside him. "Emergency bulkheads dropped to maintain an atmosphere in the portions of the base still habitable. This includes main life support. The few active maintenance bots extinguished the fires there but air-pump filters have failed and smoke is getting through."

"How we get from here to the vehicle bay?"

"Mister Jed—"

"It's Jed, K. Just Jed."

"There are over twenty Marines still in cryo. Alive but trapped since the access tunnels have all collapsed. Based on my orders and regulations, your priority is to free these men, thaw them, and make sure we're prepared for any follow-on assaults."

Jed shook his head. "*Your* orders. They're not mine."

"Marine Corps regulations are clear on this, not to mention procedures in the USMC Field Manual on Low-G Lunar Combat Operations: missile attack will likely be followed by troop assault, and bases are to prepare defenses accordingly."

Jed kicked the bot before thinking, and instantly realized his mistake; his metal foot sent an artificial pain signal, so at first Jed imagined he'd broken a toe at the same time he drifted upward into the smoke and banged his helmet on the tunnel's ceiling.

"Are you injured?" K-15 asked.

"Of course I'm not, you metal jackass; I'm almost as artificial as you. And those're your rules and procedures. Not mine. I *can* read, you know. Just because I talk like this doesn't mean I'm a moron."

"So you've read the Field Manuals."

"No," said Jed. "*Because I'm not a Marine.* I'm a civilian contractor operating under 2025 Federal Acquisition Regulations and Midas Corp's statement of work."

"I am unfamiliar with these documents. And we've lost access to networks so I can't examine them."

"Here." Jed reached into a leg pocket and pulled out a tattered document, tossing it to float downward. "My statement of work. *In the event of outbreak of hostilities, during which the base suffers catastrophic damage unrepairable by Midas maintenance contractors, Midas personnel are relieved of all obligations.* All Midas assets, including artificially augmented personnel are to extract and return to Earth as soon as possible. Paragraph eighty-three, section C."

K-15 rotated its command pod and angled it downward to stare at the papers, then rotated back to look at Jed. "These documents don't matter to me. I cannot go with you to seven-two-four. My orders are clear: I am to save these men the same way I saved you."

"Are the surviving Marines still connected to main life support? Are they still powered?"

"Affirmative."

"So the fact that they're trapped means nothing. They can survive."

"Correct. For approximately thirty-one days until backup battery systems fail."

Jed swallowed nicotine, which burned his throat at the same time he savored another wave of relaxation.

"Hell. Go with me to seven-two-four to save Ike, K. If we find out he's dead, or as soon as we rescue him, we return to get these Marines out from under all this crap. They'll keep until then. If the Russians attack in force there's not much you and twenty cybernetic combat frames can do anyway."

Jed felt the robot think. His external mics picked up the creaking of metal as the bulkhead wall before them expanded against surrounding rock and he tried to imagine the wreckage its steel barrier hid. What if they'd been nuclear-tipped missiles? He recalled the quick training he'd gotten just before going under into deep freeze, the terms used to describe radiation exposure making his brain hurt as he tried to understand what he remembered. For now his suit's integrated rad detectors registered normal background, a dim green light indicating there was nothing.

"I find the terms acceptable," the bot said.

"I thought you had to follow orders no matter what."

"I am allowed a degree of autonomy. Follow me."

The bot rotated its sphere so it faced the tunnel ceiling, where a portion of rock rotated and then shifted upward with a hiss. It swung out of the way. A dark hole formed at the same time a cloud of black smoke pulsed out, enveloping them both in soot that reminded Jed of a sermon from his childhood, a vision of the apocalypse where lions breathed smoke from their tails; his skin tingled with anticipation while waiting for the cloud to dissipate. Once it thinned he watched K-15 disappear like a wolf spider climbing into its lair where the darkness hid it except for a single red light that blinked when it spoke.

"This way."

"Okay, K," said Jed, "I'm coming. Hold your metal freaking horses."

He flexed his legs and propelled himself upward, the darkness wrapping him in a blanket of lightlessness and carbon dust so that the white fabric of his suit disappeared in a layer of charcoal black. Jed closed his eyes. He imagined himself hidden in the night-born arms of an angel, which whispered in his ears that death was all around and waiting, sure that within hours Jed would be one with the dust of lunar rock smashed into fine powder by thousands of meteors. The door shut beneath him, closing off the dim red emergency lighting and submerging him into a cramped world. Here, he thought, only rock and blackness existed.

"I can't see, K," he said. "Not even with infrared or light amp."

"My sensors can chart through over two thousand obscurant types. I can see you. We are in the main lunar base ducting network, but in a few moments I will override the safeties that sealed it off from damaged portions of the base. We will be in vacuum with only radio communications. Snap on your gauntlets, Mr. Jed."

"If you're going to break the emergency seals, why not go through the main tunnels? Why the air ducts?"

"All main tunnels between here and the rover bay are collapsed and impassible. You and I are the only active units in this portion of the base and I've been waiting for you to thaw before breaking seals."

Jed thought for a moment, a wave of fear welling up from his gut. "How did you save me?"

"Prior to full base depressurization, I was able to initiate thawing and disconnect you from systems. As soon as I dragged you to the recovery room emergency seals activated and the maintenance cryo bay collapsed."

Jed collided with the bot and cursed. "Tell me when you stop; I can't see a thing."

"Apologies, Mr. Jed." K-15's voice crackled over the radio. "Overriding emergency seals now."

The blackness evaporated in an instant, sucked out into the Moon's vacuum. Jed peered over the bot's form. He squinted at a circle of light where, a hundred yards ahead, one side of the duct had given way; a jagged hole in the rock opened onto what should have been the lunar base's main structural core of facilities, but which now was an open space where he saw the opposite side of a massive, kilometer-wide vertical cylinder bored down into rock. The pair moved closer. Jed hugged the left wall, the hole to his right, and he looked onto what was once the base; rings of steel girders protruded at regular intervals from the cylindrical walls, marking the locations of where floors had once been. A pile of rubble sat at the bottom. Jed punched at his forearm controls to zoom, focusing on tiny gray dots that caught his eye, then fought the urge to vomit. He shuffled forward, putting the hole behind him. It was too late; the memory of half-burned gray matter—the organic remains of Marines that had spewed from the tangle of wrecked cryo units—had burrowed into his brain.

"They're down there," he said.

"What are down there?"

"Marines. The dead."

"Yes. I performed a count of the visible units as we passed. Seven hundred and sixty-five, only about twenty percent of those stationed here. The rest vaporized."

"K, how much of the combat frames are actual flesh and blood?" asked Jed. "The original person who signed up for service."

"The spinal cord and brain."

Jed mentally recoiled. *Who would sign up for service like that?* The thought of voluntarily separating from his body was inconceivable after years of only wanting back what had been taken from him in fire, and he closed his eyes, trying to banish the image of the dead. Maybe it was a good thing, he told himself. The wailing of those mourning the loss of children, offspring of the Marine Corps and the Moon, would be offset by the presence of something to bury on Earth—a real connection to the young and once-animated. Parents with one last look at children, frozen in time at the age of eighteen. It was better than having no body at all.

The bot opened another hatch in the ceiling and vanished upward. Jed followed. After climbing for what felt like hours they reached a space barely large enough to hold them both where K-15 waved one limb, using it to point toward an emergency access door ahead.

"We are at the rover bay."

Frogs. Jed had heard that some frogs would freeze in the winter, between life and death where their dreams were the one thing the frogs knew, the only thing keeping them tied to the world and its blankets of snow. Mankind had become like frogs, their armies frozen in winter ice until needed.

"We're just like them," Jed grunted. "Just like animals."

He moved after K-15. A snow of white moondust had coated everything in the deep freeze of vacuum, forming drifts that sloped from the edge of a crater and cascaded over a bank of rover units. Jed bounded after the bot and squinted in bright sunlight before the auto-filters darkened his faceplate. He shivered at the thought of being frozen again and did his best to ignore the vision of a small Earth overhead, knowing that if he looked up, the urge to go home would lock his metal legs with the glue of uncertainty. He scrambled into the cab of a rover and waited for K-15 to climb on.

"Why you riding up top? There's room in the cab."

"This is the only rover not immobilized from the collapse and it's unarmored. I can defend from up here."

"You think we'll be attacked?"

"It is likely. Systems detected multiple missiles that failed to detonate and which broke up in a manner inconsistent with decoys or chaff. What we know of Russian doctrine indicates these were likely warbots, missile-delivered."

"K, do you have any fucking good news?"

"No."

Jed hit the throttle. The rover paused at first, then leapt forward to bound over a hump of rock and fly airborne for several seconds before digging into the dust and drifts, stuttering its way up a steep incline. They went flying again after hitting a line of rock at the crater lip, the rover landing with a thud.

"You will damage the axles if you continue driving aggressively."

"Have you ever driven off-road?"

"It's a standard capability."

"That's not what I asked. Have you ever driven off-road—on Earth or here on the Moon?"

"No need. Artificial units drive rovers only in cases where no Marines are capable due to their injuries. Combat units such as I have no need for rovers; we have onboard propulsion."

"Hell. You might not have a need, but I do. My pickup and I have a special relationship. All I need from you is the direction to Ike's base; otherwise shut the fuck up about my driving."

A red arrow appeared on Jed's heads-up; he navigated around the crater rim until the arrow centered in his faceplate and shifted to a small crosshair.

"At current speed, your ETA is twenty minutes."

The tobacco spent, Jed spit it out so a lump of black particles fell through the suit's neck ring and settled against his chest. "Good. That's less than the distance between my house in South Carolina and Augusta, Georgia."

"What are the coordinates of your house, Jed?"

"Hell; I don't know the *coordinates* of my house, you whacked-out metal bitch; you just keep looking for Russians while I drive."

Before long, Jed's amazement at the scenery turned to boredom. He missed the color green. A constant gray assaulted his senses with an overwhelming sensation of emptiness, its attack unrelenting with a lack of variation except in shades. An occasional black basalt or white knot of plagioclase broke it up. But greens were nowhere to be found. What was it about that color? he wondered. First the thought of hibernating frogs and now the memory of kudzu, draped like a canopy of extinction over long-dead trees. That was the first thing he'd do once this was over: drive the road between his place and the city, where he'd stop to put in another dip and just stare at all the green.

A twinkle to the right caught his eye, but before he could say anything the bot radioed in.

"Contact bearing three-three degrees. Russian comms detected."

"Bots?" Jed asked.

"Confirmed. With their current heading and speed, and assuming a standard Russian combat load-out, they'll be in range within ten seconds."

Jed's mind raced and he glanced at the pressure indicator before unlocking his helmet and tossing it to the seat beside him. He grabbed another bottle from his pouch and drained it. As the whiskey burned his throat he floored the throttle and began pounding the steering wheel to urge the rover onward.

"Incoming grenade fire, Jed."

"Goddamn it!"

"I recommend you turn left—gently so we don't spill over."

Jed spun the wheel. At this speed the four wheels on the left side lifted from the lunar surface and he felt the uneasy sensation that the rover was on the verge of rolling before it finally tipped in the opposite direction, the massive tires banging to the ground. With a free hand he grabbed another pinch of his chewing tobacco, forcing it into his lip before fumbling to snap his helmet back on. He'd just locked it in place when the grenades started detonating. Fragments of metal pinged the side of the rover and Jed flinched when the glass to his right shattered, sending a white mist out through the broken window when the cab lost its atmosphere. Red streaks flashed out from K-15, above. Jed watched as his bot's response detonated in the distance and he smiled at a direct hit; a Russian bot's magazine detonated in a white cloud of sparks.

"Those're some great fireworks, K. Keep 'em coming."

"The cab lost pressure. Are you injured?"

The rover went airborne for a brief moment, then slammed into the bottom of a shallow crater so that Jed grunted at the impact.

"Not yet, metal nuts."

"In thirty seconds they'll be in range for primary projectile weapons. They fire two-thousand fléchette rounds per minute; I anticipate loss of this vehicle once they open fire."

"You know what the strangest thing about this is?" asked Jed.

"I do not understand the question."

"The silence. I thought war was supposed to be loud. Violent. But there's nothing of that here, no sensation that anything at all is going on except for the light show; everything else is quiet."

"The rover sensors are picking up something, Jed."

"What?"

"Its signature suggests—"

A brilliant glare erupted from the direction of the oncoming Russian attackers. Then another. Jed's filters went so dark that it almost blinded him and he squinted to stay on track, keeping the rover in a gentle left turn; by now they were far off course.

"The Russians are in retreat," K-15 radioed.

"What did you shoot at them?"

"It wasn't me, Jed. One of the launch bases must have had a shuttle that survived; it just fired rockets. Get back on course and maintain top speed. The Russians may return."

"Copy. Hey, titanium dick, I have a question: how's a guy supposed to drink when I'm suited up and driving at the same time?"

"Your suit is equipped with a drinking tube but I advise against it, Jed. The danger of an accident is too high."

"Bullshit."

Jed gritted his teeth, ignoring the fact that he'd just swallowed a good portion of his tobacco. He lifted his left knee to brace the steering wheel. Jed grabbed another bottle of Jim Beam and cracked the top off, then angled it so a small tube near the bottom front of his helmet extended, touched the whiskey inside, and then kept extending until it bottomed out. Jed tongued a button inside his helmet; a moment later he pulled on a straw near his chin and grinned, swallowing loudly.

"Are you consuming alcohol, Jed?"

"Yep. *Ah...*"

"We could be in combat at any moment and you're driving a fully laden rover at fifty kilometers per hour over uneven terrain. Cease now or I'll override controls."

Jed finished the small bottle and tossed it onto the floor. "You got it, quartz brains. We're almost there, anyway; I think that's the crater up ahead."

A massive wall of rock formed in the distance. Jed's crosshair rested on a low peak at its center and he eased back the throttle so the rover slowed. His distance indicator ticked down from two hundred meters to fifty before the rover rolled to a stop, at which point Jed popped the driver's side door and jumped to the dusty surface.

Jed crept forward. He and the bot navigated their way through gray boulders, inching their way up to the crater lip. By now his suit had turned black. Soot from the burning base had coated the once white surface in black upon black, which camouflaged him perfectly in shadows.

Ike had taught him to duck hunt and had always picked Jed up at 3:00 A.M., in darkness and heavy camouflage because the birds' eyesight was so sharp, they could pick up on anything out of place. Water from the Phinizy always stayed warm through the season— rank and slippery over a matrix of goo and refuse; Jed recalled how he'd never gotten used to the nitrogen smell mixed with the stench of rot or the feeling of slime when he dipped a hand in, the decaying leftovers of animals and plants, maybe humans who'd been tossed in to decompose before other men noticed that they'd been murdered, or worse. Ike had told a story once of how the Phinizy was a favorite dumping ground for dead kids. Orphans. The ones out of St. Mary's Home for Bereaved Children and every other orphanage that sprang up once AI had taken over and parents started offing themselves by the bushel.

"Ike is alive," said K-15.

"What? How do you know?"

"I have partial net access. This lunar base wasn't fully destroyed and multiple maintenance bots are now working to restore network function to communicate with Earth."

"Where is he?" Jed asked, peering over the edge.

The base's massive cylinder descended beneath him into darkness now that the sun was at a lower angle, but it reminded him of a lamprey where smooth walls sprouted rings of girders in the shape of mangled teeth. He shifted to infrared, noting that the glowing rubble pile at the bottom was relatively close to the surface; only the topmost levels had been destroyed. A moment later his radiation alarms started blaring.

"Mother of turds," said Jed, scrambling back from the edge until the beeping quieted. "I'm cooked, K—*I'm irradiated and broiled from the inside out!*"

"Six hundred Marines are alive, Jed, along with your janitorial colleague; all in cryogenic stasis. And your dose was hardly enough to harm anyone."

"Wait a second. Who the hell are you calling *a janitor*?"

The bot turned its optical cluster to focus on Jed. "With network access I was able to access files on all of Midas Corporation's federal acquisition documentation. Your work class is listed as services, janitorial and waste disposal. If you connect to the net you'll find messages that arrived after you went under; you and Ike were downgraded and your salaries cut."

"Those sons of bitches," said Jed. "They're screwing me out of my salary and trade bonus?"

"It's all legal. Midas' contract scope was renegotiated due to impending hostilities; it included a role-shift clause in case of changes made during cryosleep. Did you not read it before signing?"

"Shut up. Just show me how to get to Ike and not get cooked."

"Follow me."

"Those motherfucking pirates," Jed mumbled to himself. "Corporate *always* gets you up the ass, K—you better read your agreement too."

The bot crawled around the crater's lip and kicked up dust that covered Jed's faceplate, forcing him to wipe it every so often. Jed's vision blurred with sweat. The whine of his leg servos filled his suit with a constant hum, which mixed with the exhaustion of stress and movement, taking him back to the cicadas and bugs of Clearwater Lake where the dam and abandoned catfish farm had been swallowed by weeds, kudzu digesting everything beneath a single green wave. Chirping sounds rode on Jed's brainwaves until the moonscape disappeared to be replaced by the shimmering summer heat over pond water. The urge to go home blossomed. It took root in the memory of cicadas and dirty water, sending vines through what remained of Jed's organic tissue until he realized that the moonscape had disappeared, replaced by the dark confines of a tunnel. Before them something moved in the shadows, scuttling forward.

"Where are we?" asked Jed. "What is that thing? And are you serious that Midas corporate cut my percentages?"

"We are in the access tunnel to main cryo storage and that is a Russian combat unit, which just sabotaged the life-support systems. Ike and the Marines are now dying." Jed started forward until the bot swung its rear leg, throwing him against the wall. "Take cover, *now.*"

Flames filled the tunnel. The Russian bot leaped forward while Jed cowered behind a girder, its thick steel curving upward in support of the tunnel at the same time it blocked the majority of chemical fire. Oxidizer and fuel mixed in midstream to form a combination of white light and colored sparks, a display that would have mesmerized him except for the fact that Jed screamed in terror. His suit temperature indicator climbed and a warning light blinked. Then the fire stopped; it went dark for a few moments before Jed realized the threat had disappeared, and he opened his eyes.

Jed peaked around the girder. "K?"

The two bots had locked in combat, their metal frames entangled in a battle for advantage, limbs swinging so fast that Jed almost couldn't see them; sparks flew when they made contact. Both robots fired fléchettes and grenades at each other. Jed ducked again behind the girder when a stream of tracer fléchettes walked their way toward him, ripping through the steel as if it was toilet paper.

"Go." K-15's voice crackled in his helmet. "Run for the cryo chamber or all the units will die, including Ike. You only have a few minutes, Samuel; I'll keep the Russian combat frame occupied. And yes; I'm serious that they changed your contract."

"*Are you insane?*" Jed screamed. "I just pissed all over my suit; my urine tube must have detached."

"There's no time, Samuel. *Now*. Go."

Jed leaped from cover and sprinted, forgetting the light gravity; he bounced close enough to K-15 that he kicked off its back, heading deeper into the tunnel. "I go by Jed, you goddamned *lawn mower!*"

When he reached the end of the corridor, a maintenance hatch slid open, twin slabs of thick steel that crept apart on roller tracks until Jed slid through and into a massive warehouse section. The chamber had been carved into black rock. It stretched off one side of the station's main vertical cylinder, a tube-shaped arm stacked from floor to ceiling with cryo units. Jed saw the flashing red lights; if the section had been pressurized, the alarm buzz would have been deafening.

"I'm in, K; now what do I do?" he radioed.

"Move through the chamber to the far end where it meets the main station. Maintenance bots are waiting on the far side of the door but can't open it. In one minute your friend and the Marine combat frames will be dead."

Jed kicked off the nearest cryo unit and bounded through the chamber, his helmet scraping against the ceiling with each step. He reached the far door where its panel hung from the wall, its wires yanked out to resemble colored spaghetti; Jed worked to reconnect them. His fingers flicked with muscle memory at the same time Jed fought back thoughts of Ike, not wanting the realization of his friend's imminent death to distract him. When the door eventually popped open, an army of small maintenance bots poured through and Jed slid to the floor, exhausted. He pulled out a whiskey bottle, using his straw to drain it. Jed repeated it until he ran out of bottles and couldn't see straight, the room spinning in a slow, creeping rotation. It took him a moment to realize that combat frames had been activated all around him, their vaguely human shapes making Jed shiver with disgust.

"The Russian unit is destroyed, Jed," K said over the radio. "Also, it appears that Ike will be fine. The bots pressurized the chamber and put him into a pressure suit. He's being moved to sick bay now and should wake within an hour."

"That's great, K. Thanks."

"What's wrong?"

"How long will I be stuck here, on the Moon?"

"It could be months, Jed. It depends on how long it takes to repel Russian forces; if we can't, and they defeat us, you'll likely perish here. Why?"

"I just drank all the Jim Beam in this suit and I think the rest of it got destroyed in the attack."

"At least Ike is alive, though."

"Screw Ike, K. I thought you got me—like we had a connection. This is a bigger problem than making sure Ike is okay."

"I'm sorry but I don't understand."

Jed sighed and pulled himself up off the floor; he swayed and almost fell, his leg servos whining erratically. "I was supposed to save some Jim Beam for Ike; half was his. He's gonna be pissed off like a demon when he comes to."

THE PINOCCHIO GAMBIT
Brad R. Torgersen

The tape over the left breast of my uniform pocket said U.S. SPACE FORCE. I still wasn't quite used to that. For the entirety of my career I'd had U.S. ARMY displayed there, going all the way back to the splotchy green-on-brown-on-black Battle Dress Uniforms I'd worn in Basic Combat Training. Like several other Army personnel who'd formerly worked in the ODIS program—ODIS being the acronym for the joint Air Force and Navy project technically known as the Orbital Defense Initiative Station—I was a rather new transferee to what was a rather new service under the Department of Defense. Everything in ODIS had been quickly rolled up within the Space Force, per presidential directive. And now the Space Force operated under the aegis of the Air Force, much as the Marine Corps operated under the aegis of the Navy. To include all of us proxy Operators.

Brigadier General McConnell—also newly assigned to the Space Force—sat at the head of the conference table, while a wall-sized screen opposite her showed a similar table of uniformed Space Force personnel on the other side of the country. McConnell had been my first boss at ODIS, back when she'd been a colonel. Hard to believe so much time had passed so quickly. I'd heard McConnell successfully scrolled for her second star, and now hoped to achieve a third before she retired.

But first came the Chinese problem, which had bedeviled us ever since I'd initially become involved as an ODIS exchange officer.

"Technically," McConnell said, "we've never been at war. Though everyone on this top secret call knows otherwise. We've lost people and equipment to the fight, and so has Beijing. None of which ever gets openly acknowledged by Washington, nor the Chinese Communist Party. But our funding within the Space Force is continually supplemented from 'black' budgets, which is a tacit acknowledgment by the secretary of defense that Operation Dark Falcon will continue to be prioritized. I've asked Chief Jaraczuk to sit in on this meeting. He and a Marine Corps warrant officer by the name of Stoddard were the first to put proxy combat capability to the test in an orbital environment. Now that the new shadow proxies are being tested, I want him and his experience put to good use."

All heads and eyes turned toward me. Internally, I felt a moment of panic. If this crowd was expecting some kind of tactical or strategic wizardry from me, I knew they were going to be disappointed. I'd not even managed to qualify for astronaut service, though Mavy Stoddard—my old friend from the ODIS days—had made it. I'd been unable to cope with zero-g in the astronaut examination process, while Mavy had sailed through. She'd done three missions in orbit, before finally retiring to teach at a local university near her home town in North Carolina.

Me, I'd licked my wounded ego for a short tour at the Pentagon—advising the secretary of the Army on space combat tactics—then gotten the hell out of D.C. the moment it had become convenient. The atmosphere at the Pentagon had made my skin crawl, and the secretary of the Army had quickly concluded—as no doubt the Space Force itself would also conclude—I was no genius when it came to employing proxies in an orbital fight against determined Chinese aggressors. My one and only act of space heroism had hardly been heroic. More like, desperate. And we'd lost an entire platform in the process, while also taking down a Chinese team determined to seize both the platform, and all the U.S. proxies on it—the latter being the fully robotic man-sized machines used by ODIS Operators, with the new stealth "shadow" units being our latest iteration.

I cleared my throat.

"Not sure I can offer anything earth-shattering," I said for all ears. "A few years ago I was just lucky enough to remember something from ODIS training which helped me keep Grissom Platform out of Beijing's hands. Not like that prevented them from eventually getting access to the technology which made both Grissom Platform and the original proxies possible. We've known they're using their own proxies now—have been using their own proxies for years. It never takes Beijing very long to catch up to, nor keep up with us. Mainly because they can usually buy whatever secrets they need on the international market. Half or more of our equipment isn't US-made anymore, and it doesn't take Beijing much effort to put the technology together in ways which mirror ours."

A little ripple of conversation went through the room on the other side of the top secret connection to our sister office in Florida. On that end, Brigadier General McConnell's boss was still trying to figure out how the remnants of ODIS——and the shadow proxies—fit into the bigger scheme of Space Force–crewed operations. There was plenty of hardware to go around, especially now that private enterprise down in Texas was making so much progress with its public Moon initiative. But there was speculation that Beijing was going to do everything in its power to thwart crewed US landings on the Moon before the end of the decade—be they private, or military.

"Don't be so modest, Chief," said Major General Dalton, sitting at the head of his own conference table on the screen. "Your bona fides speak for themselves. I know the Army couldn't necessarily make much use of your experience with ODIS, but now that you're Space Force officially, I think you'll find things will be a lot different. Everything you've done up to this point is going to be hugely influential on the Space Force's continued focus for remotely piloted operations, both near-Earth-orbit, and eventual lunar missions."

"If you know my record that well, sir," I said hesitantly, "then you also know I flunked the astronaut exam. Couldn't take it on the Vomit Comet. If the shadow proxies are going to be our edge on the Moon, proxies won't work on the lunar surface with more than half a second signal lag. You need Operators who can be on the Moon too, or at least be in lunar orbit, for that. Which crosses me off the list."

"We're not thinking of sending you to the Moon," the two-star said.

"I also can't offer any technical advice on shadow proxy development," I added. "I think General McConnell and the other former Air Force officers are your best resource in this regard."

"Chopper," McConnell cut in, using my old ODIS call sign, "they don't need you for Moon missions nor to test-drive the shadow proxies. They want your help with the defector."

"Beg pardon, ma'am?" I blurted.

"We've got someone who fled the Chinese military space program by way of Hong Kong a few weeks ago," Major General Dalton said. "Somebody who claims to know all about Beijing's plans for its own proxies. To include an advanced prototype which would theoretically leave our shadow proxies in the dust."

I sat up straight in my chair, mouth partially open.

"I'd think the CIA should be all over this, sir," I said.

"The CIA wants her, alright," Dalton replied. "But I convinced the secretary of defense to convince the President to let us have the defector first. She's motivated to work with us because she fears the CIA by reputation, and that's an advantage you'll have to press if you want to get out of her what we think she knows."

"I am the last man you want pumping a foreign officer for information," I said, pushing away from the table and holding up my hands in a placating fashion. "I enjoy working with machines. It's the whole reason I got into ROVs in the first place. Working with people is not necessarily my strong suit—just ask Mavy Stoddard, whom I worked with in the beginning!"

"You've got your assignment," General McConnell said, raising her eyebrow at me.

I slowly lowered my hands, and sighed deeply.

"Fine. Where is this supposed defector, and can she even speak English?"

As it turned out, Jennifer Cheung spoke very good English, courtesy of having been born and attending school in Hong Kong before being scooped up by the Red Chinese Army's space operations people. They'd wanted her for her robotics expertise, which she'd originally intended to ply overseas for one of the several multinationals who'd been entertaining her résumé at the time the Red Army came calling. After that? Nothing had been her own anymore. Not her time, and not her work. Like so many other cutting-edge professionals in that beleaguered city, she'd become human property of the People's Republic of China.

They flew me to Joint Base Lewis-McChord to meet her, at a small section of base housing which had been reserved by the Department of Defense for "sensitive" individuals—while the State Department did its best to cover Jennifer's tracks and blur the line leading from Hong Kong, across the Pacific, to the United States.

I showed up at Jennifer's doorstep with Brigadier General McConnell and two Security Forces airmen at my back. Which should not have made me nervous. But it did anyway. Jennifer's presence on post could not be officially acknowledged, which also meant that she officially had no legal status. She was essentially a secret prisoner of a secret war, and I was more than a little hesitant to meet someone being kept under such circumstances.

When the door opened, a winsome young Chinese face greeted me. She was easily a foot shorter and twenty years my junior. She did not smile, but she nodded her chin to her chest and said—with a mildly British accent—"They told me you were on your way, and to expect and welcome you. Come in."

We were all in civilian clothing—which would not have fooled anyone used to spotting US military personnel dressed in plain garb—and I took off my ball cap as we entered the small single-family dwelling. Looking around, I marveled at how much more spacious and luxurious on-post housing at Lewis-McChord had gotten since the first time I'd set foot on the installation as a private first class. Then I followed Jennifer from the entryway to what appeared to be a hastily furnished living room. The two SF airmen promptly posted themselves at both the front and back doors of the house, and one of them talked quietly into a secure radio which ran a wire into her ear.

General McConnell and I both took a seat. The leather furniture was brand-new, and smelled accordingly.

"Are they treating you okay?" I asked, ignoring the pinched expression on my boss's face.

"Yes," Jennifer said. "Better than the minders in Beijing."

"Minders?" I asked.

"People assigned to make sure I didn't talk to the wrong people, nor could ever travel without state escort."

"Seems like you've exchanged one set of minders for another," I said, tipping my head in the direction of the male airman who peered outside through the glass of the small window in the front door.

"Perhaps," Jennifer said. "But here there may be a chance of eventual freedom. Something you've had your whole life, Mister . . . ?"

"Jaraczuk," I said carefully.

"That's not your first name," Jennifer said, raising an eyebrow.

I laughed nervously. "No, you're right. Daniel is my first name. My friends call me Dan. You can call me Dan, too."

"But I'm not your friend," Jennifer said.

"Hope to change that," I said, and again laughed nervously.

General McConnell cleared her throat.

"Ma'am," she said, "I can't say how long it will take the Space Force to work with the State Department to get your status in our country worked out. Technically, since you'd be considered a high-profile target for any of Beijing's operatives working on US soil—and we know there are a lot of them—it's risky to have you out in the general population. Someone might spot you, and decide to act."

"Meaning, they would kill or kidnap me before you obtained the information you need," Jennifer said coldly.

"That's a blunt way of stating it, but yes," my boss said.

The two women locked eyes for a long moment.

Jennifer's eyes dropped, and she allowed herself a deep breath, then puffed out her cheeks.

"Fine. It's still better than Beijing."

"Good," I said. "And I meant it when I said I hoped we could be friends."

"Why?" she said. "I matter to you only as much as the contents of my memory matter to you—what I can tell you about China's space robotics effort, and the autonomous learning machines Beijing has deployed."

"Autonomous learning machines?" I asked, and now it was my turn to give my boss a pinched look. "Is that what I think it sounds like?"

"That's for Jennifer to tell us," General McConnell said, coming to her feet. "Your job, Chief Jaraczuk, is to assist Ms. Cheung."

My boss handed me a small manila envelope.

"Here's access to the other side of this duplex, and keys to a vehicle, plus post privileges to the lab near Gray Army Airfield—some of the old ODIS equipment is in storage there."

"I didn't realize they've evacuated the old site at Hill," I said, taking the envelope.

"Once Space Force consumed us, a lot of things changed," McConnell said. "You're to report to me daily at the lab."

"Rog," I said. "Even if I've got nothing to report?"

"I am sure Ms. Cheung didn't come all this way just to waste our time," McConnell said, and again locked eyes with Jennifer. They stared at each other for a couple of seconds, then my boss walked to the front door and exited, while the SF followed. Though I got the feeling those two weren't the only ones around. Most probably there were other plain-clothed Air Force or Army MPs lurking outside. If Cheung was the high-profile refugee it seemed she was, my boss had been right. Beijing would want her silenced before she could tell me—any of us—anything of value.

"I'm sorry it has to be like this," I said lamely, motioning my hand around the living room, which suddenly seemed like a very comfortable prison.

"Being stuck at home and unable to go anywhere?" she said, half mocking. "Isn't that how all of America was living not too long ago?"

"Some cities are still like that," I said, "though the people living there are damned tired of it. There's taking precautions to stay safe, and then there's enduring house arrest because some unelected bureaucrat ordered it. I hate to say this, but since the pandemic hit, I am not sure the United States is as free as we like to think we are."

"What does that mean?" she asked.

"It means that people who've no business suspending our freedoms, have been busy suspending our freedoms."

She looked around, then said, "This is still better than Beijing."

"Well," I responded, "let's hope to hell it stays that way. Now, I'll tell you a quick story of myself, and you tell me a quick story of yourself, and we'll see if we can make this a pleasant relationship."

I gave Ms. Cheung the short version of my time in the Army, my deployments, working with both military remotely operated vehicles, and the specific proxies developed for ODIS. I even told her about having brought down Grissom Platform, though I was not entirely sure the event was mine to reveal to a nonclassified source. Was Cheung a plant? A ringer? Somebody Beijing had dispatched to play victim in our midst—get us to tell her or show her things, and then she'd be disappeared back across the Pacific? McConnell had discussed the possibility with me in the car on the way over. I had to admit it was a disquieting thought which deserved sussing out. But if she was a plant, nothing about the events of Grissom Platform would be a secret to her. So I told her the truth, hoping to receive some truth in kind.

Jennifer's eyes widened.

"So that's what they were talking about," she said. "The generals who supervised me used to occasionally mention the first man-to-man combat ever experienced in space. Only, their version of events made it sound like United States robots had attacked a Chinese space platform, and one of the noble Chinese soldiers had to bring the whole thing down in order to keep the Chinese platform out of American hands."

"Which version do you think you believe, now?" I asked genuinely.

She bit her lip, and wrapped her arms around her chest—almost like she'd grown cold—and said, "I believe yours. The generals . . . I learned not to believe anything they told me. After a while."

"Fair enough," I said. "Now, I need you to help me believe that you somehow escaped without Beijing helping you."

"You think I'm here falsely?" she said, jutting her chin out.

I held my hands up in a placating gesture.

"How is it possible they let you go if you're so vital?" I asked.

She kept her chin thrust out—indignant—but seemed to be running the question over and over again through her mind. Then she said, "I have asked myself the same question many times since I left Hong Kong. Getting their permission to visit an uncle they should have known had been dead for years. Making contact with the underground. Getting onto the container ship. I feared for my life at every step, and at every step it felt easier and easier. Arriving in Seattle . . . your government was waiting for me—prepared, they said, by the underground forwarding word—and now here I am. Thousands of other people from Hong Kong have not been so lucky. Thousands who are far less important to Beijing's strategic plans than I am."

"So what's the gimmick?" I asked.

"Gimmick?"

"The spoof. The catch. The angle. What's in it for them to let you go?"

"I don't have a mind for spy games," she said, and stood up from her armchair, then began to pace—still keeping her arms wrapped protectively around her chest.

"Frankly," I admitted, "I don't either. But my boss—whom you just met—would have unkind words for me if I didn't broach the subject. For whatever reasons, Beijing didn't stop you. Could be a mistake on their part. Could be intentional? It's those bigger 'strategic goals' you're talking about, which concern my boss, and her boss, and her boss's boss, the most. That, and the autonomous robotics you mentioned. Let's start there."

Jennifer gave me the rundown. They were the latest in Chinese proxy technology—man-shaped machinery designed to go places and do things where men find it difficult or impossible—but they were designed to "unplug" from their Operators and work independently on certain things. More importantly, the more these autonomous proxies performed on their own, the better they learned how to work on their own. Solve problems. Deduce plans of action. Make choices without direct human guidance. It wasn't exactly artificial intelligence, but it sounded way ahead of anything General McConnell had ever had me work on at ODIS—where every proxy sent to space needed a man or a woman in an Operating booth to control it.

"We still have those," Jennifer said. "They're very expensive."

"So are ours," I said. "It's why we've never been able to field very many of them at any one time."

"Beijing has the same problem," she said.

"But a self-learning version might make it easier to field-and-forget?" I speculated.

"What does that mean?"

"Suppose you put these things on the Moon, and run them manually just long enough for them to get good at doing some very basic tasks over and over and over again. Then you let them go, and your Operators use new proxies to do the more detailed work, while the autos do the dumb lifting."

"These aren't pack animals," Jennifer said, pausing to stare out her window.

I looked over my shoulder and observed the unmarked sedan parked across the street. There were two people in the front seats, idly watching us from behind sunglasses. I assumed they were American, given our location on the base. But a little creepy feeling up the back of my neck made me wonder how hard it would be for a

Chinese spy—a couple of Chinese spies, or someone being paid off by the Chinese—to get through the Lewis-McChord gates.

"If not pack animals," I said, "then what? Surely these machines aren't thinking the way a man thinks."

"Not all on their own, no," she admitted. "But my research in Hong Kong wasn't on singular artificial intelligence. I was doing work on hive-mind intelligence. Many machines, joined wirelessly, and acting as one. Like an ant colony. Or bees."

The creeping sensation on the back of my neck got worse.

"So these proxies still need people to run them, until you get them organized in a group . . . and the group does the thinking?"

"That's the idea," she said. "I was getting good at making insect-sized robots work together in teams—overcoming different obstacles—when Beijing grabbed me. I was promised special privileges and status if I could adapt my research for larger robots. It didn't take long. Though the special privileges and status never materialized. That's when I knew I had to find a way to disappear."

"There are other places in the world you could have gone," I said. "Why choose the United States? Do you have friends or family here?"

"No," she said. "But your former President spoke out on our behalf. He risked making Beijing angry. Very few people around the globe these days seem interested in making the Party in Beijing angry. I want to help you. I want to make the Party people pay for what they have done to my city."

We spent three days talking about technical specifics—a lot of it way over my head. Jennifer let me record it all on digital, which I obediently handed over to General McConnell every night. The lab itself was more like a small warehouse, and a lot of familiar equipment I had not seen in years was mothballed under tarps or sealed in protective plastic. Operating had gotten a lot more sophisticated since I'd first worked with my boss at ODIS back in Utah. The human-machine interface had become more refined, less bulky, and had better responsiveness. Plus the new "shadow" stealthing made our best proxies undetectable to foreign radar, as well as other sensors. Or so we thought. Though I didn't talk about that much with my young companion during our daily afternoon chats.

"I'd not expect a name like 'Jennifer' in China," I said to her as we sat down on the fourth day.

"Lots of English first names in Hong Kong," she said. "We were British in many ways, and not Chinese in other ways. Which was another reason I decided I had to vanish. The Party leaders in Beijing want their kind of China to become the new normal for not just Hong Kong, but Taiwan as well, plus Tibet, and many other places. What they cannot conquer outright, they buy. Fast, or slow. Your government has been foolish to try to placate Beijing."

"Tell me about it," I said, embarrassed. "But one thing about Washington D.C., the leadership is schizophrenic."

"What does that mean?" she asked.

"It means we don't have the same political leadership for year after year. Every four to eight years, it tends to flip-flop dramatically. Everything hinges on our two parties—wretched bastards that they are."

"You don't like your parties?"

"Some days I think they're worse than your Party you hate in Beijing," I admitted.

"You're allowed to say that?" she remarked, with an honestly surprised expression on her face.

"We don't have political officers in our military," I said. "Not yet at least. I'm gonna think and say any damned thing I please, as long as it's not risking my clearance. And there's nothing secret about hating the two parties. Everybody here hates them. To one degree or another. Only difference is, up until now, our system of government has managed to restrict the kind of damage they can do to the American citizen. Though, the pandemic has taught them that millions of Americans are ready and willing to take the yoke."

"A great many in Hong Kong as well," Jennifer admitted. "They wanted to believe the promises Beijing made. They are still learning the awful truth."

I sighed, and took a long sip from my can of fizzy caffeinated soda. I had to admit, having only known her for a short while, I was getting a warm fuzzy off this woman. And not from anything inappropriate—she'd been as formal in that way as a school teacher—but because she had been as forthcoming as either myself or my boss could hope, and didn't seem to contradict herself on any of her information. To include bits and pieces about her story of escape, which inevitably tucked themselves into our conversation.

The container ship had been the worst. Hiding out in a steel CONEX with barely any fresh air, very limited water, and just a bucket into which she could empty her bowels. After a while the CONEX had become rank with terrible smells; and the motley gang of Chinese folk who'd all stowed away? Clung to the idea that landing in Seattle meant a new chance at a better life. Something apart from the tender mercies of the Party back home.

"The day people like you stop risking life and limb to come here," I said to her, "is the day we'll know the United States has truly ceased to be the United States, and become something else."

"You don't sound hopeful," Jennifer pointed out, her legs tucked under her as she perched on her couch—a cup of tea in her hand.

"I think I'm just getting old," I admitted. "When I joined the Army a long time ago, I was still an idealist. I wanted to defend what seemed worth defending. There are times lately when I have to ask myself if it's been worth it—because, again, of those two parties in Washington. I love my brothers and sisters in uniform. But sometimes I think we serve a very unworthy set of masters."

"The Party in Beijing," she said, "tells us that America is a corrupt tyranny, where the very rich prey on everyone else who is not, and you blunder about the globe doing great wrong to other nations—in your attempt to maintain a faltering position of supremacy."

"Would it shock you to learn that Americans with doctorates often say exactly the same thing? These are highly educated men and women, who have no idea how good we've got it here. And talk like they want to rip it all down."

"Well," Jennifer said. "I hope I am lucky enough to have come before the best parts of America are beyond my reach."

"From your lips to God's ears," I said.

At the end of the first week, I got my boss's permission to bring Jennifer to the lab, where I rigged up one of the old proxy booths—with a proxy to match—and put the ODIS-era technology to work. Thankfully my "fingerprint" in the system was still good. It takes a lot of effort to get the proxy system to learn an Operator's specific signature. Then I put Jennifer in an adjacent booth, and started her with some initial exercises. She'd only ever seen the Chinese equivalent from the outside. Never had her Chinese minders ever allowed her to actually operate any of the equipment. Jennifer was startled, and then delighted by the show. So much so, that by the end of the second week she'd managed to train one of the booths—or rather, the software running the booth-to-proxy setup—to recognize her. She hopped, jumped, crawled, performed calisthenics, and took the old proxy through its paces.

"You could climb to the top of Everest with this," she said, draped in the old proxy sensor web, with attendant cables and headpiece which showed her the camera-eyes view of her proxy unit.

"A few have," I said.

"Really?"

"It was a test," I admitted. "Just to see what was possible."

"Other countries are using your technology?"

"We've discreetly loaned it," I said. "It was damned difficult to keep anything like this secret, once the various intelligence communities of the other nations figured out what ODIS was doing. So we carefully arranged to have ODIS bring in some exchange officers from friendly militaries, while loaning some proxies and equipment to countries in Europe, and elsewhere. Most of this is still kept out of the public eye, though there are commercial industrial applications for which various private interests want licenses. It's a complicated arrangement between the contractors who make the technology, and what our government believes is wise to let loose for commercial interest."

"In China," she said, carefully walking her way around the storage center—her proxy doing the walking while Jennifer's feet moved in place on the booth's treadmill-like flooring—"nothing like this is ever admitted to being possible. The state owns all, and while I am sure many civil engineers would be quite interested in the technology for a range of applications, the state has not yet made it so."

"That you know of," I reminded her.

"True. Who knows if what I have been told is a lie, or the truth, or somewhere in between? That's what it is to be Chinese, Chief. You know the state is always lying to you somehow, in some way, but you're never quite sure when, or how."

"I hate to break it to you," I said, "but our government isn't much better. Especially lately."

She stopped mid-stride and pulled the headpiece off, leaving her hair mussed, and stared at me.

"If you do not trust your government, why do you still wear that uniform?"

I stared back at her, then dropped my eyes to the floor.

"Some days I ask myself the same question," I admitted, "and I don't necessarily have a good answer. For the retirement and benefits, obviously, but that's a shitty reason to serve. I guess . . . I guess it's because I have to believe our Constitution will somehow survive those boneheaded idiots in Washington D.C. It's survived such boneheaded idiots before. I have to think our founders—some of us still revere them—were insightful enough to design a system which is proof against political morons."

"How will you know if the answer is 'yes'?" she asked.

"If ever this nation becomes one where I am climbing into a CONEX on a boat out in that ocean, risking my life to sail to somewhere else I think might possibly be better . . . then we'll know."

She put the headpiece back on, and kept her proxy moving. At the far side of the secure storage bay she found several partially crated weapons, with stacked boxes of ammunition on pallets.

"What are these for?" she asked.

I took a long walk over to where the proxy peered down at the collection of squad weapons, including a monstrous Browning M2 heavy machine gun.

"I think the Army may be thinking about buying and converting these older space-rated proxies for ground combat use."

"The biggest one," Jennifer said through her proxy's speakers, and pointing a mechanical finger at the M2. "How does it work?"

"You really want to know?"

"You started this," she said. "Show me everything."

"How come it feels like I've heard that line before?" I asked, half smiling.

Third week found us talking mostly to the engineering eggheads who'd been grandfathered from ODIS. In this regard, Jennifer ran circles around me. So much so that I dropped back and just kind of let her go. She became so engrossed in discussing the design of processors, the speeds necessary for multiprocessor computing, the types and kinds of materials needed to make the kinds of chips she knew would work in a learning computing system, that I had to pry her away from the men and women in lab coats, and drive her home—exhausted, falling asleep in the seat next to me. If she'd been fascinated operating a proxy, she became absolutely exalted discussing the application of her hive-computing theory to multi-proxy operational methods. So much so, any reticence she'd once felt about working with myself and General McConnell melted away.

"She's a true lover of what she does," the boss said to me one night, after I'd gotten Jennifer through her front door, and into bed, then driven back to debrief at the lab.

"You noticed?" I said, half mocking. "No wonder the Communists wanted and used her. All they had to do is put her into a room with a bunch of other like-minded techies, and she's off and running. So eager to share her thoughts and concepts. She doesn't care about the political ramifications as much as she's excited by the possibilities of the concept itself. She wants to see it made real. Know that a thing can be done. She almost demands that it become so. Glad we have this chance to work with her, though I do wonder if part of the reason she escaped is the Chinese got what they needed from her, so she wasn't essential after a while?"

"Maybe," McConnell said. "But I'd assume they just lock her away or kill her, versus letting her escape."

"You still think they let her go for some ulterior motive?" I asked.

"Don't you?" my boss asked, sitting up in her chair at her desk, her Space Force uniform still crisp even after having been worn for fourteen hours.

"I dunno," I admitted. "Sometimes the simplest answer is the answer. No state security apparatus is foolproof. Maybe the Red Chinese just . . . fucked up. Or something? It's not like our national security doesn't endlessly screw the pooch all the time, and we know ours is better than theirs."

"Or so we tell ourselves," McConnell murmured, stifling a yawn.

"Yeah," I said, drumming my fingers on her desk—while seated in one of two office chairs for guests.

"I liked what you said," McConnell told me.

"About what?" I asked.

"About the Constitution, and the founders."

"How the hell did you hear that?"

"Duh, stupid, we've recorded every second of her activity with the old ODIS proxies. Including every second of your conversations with her. Don't worry, I'm in complete accord with your opinion of Washington D.C., though I can't admit it in mixed company. They don't put these stars on your chest if you can't at least appear to be a 'player' the way they want you to be a player. But you should know I hope it too: that the Constitution can survive the current idiocy, and see us all through. Because if not? Better save a seat for me in one of those CONEX boxes bound for Australia or New Zealand, or something far away from here."

Week four saw more of Jennifer working with our prior ODIS lab-coats, and I brought up the fact she wasn't being paid for her time. My boss seemed to think getting free food and board was more than generous compensation, all things considered, but I reminded her sternly that Jennifer would eventually deserve a life beyond the confines of either her little duplex, or the lab. If what she was giving us was even half as useful as I thought it would be, she'd earned the highest paycheck possible, and a guaranteed path to some kind of official legal status—even if the State Department wasn't yet ready to publicly admit she existed.

We debated the fact out on the lab loading dock as an unmarked eighteen-wheel truck pushed its trailer up to the dock's rubber bumpers. Space Force was constantly shuffling ODIS and post-ODIS equipment in and out of the lab on an almost daily basis, and when the young enlisted soldier with the clipboard cranked open the back of the trailer, I didn't think twice about the proxies arrayed inside.

Until all of them sprang to life at once, and began shooting at us.

The young enlisted troop, General McConnell, and two other Space Force personnel went down in heaps as the sleekly built proxies—armed with what looked like modified submachine guns—marched out of the back of the trailer and began to swarm through the bay loading door which opened into the larger lab facility behind.

I'd have been hit too, except I'd leapt off the dock the instant the first shot rang out, and was running toward the cab of the truck—in the opposite direction, away from enemy movement. But there was a very good reason. Whoever was running those units, the driver was obviously part of it. Stopping a machine many times my own strength—and armed with a weapon—would be impossible. But if I could get to the Operators...

The driver had seen me coming. The eighteen-wheeler began to pull away. I reached the steps up to the driver's door on the tractor, and hurled myself upward. The latch on the door was locked, and the driver's eyes were wide as I slammed my fist on his window repeatedly, commanding him to stop. He ignored me and kept shifting, trying to build speed as the big truck horsed its way around the lab's parking lot, and aimed for an exit through the fence which surrounded the building. The airfield itself had separate security, but the ODIS lab just had military police at the doors—who'd probably stand little chance against the mechanized, bulletproof enemy.

I put a hand to the butt of my weapon. Carrying on base was not permitted for most, but since I'd been charged with being Jennifer's keeper, I'd gotten the boss's permission to keep a compact semiautomatic in a waistband holster. I plucked it from its stowed position and put the muzzle to the driver's door latch, firing twice. The .40-caliber shots were insanely loud in my ears, at that range, with no ear protection, but the latch came free and I flung the driver's door open.

A slightly terrified man of unspecified Asian extraction stared at me for a moment, then his counterpart in the passenger's seat was aiming a carbine across the driver's lap. I threw myself away from the flapping driver's door—just managing to keep a hand on one of the safety grips at the door's edge—and let the mid-caliber carbine shots hit air. Again, the noise was astoundingly loud, at that range, and with no ear protection. My head was ringing like a bell. But I holstered my semiautomatic and wrapped a hand around the barrel of the carbine just aft of its triangular front sight post, and pulled. The man in the passenger seat pulled back, shooting crazily as I attempted to wrestle the weapon out of his grasp.

The driver was screaming in a language definitely not English. Hot cartridge casings were ejecting all over the cab and into his face.

I suddenly realized the rig was no longer headed for the exit in the fence, but toward the fence itself—beyond which was the storm ditch which ran into the culvert under the road. I experienced a moment of clarity, and stepped down off the tractor—unsure of how fast it was moving—and feeling like the world's biggest idiot as my shoes touched the pavement.

I immediately went down like a sack of potatoes.

The pain was unbelievable. Worse than the time I'd gone over the handlebars of a motocross bike out on the sand dunes back in Utah. For two or three seconds there was only flailing and tumbling, with my arms wrapped over my head, then I was flat on my back with the wind knocked out of me, and the sure knowledge I'd messed up at least one ankle, if not both, plus earned myself some epic road rash.

I struggled to my knees—trying to ignore the ankle—and watched as the tractor and trailer smashed through the fence and hurtled into the ditch, impacting the ditch's grassy opposite side. There was a horrendous crashing sound as the trailer pancaked into the back of the tractor, and then fumes billowed up from the engine as the tractor lay still—its driver's door still hanging wide open.

I willed myself to get up—fuck, that ankle!—and limped as quickly as I could to the hole in the fence. I pulled out the compact semiauto and aimed it at the driver's open door, smelling diesel fuel and oil, as well as the acrid stench of burning plastic. Groans from inside the cab told me the driver and passenger were still alive, and possibly still coherent. I used my good ankle and free hand to get back up on the steps to the cab, then swung around—gun first—into the cab proper.

The driver and passenger partially dangled by their seat belts. The passenger's carbine had fallen out of his reach to the cab floor above his toes. Blood stained the driver's left leg where an errant carbine round had penetrated. Lots of blood. Too much blood.

I aimed my pistol at the passenger—also of unknown Asian extraction—and shouted, "Talk now, or die!"

He coughed several times, and forced a grin.

"It's too late, American," he said in heavily accented English, and began to laugh.

"The proxies!" I continued to shout. "Where are their Operators?"

His laughter grew hysterical.

I'd never killed a man face-to-face. As an ROV operator, I'd only ever killed from behind a screen. Away from the violence. With a cold drink or a cup of hot coffee within reach. Never seeing the blood. Never hearing the screams. Never seeing the hate in another man's eyes—the hate of someone who considers you his mortal enemy.

The passenger's brains made a pink mist exiting the opposite side of his skull.

I put the barrel of the compact semiauto under the driver's chin.

"Talk," I said into his ear, as he continued to bleed dangerously from his leg wound.

"Too late now," he said. "Too late for all of you."

I felt my finger began to pull the semiauto's plastic trigger back to the point it would send the weapon's internal striker pin plunging into the primer on the back of the .40-caliber cartridge in the chamber.

Then I lifted my finger.

"Yeah," I said, looking down at the incredibly dark blood pooling on the cab's floor. "I imagine it is."

Climbing down from the cab—shit, that stupid ankle!—I hobbled back up the ditch and headed back toward the loading dock. I could see General McConnell and the others lying where they'd fallen. It took me far longer than I'd have preferred to reach her, but when I did, she was still gasping for breath.

"Compromised," she whispered to me as I began to search her body for the wound. I found two wet holes in her stomach, and ripped her uniform blouse top off, then pushed the wadded-up blouse onto the wounds and held it tight. She gasped with pain, but feebly managed to get her blood-covered hands over mine.

"Sound the alarm," she commanded, still whispering.

The noise of gunshots and mechanized machinery moving rapidly from deep inside the lab told me that the proxies—I'd never gotten a clear look at them before they'd attacked, but was now firmly convinced they were not ours—were making quick work of anyone who opposed them. What could men do against fighting mechanisms which were faster, had better reflexes, quicker, more accurate targeting, and would shrug off hits from practically any small arms?

I reached to my back pocket for my phone, and pulled it out, only to discover that the face was hopelessly smashed—a victim of my fall from the truck.

"Under me," McConnell said weakly. "My phone."

I pushed my fingers under her butt until I felt the solid rectangle in her back pocket, and wormed it out. Thankfully, it was still intact.

I tried to log into the device, then quickly flashed its front at her face. Then opened the little Department of Defense app which would let me quick-dial for on-post disaster or emergency.

Gunshots continued to ring out from inside the lab. As men and women yelled or screamed.

"Nature of emergency?" said a computerized voice through her phone.

"Multiple assailants, gunshots, require immediate military police response!"

"Affirmative," said the computerized voice. "Sending to your present position via global positioning. Stand by . . ."

I kept the blouse wadded over my boss's double-entry wound. Her face was white as a sheet, but her eyes were open.

"How . . ." her lips asked, without making a sound.

"I dunno, boss," I said, "but you better not fucking die on me like this. Whoever sent them is after the lab, and not even the guards have the kind of armament necessary to take down a proxy! If they even are what I think they are. Boss . . . what if these are the machines Jennifer told us about? How in the hell did they get here? And why attack now?"

McConnell's phone began to buzz with an incoming call. It was Jennifer's government-issue phone they'd given her during the second week.

"Dan?" her voice shouted through McConnell's phone.

"Jennifer, what the hell is going on?" I shouted. "Did you—?"

"Not me, Dan!" Jennifer shouted. "Never in a million years! But somehow they tracked me. Must have waited until they thought they could get you, or a whole bunch of you. I don't know who they bribed, but—listen, Dan, I can't—"

Gunfire cut her off.

"Jennifer, you've got to get out! We can't stop these things!"

"—wait where you are, I'm coming!" Jennifer's voice shouted, and then the call dropped.

Moments later, an altogether louder, much more concussive weapon could be heard firing. Beyond either the submachine guns carried by the enemy, or the carbine back in the tractor trailer. I hadn't heard that sound in a long time. Not since the Middle East. My jaw gaped open as I heard the blasts—repetitive and deafening—grow louder.

Two of the enemy proxies backed out of the open dock door, facing the new threat. Their submachine guns chattered crazily, but one of the two suddenly burst apart as if exploding—pieces of itself flying in all directions as it crumpled to the dock's surface. Then the other one backed up to the edge of the dock and toppled, clattering to the ground below.

A shape emerged from inside the dock. Not quite human. But definitely not one of the enemy proxies. This one was American-made. Older. Not nearly so quick nor agile as the new ones which were attacking. But heavy, and built to stand up to micrometeoroids if necessary. Its plated torso and limbs were marred by the impacts from hundreds of pistol-caliber bullets, and it wielded from the hip a Browning M2 heavy machine gun with an ammo box tucked up against the receiver.

The old space-rated proxy calmly walked to the edge of the dock and mowed down its target with a five-round burst.

"Gotcha," said Jennifer's voice through the old ODIS proxy's speaker system.

Submachine gun rounds pinged and panged off the back of Jennifer's proxy. She whirled on a heel and marched back into the open dock bay, her proxy's head turning to face me as I ducked over McConnell's body.

"I got to the booth before they got to me," Jennifer's voice announced loudly with the proxy's speakers. "Now it's time to clean up the rest of them."

The M2 began to thunder annihilation at the oncoming enemy, while I wondered what it would be like to file for hearing disability.

A quick glance over my shoulder showed a string of post police vehicles zooming up, as well as two ambulances, their lights flashing and sirens blaring. There hadn't been time to warn them what they were facing. But it seemed Jennifer was taking care of that. What might come after? Anyone's guess. Never before had any ODIS Operator or facility ever been directly targeted. But now? The secret war with Beijing had become a lot more personal than I'd ever thought it would.

NIGHTINGALE
Stephen Lawson

Leonard Murrow sat in an uncomfortable wooden chair in a dimly lit room with drab cement walls. He wanted to get out of the chair, but his ankles were tied to the chair's legs. Leonard wanted to pull the matted hair out of his eyes and check for bleeding from a head wound, but his hands were tied to the chair's back.

"It'd be a mistake to kill me," Leonard said to the bald man with the purple latex gloves.

The man's steel-framed glasses reflected the single incandescent bulb above Leonard's head.

"Really," Purple Gloves said. "Why's that?"

"I'm a valuable asset to my employers," Leonard said. "People are going to come looking for my body."

Purple Gloves half smiled. He pulled a table closer to Leonard and opened a laptop screen.

"Watch," Purple Gloves said.

Leonard watched a video of himself in a tuxedo, walking through a crowd of men in tuxedos and women in little black dresses. A young woman in a dress shorter than the others hung on his arm as they left the mansion. Leonard had never seen the woman before, much less left Maurice Bloodworth's fundraiser with her.

"That's not me," Leonard said.

"Of course it is," Purple Gloves said. "Certainly your friends will know where to look for you—with the transmitter we found in your watch, and the backup in the sole of your shoe. Those probably survived the flames of the car wreck fifty miles south of here. You were seen by several eyewitnesses leaving the party with Miss Meadows, and, well—here's the video evidence. Both of you died on impact, I'm afraid. It'll be a shame when your wife finds out. Ellie, is it? Such a pretty thing. She'll certainly curse your philandering."

Leonard glared at Purple Gloves. He strained, impotently, against his bonds.

"Even if you have some secret microchip in your hair or skin," Purple Gloves said, "this wing of the building is a Faraday cage. No signal would get out. No one is coming for you, Dr. Murrow, and if they did—this building is guarded by a hundred state-of-the-art killing machines."

"This is a misunderstanding," Leonard said. "The Pegasus Foundation is interested in Bloodworth's work in robotics— potentially in acquiring it. I was at the fundraiser to assess the crowd and see what sort of competition we might have. The trackers are a standard precaution at Pegasus. Sometimes we have to travel overseas. Those trackers have been in my clothes for over a year."

"Innocent circumstances, sure," Purple Gloves said. "My client's facial recognition systems are linked to all the databases—even the databases that don't get scrubbed for government assassins. We know that Pegasus is a shell. Perhaps you're here because of Mr. Bloodworth's flaunting of the Laws of Military Robotics?"

Isaac Asimov's imagining of laws had gone out the window when the realities of human violence were applied to robotics. Other regulations had replaced them.

"Span of control," Purple Gloves offered. "'No human may have simultaneous control of more than ten robotic soldiers of any size or capability.' Am I getting warm?"

Leonard knew the thesis behind the regulation by heart, because he'd written it.

Humans are moral agents and are expected to question immoral commands in warfare. Robots cannot be moral agents, because they are inherently amoral. The span of control regulation limits the amount of damage one human can perpetrate without another moral agent in the decision cycle.

"Those regulations also only apply to the sovereign states that signed the pact," Purple Gloves said. "They don't apply to private business ventures. Regardless, Mr. Bloodworth's children aren't weapons of war. You can see that he needs a substantial amount of private security."

"Tell me—" Leonard said. "What did the girl in the video—Meadows, you said—what did she do? She can't have deserved to die."

Purple Gloves considered the question.

"Mr. Bloodworth doesn't like to be told 'no,'" he said, "by governments, or by women."

Thick fog hung over Lake Melloan, and the sprawling island at its center. Inside the fog, a single helicopter flew forty feet off the lake's surface at sixty knots. Its rotor noise was rendered all but silent by stealth technology, and it was escorted by a pair of similarly equipped drones that were linked to its airframe network. The helicopter, an MH-84 Kestrel, held a crew of five—two pilots, two crew chiefs—and the brigade's flight surgeon, Ellie Murrow.

Captain Stanley Cooper scanned the glass cockpit displays, from the moving map to the radar altimeter, to the airspeed indicator, and then over to the TGT, engine oil, and transmission oil displays. He shifted up to the windshield, which was overlaid with the blue and magenta lines of Lockheed Martin's artificial-vision system. Though he couldn't see the two drones—Calvin and Hobbes—through the fog, he saw blue outlines of them with distance indicators in augmented reality. He glanced back down to the moving map as a GPS waypoint began to blink.

"Land in six hundred meters," Cooper said. "Slow to fifty."

"Roger. Slowing to fifty."

CW3 Wesley Sloane disengaged the coupled flight director by pressing a button on the cyclic in his right hand. He eased back ever so slightly on the cyclic while lowering the collective in his left. Few pilots trusted the electronic flight director during confined hover work or nap-of-the-Earth (NOE) flight, and Wes wasn't one of those few. The computer never corrected for wind as fast as a human could.

Calvin and Hobbes slowed to match the MH-84's new airspeed.

Cooper leaned to his right across the lower console to look back into the cabin. Ellie looked up, held his gaze for several seconds with heterochromatic eyes—one pale blue, one gray—and then looked down to her right hand. Cooper couldn't see it from where he sat, but he knew it was shaking. She wouldn't be scared—the tremor was a nerve disorder—but it wasn't something she'd had when they'd come in as second lieutenants, before she went off to med school and he left for flight training.

Cooper looked back to the map.

"Land in four hundred meters," he said. "Looking good. We're lined up on the valley. Artificial vision IBIT's a go. Proceed into NOE."

The terrain rose on either side of the Kestrel as they flew into the valley, twenty feet above the tree line. They would be shielded from radar here, and from any other imaging sensors that could penetrate fog.

Cooper wanted to look back again, to somehow convey that he wouldn't let her down. He wanted to say something over ICS—to tell her this would be fine—but he held his tongue. He had to focus on the map. NOE flight in a fogbank was no time to chat.

A memory surfaced, ever so briefly.

Cooper remembered opening his eyes and seeing her face—pale, with black, sweat-soaked hair stuck to her forehead. A tube ran from her arm to his, with red fluid inside. He'd been disoriented, with no idea how he'd arrived in the grassy field. He smelled burnt metal and jet fuel. When she saw his eyes open, a smile flitted briefly on her lips, and she let her own eyes close. She'd accomplished something, perhaps, with her last ounce of strength.

The sound of rotors came from far away. How long had they been lying there? An ugly laceration ran down the side of his torso, and another down his left leg, but they'd both been stapled shut. His left leg seemed to be splinted, perhaps from a compound fracture. His right pants leg hadn't been cut away, but a patch of the Nomex had been burnt to ash. The leather of his right boot had charred a bit. His head felt foggy, like someone had pumped him full of painkillers.

Barely audible over the approaching rotors, he heard a faint click as the auto-valve on the transfusion snapped shut. Ellie didn't open her eyes or move to pull the needle out of her arm.

"How much blood did she give me?" he asked the medic when Dustoff loaded them into litters and shoved them in the cabin. The soundproofing on HH-84s was a vast improvement over the HH-60 Black Hawk, and allowed speech between patients and medics without yelling.

The medic shined a penlight in Cooper's left eye, then his right. "More than she should have," the medic said, "but she'll live."

"Harper? Gurney?"

"I'm sorry, man. Nobody else made it out of the fire. Looks like Doc dragged you a hundred meters with her own wounds and fixed you both. Once the local anesthetic wears off, I'm probably going to have to hit you with Special K, so you might not remember any of this. Probably better that way."

But Cooper had remembered. He'd dreamed about that crash many times.

Once, the transfusion tube had been an umbilical cord running from her arm to his.

The crash had been traced to a mechanical failure. Cooper had been riding in a crew chief seat after a PI-swap, so he was completely in the clear, and returned to flying duty. Ellie had become something of a local legend.

Now, as they transitioned from lake to valley, Cooper watched Calvin and Hobbes tighten their spread to match the rising terrain on either side.

"We've got wires ahead," Wes said. "Three hundred meters."

Without command, Calvin and Hobbes launched micro-rockets with incendiary payloads at the anchor points of the wires.

Cooper watched in the cockpit glass as the wires emerged as magenta (danger) lines across the flight path, then abruptly fell into the valley below. The magenta lines shifted to blue as they fell below the MH-84's flight path, and were no longer deemed a hazard.

"Might be an early warning system," Wes said. "We might've just tipped them off that we're here."

"Let's hope not," Cooper said, "but they're going to know eventually either way."

ICS picked up a stressed sigh through a voice-activated microphone. Cooper had heard it before.

"It's going to be fine, Doc," he said. "We'll get him out."

A second memory surfaced in Cooper's mind.

"Are you sleeping at night, Cooper?"

Ellie had asked him that one year to the day after the crash.

He'd started smoking again, and dark bags had developed under his eyes. She and Leonard had been married for four months.

"Three hours last night," he said. "Can you write me a script for Ambien?"

"I have to down-slip you if you take anything for sleep," she said. "You wouldn't be able to fly."

"I haven't flown in a month anyway," he said.

"I noticed," she said. "You were on the schedule and I signed up to get hours. And then you came off."

"Sorry."

"Is it the crash?" she asked. "Is something else bothering you?"

Cooper closed his eyes for a long moment. Then he opened them again and stared at the floor.

"I have to come to you for help, but—"

He didn't finish the thought.

"But I'm the problem?"

"You're not a problem, Ellie," he said.

There had been a month, shortly after the crash, when Leonard and Ellie had broken up. Cooper had debated making a move, but decided ultimately to simply be her friend and see how things evolved. When they got back together, he saw that brief window of opportunity for what it was. They'd always been close, and when she and Leonard married, Cooper knew he'd missed something that would never present itself again.

Now, Ellie picked up his hand from the edge of the examination table. She just held it for a moment until he looked up and made eye contact.

"It's okay to love somebody and not make babies with them," she said. "It's what responsible adults do in the military. We rely on each other in ways civilians don't, and emotions are what they are. Things get power over you if you can't talk about them, Cooper. They knot up in your chest and take your sleep away. Is that what it is? You love me?"

"A bit," Cooper said softly.

Then she lifted his hand and kissed the palm, just at the base of his thumb.

Cooper found that he was quite unable to move.

"There," she said, and returned her eyes to his. "I made it better. It's time-release medicine."

She held his hand in hers and ran the index finger of her other hand down his arm. Her fingertip hovered over his lips for a moment before she smiled and pressed her finger to his nose.

"Boop," she whispered, and he laughed despite himself. "You'll have enough time to get home and into bed before it gets all the way to your brain. You're not going to have problems sleeping anymore."

"This seems unorthodox," he said.

"You have doctor-patient confidentiality with me," she said. "I'm pretty fond of you too, Cooper. I'll look after you. Now go home and get some sleep, you overgrown man-child."

Cooper almost laughed again, tired as he was.

"And Cooper?" she said as he slid off the examination table.

"Yeah."

"Quit smoking. I like having you around."

"Okay," he said.

Cooper drove home, showered, and climbed into bed despite it being three in the afternoon. At the instant he pulled the sheets up to cover his cheek, he felt something unwind in his chest and a deep sinking in his mind. He felt as though he was being pulled down into the cool depths of the mattress, like being swallowed in a pool of black ink.

When he looked at the clock next, fifteen hours had passed. He picked up his phone.

Well, he wrote in a text message, *it worked.*

A minute passed before she replied.

Of course it did, she said. *But was it medicine . . . or something else?* <|;-)

Is that a witch hat?

But she didn't reply. He remembered that some of her blood flowed in his veins, and he wondered if that joined them on some deeper level. He imagined her face with the smirk she got when she was amusing herself, and shrugged off the mild discomfort of knowing how easily she slipped under his skin every time she wanted to.

He got up, went online, and ordered a flight patch that read:

Ellie "Nightingale" Murrow
CPT   US Army

Nightingale—after legendary healer Florence Nightingale—because *Person-who-can-reach-into-Cooper's-subconscious* scared him too much. *Nightingale* let him believe she was just very good at basic psychology, and that he still had some autonomy.

He tossed his cigarettes in the trash can. After a week, Cooper found that his insomnia was gone.

The name stuck, and she wore the patch on her A2CUs when she flew.

"Calvin and Hobbes are one hundred meters from the target," Cooper said. "Looks like fifteen robotic sentries on the roof, but they're not moving. No indication they've detected us."

The paradigm of attack helicopters paired with UAVs in manned-unmanned teaming (MUM-T) had given way to two scout/attack UAVs paired with one manned aircraft. Humans no longer flew scout or attack. Human passengers demanded human pilots, though, so lift and medevac pilots still had a job.

"Left cabin window's coming open," SSG Ross Bedford said. He slid the window open and latched it, then swung the fifty-caliber machine-gun mount into place. The thing was a monstrosity, with a long metal cylinder mounted on each side of the gun's barrel. "Gun's in place. Say when, Coop."

"Get ready to turn," Cooper said to Wes.

"Ready."

"Hard right in three . . . two . . . one," Cooper said. "Bank right."

Wes pulled the cyclic right, and the Kestrel swung into a forty-five degree roll.

"Ross, ready on guns," Cooper said.

"Ready," Ross whispered. He'd already pulled open the safety cutouts on the cylinders.

When the Kestrel was lined up exactly abeam the fortress with the left cabin window forty-five degrees high, Cooper announced, "Clear to fire. Do it now."

One faint pop, then another, came from Ross's gun mount.

"Bots out," Ross said.

Then, to return the Kestrel to a clean stealth profile, Ross pulled the gun back in and closed the window.

Wes rolled out of the turn and dropped back into NOE.

"Loiter area's in two klicks," Cooper said. "Calvin's going to clear it for us, then return for wide orbit with Hobbes."

"So far, so good," SGT Marco Sanchez said from the right crew chief seat. Next to him stood an M134 minigun, which was mounted on a servo-assisted arm with an articulated ball just behind the barrels.

"This was the easiest part of the night, Marco," Cooper said.

"I know, sir, but I like to be optimistic."

Two tiny humanoid robots—commonly known as homunculi by those in the robotics field—reached the apex of their flight path. Each was roughly as tall as the length from your elbow to the base of your wrist. As their arc flattened and gravity began to take over, each of them snapped their arms and legs wide to spread the webbed fabric between them. Mimicking flying squirrels better than any human in a wingsuit, they rode the air. Hobbes provided external thermal and radar guidance to them as it circled the fortress until their micro-cameras locked onto an air vent.

The homunculi shifted in the air to make a course correction, folded their limbs to drop rapidly, then expanded them again to fly directly into the vent. They shifted again, flared for air resistance against their flight path, and rolled onto the aluminum floor. The ventilation system, as virtually all ventilation systems are, was much too small for a human to crawl through. It was, however, the perfect size for two MX-47 Infiltrator robots to stand upright, side by side.

Each of them tore the fabric from the other, and they did visual inspections of each other's chassis for damage. One carried a polymer-framed, seven-round .22 pistol—loaded with subsonic .22 short—and a transceiver earpiece on its back. The other carried lock picks, a diamond saw, and a small shaped explosive charge. MX-47s had many load-out options. These were deemed most likely to enable them to rescue Dr. Murrow—or at least facilitate his self-rescue. Each homunculus also had a coil of fine Kevlar thread for climbing and rappelling, and an extremely sharp blade concealed on one arm. For tracking purposes, the one with the pistol and the transceiver had been designated "Randy," and the other had been designated "Gordy," after two of the most majestic human beings to ever grace the Earth. With their inspection complete, the two homunculi started down the ventilation shaft to find their target. After the first turn in the shaft, they came to an aluminum mesh barrier—part of the Faraday cage's seal—and they worked in tandem to cut an X in its center before proceeding through.

With the Kestrel safely nestled between trees in a narrow valley, Cooper pulled the engine power control levers to idle and watched as engine and rotor RPM decreased.

"Randy and Gordy are inside," Ross said, looking down at a console behind Cooper's seat.

"Are you going to tell us how you know which building he's in, Ellie?" Cooper asked. "I saw a leaked video of him leaving that fundraiser with a girl, and saw an initial intel report that the two of them died in a car wreck."

Ellie cleared her throat. She didn't answer right away.

"The video's a deepfake," she said. "That wasn't Leonard's walk, so that's how I know it wasn't him. He started getting nervous a few days before he left, and I trust his gut as much as he trusts it. He knew something wasn't quite right. As for how I knew the building—I got him pretty drunk and, um—"

"You used your lady powers on him?" Ross offered.

Cooper knew without looking that her cheeks would be flushed red right now.

"Sure," Ellie said. "He's usually a light sleeper, but he was out. I injected a K-FIND tracking pellet in his butt. The pellet has a transmitter in it. When the other tracking devices from Pegasus showed up fifty miles down the road, mine didn't. The pellet doesn't have much power, so it sends a parasite signal to cell phones when they come in range. Even if it gets stuck in a cave or something, the phone will transmit the pellet's location when it reconnects to the network."

"That sounds expensive," Ross said. "You'd have to have doctor money to afford something like that."

"Well, I've got doctor money, Sergeant Bedford. And I want my husband back."

Flight crews generally revert to a casual first name or nickname basis, as do all small military groups that work in tight quarters and in positions that require absolute mutual reliance. Flight surgeons, while required to maintain flight hours, do not fly as often, and the same demands are not placed on them. Her use of Ross's rank exerted a subtle formality that let the rest of the crew know how on edge she was.

"Wouldn't it have been better," Ross said, "to bring a flight medic? Somebody a bit more detached emotionally? And I mean you've got that hand thing—"

"Ross—" Cooper said.

"It's fine," Ellie said quietly. "If Leonard's going to die, I don't want it to be because anybody else screwed up. My hand won't be an issue when it matters."

She held up a pneumatic injector and wiggled it for Ross to see.

"What is that?" Ross asked. "Tranquilizers?"

"Short-life nanomachines," Ellie said. "Only way I can do surgery now."

"Doctor money," Ross said. "Doctor toys."

A message arrived in Gordy's core processor, then in Randy's. Signals relayed from Calvin, Hobbes, and the humans aboard the Kestrel had ceased due to electromagnetic interference. They were alone now, with only the learned tactics in their Evolved Sentience 2.0 to guide them.

They came to a vertical drop in the ventilation system, and their last stored location from the K-FIND pellet showed the target three floors below them. They communicated through a brief series of ultrasound clicks and chirps that would be inaudible to humans. Then Randy removed his coil of Kevlar thread and handed it to Gordy. Gordy knotted the two strands together.

Randy searched for a suitable anchor point, and, not finding one, briefly suggested that they use the .22 pistol to shoot a hole in the aluminum.

Gordy clicked and chirped his disapproval due to noise and the depletion of resources available to their principal. He elaborated with the fact that neither of them had fired a handgun and that now was not the time to figure out if they could handle the recoil.

Randy conceded, then snapped the knife blade on his right arm forward. He used this to stab holes in the aluminum, and began to bend the jagged openings down to create smoother contact points for the Kevlar. In the act of prying the second hole open, the tip of his blade snapped, and Randy was left with a jagged point and only two thirds of his cutting surface when he retracted it.

Together, they threaded the Kevlar through the holes, attached it to loops on the front of their chassis, and rappelled into the darkness below.

A third memory surfaced in Cooper's mind.

It was December, several months after Ellie had cured him of insomnia. He stood on a porch, alone, and sipped a beer. It was good beer, because he'd done well the last week and he felt he deserved it. Inside the house, people laughed and carried on at the unit's Christmas party.

The door opened and Ellie came out.

"Cooper?" she said. She staggered a bit. She rarely drank so much. "Are you smoking out here?"

He smiled.

"No ma'am," he said.

She stepped close, lowball glass in hand, and sniffed him.

"Okay," she said. "Just making sure. Good boy."

She didn't step away.

Almost without thinking, Cooper leaned in and kissed her. She pressed her body into his for a moment, with her free hand on the porch railing. Then she stepped away.

Those eyes held a look that almost scared Cooper.

"What are you thinking," he asked, "right at this moment?"

Ellie sniffed. She took a step back and looked him over.

She was about to speak when the door opened again, and Leonard appeared.

"Babe?" he said. He looked between them. "You wandered off."

She didn't break eye contact with Cooper. Neither of them blinked.

"Yeah," she said, before finally looking away. "Just making sure Coop wasn't out here smoking. Sometimes he's bad."

Then she walked back inside with her husband. Cooper left without finishing the good beer.

The next time he saw her, in the daylight, her cheeks flushed. She didn't look away, but there was tension in her eyes. He extended a hand, and without looking down at it, her fingers slipped into his palm.

He gave her hand a squeeze. "It's fine. We're friends. Emotions are what they are."

She sighed, nodded silently, and went back to her work. And they never spoke of it again.

A knock came at the door behind Purple Gloves. He opened it, listened to a few whispered words from someone Leonard couldn't see, and then went out. The bolt clicked shut again from the other side.

Minutes passed.

Purple Gloves returned. A scowl had replaced his sadistic smirk.

"Have you ever heard of a tracking system called K-FIND?" Purple Gloves asked.

"Eh, maybe," Leonard said. "Not really my field."

Purple Gloves walked to Leonard's side and stared down at him for several seconds. Then he kicked Leonard's shoulder with such force that the chair tipped over and Leonard landed on his arm. He barely avoided slamming his head into the concrete.

Leonard grunted at the impact.

"Let's see," Purple Gloves said. "Where would they put it?"

"What are you talking about?" Leonard asked through clenched teeth.

"The pellet," Purple Gloves said. "Mr. Bloodworth has access to all the networks. Someone's tracking some sort of locator in this room."

Leonard heard a switchblade snap open near his feet. He braced himself as Purple Gloves dragged the point across the bare sole of his foot.

"No, no," Purple Gloves said. "They wouldn't put it in your feet. It would cause irritation when you walked. Not a lot of fat on you either. Calves? Forearms perhaps?"

Purple Gloves slid the blade inside Leonard's right pant leg—just above the tape and zip ties that held his ankle to the leg of the chair—and began cutting upward. The point of the knife nicked Leonard's skin, and he flinched.

"Relax," Purple Gloves said. "It's only your skin. It's not like you're going to need it much longer anyway."

He ran the knife's edge over Leonard's right calf, feeling for bumps. Then he stood.

"You know, if I was going to track you, I'd probably go with the penicillin method. Plenty of room to stick a pellet in one of your glutes."

Purple Gloves slashed upward, cutting away the right leg of Leonard's pants through the waistline. He began running the edge of the knife over the skin of Leonard's left buttock.

"You waited all this time to tell me you're gay?" Leonard said through gritted teeth. "I mean you've had me tied up for three nights. Not like I could get away from your butt fetish if I wanted to."

"Funny," Purple Gloves said.

The edge of the knife hit a bump, and Purple Gloves stopped. Leonard felt it too. Until that moment he'd thought it was a spider bite.

"What've we here?" Purple Gloves said. He dug the point of the knife into the skin, just a bit deeper than was necessary, twisted, and then withdrew the knife.

Purple Gloves held the tiny black pellet—roughly the size of an apple seed—between his thumb and forefinger for Leonard to see.

"Who's coming?" Purple Gloves asked.

"I'm telling you," Leonard said, "I had no idea that was there."

"Stay there then. I'd even considered giving you a last meal. You can die hungry."

Purple Gloves left the room and locked the door behind him.

Leonard struggled to move the chair, and groaned against the pain in his shoulder. He tried moving his legs, and found that he could, at least, begin to loosen the tape.

Cooper watched the artificial-vision feeds from Calvin and Hobbes on the center console. The mix of forward-looking infrared (FLIR) and radar could paint any environment through mist, darkness, sandstorms, or snow.

He sighed. Despite the seat and the space between them, he could feel Ellie's presence behind him in the cabin as surely as if he had some sort of artificial vision of his own.

Cooper had tried to have normal, healthy relationships. He'd dated a rather passionate Cuban girl for nine months, but it ended badly. She'd said he was too distant. He'd dated Wes's sister, which Wes had forgiven him for since it never got very serious. He'd serial-dated a string of girls for several months, and then given up on it and reverted to a sort of monastic isolation.

"They're moving him," Ellie said, pulling him out of his reverie.

"What?" Cooper asked.

"The K-FIND pellet's moving north toward the bridge," she said. She moved the map on her tablet computer with her forefinger. "I think they might be putting Leonard in a vehicle."

Wes cursed quietly, but the VOX still picked it up.

"Don't have visual on the truck from Calvin or Hobbes from current positions," he said, leaning in to look at the drone feeds. "It'd be another thirty seconds before we can get eyes on it."

No one spoke for those thirty seconds.

"Truck's moving," Wes said. "We missed them loading him."

"Okay," Cooper said. "Adapt, improvise, overcome. We've still got two Infiltrators, right?"

"Yeah," Ross said. "Gimme a sec and I'll get 'em loaded."

"We can wingsuit our last two onto the truck," Cooper said, "then shoot out the engine block on the truck while it's crossing the bridge to immobilize."

"What if it goes into the water?" Ellie asked, her voice tense. "If he's in restraints he'll drown before we could get to him."

"Fine," Cooper said. "We launch the bots while it's on the bridge, before trees get in the way. Interdiction with the fifty-cal when the truck hits the far side so it crashes on land."

"We should've brought real ground troops," Marco said.

"We're not even supposed to be here," Cooper said. "Okay, before takeoff—"

He reached up and moved the engine power control levers fully forward, and the rotor accelerated silently back to one hundred percent RPM.

"—PCL's to fly, stealth enabled, systems all green, crew, pax—"

He didn't wait for everyone to respond, though they did so rapidly.

"Clear up," he said to Wes. Wes pulled the collective upward, and they leapt into the fog once again.

⊕⊕⊕

Randy and Gordy came to a T-intersection in the ventilation duct. The stored waypoint for their target hadn't moved when Purple Gloves removed Leonard's K-FIND pellet because they were using cached information. The waypoint was, however, directly ahead of them—outside the duct system—and they didn't have a schematic from which to navigate.

They chirped and clicked briefly before deciding that—based on the building's external structure and laws of probability—left was the most likely direction to lead them where they wanted to go.

They had not gone very far to the left before Gordy chirped quietly that they should stop. Something had vibrated the floor of the conduit. Almost inaudibly, Randy suggested that it might be a fan system powering up. More vibrations came—more frequently, and with greater force. Something else was in the conduit, and it was getting closer.

Leonard freed his legs from the legs of the chair, despite his left hamstring cramping in the process. He hadn't eaten in three days, had minimal water in his system, and he was weak from lack of sleep. He managed to roll the chair so that he was on his knees and the weight of his body was not on his bruised shoulder. Then he pulled one leg up, and stood in a crouch. He tried to move his right wrist to loosen the tape, but the effort threw him off-balance and he landed back in a sitting position.

He was exhausted. Perhaps dying would be a relief—provided it was quick.

Leonard had landed close to the door—close enough to put his ear to the metal, which he did. That didn't require much exertion.

"One of the power lines came down on the south end of the island," a man's voice said. "It runs the lights at the marina, so we didn't know about it until the patrol boat came back."

"Any idea what caused it?" Purple Gloves asked.

"No," the man said. "We sent a couple of bots to check it out, and it looks like it was severed at both ends. That's as much information as we got."

"Could be to clear passage for an air assault," Purple Gloves said. "Keep your eyes peeled. They may have a recon element on the island already."

"Will do, boss," the man said. "The truck with the tracking thing just rolled out also."

"Good," Purple Gloves said. "We may need to dispose of Dr. Murrow sooner than we'd planned. I don't think there's anything else we're going to get out of him anyway."

Footsteps approached the door, then stopped.

"Hey, Mike," Purple Gloves said.

"Yeah?"

"Have them flip the truck halfway across the bridge. See if anyone comes out to look for a body. Better yet, set it on fire too to increase urgency. It'll be a perfect engagement area. If anyone comes looking for the doctor, kill them."

"You got it, boss."

"When you're done, I need you back here to help me clean up."

Randy and Gordy both extended the knives on their arms. When they saw the thing, though, they knew knives weren't going to do much good. It had overlapping carbon fiber armor plates all over. The robotic sentry was roughly the size and shape of a common house cat, but it had six cameras on its head where eyes would've been, and a reinforced jaw that looked like it could crush either of them easily. As it approached, retractable claws slid out of their hiding places in its forepaws. Given the relative size of its limbs, they knew they wouldn't get far if they tried to run.

"Get ready to launch bots," Cooper said. "The bridge is a lot lower and we don't have to avoid sensors, so we'll launch without banking for arc."

"Roger," Ross said. "Left window's coming open."

Cooper glanced down at Hobbes's camera feed, which showed the truck from another angle.

"Stand by to launch," he said.

"Standing by."

"Launch bots in three . . . two . . ."

The truck wove left, then overcorrected and flipped onto its side.

"Hold fire," Cooper said.

"Roger," Ross said. "Holding."

"What's happening?" Ellie asked.

"The truck just flipped," Cooper said. "Looks like a fire's spreading from the engine. I don't see movement from anyone inside."

"We have to get Leonard out," Ellie said.

"I'll stand by for hoist," Marco said. "I'll take the remote and lower myself to grab him. Keep Ross on his gun for cover fire."

"Okay," Cooper said. "Let's do it quick. We're going to be exposed once we drop below the scud."

Purple Gloves opened the door.

"Well, look who's up and about," he said. "You even got your legs free."

He pulled a case out of his pocket, opened it, and withdrew a syringe.

"You don't have to do this," Leonard said.

"Perhaps," Purple Gloves said, "but I want to."

Leonard kicked out at Purple Gloves' knee, but Purple Gloves sidestepped easily. He backed away, out of range, as he pushed the plunger to clear the air from the needle. A thin jet of liquid spurted from its tip.

"The air bubbles would kill you too quickly," Purple Gloves said. "This way I can be sure the pain will last. You should've been more cooperative."

A squeak from the back of the room drew Purple Gloves' attention, and Leonard followed his gaze to a small vent as it slid open. What looked like a robotic cat stepped through it. In its jaws, it carried a small humanoid robot—one of the Infiltrators Leonard had written code for.

"Interesting," Purple Gloves said. "I told Mr. Bloodworth he was being paranoid when he said he wanted cat sentries in the vents, but it looks like they paid off. Doesn't seem your friends cared enough to send full-sized commandos to rescue you."

The cat-bot dropped the homunculus in the middle of the floor.

"Don't leave that there," Purple Gloves said.

The cat-bot padded closer, then abruptly sprang into the air, claws extended. Purple Gloves dropped the syringe and managed to catch the cat-bot by the chassis, but it clawed at his face and wrists. Gordy sprang to his feet and sprinted across the cell floor as Randy climbed out of the vent. As Purple Gloves tangled with the traitorous cat-bot,

Gordy used his knife to slash both of Purple Gloves' Achilles tendons. He screamed and dropped to the floor.

Simultaneously, Randy leapt onto Leonard's chair to slice through the tape and zip ties that held his wrists. Randy then climbed onto Leonard's right thigh and offered his back, with the .22 pistol and the earpiece.

Leonard grabbed the pistol, which thankfully didn't use a Browning action. One bullet just behind Purple Gloves' ear—with the barrel pressed into the skull—made almost no noise. Purple Gloves crumpled, dead, on the floor.

Leonard knelt next to Randy.

"Take the cat-bot and get back in radio range as fast as you can," he said. "The helicopter's flying into a trap."

Randy leapt onto the cat-bot's back, and they disappeared through the vent once again.

"Too bad you're running a low neural-density AI on your cat-bots," Leonard said to the pile of blood, bone, hair, and gray matter that had once been his tormentor's head. "I just wrote the Dominate program for Infiltrators last week. Looks like it works okay."

It also meant Ellie was there, because he hadn't distributed the program yet. Only she would've known where to access it to upgrade the Infiltrators.

He searched Purple Gloves, and found an ID badge just as a knock came from the door.

A moment passed, and another knock came.

"Boss?" Purple Gloves' henchman—Mike, he'd called him—had returned to dispose of Leonard's corpse.

The door opened. With it open, the noise of a shot might carry. Others might come.

Leonard picked up Gordy and threw him at Mike. Mike tried to scream, but Gordy sliced through his trachea and the scream came out as a muted gurgle. Gordy kept stabbing as they fell to the floor together, giving Mike a mercifully quick death as his arterial blood sprayed up the wall.

Leonard looked between Mike and Purple Gloves, decided that Mike was a closer match for pants size, and began tugging them off of him.

⊕⊕⊕

The Kestrel descended next to the burning truck as Wes lowered the collective. Marco stood at the open door, already clipped into the hoist.

"Ten more feet and we'll be out of the fog," Cooper said.

"Ready when you are," Marco said.

A message appeared on the central screens.

"Hold descent," Cooper said.

"Cooper," Ellie said. "He's right there."

"Holding here," Wes said, and pulled hover torque back into the collective.

Cooper watched the artificial vision for a moment, then the feed from Hobbes. Something was definitely wrong. He tapped a button on the center console, and Hobbes' feed displayed FLIR only. The heat signature from the truck showed orange-hot where the flames came out of the engine compartment, but there were no other strong heat signatures.

"The driver wouldn't have gone cold this fast," he said.

"Could've been a bot," Wes said.

"True, but we'd see *something* from Leonard. Climb. Get us out of here. Randy just came online and said he's still in the main compound. He said they pulled the pellet out of Leonard. He's out of his restraints and should meet us on the roof."

Marco unclipped from the hoist, closed the door, and hooked the remote to a tie-down ring next to his seat.

"Okay," Wes said. "Moving."

Leonard crept down the hall, barefoot. He'd half expected a squad of bots to come after him, but this was one of the ironic upsides to having so many bots under the control of so few humans. Whoever Mike had relayed commands to was unaware that Leonard had escaped, so the island's security force was still entirely focused on the unknown external threat. Centralized command meant slower changes in the system.

At the end of the hall was a security camera. From its angle, Leonard didn't think he was in its field of vision yet. He whispered to Gordy, who rode on his shoulder.

"I can't throw you that far," Leonard said. "Think you can climb? Dominate might work on it."

Gordy tapped Leonard's ear, knowing he wouldn't understand chirps and clicks, even if he lowered their frequency into an audible range.

Leonard picked up Gordy in his hand so he could see his arms.

"We really need to install a full voice circuit on you guys," Leonard said.

Gordy, once he was in Leonard's view, pointed up to the tiled ceiling.

"Of course," Leonard said. "I should've thought of that. I'm tired."

Leonard stood on his tiptoes against the wall and lifted Gordy to the tile. Gordy pushed the tile upward, pressing his feet down against Leonard's fingertips. Then he disappeared.

Seconds later, a tile eased upward above the camera. Gordy dropped onto its mount and—after what seemed to be a failed attempt to take over the camera with the Dominate field—he stripped the insulation from wires on the power cable with his knife. Then he sliced through a wire. He waved his arm down toward the door as a signal to Leonard.

The door opened when Leonard held Purple Gloves' ID badge against an RFID scanner on the wall. Leonard went through and extended his arm in the open doorway. He figured it would take at least one second from the time Gordy twisted the wire back together and the time the camera rejoined the network.

Gordy leapt onto Leonard's outstretched hand and scurried up to his shoulder as Leonard closed the door behind them. Ideally, it would appear that a momentary glitch had caused the camera to lose connectivity.

"—any—ody—ear me?"

Leonard's voice came in broken, but they knew it was him.

"Hightower," Cooper said, "This is your extract. You're coming in broken but readable. Can you get to the roof?"

"—an certai-ly try," Leonard said. "—eading—at way."

Wes brought the Kestrel to a hover fifty feet above the roof, still within the fog. Two robotic sentries remained, the others apparently having been re-tasked.

The flat bottom of the aircraft would reflect radar, so if the bots were equipped with more than optical sensors, they'd see the Kestrel if they looked directly up. Fortunately, their machine minds seemed to have the same instincts as humans.

"I'm tracking Gordy now," Ross said. "Provided he's with Leonard, they're one floor below the roof and it looks like they're moving up a stairwell. Randy's at the edge of the vent, just out of sight of the guards."

"Wait until he's almost on the roof," Cooper said quietly. "Then hit 'em with the minigun. I'll put one wheel on the roof where we have rotor clearance, and you pull him in."

"Got it," Marco said, slaving his holographic sight to the Kestrel's artificial vision system so that he could shoot through the fog. "Gun's ready."

Ellie pulled the pneumatic injector from her gear, held its tip against her wrist, and pulled the trigger. She winced as the short-life nanomachines flooded into her bloodstream. Moments later, her hand tremor stopped.

Ross counted down Leonard's approach to the roof, then gave Marco the command to fire. The two sentries dropped, and Wes eased the collective down.

Leonard was halfway across the roof when a short burst of gunfire stitched up the back of his leg. One sentry, then another, then five more swarmed onto the roof from another stairwell. Leonard fell, tried to get up, and fell again. The bots set up a perimeter around him, but didn't shoot again.

"They've wounded him," Cooper said. "They're using him as bait."

The cockpit glass went abruptly black. All the lines showing the building's structure disappeared. The radar altimeter showed the ground sixty feet below them, but not the roof. To move closer, over the roof, would slam the rotors into the antennas and structure above the roof. Outside the glass was fog and the night.

"Just lost artificial vision," Wes said.

They all knew the emergency procedure—initiate a straight vertical climb. They had to leave Leonard behind. If they drifted in the fog, they could easily crash.

Wes pulled on the collective, or tried to. He looked to Cooper, who held the co-pilot's collective in place.

"Cooper—" Wes said.

"Wait."

"Ellie's on the hoist," Marco said.

"Well, get her off of it," Wes said.

"Can't," Marco said. "She grabbed the remote when I was on the gun sights. She's ten feet . . . fifteen . . . twenty feet . . ."

"Wait until she's on the roof and cut the cable," Wes said.

"No," Cooper said.

"Coop—"

"No."

Fifty sentries swarmed onto the roof, though Cooper could only see them through Calvin and Hobbes' drone feeds. Then he saw Ellie descend out of the fog. The bots aimed upward, following the cable into the fog, though apparently they didn't have radar. They would shoot any second, and a series of scenarios flashed through Cooper's mind almost simultaneously.

If Calvin and Hobbes fired rockets at the bots, Leonard and Ellie would certainly get hit.

If they ascended with Ellie on the cable, she'd be slung into something and be injured or killed.

If they cut the cable, they would have no way to get her or Leonard off the roof without artificial vision. Even if the bots didn't shoot the Kestrel down, and even if they didn't shoot Ellie and Leonard, they would have Ellie as an additional hostage. She would certainly be tortured.

There wasn't nearly enough time for her to secure Leonard and ride the hoist back up the Kestrel.

There was only one other option.

"Calvinball," Cooper said. It was a reference to the make-up-rules-as-you-go game from Bill Watterson's comic strip.

A light glowed green near the minigun's triggers as the aircraft's main processor recognized the voice command.

"You sure?" Marco asked. "The proximity—"

"Now," Cooper said.

Marco hit a button next to the green light, and the servos on the minigun's mount took over. Marco pulled his hands well clear.

The Kestrel had lost artificial vision, but Calvin and Hobbes had not. They locked onto the fifty sentries in one fraction of a second. In the next fraction of a second, the minigun roared to life. NATO 7.62 mm bullets ripped through the bots at a rate of four thousand rounds per minute. A couple of bots managed to fire short bursts before they were shredded by the onslaught. Three bullets impacted the floor of the Kestrel, but Wes held the hover.

More bots swarmed onto the roof at a sprint. The minigun shifted and began firing again, slaughtering Bloodworth's robot army as they poured through the choke point.

Then they stopped coming.

The minigun twitched, almost like a nervous tic, between the pile of shredded bots at the stairs and the bots around the Murrows. None stirred.

Randy emerged from the vent, gave the cat-bot a hibernate command, and ran to join Gordy at Leonard's side.

Ellie clipped her husband into a harness, helped him hobble to the place where she'd initially touched down, and pressed a button to begin reeling them back in.

"Let me know when they're secure," Cooper said. "I'm going to fiddle with a couple of circuit breakers."

Wes held his hover as the minigun continued to twitch between target reference points.

Cooper reset four breakers, with no effect. He sighed audibly and began punching buttons on the lower console's computer interface.

Lines appeared on the cockpit glass.

"I can see," Wes said, but Cooper could tell from his voice that he wasn't happy.

"Pax secure," Marco said, as he slid the cabin door shut.

Cooper turned to look behind his seat, and found Randy and Gordy sitting in the seat directly aft of Marco's crew chief seat. Ellie was working furiously on Leonard's leg, packing entry and exit wounds with hemostatic gauze. Seconds later, she had a saline IV hanging from a ceiling tie-down ring to rehydrate him.

"My beautiful husband," she whispered as she worked.

Leonard, who could give life to homunculi and teach them mind control—what was he if not a modern alchemist, or a warlock? And Ellie—whose healing powers bordered on the supernatural . . .

He flew a helicopter. They bent the edges of reality.

Cooper shook the thought from his head.

"Coop," Wes said, "there's a boat leaving from the marina."

Cooper looked down at the video feeds from Calvin and

Hobbes. A small go-fast boat was indeed gaining speed away from the island.

"Think Bloodworth's making a run for it?" Wes asked. "We could have Calvin or Hobbes sling a rocket at him."

Leonard heard the conversation, thanks to the sound-dampened rotors.

"Need positive ID," Leonard said weakly. His burst of adrenaline had clearly run its course.

"We've got artificial vision back," Cooper said. "Let's drop down and have a look."

"Fifty cal's better for boat interdiction," Ross said.

"Roger," Cooper said. "We'll put him out your door. I have the flight controls."

"Your aircraft," Wes said, carrying through on a three-way positive transfer of flight controls. He pulled his hands away from the cyclic and collective, and his feet away from the pedals.

"I got 'em," Cooper said. "Prop Leonard up in a seat so he can see."

They dove below the fog, gaining airspeed as they fell. Cooper leveled off ten feet above the water and banked into an arc around the front of the approaching boat.

"Set the searchlight to target-track," Cooper said quickly, and a light snapped on. It swung to the left, blinding the boat's occupant.

Ross tapped a button on the console to his right, and the camera view from his gun mount displayed. White squares snapped in around the face of the boat's driver as the pattern-match algorithm ran. Lines snapped around his figure for height, weight, and body composition biometrics.

"Ninety-three percent match from the database," Ross said.

Leonard looked through the cabin window. He squinted as the boat turned to avoid the helicopter.

"That's him," Leonard said.

"Light him up," Cooper said.

Ross stitched the boat from the bow, up through the cabin, and down to the stern. Bloodworth crumpled inside. Ross held down the triggers and kept the barrel on the engines until they exploded. He swept the barrel back and forth across the hull at the waterline, where Bloodworth's body most likely lay. The starboard bulkhead disintegrated, and for an instant, Leonard could see Bloodworth's shredded corpse behind it. Until that moment he'd wondered if perhaps Bloodworth might send a robot body-double out as a decoy. But now he knew.

Then the boat tilted and began to sink. Leonard sunk back to the floor, and Ellie cradled his head in her lap.

"Left gun's Winchester," Ross said, indicating that he was out of ammo.

"Roger," Cooper said. "Don't think we'll need any more anyway."

Cooper pulled back on the cyclic, trading off airspeed for altitude, and climbed back into the fog.

"Your flight controls," he said to Wes.

"I got 'em," Wes said.

"All yours."

The next day, after an intel debrief and a fitful five hours of sleep, Cooper stopped by the hospital where Leonard was being treated for internal bleeding, a broken rib, and a host of other injuries.

"Thank you, Captain Cooper," Leonard said.

"I'm just glad you're okay," Cooper said. He glanced at Ellie in the chair next to Leonard's bed. "I know the doc's happy to have you back."

Then Cooper left.

He got halfway down the hall before he heard soft footsteps behind him. He turned.

"Thank you," Ellie said. Tears welled in the corners of her eyes, and she seemed very unsure of what to say next.

"For what?" Cooper asked. "You could've killed us."

"I heard you on ICS," she said. "You stalled for me."

"I endangered my aircraft and its crew," Cooper said. "I shouldn't have."

"It worked, Cooper," she said. "Don't beat yourself up. I asked for you, you know—by name. I knew you'd endanger yourself for me if you had a choice to make. The best possible thing happened because you did."

And Cooper considered the awful choice that had flashed through his mind when the artificial vision had failed. If he hadn't stalled for her, Leonard would be dead. Ellie would grieve, but she would recover in time.

"If that's what you think that was," Cooper said quietly. "I just know what the aircraft can handle."

"Well thank you just the same," she said. She dabbed the corner of her sleeve at the tears. "Will I see you in a week?"

"Sure," Cooper said. "Maybe."

Ellie's brow furrowed.

"I don't think I should be doing this anymore," he said. "I need you to be whole more than I need me to be whole, and I don't like what that means. I'd burn the whole damned world for you. It's too much risk for people that haven't signed up for it."

Ellie cleared her throat and looked down at the floor. She seemed about to say something, but Cooper turned and walked away.

Cooper left the gas station with a pack of cigarettes and a twenty-two-ounce can of cheap beer. He didn't deserve good beer.

He sat on the curb, just out of the glow of the street light. He didn't deserve the light either. He put a cigarette in his mouth—the first in years—and lit a match.

"I'm not a robot," he said quietly.

He stared at the match, shook it out, and tossed the cigarette on the ground in front of him. He fixated on it for several seconds until the squeaky wheels of a shopping cart drew his attention to the sidewalk. A homeless black man in overalls stopped pushing the cart and looked down at him.

"Shame to waste good smokes like that," the man said.

"Won't get me where I need to go fast enough," Cooper said. "Take 'em if you want 'em."

He tossed the pack to the man, who would probably trade them for something else.

"Man, you are one sad, pathetic loser, ain't you?" the man said.

"I guess," Cooper said. "I saved the world yesterday, though."

"The whole world, huh?"

"The bit of it that mattered to me."

The homeless man looked at Cooper's haircut, minimal stubble, and athletic build. He was a dead giveaway as a military man in civilian clothes.

"Well, uh," the man said, "thank you for your service, good sir. And the smokes."

"Sure," Cooper said. "Godspeed."

The man rolled his shopping cart away. He laughed about something, then began talking to himself in a strange, agitated voice.

Cooper remembered closed-casket funerals for Harper and Gurney, years ago. He wondered how much he and Wes had drifted in the fog last night—how close he'd come to killing his entire crew.

And he knew that if he'd made the other choice—if he hadn't stalled, and Leonard had died—he'd be punishing himself the same way. If the aircraft hadn't failed, he wouldn't have even had a choice to make. But it did, and he had.

Cooper's phone buzzed, and he lifted it to see a text message.

I can literally feel you overthinking this, Ellie said. *Come back to me. I'll make it better. It's what we do, Cooper. We look after each other.*

Cooper's hands shook. He'd survived so many things—things other people didn't, things he probably shouldn't have. Why was this the dumb thing that hurt him the most? It was like a song he'd never heard the end to, so the chorus just kept playing in his head. He wanted to hear the end and he loved the tune when he heard it, but he wanted the music to stop too.

In the second-worst impulsive gesture he could remember, Cooper threw his phone as hard as he could toward the river. He heard a faint splash, but his hands didn't stop shaking for five minutes.

Then he sat back down, just outside the glow of the street lamp, with only his own thoughts for company.

OPERATION MELTWATER
Philip A. Kramer

The first thing Dr. Dale Stratford learned as a scientist was that no experiment ever went exactly to plan. Now, four years into the most anticipated experiment of his career, he was still waiting for the ball to drop. The anxiety chilled him more than the bitter cold of the Antarctic.

His technician did not share his concerns. Gideon sat in a lawn chair, cradling a tablet in his arms. Occasionally he would withdraw a gloved hand from the warmth of an armpit to probe or swipe the screen with a finger.

"We just passed five hundred meters," Gideon said. Smiling like a schoolboy at lunch bell, he sprang from his lawn chair and approached a flimsy rope barrier.

Dale pulled the collar of his survival suit tighter and shuffled across the hard-packed snow after him.

Steam billowed up from a two-by-two-meter hole on the other side of the barrier. At one corner, a ten-centimeter-wide hose snaked up and away to deposit millions of liters of meltwater at a distance.

Their NASA prototype, HESTIA, melted through the ice at a rate of two cubic meters per minute. The cube-shaped probe, named after the Greek goddess of the hearth and its fire, contained a fast nuclear reactor with highly enriched uranium and a molten lead-bismuth coolant. By directing the flow of coolant into the probe's ceramic composite exterior, they could melt through the ice in any direction they chose. Between its thermoelectric generator and steam turbine, it produced more power than its onboard instruments and sensors would ever need.

Back at its earliest inception, the project had been little more than a chance to bring in non-dilutive capital for his scientific instruments company. NASA was planning an exploratory mission to Enceladus, the icy moon of Saturn, and they needed a probe capable of tunneling through the ice. Before he knew it, they had completed phase three of the grant and signed a contract with NASA to construct the final prototype. Now, a year before the planned launch, he stood with his assistant and a small team of NASA engineers just outside the eightieth parallel, putting the prototype through its paces. The East Antarctic Ice Sheet was their closest analogue to the frozen moon, with ice as pure and nearly a third as deep.

Beyond the ice pit, a small geodesic dome stood alone on the featureless windswept plains. From this distance, it looked like a faceted blue gem on a glittering white sand beach. For the next two weeks, it would be their base of operations and the only escape from the cold.

"What's the matter?" Gideon asked, glancing away from the column of steam and at his mentor's pinched features.

"Waiting for something bad to happen."

Gideon chuckled.

"You worry too much. Lighten up a little and enjoy the success."

That was easy for him to say, Dale thought as he grumbled. Gideon had had the luxury of experiencing only the golden years of their endeavor. He never knew the sour taste of a project's failure or the endless months of wondering what he could have done to prevent it.

Dale, on the other hand, had a lifetime's worth of failure and all the intuition it granted. Even now, as he blew warm air into his gloved hands, that sense niggled at him, urging him to take notice.

A moment later, he finally pinpointed the source of his unease. About thirty meters away, where the pump disgorged over two thousand liters of water a minute, stood one of the three NASA engineers. She held the nozzle of the hose in one hand as she oscillated back and forth like an enthusiastic yard sprinkler. The thing had to be exerting as much force as a fire hose, but she had been at it since they began a little over four hours ago. How strong was this woman?

Now that he thought of it, all the NASA engineers seemed a bit off. He had worked with his fair share of engineers over the years, but he did not recognize the three they had saddled him with. They carried about their tasks with a silent efficiency, setting up the shelter, unpacking the equipment, and aiding him and his technician without question. Quiet, strong, and obedient were certainly not the qualities of any engineer he had ever met. If he did not know any better, he would guess they were soldiers.

Unable to shake the thought, Dale casually circled the pit in search of the second NASA engineer. A man stood on the other side of the steam column, quietly regarding his own tablet. His name tag identified him as Adrian Hendricks. He was a few centimeters taller than Dale, with a crooked nose and cold blue eyes.

"Doctor," Hendricks said without looking up from his screen. "Can I help you with something?"

"I thought I'd get to know the people I'll be bunking with the next two weeks. What's your opinion on nuclear reactors under the control of autonomous systems?" It was not a baseless question; he and Gideon had been arguing about that very thing for the past hour.

"I don't have an opinion."

"Really? I've never met an engineer who didn't have a lot to say on the regulation of AI."

"Sorry to disappoint," he said. Still not looking at him, he promptly turned and walked toward the humming water pump a dozen meters away.

"Now hold on. I have another question," Dale called. He shuffled after him in his baggy survival suit.

"What's that?" he said, not turning around or slowing in the slightest.

"What's your opinion on military interference in purely scientific endeavors?"

There was a slight stutter in Hendricks' step. Dale had finally scored a reaction, but he did not celebrate. If he was right, what did it mean for their project?

"You think I'm with the military?"

"Tell me you aren't."

This time he stopped and turned to face him before answering.

"I can tell you with complete honesty that I am not, nor have I ever been, associated with the military."

Dale drew up short. He had not expected that response.

By this time, their conversation had carried to the woman holding the hose. She anchored its nozzle into a bracket hammered into the snow and approached at a brisk walk. Just as the crunch of her boots became audible, Hendricks' right hand extended a few inches from his side and squeezed into a fist. Within a fraction of a second, she came to a complete stop.

"Then explain that," Dale said, pointing to the offending hand.

Hendricks looked down at the "freeze" signal, then over his shoulder at the woman standing stock-still behind him. He shoved his hand in his pocket and the woman developed a sudden fascination with her boots.

"Look, I don't care," Dale said with a dismissive wave. "I'm relieved you're here, actually. I'm sure you have loads of survival training and enough guns to give every blood-crazed penguin second thoughts. I just want to know why NASA sent the military to help me instead of the other project's engineers. Wait, is it because Ryabov is Russian?"

Hendricks tensed at the mention of the Roscosmos scientist. Anton Ryabov had helped design their fast reactor to meet the heat and power requirements. It was an area in which the Russians excelled. Or was it the mention of Anton's motherland that put Hendricks on edge? NASA had gone to great lengths to convince the Russian government to allow them to test their prototype on the deepest ice in the Antarctic. Nearly everyone disputed Russia's claim on the southernmost continent, but so long as they allowed scientists access, Dale could not care less.

"We are not military, and we have no problem with the Russians," Hendricks said, with a menacing tone.

Just then, the voice of the third NASA engineer sounded on the small radio attached to Hendricks' belt loop.

"Sir, two Russian birds inbound at ninety-eight degrees. Forty klicks. ETA ten minutes."

Dale crossed his arms and raised his eyebrows. They did not meet his eyes.

"Just tell him, sir," the woman said, stepping forward. "He'll find out as soon as we deviate from the plan tomorrow." Beneath the NASA logo, her name tag read April Drake.

What had she said about deviating from the plan? This was his project. He would not let them take it from him so easily.

"Okay, fine," Hendricks said, holding out a hand as if to ward off a rabid dog. "We are military engineers. But officially, we work for NASA and are here to test a prototype. You don't need to know more."

"I don't need to know? I am the head of this project. I built this probe myself," Dale said, pointing unhelpfully to the space where the prototype had sat a few hours ago.

Beside the hole in the ice stood Gideon, his mouth agape as he watched their exchange.

"Sir, we don't have much time. If they knew the gravity of the situation, they'd be more willing to keep our identities a secret when the Russians show up."

"Thank you, April. If that is your real name," Dale said, trying to inject equal amounts of gratitude and derision into the words.

Hendricks stripped off his cap and raked his hand across his bristly hair.

"Let's head inside," Hendricks said, motioning to their shelter with his cap.

"The prototype—"

"Drake will handle it."

April shrugged in apology as she took the tablet from Gideon. The device practically fell out of his technician's slack fingers. He continued to stare in awe as she settled into his lawn chair and flicked through the HESTIA's readouts like she had been doing it for years.

Together, Hendricks, Dale, and Gideon followed the narrow trail of footprints to the shelter. The shallow angle of the sun made the solar panels gleam on each of the structure's faceted surfaces. It had only taken thirty minutes for the engineers to unload, unfold the triangular pieces, and raise them into a dome that morning. It was a good thing, too. As soon as its hold was empty, their cargo plane had promptly departed, leaving them with no other shelter to speak of.

Once inside, Dale took stock of all that had changed since that morning. Collapsible tables, cots, and dozens of crates took up most of the rubber-tread floor, and drawn curtains divided the space into a dining, bathroom, and sleeping area.

The third engineer sat at a small desk constructed from empty crates and covered in radio equipment. He had stripped out of his survival suit in the heated confines of the shelter and was tapping at a computer with fingers that flashed over the keyboard. He too seemed unreasonably well muscled. His computer displayed a map of the Antarctic. Surrounding the lone blue dot in the center of the East Antarctic Ice Sheet was a scattering of red dots against the white expanse. Two of the dots were moving in their direction.

Hendricks sat at the dining table, propped up his elbows, and tented his hands. Dale flashed back to his thesis defense nearly three decades ago. Like his thesis committee, Hendricks held the fate of Dale's career in his hands, and he knew it.

"You should sit down," Hendricks said.

Gideon's knees bent as if he might sit directly on the floor. When his wits caught up with him, he cautiously took a chair. Dale stood stubbornly in place, taking satisfaction in the act of slowly pulling his gloves off one finger at a time.

"We were not made for this weather," Hendricks began, glancing significantly at Dale's gloves. "The Russians were. They've occupied Siberia and a full half of the Arctic circle since the age of the Vikings. For the last hundred years, they've had more arctic-capable vehicles and icebreakers than any other country in the world. We should have known they weren't going to decommission all of that hardware when the last of the arctic sea ice melted. When the Antarctic treaty expired in 2048, the Russians finally had the chance to expand their military operations to this continent. Seemingly overnight, they had such a strategic foothold, nobody could dislodge them. With China's conditional aid, they began stripping the Antarctic and its surrounding seas of oil, minerals, fish, and krill, and choking all trade and military traffic south of Cape Horn. If they retain control over both poles, they will have the mobility advantage in any conflict. And we believe conflict is what they're after. Until now, the United States and its allies had no way to turn the tables."

"Until now?" Dale asked as he began piecing the puzzle together. "You plan to use NASA as your passport onto the continent? And then what? Spy on them? But why not do this years ago? Why wait for HESTIA?"

"HESTIA *is* the mission, Doctor." Hendricks waited for Dale and Gideon to share a look before elaborating. "They didn't send military engineers on a lark. This was planned years in advance. NASA's funding-opportunity announcement and the proposed mission to

Enceladus was all orchestrated to get us onto the Antarctic ice sheet with a probe capable of rapidly melting through the ice."

Dale's knees felt weak, and he decided he would like to sit down after all.

It had all been an elaborate lie. He knew the grant and the resulting NASA contract had been too good to be true. They were doing what the military had always done, stealing groundbreaking innovations in science and using them for war.

"Don't worry," Hendricks said. He met Dale's angry glare with a placating hand. "You'll still get to Enceladus. It's an important mission and there's nothing the government likes more than killing two birds with one stone."

The assurances had the desired effect, and the cold knot of despair in his chest melted away. Once he had a tight rein on his emotions, he voiced his next question.

"And how is the HESTIA supposed to solve your problem with the Russians?"

Hendricks smiled, an expression that looked uncomfortable for him.

"We'll be using it to construct a military bunker under the ice." He paused a moment to let that sink in. "When the conflict starts, and it will start soon, we will use it as our foothold in the Antarctic. Nothing they throw at us, not even a nuke, will reach us that far under the ice."

Dale shook his head in disbelief. It all made sense now. The original designs for the HESTIA had changed dramatically once NASA obtained them. At first, he had seen their odd modifications as a challenge and had integrated them with little thought. After all, they knew more about the challenges they would face on the icy moon than he did. Now, he saw them in a new light. They had to make sure the probe could carve out an entire military bunker in the span of a couple weeks.

"This is better for us, isn't it?" Gideon asked tentatively. "I mean, if we could build a base here in the Antarctic, couldn't we do the same on Enceladus? Prepare the moon for colonization?"

Gideon was right for a change. Dale had been thinking too small. A part of his subconscious was already drafting a proposal to NASA to add a subsurface base to the mission objectives. They would be fools not to approve it. It was not an ideal location for colonization with the gravity so low, but all that ice would protect colonists from radiation and any other dangers space could throw at them. The base could also serve as a refueling hub for the entire outer solar system.

This was not the terrible event he had feared. It was another stroke of good fortune. Better still, in testing the prototype, they would do something meaningful instead of boring a useless hole in the ice.

There was still one missing piece of the puzzle.

"Why go through NASA? Why not build the probe yourself and keep everything classified?"

"As you have seen for yourself, melting through the ice results in a lot of steam. The Russians have eyes in orbit monitoring every inch of the Antarctic. We were never going to be covert about it, so why not hide in plain sight and recruit the world's most brilliant scientists to build it for us?"

Gideon, who had been cowering like a turtle in its shell since learning the engineers' identities, emerged at the unexpected flattery. Dale stroked the white stubble on his chin.

That explained why they did not seem surprised by the inbound Russian forces.

"And when the Russians get here?" Dale asked.

"ETA Becket?" Hendricks asked, glancing at the back of the third engineer.

"One minute, sir."

"They will search the place, but they won't find anything to alert them of our intent," Hendricks continued. He leaned forward as if to impart the most important information of all. "And all of us will play our roles. Just be the scientists you came here to be. With any luck, they will leave us to our business and never come back. When we reach three and a half kilometers, Drake and I will take over the design of the base. It is top secret after all, and we can't have a couple civvies knowing the layout."

"You expect us to sit back and do nothing for the next two weeks?" Dale asked, disheartened. The rollercoaster of competing emotions was dizzying.

"You will have access to all the sensor data on the probe. That should be more than enough to keep you busy."

Just then, a rumbling sound in the distance reached a volume he could not ignore. The Russians had arrived.

Becket stood and shrugged into the top half of his survival suit. "We should meet them outside."

Picking up his gloves, Dale gave one last look at their shelter. Sure enough, he saw nothing that could be construed as military hardware. That also worried him. If the Russians discovered their purpose here, Dale and his small team would have nothing with which to defend themselves.

His mind swimming with uncertainties, Dale followed Gideon out the door and into a biting wind. The snow kicked up by the helicopters' rotor wash formed long streamers under their feet. Dale pulled his hood around his neck and face as he examined the two rusted relics settling onto the packed snow. The feet of six soldiers hit the ground a second before the helicopters' wheels. Between their large goggles and balaclavas, their faces were completely concealed, and the fur-lined hoods had all the appearance of a lion's mane. Dale barely noted those details, his attention drawn to the large guns dangling from slings on the Russians' shoulders.

The speed and grace with which the soldiers ran across the snow spoke of many years of practice and perhaps one or two artificial enhancements. Before Dale knew it, they were standing in front of them.

"Welcome to NASA's temporary prototype testing facility," Hendricks said, shouting over the roar of the helicopter's blades. A packet of paper fluttered madly in his outstretched hand. "I believe all of our paperwork is in order. Please feel free to have a look around."

The forward-most Russian soldier removed his goggles and balaclava. Instead of acknowledging Hendricks, his eyes lingered on the distant column of steam billowing up from the pit and the growing lake nearby. April was a mere silhouette against the white cloud of vapor. With a quick flurry of hand signals, he sent two of their number toward her and two inside their shelter. Only then did he reach out and grab the packet of papers.

"If we can wrap this up quickly, we have several sensitive experiments to . . ." Hendricks began before trailing off under the soldier's glare.

The two remaining soldiers consulted the paperwork for a few minutes as their comrades made a racket inside the shelter. After a moment, one soldier pointed at a line on the paper while the second withdrew a tablet from his jacket's interior.

A few moments passed as the soldier connected with someone over the tablet. A lengthy conversation followed in Russian, which Dale could not understand. He did, however, hear his name mentioned a few times.

Just when Dale and the others started to shuffle on their feet, the leader of the Russian outfit stepped forward and flipped the screen of his tablet around. This placed Dale a half meter away from the imposing soldier, who stared at him with narrowed eyes.

Dale tore his eyes away from the grim face and immediately brightened at the sight of his long-time colleague on the screen.

"Anton! What a pleasant surprise."

The Roscosmos scientist wore a magnificent grin on his chubby face.

"You look chilly, my friend. I hope the Antarctic is treating you well. How is our HESTIA performing?"

"Better than we could have expected. We reached five hundred meters in a little over four hours. I worried the torque of the serrated wheels wouldn't stand up against the pressure of the steam, but it's performing admirably."

"I told you it would."

"I shouldn't have doubted you, Anton. Of course, we have a long way to go before three and a half kilometers and we still have to test the coolant transfer during locomotion along the X and Z axes."

"Don't forget to send me the cosmogenic nuclide dating from the descent," Anton said as he leaned forward, his interest piqued.

"Gideon still thinks counting the strata will be superior to beryllium-10 dating."

"At that depth? Imbecile."

"But Dr. Ryabov," Gideon whined as he leaned into frame. "That might be true on Earth, but Enceladus doesn't have an atmosphere to support significant cosmic spallation. The low gravity and regularity of its plumes should ..."

Despite the soldier's poor grasp of the English language, he seemed to detect the start of a long and unproductive conversation. He cleared his throat.

"Yes, well. How long before we can get back to it?" Dale asked, eyeing the soldier warily. He nudged Gideon out of frame with an elbow.

"They just worry. Ignore them," Anton said, waving a hand as if they were a few mosquitos and not six anxious soldiers with big guns. "You are close to Vostok. It is their"—he took a moment to find the right word—"their hub of operations. They see this is nuclear powered. They can't sleep until they know more."

"Where else could we go? The deepest ice is right here. Anywhere else would be a lesser analog."

"They know this. Vostok was a research station once. It collected some of the deepest ice cores on record."

"You told them what the HESTIA is then? They know it will be several kilometers down and dozens of kilometers away? Radiation could never get through that much ice."

"They know this now. I tell them so they can sleep, but they want to keep someone there to monitor. Will this be acceptable? There is no Russian there. They worry."

"We wouldn't be having this problem if you were here, Anton. HESTIA is your project too."

"I will be there for the real thing. For Enceladus. You do the hard work in the cold."

"Alright, my friend. You take it easy."

"Easy. That is what I like. You, don't blow up the south pole."

Anton's cherubic face disappeared and after a moment, Dale nodded to the soldier with a nervous smile.

Hendricks had fished out his own tablet by then and held it up to his mouth as he spoke.

"You stay here?" he asked as he first motioned to the Russian soldiers and then the shelter. The Russian translation followed a moment later. Whether from an inaccurate translation or a sullying of his mother tongue, the soldier scoffed and turned his back to them. On his way back to the helicopter, he barked a few orders, and his subordinates came running out of the shelter and back from the rim of HESTIA's pit. Their brief huddle ended with the leader and three of the soldiers piling onto a single helicopter and leaving back toward Vostok. The remaining two soldiers and the last helicopter's pilot set about unfolding long awnings from the side of the helicopter. The thick fabric stretched all the way to the snow to form a sort of tent.

Hendricks led them back inside the shelter. The once orderly interior was now a jumble of supplies, with crates on their sides and MREs strewn across the floor. Hendricks did not appear to notice the mess as he motioned to the four of them to create their own huddle.

Holding his tablet between them, the military engineer typed out a message for all to read.

Could have planted something. Assume they are monitoring everything we say. No word of our mission here. It's business as usual.

With that, he deleted the text and broke the huddle.

A part of Dale wished they had never told him of their mission. Now he had nothing to do but worry and plenty of time to do it.

The next week passed in what felt to Dale like one extremely long day punctuated by monotonous data collection, stress, and exhausted naps. The perpetual sunlight was the primary culprit. This time of year, it never fully set but skipped off the flat horizon like the ball on a spinning roulette wheel. Their three Russian neighbors brought with them as much stress as their own particular brand of roulette. They would frequently walk into the shelter unannounced, perform a circuit around the room, and leave. In one particularly nerve-racking encounter, one of them asked to see, in halting English, the display on April's tablet and then stood mutely over her shoulder as she worked.

The drone was the most intrusive of all. The small device was about the size of Dale's palm. It came out of nowhere on the second day and maneuvered throughout their shelter. It appeared to be controlled by the helicopter's pilot, though not by any means Dale could see. The man simply stood there, tilting his head this way and that in time with the drone.

"Neural interface," April told him one afternoon by HESTIA's pit. Between the blanket of fog and the noise of the water pump, it had become the only place nearby with any privacy. The one time the drone had come to explore the area, the wind emerging from the pit had sent it off into a tailspin to clatter against the ice. "Corneal implants too. If you get close enough, look for a glimmer in his dilated pupils and a small red wire in his sclera that looks like a vein.

He's controlling the thing with his brain waves and seeing everything it sees."

"Do you have any implants?" Dale asked as he leaned forward to look into her eyes.

Gideon snickered from where he sat in his lawn chair nearby.

April winked, but then glanced away. She went back to wrangling a length of the hose down into the pit. Addressing Gideon, she asked, "How did you plan to deal with all this water on Enceladus?"

"Liquid water doesn't exist under low pressure. Without an atmosphere on Enceladus, the ice will instantly transition to a vapor when heated," he said absently. "It's in HESTIA's name, Hexahedral Enceladus Surveyor with Thermal Ice Ablation."

She lay down the hose and brushed the snow from her gloves.

"Funny. I just thought it was a forced acronym." With that, she set off toward the ever-expanding lake of meltwater, examining the hose as she went.

She had struck a little too close to the truth for comfort. Being the scientists they were, though, they would defend the acronym to their dying breath.

"Go make me a coffee," he told Gideon before the man's blush robbed him of all the blood in his limbs. His technician slumped, stood, and set off for the shelter.

Alone, Dale had nothing better to do than analyze data from the thermal ionization mass spectrometer. True to Hendricks' word, he and April had taken full control of the HESTIA, leaving Dale with little to occupy himself. A day earlier, he had noticed an anomaly in the isotope readings and had been spending the day troubleshooting. Best he could figure, the HESTIA was slowly climbing back toward the surface. While the incline would allow water to drain back toward the entrance and the inlet for the pump, he cringed at the thought of a military bunker with steep hallways and sloped floors.

He powered off his tablet and headed back to the shelter and the coffee that awaited him. He secretly hoped Hendricks bungled the job. That would teach him for not consulting Dale on the bunker's design.

By the time their two-week stay neared its end, the poor sleep quality, lack of stimulating work, and the close quarters of the shelter had left their mark.

Dale's relationship with Gideon had taken a turn for the worse. Little things like the way he breathed at night, the order in which he prepared the coffee and rehydrated the freeze-dried meals made him want to strangle the man. Their conversations quickly devolved into arguments, requiring him to distance himself lest he be tempted to test the depth of HESTIA's pit with his technician's corpse.

He was on his third sanity-preserving excursion of the morning when he noticed Hendricks kneeling beside the pit. A rhythmic clanking sounded with each rise and fall of his arm. He was pounding stakes into each corner of a toaster-sized device that looked uncannily like a large fishing reel. Instead of fishing line, it contained several kilometers worth of a thin metal wire.

A winch to help pull out the HESTIA, Dale guessed. This came as a relief. While the prototype should be capable of extending its many serrated wheels and driving up the pit on its own, he worried the heat of the steam had enlarged the pit's diameter. The presence of the winch also signified the end of their time on the godforsaken continent.

"Time to haul out the goddess?" Dale asked, using a phrase for the probe he had heard the military engineers throw around. "I saw you switched it into idle this morning."

"Just about," Hendricks said, without looking up. He finished pounding the last stake into the ice and pulled out a short length of wire from the motorized winch.

"Becket said the cargo plane is due to arrive tomorrow night. Well, as night as it gets around here. It's a shame, you know. I always wanted to see the stars of the southern hemisphere. The southern cross is . . ." Dale's train of thought completely derailed when Hendricks stood to his feet. He had clipped the wire to a harness around his waist. "What are you doing?"

"I need to inspect the probe before we bring it up. It'll take me most of the day and maybe some of tomorrow."

"You're going down there?" The thought made Dale shudder. It would be about as hospitable as Dante's ninth circle of Hell. Before he could ask why he would do such a thing, the reason for the risk became obvious. He was going to inspect the military base to make sure it had taken shape with no mishaps. "Do the others know?"

"Becket will monitor the radio. I'll be on the same frequency as the HESTIA, so we know the signal will get through the ice."

Hendricks bent to pick up a small backpack Dale had not noticed. He recognized the familiar bulge of MREs and a tablet inside.

"And our guests? What do I tell them?"

Hendricks glanced to where the Russian helicopter sat. One of the men was shoveling away a bank of snow that had accumulated in the lee of its tent.

"You don't tell them anything. Let Drake do all the talking."

As if her name had summoned her, April pushed through the door of the shelter and hurried toward them. She was not wearing her survival suit, but the one-piece thermals they all wore beneath. She looked less than happy. At first, he thought Gideon may have said or done something to offend her. Maybe Dale was not the only one who hated how the technician ground the coffee beans before heating the water. Then she drew close enough for Dale to see wet hair and skin pinkened by a recent shower. In her left hand she clutched a small drone.

The Russian pilot stormed out of his tent a moment later. Even from a distance, his face looked red with fury. He caught sight of April and immediately gave chase.

"He sent his drone into the shower," April spat when she reached the pit. She threw the drone to the ground where it fell into two pieces.

Hendricks set his jaw.

"Did he see them?"

It was the last thing Dale expected the man to say. He opened his mouth to rebuke him, but the words fell away when he noticed the fear in April's eyes. She let out a steadying breath through her nose and pinched her lips together.

"I'm not sure."

"Uh, see what?" Dale asked lamely.

They said nothing more as the enraged pilot stormed up to them. He did not spare a glance at his demolished drone; instead, he stepped close to April and searched her eyes like he might see something in them. Then, faster than Dale could follow, he grabbed her wrist and stripped off the unassuming smart watch all the engineers wore.

Barely visible against the pale skin of her forearm was a pattern of raised pink welts. If not for their number and regularity, he would have dismissed them as small veins. These looked more like a circuit board.

The Russian looked just as surprised as Dale felt. He took a step back, his hand reaching over his shoulder to grab the ever-present assault rifle. He trained it on each of them as he created some distance.

Dale did not realize his hands were in the air until Hendricks and April followed suit.

The pilot stopped his retreat when he spotted the motorized winch at Hendricks' feet. Glancing between the pit and Hendricks, his brow furrowed. A few lateral steps took him past the safety barrier and to the edge of the pit. He held out his hand as if to search for a breeze, then he smiled. Even if the HESTIA hadn't been on idle, its depth prevented any steam from emerging. Instead, all that moist air reached its dew point and crystalized into a downy white blanket along the inside of the pit.

"I. See. Down," he said, emphasizing each word as he pointed to his own eyes and then into the pit. Those same eyes dilated, and his hand reached into his breast pocket to pull out the twin of the broken drone. With no controller Dale could see, the drone activated and lifted from his hand. In seconds, it had disappeared down the pit, its steady whirring slowly fading to nothing.

Dale gulped. This was the worst-case scenario, the moment he had experienced in his nightmares every night. It was the moment their guests learned the NASA engineers' true identities. Somehow April's implants were the giveaway, and now the Russian pilot was about to discover the military bunker beneath the ice. Dale resigned himself to the terrible reality. He would not be returning home. They would lock him in some frigid prison cell for the foreseeable future.

When the pilot squinted and stepped closer to the pit, Dale experienced a flicker of hope. If the drone could not travel that far, or if its radio was incapable of penetrating the ice, all might not be lost. So long as they stayed friendly and came up with an excuse for April's implants, they could . . .

Hendricks darted forward, his body a blur in Dale's peripheral vision.

The pilot, his eyes narrowed in concentration, failed to react in time. The gun let out a rapid staccato, and chunks of snow sprayed into the air near Dale's feet.

Then Hendricks was flying through the air, tackling the pilot to the ground. Except there was no ground. Before Dale could register what had happened, they were both gone. The gaping hole HESTIA had left in the ice looked much the same as it had before.

April was faster on her feet. She slid across the snow to kneel beside the motorized winch. The reel was spooling out at a rapid pace. She turned it on, and the motor let out a loud squeal as it applied torque to the line. The thin wire cut deep into the rim of the pit.

April scuttled forward on her hands and knees to peer over the edge.

"Sir? Can you hear me?"

Dale finally let his limbs respond to signals from his brain and went to lie on the snow beside April.

"... got me in the leg," came a calm but pained voice from below. Looking down, he saw nothing but light blue walls fading into an impenetrable black curtain.

"The pilot?" April called back.

"Gone. But his friends will have heard the shots."

Sure enough, a commotion was stirring at the helicopter. The man Dale had seen shoveling snow was rushing toward them with rifle drawn. The last soldier had also emerged from the tent. He wore little more than April, his white thermals creating the illusion of a disembodied head and floating gun against the snow-covered landscape.

The pilot was dead, and his fellow soldiers would make them answer for it. The analytical part of Dale's brain argued that the pilot would not be dead for another minute. It would take that long for him to hit the bottom of the 3.5-kilometer pit.

"They heard it all right," April said. "The motor is on, come back up and we'll deal with them."

"They have guns, Drake. And we don't. The mission is the priority." His voice trailed off for a moment and then returned, quieter than before. "Becket, do you copy? Operation Meltwater is a go, I repeat, Meltwater is a go. Call for backup and get yourself and the civvy out of there."

April did not stay to hear Hendricks' instructions. She had rolled across the ice to snag the small backpack and then returned.

"I've got the gear. I'm coming down."

"Negative. You don't have a survival suit."

"With all due respect, sir, you don't have two good legs anymore. You can't complete the mission on your own, and like you said, the mission comes first."

Dale, unsure what they were talking about but absolutely positive he wanted no part in it, was pushing away from the pit.

Apparently, seeing April make her escape down the hole in the ice was all the excuse the Russians needed to open fire.

Reversing direction, Dale mindlessly fled toward cover. The sight of Dale making to escape the same way prompted another spray of bullets.

April, having no means by which to grip the thin wire, looped her arms and legs around the bloated water hose. Dale followed and quickly lowered his feet over the side. Seeing the wall of darkness beneath him nearly made him take his chances with the bullets, but April reached up to grip his boot and pulled him out of harm's way.

Hugging the water hose for dear life, he slid down at a terrifying speed. Whenever his momentum slowed, April tugged his boot harder, and he would start sliding again.

The powdery snow on the walls of the pit fell away when he brushed by to reveal a remarkably smooth surface of ice, its strata depicting years of Earth's history in every inch. In a very real way, many millennia flew past every second.

Then it was too dark to see anything.

The square-shaped section of blue sky above them had shrunken to the size of a postage stamp. Two shadows passed over its surface as the Russians arrived at the edge of the pit. They called for their comrade and waited long enough to be certain of his demise before opening fire. The sound issuing from the flashing barrels was barely audible, but the bullets ricocheting off the ice were harder to ignore.

A bullet struck the hose above, raining water down on them. The hose shrank in size as air rushed in through the puncture and gravity pulled the contents of the hose back down into the pit. The diminished size of the hose had the unexpected benefit of being easier to grip, but he was not about to call out his thanks.

After several seconds of near constant fire, the shooting stopped. Either they were out of ammunition or confident they had hit their targets.

"Don't slow down," April called from below. "They could sever the hose any second."

Reluctantly, Dale loosened his grip and began descending again.

"You brought the scientist?" Hendricks asked incredulously, as if Dale were an extra bag she had brought on their vacation.

"We were under fire," April said in her defense.

"Give me the backpack."

A light flickered on from below and then Dale was passing it. It was Hendricks, who conveniently had a headlamp and a line of his own with which to descend. For some inexplicable reason, he had snatched the bag from April and let them pass. As soon as they were beneath him, the military engineer reached over to grab the deflated water hose and began hammering something into it. It had the familiar metallic clang of a stake being driven into the ice.

A moment later, something struck Dale's back. It thumped and thrashed for several seconds until it stopped and settled beside him. Confused, Dale reached out and felt it with a gloved hand. It was another hose. No, it was the same hose. Despite all odds, Hendricks had staked their hose into the ice before the Russians had severed it from above. Not a second too soon.

Then the Russians severed the line holding Hendricks. Had he not had a grip on their hose, there would have been two bodies lying at the bottom of the pit. They now had only one anchor to the wall, and it no longer reached the surface. Unless the rescue party brought an insanely long rope, Dale might never see the sunlight again.

Above him, the patch of sky had shrunken to the size of a bright but dimming star. *This is what the HESTIA will see when it flies away from the sun and out to the dimly lit moons of Saturn.* It was a peaceful thought, but he hoped it would not be his last. He needed to survive this. He needed to make sure his probe made it that far.

The pressure built in Dale's ears until finally, April told them to slow. When they came to a stop, she asked for Hendricks' headlamp. Dale transferred it between them without dropping their one and only light source. With their eyes focused on the illuminated shaft below, they continued down at a more sedate pace.

A few minutes more, and the glimmer of water reflected up at them. It was about time. Dale's hands cramped with the strain of holding on to the deflated hose. He was about to voice the complaint aloud until he saw the prone form of the Russian pilot floating facedown on the surface. His aches and pains seemed trivial all of a sudden.

April landed in the water and let out a gasp as she sank to her neck. The light from her headlamp revealed an opening in the wall of ice. It appeared to be a long tunnel with just enough of an incline to channel the water back to the pump's inlet. On her way up the tunnel, April grabbed the Russian's collar and dragged him with her.

Dale gritted his teeth and made the plunge. He swam as fast as possible to prevent water from seeping into his survival suit. Hendricks followed and soon they were both staggering out of the water.

When Hendricks had nothing but the ice beneath him, he pressed his back to the wall and slid down. Blood oozed out of a hole in the pants leg of his survival suit.

"Don't bother. It's already taken care of," he said, waving Dale away as he came to help. He tapped at the watch on his wrist instead of applying pressure to the wound. Then the man's face relaxed, and he started breathing easier. A few seconds more, and the blood oozing from his leg eased to a stop. At Dale's confused expression, Hendricks elaborated. "Implant. I just got a dose of its anesthetic, artificial blood, and coagulants."

"Implant? Like the one in April's arm?" Dale asked, less out of curiosity than desperation. If his companions had any superhuman enhancements, they might be able to get him out of this alive.

A few steps away, April had stripped the Russian of his outerwear with concerning efficiency and donned it just as quickly. That the clothes had just been on a dead person seemed irrelevant to her when faced with hypothermia. Fully clothed, she curled up on the ice on the other side of Dale.

"No, this one's more of an artificial spleen. Here, give this to her." Hendricks took off the ever-present watch at his wrist and handed it to Dale.

April took the watch from him with trembling fingers and strapped it on. She tapped the face of the device a few times and then instantly stopped shivering. It was as if every muscle in her body had tensed.

"That's the subdermal muscle stimulator. And it's not just the arm. That's just where it converges on the watch, the power supply, inductor, and controller. The circuitry extends into all major muscle groups. We use it during training to stimulate the muscles opposite of the ones being used. It makes you feel like you're moving through molasses, but it's great for building muscle and generating some heat. In combat, it stimulates more motor units than your nerves can at any one time, allowing for bursts of speed and strength."

"You all have these?" Dale asked, seeing the faint trace of lines on Hendricks' now exposed wrist.

"And corneal and neural implants. They all work together. I can see my team's biometrics on my HUD, assign targets, and if I'm looking down the sight of a gun, it will coordinate with my muscle stimulator to steady my aim and center the reticle on my target."

"Don't they make exosuits and helmets that do all of those things? Why implants?"

"Those aren't exactly nondescript for a covert mission specialist."

Dale nodded as he too settled against the wall of the tunnel. Despite the layers of insulating fabric, the ice seemed to suck the heat right out of him. None of their implants would help keep Dale warm. Deciding he could just huddle close to the HESTIA until rescue arrived, he looked for the NASA probe. It was nowhere in sight.

"Where's the HESTIA? We were scheduled to bring it out tonight. It should be right here. Is it somewhere deeper in the bunker?"

He realized then that nothing in the circle of light looked remotely like a bunker. There was just the single long tunnel extending into the darkness.

"About that . . ." Hendricks said, grunting as he shifted and pointed up the tunnel. "It's about forty kilometers in that direction."

"What? How?"

"We aren't building a bunker," April said. Her teeth no longer chattered, but her words sounded strained.

"You lied? About all of it?"

"We are military engineers, I was not lying about that," Hendricks said. "But there is no military bunker. We told you that in the event something like this happened. If they made the two of you talk, you wouldn't give away our actual goal."

It was the best kind of lie, Dale admitted, so attractive he could not help but believe in it. But did Becket get Gideon out of there? Or was his technician even now spilling the beans like the first time he had made Dale coffee?

"Then why did you need the HESTIA?"

"We are sappers," April said. "We clear the way." It had all the ring of a mantra, but not one Dale had ever heard before.

"Is that like a plumber or something?" His frustration only mounted at the lack of a straightforward answer.

"Military engineers aren't only good at building bridges and fortifications on the fly. We are experts in tunnel warfare. That means building covered trenches or tunnels under enemy fortifications and planting loads of explosives. As sappers, our job was to clear the way for the rest of the troops. And that's what we plan to do here."

Dale closed his eyes, wondering why he had never considered the possibility. Two weeks was a long time in the field to test a prototype, even considering the to-do list NASA had given them. They never needed all those tests; they needed the time. At two meters a minute, it would take the whole of two weeks to move forty kilometers under the ice. The same distance away as Vostok.

"You're going to blow up the Russian base."

Hendricks sighed.

"Another war is about to start, and like it or not, you're going to help us deal the first blow. The first thing the Russians did when usurping the continent was to surround it with enough antiair defenses to make sure the Antarctic will never see a penguin that flies. We would never sneak a missile past them. But they'll never see it coming from below."

"It's not possible. I've been through every crate in the shelter twice by now. I would have seen explosives."

"Oh, there are explosives," he said, patting the backpack beside him. "But not nearly enough to do what you're thinking. I hate to be the one to break it to you, Doctor, but your prototype is the bomb. The fissile material in the reactor is not weapons grade, but near enough. Packaged with a bit of neutron reflector and some plastic explosive to bring it all together, it will reach criticality."

Dale's heart sank. From the angle at which the tunnel climbed, he guessed the probe was right beneath Vostok. They were planning to turn his HESTIA into a primitive atom bomb under the Russians' feet. The greatest invention of his career would be used to kill hundreds of people.

April had dialed down the settings on her watch enough to regain some motor control. She sat up and gave Dale a sympathetic look before addressing Hendricks.

"We need to beat feet, sir. We've lots of distance to cover."

"You'll have to do the dirty work I'm afraid. I won't be able to keep up. It's best I take the gun and follow at my own pace, cover the rear."

"You sure?"

Hendricks took back the watch in exchange for the backpack and then picked up the Russian's assault rifle.

"You've got the explosives training and you know how to make it work. Take the backpack and get moving. And take the doctor with you. He's no use to me back here, but he might be able to help you disassemble the probe."

Dale blinked. They could not really expect him to go along with this. He wanted to be right here when the rescue team arrived. Then again, Hendricks seemed convinced the Russians would come looking for them before that happened. Thinking back on the previous gunfight, he wanted no part of that action. Reluctantly, he stood up to follow April.

"Catch up when you can, sir."

"Clear the way, Drake," Hendricks replied.

April grinned and nodded before setting off down the tunnel. Dale staggered as he tried to keep pace. Unlike the tunnel walls, the floor was uneven, a deep runnel having formed to carry the meltwater down the slope from the NASA probe.

Behind them, Hendricks switched on a light on the rifle and was checking to make sure it was in working order. That light soon became a dim spark as they ascended the shallow incline.

They walked for five hours. In his younger years, he had once run a marathon in that time, but this made that experience feel like a relaxing jaunt along the beach.

"You have food in there?" Dale asked, eyeing the backpack bouncing lightly off April's back as they walked.

"Not exactly. It's plastic explosive. They added a funky smell so it would look like a package of noodles gone bad. Their heater packs work, though."

"Great. Maybe you can use them to thaw my emaciated corpse."

"You really are a pessimist, aren't you? Gideon's said it more than once."

"It seems I wasn't pessimistic enough," he said, breathless from their strenuous hike. He slowed to a stop and leaned against the wall. The fuzz of ice clinging to the surface fell away at his touch.

April frowned and returned to his side. She withdrew the hammer from her bag and used the spiked end to chip some ice from the wall and into a metal cup. Placed on an activated heating pack, the ice quickly melted.

Dale took a grateful sip.

"You know, the last time this was liquid water, humanity didn't exist." Dale's voice became longing. "There were no wars back then."

"There weren't hammers or heating packs either," April reminded him. "Don't forget that it was the need for war that brought about many of these innovations, including your HESTIA. Civilization needs soldiers as much as scientists."

Dale did not like it, but he did not disagree.

By the time they got moving again, Dale had decided not to assist her with Operation Meltwater. He would not help her dismantle the HESTIA, use it to take hundreds of lives, or destroy this pristine albeit detestable environment. Those same principles told him that doing nothing was just as bad as making them happen. Common sense told him he could not stop her if he tried.

It was another five hours before they made it to the end of the tunnel. Dale could barely feel his legs and considered removing the survival suit to keep from overheating. But the heat wasn't entirely from the exertion. The walls of the tunnel were no longer covered in frost but a thin film of water. The white ceramic cube of the HESTIA sat directly ahead. On idle and with its control rods lowered and coolant distributed equally throughout each side of its cubed surface, its radiant heat had melted a small chamber out of the ice.

When April's light fell across it, he nearly cried with relief. The sight of the probe was only half of the reason. He knelt and began scooping water into his parched mouth. They had run out of the heating packs hours ago.

While he slaked his thirst, April went to work on the probe. At first, all she did was take out a tablet from the backpack and type in commands. She must have ordered the coolant purged from the topmost face of the cube, as she immediately started splashing water on the steaming surface. When it had cooled sufficiently, she unbolted the ceramic cladding with a wrench from her backpack.

Dale, steadfast in his decision not to help her, could not resist getting one last peek inside before it was reduced to a cloud of ionized particles. He leaned over the half-submerged cube to see the imposing sight of over a dozen circular sawlike wheels. Ryabov's team designed them to grip the icy surface and propelled it forward against the force of the steam. Beyond them were innumerable insulated wires and pipes. His focus, however, was on the reactor housing.

It was unremarkable on the outside, but the three-foot-wide metal cube held all the control and fuel rods within. Enough power to level an entire Russian military base.

April unbolted a strut to access the housing and immediately set to work opening it. After removing the metal casing, she reached into her backpack to pull out four MRE pouches. She ripped them open and stuck them down into the four sides of the reactor core. As promised, the stringy substance inside had a rank odor, like a spoiled noodle dish. Jumping back down to the discarded cladding, she collected some of its radiation shielding, thick metal sheets of tungsten carbide. She deftly slid these into the housing between the fuel rods and the plastic explosive. If Dale had to guess, they would serve as both the tamper and neutron reflector of a nuclear bomb. Lastly, April attached a lead from the HESTIA's radio receiver to the plastic explosives.

The idea that someone might trigger the explosives remotely and without warning made him feel sick. *At least the control rods are still in place*, he thought. Those would prevent a criticality event. So it was with some trepidation that he watched April raise and detach the control rods and throw them into the water. She then did the unthinkable and lifted out one of the fuel rods to insert it in the vacated space, bringing all the fissile material closer together. It was as if all the components had been designed to slide perfectly into place, converting a NASA probe into a nuclear weapon in under ten minutes. He could see now why NASA had been so adamant about some of the components' dimensions and not others.

It was getting hot in the small ice chamber and more and more water dripped down from the rounded walls and ceiling. He hoped none of it got inside the exposed reactor core. Adding a neutron moderator to the core of a fast reactor was a quick way to cause a meltdown and boil them alive.

He was so on edge that when a gunshot sounded in the distance, he dove straight into the water at his feet.

Spitting out a mouthful of the tepid water, he splashed over to the nearest wall, out of the tunnel's line of sight.

April's brow drew together as she jumped from the top of the HESTIA and placed her back flush to the wall opposite him.

Several tense minutes passed as they listened, and more gun shots rang out. Then Hendricks stumbled into the chamber, falling flat into the water. He breathed raggedly, like he had been running for hours. The gunshot wound in his leg had started bleeding again, turning the water pink around him.

"They're a few minutes behind me. No more ammo. You need to . . . hurry." He wheezed out the words in April's direction. His eyes fluttered closed as he fell into unconsciousness.

As Dale stumbled forward to help April pull Hendricks out of the water, the man's words tumbled through his head. They were trapped between an armed nuclear weapon and armed Russian soldiers. And they were defenseless.

April had also run the odds. She yanked the radio from Hendricks' belt.

"Becket. This is Drake. Operation Meltwater is still a go. The goddess is armed," she squeezed her eyes shut, and let out a shuddering breath. "If you don't hear from me in ten minutes . . . detonate."

Dale shouted over Becket's solemn confirmation.

"What are you doing? That's not enough time to get out of here. Are you trying to kill us?"

"I'm sorry, Doctor Stratford. This mission is too important. If we fail here, if we don't get them off of this continent, the coming conflict will not end in our favor."

"But the reinforcements may already be here. We just have to—"

"We can't afford to wait. They only need a few minutes alone with the probe to disarm it. I really am sorry."

He could not tell if the streak of water running down her face was a tear or dribble of water from the ceiling.

"That's it then? We're just going to die here?"

The sorrow in his voice seemed to get through to her. Her jaw tightened and she clenched her fist.

"Maybe not. If I can take them down, we'll radio Becket, tell him not to activate the bomb."

"You heard Hendricks. That gun is useless."

"I don't need a gun to deal with them," she said, hefting her wrench in emphasis. "I can ambush them when they come out of the tunnel. We have a chance."

As April stared down the dark tunnel, Dale took in the chamber. Shame welled up in him when he realized he was looking for something to hide behind. That was not him. He was a scientist. Whenever he encountered a problem, he would troubleshoot the hell out of it. That was all this was. A problem.

As he examined the half-submerged HESTIA, pieces of an idea formed in his mind. When they finally came together, goosebumps cascaded over his skin. Maybe there was a way to give them both what they wanted and earn them a ticket out of this pit. It would be crazy, but it just might work. Unless April tried to stop him.

"What are you doing?" April asked when she noticed him fumbling with something at Hendricks' wrist.

Dale examined the watch in his hands and flipped through some settings.

"Hendricks said this thing makes you faster and stronger. That should improve your odds, right? Okay. I think I got it. Give me your wrist."

Psyching herself up with some rapid breathing, she absently held out her arm.

Dale latched the watch to her wrist.

April froze in place, every muscle in her body going rigid.

"What the hell," she growled through gritted teeth. When she tried to retract her arm, her triceps flexed and resisted the motion.

"I agree with you, you know," he said as he pried the wrench from her stiff fingers. "The world needs people like you to go to war for us. But the world needs people like me too, to give you other options."

He loosened the bolts holding a piece of HESTIA's outer cladding in place until it sprang a leak. As water slowly filled the interior of the probe, he reached inside to remove the open MRE pouches containing the explosives and plucked free their trailing wires. He did not think he was missing anything, but it was hard to concentrate over the stream of imaginative curse words coming from April.

Dale splashed over to the cast-off pieces of the HESTIA and dragged the ceramic lid to the entrance of the tunnel. With some effort, he levered the limp and stiff forms of Hendricks and April on top. April tried to fight him, but it was no use. Her body trembled in impotent rage.

The last thing he did was turn off April's headlamp. Without it, the Russians would never see them coming. When the light went out, several flickering lights became visible down the tunnel. The dread the sight caused was nothing compared to what lay behind him.

The iconic blue of Cherenkov radiation illuminated the HESTIA from within. Water had risen to the level of the reactor's housing and was pouring inside, sending steam billowing into the air. Far more heat radiated from the probe than it ever had before. And it was only going to get worse.

He knelt and pushed on the edge of the cladding and then jumped onto the makeshift sled.

The smooth, still-warm ceramic surface slid along the ice with little friction. On the eight-percent grade, they quickly built up speed as they raced down the tunnel.

Dale threw his arms over the two other passengers and ducked when he glimpsed the lights of the Russian soldiers just ahead. They plowed right through the men without slowing, the sound of breaking bone and muted screams all that marked their passage.

The wind rushed past them as they barreled onward. He could not see what lay ahead in the darkness, and that scared him more than the bomb ever had. Dale tried to slow down by raking his fingers across the floor of the tunnel, but they skittered uselessly off the slick surface.

After endless minutes of heart-thumping terror, Becket's voice came over the radio at April's belt.

"Drake. That's ten minutes. I'm so sorry. I'm detonating. It was an honor to serve with you."

Dale squeezed his eyes shut, and an instant later, he was flung into the air. When coldness enveloped him, he feared he had miscalculated, that a thermonuclear explosion had just incinerated him. Then he recognized the cold for what it was. He thrashed until he broke the surface of the water and breathed in a lungful of fresh air. The jumble of hose floating around him and the pinprick of light above told him all he needed to know. They had reached the base of the tunnel.

He did it. He had prevented the detonation. It would be another few minutes before he knew if his plan had succeeded. That was assuming April let him live that long.

April.

Dale dove. He found both Hendricks and April by feel a meter below. Unable to haul them both, he unstrapped April's watch and then grabbed the collar of Hendricks' survival suit. Together they swam to the surface.

"What the hell did you do, Dale?" April said between fits of coughing. She switched on her headlamp and swung the beam toward him. The sight of him struggling to keep Hendricks' head above the water must have reordered her priorities. From the way her eyes blazed as she swam over, he thought she might try to strangle him just as soon as Hendricks was seen to.

"I did you a favor," he said as she checked Hendricks' vitals on her HUD. "Atom bombs are hugely inefficient. Little Boy, the bomb that detonated over Hiroshima, resulted in less than two percent uranium fission. And it was designed to blow up, not pieced together from a fast reactor. My way is much more efficient and it won't kill anyone. Unless the Russians can't swim. Oh God, they will know how to swim, right? Tell Becket to send over some rescue teams. Take lots of towels."

"What are you talking about?" she growled. Her eyes outshone the headlamp in their intensity.

Dale took a calming breath.

"I stopped your nuclear explosion and gave you a nuclear meltdown. All it needed was a bit of water. It's the neutron moderator of choice in most nuclear power plants. It slows down fast neutrons, releasing enormous amounts of heat and gives the resulting thermal neutrons a better fission cross-section with U-235. The HESTIA has more enriched uranium than any nuclear power plant in the world and is surrounded by a nearly infinite supply of water."

"You're saying ... ?"

"I'm saying that in a few hours, Vostok will be the name of the largest freshwater lake in Antarctica."

Her eyebrows climbed into her mop of wet hair.

"I suppose that's something," she said grudgingly. "But I'm not the one you have to answer to. Assuming we ever get out of this hole."

"About that ..." He gestured up the tunnel where a wall of fog rolled toward them. "That should be our lift now." In seconds, the air became thicker than the muggiest day in Texas, and all he could see of April was a halo of light from her headlamp.

The sound of water trickling into their small pool came next and steadily grew until it was a turbulent river. Before he knew it, the tunnel entrance sank beneath the surface and they rose ever so slowly up the pit. Dale tried to swim, but whenever he strayed too close to a wall, an undercurrent threatened to pull him down. Once again, the water hose came to the rescue. With air now in the line, the slack of the hose formed a tangled raft for them to cling to.

They shot higher and higher up the pit until at last, their speed slowed. The white haze of fog no longer appeared in the cone of April's headlamp but seemed to come from all around them. Then there was blue sky.

Dale, April, and Hendricks rose out of the pit on a cushion of water and partially inflated hose. It gently spilled them onto the snow and ice and under the ever-present sun.

A literal army of people stood nearby, all wearing the uniforms of one branch of the US military or another. They all turned to stare in slack-jawed amazement at the people they had given up for dead. As several uniformed personnel splashed over to aid April with the still unconscious Hendricks, Dale stood on shaky legs and staggered away from the pit.

Gideon stood a few feet away, water sloshing over his boots. He did not seem to notice. His wide, tear-brimmed eyes looked as though they had just seen a ghost.

Dale took the steaming cup of coffee from his limp fingers and collapsed into the lawn chair.

"Who's the pessimist now?"

ABOUT THE AUTHORS

M.T. Reiten grew up in North Dakota where he discovered science fiction. He left grad school to join the Army and jump out of airplanes. He went into the Signal Corps, because they wanted electrical engineers. He spent time in Germany and Bosnia before returning to finish grad school. In the middle of his PhD, he got an opportunity to serve in Afghanistan with an infantry battalion. While deployed, he was a winner of the Phobos Award and Writers of the Future.

He returned to finish his PhD in electrical engineering (really physics, but don't tell anyone.) His stories have appeared in anthologies to include S. M. Stirling's *The Change: Tales of Downfall and Rebirth*, and The Post-Apocalyptic Tourist Guide series, and in SF magazines, such as *DreamForge* and an upcoming issue of *Analog* (a lifelong goal recently fulfilled.) He is also a grand prize winner of the Jim Baen Memorial Short Story Contest in 2020. He lives and writes in New Mexico with his wonderful wife and daughter and works at a government laboratory on national security technology.

Martin L. Shoemaker is a programmer who writes on the side . . . or maybe it's the other way around. He told stories to imaginary friends and learned to type on his brother's manual typewriter even though he couldn't reach the keys. (He types with the keyboard in his lap still today.) He couldn't imagine any career but writing fiction . . . until his algebra teacher said, "This is a program. You should write one of these."

Dr. Doug Beason, a PhD Physicist and Fellow of the American Physical Society, has written sixteen novels, two nonfiction books, and over one hundred scientific papers and short stories. His novels include *The Officer, Space Station Down* (with Ben Bova) and *Ill Wind* (with Kevin J. Anderson). A Nebula Award finalist for Best SF Novel of the Year, he has written for publications as diverse as *The Wall Street Journal, Analog, Physical Review Letters, Amazing Stories, Physics of Fluids, There Will Be War,* and *Journal of Computational Physics.* A retired USAF colonel, Doug served on the White House staff for both Presidents Bush and Clinton, and was commander of the Phillips Research Site/Deputy, Directed Energy, USAF Research Laboratory. He was previously the associate laboratory director of Los Alamos National Laboratory and was recently Chief Scientist of Space Command.

Doug served on the United Kingdom's Threat Reduction Advisory Board for the Atomic Weapons Establishment; was a member of the USAF Science Advisory Board; was the Principal US Representative for the US/UK/Canadian Satellite Program; and was VP of the Directed Energy Professional Society.

Doug is a 1977 graduate of the United States Air Force Academy (dual BS Physics and Mathematics), and was a senior service school Distinguished Graduate of National Defense University. His book *Science and Technology Policy for the post–Cold War: A Case for Long-Term Research* was awarded the NDU President's "Strategic Vision" award and was used as a textbook at both the National War College and Air War College.

More information can be found at DougBeason.com.

Richard Fox is the winner of the 2017 Dragon Award for Best Military Science Fiction or Fantasy novel. He's best known for The Ember War Saga, a military science fiction and space opera series.

His writing draws extensively from his experiences in the United States Army, where he served two combat tours in Iraq and was awarded the Bronze Star, Combat Action Badge and Presidential Unit Citation.

He lives in fabulous Las Vegas with his incredible wife and three boys, amazing children bent on anarchy.

Subscribe to Richard's spam free email list and get free short stories set during the Ember War Saga (and more as they become available) at: eepurl.com/bLj1gf.

Visit his website at RichardFoxAuthor.com.

Sean Patrick Hazlett is an Army veteran, speculative fiction writer and editor, and finance executive in the San Francisco Bay area. He holds an AB in history and BS in electrical engineering from Stanford University, and a Master in Public Policy from the Harvard Kennedy School of Government where he won the 2006 Policy Analysis Exercise Award for his work on policy solutions to Iran's nuclear weapons program under the guidance of future secretary of defense Ashton B. Carter. He also holds an MBA from the Harvard Business School, where he graduated with Second Year Honors. Over forty of his short stories have appeared in publications such as The Year's Best Military and Adventure SF, Year's Best Hardcore Horror, Terraform, Galaxy's Edge, Writers of the Future, Grimdark Magazine, Vastarien, and *Abyss & Apex*, among others. He is the editor of the *Weird World War III* and *Weird World War IV* anthologies. Sean also teaches strategy and finance at the Stanford Graduate School of Business's Executive Education Program. He is an active member of the Horror Writers Association and Codex Writers' Group. If you enjoyed "Manchurian," check out other World War IV stories in *Weird World War IV*.

Monalisa Foster won life's lottery when she escaped communism and became an unhyphenated American citizen. Her works tend to explore themes of freedom, liberty, and personal responsibility. Despite her degree in physics, she's worked in several fields including engineering and medicine. She and her husband (who is a writer-once-removed via their marriage) are living their happily-ever-after in Texas. Her current works, including her Ravages of Honor space opera series, are listed at her website, MonalisaFoster.com.

Commander Phillip E. Pournelle (USN–Retired) was a Surface Warfare Officer and analyst in the Navy for twenty-six years. He served on cruisers, destroyers, amphibious ships, and a high-speed vessel. He completed three tours in the Pentagon: one at the Navy staff conducting campaign analysis using modeling and simulation; another at OSD CAPE doing mobility and naval analysis; and his last uniform assignment was a five-year tour at the Office of Net Assessment (ONA). He worked at the Long Term Strategy Group for three years doing wargaming and analysis for ONA. He is now a senior operations analyst and wargame designer at Group W supporting the Joint Staff and USMC. He has a master's degree in Operations Research from the Naval Postgraduate School in Monterey.

Weston Ochse has spent the last thirty-five years in and out of various military organizations. Most of his work was with special operations, but he was also no stranger to nuclear artillery and mechanized infantry units. He's been to Afghanistan several times and knows the special sound of silence after an IED has been blown. He's trained soldiers all over the world, including Papua New Guinea and Thailand in advanced weapons, special operations techniques, and various small-unit tactics. His fascination with robotics was spurred by the advancements of Boston Dynamics and companies developing similar technologies. Combined with his love for real living dogs, merging the two ideas to create this story was the only way the story could progress. The author of more than thirty books, his SEAL Team 666 books have been optioned by Dwayne Johnson to be a major motion picture. He has also worked on the franchises of *Hellboy, X-Files, Predator, Aliens, V-Wars,* Clive Barker's Midian, and Joe Ledger. When not trying to take over small countries, you can find him hunkered down in southern Arizona with his wife and rescue Great Danes.

While **David Drake** was studying at Duke Law School, the Army changed his immediate career path to a choice between interrogator or grunt. Dave chose interrogator. He was assigned to the 11th Cav, the Blackhorse, and spent much of 1970 riding armored vehicles through jungles instead of slogging on foot.

During his service, Dave learned new skills, saw interesting sights, and met exotic people who hadn't run fast enough to get away. He returned to Duke, completed his law degree, and became Chapel Hill's Assistant Town Attorney while trying to put his life back together through fiction that made sense of his Army experiences.

Dave describes war from where he saw it: the loader's hatch of a tank in Cambodia. His military experience, combined with his formal education in history and Latin, has made him one of the foremost writers of realistic action SF and fantasy. His best-selling Hammer's Slammers series is credited with creating the genre of modern Military SF.

He would rather be a moderately successful lawyer with a less interesting background.

Dave lives with his family in rural North Carolina.

A former CIA weapons expert, **T.C. McCarthy** is a recognized authority on the impact of technology on military strategy and is a regular speaker at USSOCOM (US Special Operations Command) and other commands on future warfare topics. Before embarking on a national security career, he earned a PhD in geology and bachelor's degrees in environmental science and computer science—in addition to being a Fulbright Fellow and Howard Hughes Biomedical Research Fellow—and worked as a patent examiner in complex biotechnology and combinatorial chemistry.

Brad R. Torgersen is a multi-award-winning science fiction and fantasy writer whose book *A Star-Wheeled Sky* won the 2019 Dragon Award for Best Science Fiction Novel at the 33rd annual DragonCon fan convention in Atlanta, GA. A prolific short fiction author, Torgersen has published stories in numerous anthologies and magazines, to include several Best of Year editions. Brad is named in *Analog* magazine's who's who of top *Analog* authors, alongside venerable writers like Larry Niven, Lois McMaster Bujold, Orson Scott Card, and Robert A. Heinlein. Married for over twenty-five years, Brad is also a United States Army Reserve chief warrant officer—with multiple deployments to his credit—and currently lives with his wife and daughter in the Mountain West. Where they keep a small menagerie of dogs and cats.

Stephen Lawson served on three deployments with the US Navy and is currently a helicopter pilot and commissioned officer in the Kentucky National Guard. He earned a Masters of Business Administration from Indiana University Southeast in 2018, and currently lives in Louisville, Kentucky, with his wife.

Stephen's writing has appeared in *Writers of the Future Volume 33, Orson Scott Card's InterGalactic Medicine Show, Galaxy's Edge, Daily Science Fiction, The Year's Best Military and Adventure Science Fiction Volume 5,* and *Weird World War III.* He won second place in the Jim Baen Memorial Short Story Award in 2017 and won the grand prize in 2018. He's written two episodes of *The Post-Apocalyptic Tourist's Guide*, which he also edits. His blog can be found at stephenlawsonstories.wordpress.com.

Philip A. Kramer, PhD, is a biomedical researcher who studies muscle, aging, and metabolism. In addition to his academic works, he has published several hard science fiction short stories and nonfiction articles. In 2017, he won the Jim Baen Memorial Short Story Award sponsored by Baen Books and the National Space Society. His blog (pakramer.com) is an educational resource for writers who seek to more accurately represent science in their fiction. He currently lives in North Carolina with his fiancée, dog, and way too many birds.